Praise for *Doesn't She Look Natural?*

". . . a lighthearted read that is simply to die for."
—**Sandra Byrd, author of *Let Them Eat Cake* and other novels**

"*Doesn't She Look Natural?* proves the point that Angela Hunt is one of the most versatile authors writing today. . . . I loved this book."
—**BJ Hoff, author of the Mountain Song Legacy series, the American Anthem series, and the Emerald Ballad series**

"Not only did this story entertain and pull me into the lives of a family in the midst of a huge season of testing and trial—it also challenged me spiritually and twisted my heart."
—**Novel Reviews**

". . . a top-notch inspirational plot that maintains a lighthearted touch."
—*Library Journal*

"Angela writes with humor, tenderness, and creates such emotional tension that I had to remind myself to take a breath! I can't wait to see where Angela takes her Fairlawn series—*Doesn't She Look Natural?* is highly recommended."
—**CBD reader**

"*Doesn't She Look Natural?* is an entertaining and thoughtful read and a promising beginning to a new series."
—**Faithful Reader**

Doesn't She Look Natural?

➤❖◄

ANGELA HUNT

TYNDALE HOUSE PUBLISHERS, INC.
CAROL STREAM, ILLINOIS

Library of Congress Cataloging-in-Publication Data

Hunt, Angela Elwell, date.
   Doesn't she look natural? / Angela Hunt.
      p. cm.—(Fairlawn ; #1)
   ISBN-13: 978-1-4143-1169-2 (sc : alk. paper)
   ISBN-10: 1-4143-1169-9 (sc : alk. paper)
   1. Divorced mothers—Fiction. 2. Funeral homes—Fiction. I. Title.
   PS3558.U46747D64
   813'.54—dc22   2007011050

ISBN-13: 978-1-4143-2605-4
ISBN-10: 1-4143-2605-X

Printed in the United States of America

15   14   13   12   11   10   09   08
  8   7   6   5   4   3   2   1

"There's no great loss without some gain."
—PROVERB

Death gives life its fullest reality
—ANTHONY DALLA VILLA

A grieving woman, I've decided, is like a crème brûlée: she begins in a liquid state, endures a period of searing heat, and eventually develops a scablike crust.

By the time we sell the house I am pretty much crusted over, so I'm honestly surprised when the real estate agent slides a check toward me and tears blur my vision.

Ms. Nichols doesn't seem to notice my streaming eyes. "That's a tidy little profit, even if it is only half the proceeds," she says, eyeing the bank draft as if she can't bear to let it slip away. "If you're in the market for another property—"

"I'm sure we'll be renting for a while." I lower my gaze lest she read the rest of the story in my tight expression: *This money is all we have.*

Apparently oblivious to the rough edges in my voice, the Realtor babbles on. "Our agents also handle rental properties. If you're interested, I have a nice listing inside the Beltway—"

"Anything I could afford near the District wouldn't be big enough for me and my boys."

Ms. Nichols frowns, probably wondering how a woman who's just been handed forty thousand dollars could be so miserly; then she shrugs. "I'm in the yellow pages if you want to take a look. I'm here to serve." She stands and thrusts her hand into the space above the desk. "A pleasure to work with you, Mrs. Graham."

I stifle a grimace. Do I still have the right to be called Mrs.? The title fits about as well as my wedding band, now two sizes too big and consigned to a box at the bottom of my underwear drawer. Stress has whittled flesh from my fingers and added years to my face. My boys haven't noticed, but my mother certainly has. Before we turn out the lights tonight, I can count on a lecture ranging from "Why You Shouldn't Have Married that Louse" to "What Will Become of My Poor Grandsons without a Father to Play Ball with Them?"

I can't deny the truth any longer. I am now not only divorced but homeless as well.

Good thing I've developed that crust.

I stand and accept the real estate agent's outstretched hand. "If the new owners have any questions, they can reach me at my mother's house. We'll be there until we find a place to rent."

Ms. Nichols laughs. "Oh, we don't encourage interaction with buyers after the sale. If one of their pipes bursts next week, you don't want to be around. Walk away and don't look back—that's the best thing for everyone."

Easier said than done. I give the woman a stiff smile and leave the office. I'd love to stride into the future without looking back, but it's not easy to ride away from sixteen years of marriage without at least glancing in the rearview mirror.

I reach the van and catch my reflection in the driver's window. At this point some women might be tempted to throw themselves a pity party, but I'm not in the mood for pity *or* parties. I'm ticked at my husband for forcing us to sell our house, and I'm tired of living at my mother's.

To be completely honest, I'm feeling a little irritated with God. Why did he endow perfectly nice men with hormones that create an insatiable yearning for sports cars and nymphets about the time they spy their first gray hair?

I meet my mirrored gaze and order up a lecture in the same no-nonsense vein I'd use with one of my boys: "Look forward, not back. You'll find someplace to live; you'll find another job. Thomas will get through this midlife crisis and come back to his senses. Until he does, you can depend on your mother."

Oh yeah, I've come a long way, baby—from chief of staff for a respected U.S. senator to a woman who goes around talking to her reflection.

I lift my chin, unlock the door, and toss the check for forty thousand into my aging minivan.

※ ※ ※

My youngest, Bradley "Bugs" Graham, is playing fetch with our Jack Russell terrier when I pull into the driveway. My son turns his head long enough to recognize the minivan; then he plops his fanny onto the front porch step, props his elbows on his blue-jeaned knees, and plants his round cheeks in his hands. Even at five, he knows that little-boy-dejected pose is guaranteed to wring my heart.

Bugs doesn't budge as I shut off the engine and step out of the van, though I do catch him shooting a curious glance in my direction. As I walk toward him, though, his gaze remains fixed on the brick step under his feet. Skeeter pops out from beneath a bush and scampers to greet me, his favorite red ball in his mouth.

I take the spit-slimed ball, give it a toss, and look at my son as the dog darts away. "Hey, kiddo." My purse slides from my shoulder as I stoop to his level. "Got a hug for your mama?"

His blue eyes roll toward his coppery bangs, but he doesn't move.

"Something wrong?"

He nods, so intent upon maintaining his hands-on-cheeks posture that his elbows rise from his knees with each up-and-down motion.

I sink to the step. We sit together, two melancholy souls staring at the yawning emptiness of the sky. A pair of birds flies by—ducks or something—and I wonder if they've mated for life.

"The redheads are in there." Bugs's voice startles me.

"The redheads?"

"You know, those ladies. They're all actin' silly."

His meaning eludes me until I remember why the street is glutted with cars—my mother is hosting a meeting of the Fairfax chapter of the Red Hat Society, a group of over-fifty ladies who vow to have fun in their golden years. I've never actually witnessed what they call a get-together, but I've seen Mom gussied up in her red hat and purple feather boa.

And she thought my teen years were bizarre.

I'm sure the Hatters inside are lovely women, but right now I'm not in the mood to face a faction of females who are bound to be curious about why my kids and I have moved in with Mom.

Skeeter rushes off to chase a squirrel as I slip my arm around my son's narrow shoulders. "Are the Red Hats in the living room?"

He nods.

"Then we'll go in through the kitchen, okay?"

Like cat burglars we sneak into the garage and creep down the narrow aisle between a wall of storage boxes and the side of my mother's Buick. When we reach the door that leads to the kitchen, I turn and press my index finger to my lips. Bugs's eyes are shining, and I'm so grateful for this evidence of happiness that my voice wavers. "Ready, Fred?"

"Ready, Ted."

I open the door and slip into the kitchen. Bugs tiptoes behind me. The dining room table, visible over the kitchen bar to our right, bears the remains of finger sandwiches, cookies, and a variety of congealed salads.

When I turn to check on Bugs, I see that my coconspirator's eyes have drifted toward the delectable detritus. "Hungry?"

He presses his lips together as his gaze lingers on a mound of sausage balls.

"Tell you what, kiddo—I'll cover you if you want to sneak in there and grab a couple of goodies."

I understand why he hesitates. Mother's friends seem to think the good Lord dropped me and my kids at her house so she can enjoy unlimited time with her grandchildren and they can sneak hugs and kisses.

Bugs focuses on me. "I'll be quick."

"Okay, sport. Make a run for it."

He's off with a squeak of his sneakers, but the laughing ladies in the living room don't seem to hear this evidence of our trespassing.

After a moment, my mother's voice commands their attention. "Do you agree to handle growing more mature with humor and to take your silliness seriously?"

Someone giggles in answer.

"In the spirit of friendship and sisterhood, do you join your Red-Hatted sisters as we sassily go forth, bonded affectionately by the common thread of 'been there, done that,' and with real enthusiasm for whatever comes next?"

A hushed voice: "I do."

"Do you promise to learn to spit and not be afraid to sit on the sidewalk if you get tired?"

"I do."

"Do you pledge to never, *ever* wear nylons with open-toed sandals?"

"I do."

"Then place your right hand on your hat and repeat after me. I do lightheartedly swear on my hat to do my best to uphold the spirit of the Red Hat Society. This I pledge with a Red Hattitude. . . ."

Alarmed that Bugs might have accidentally violated the sanctity of the initiation ceremony, I peek over the kitchen bar. My son's pockets are bulging, presumably with sausage balls, and he's heading for a plate of chocolate chip cookies.

"Bugs!" I whisper as loud as I dare. "You'd better hurry!"

He grabs a cookie, takes a bite, and stuffs the eclipsed remainder in his shirt pocket. He's eyeing a bowl of red M&M'S when the relative calm of the living room erupts into a babble of voices.

I hiss a command to my offspring. "Move it, boy!"

Like the hero of every B movie, Bugs reaches for one treasure too many. His fingers have just invaded the crystal candy bowl when the tide turns and the sea of Red Hatters swells toward the dining room.

Mother sings out above the bedlam, "Bugs Graham! You'll spoil your appetite—"

But a crush of swirling compliments drowns out her reproach.

"What an adorable child!"

"Let the boy eat what he wants."

"Oh, you sweet darling! Come give me some sugar."

I gesture to Bugs, but he's caught in the riptide.

One woman pinches his face while another bends and wraps her arms around him. My little eel squirms, though, so when the latter Red Hatter attempts to kiss his cheek, her lips smack his ear instead.

Too late, I realize that I am also exposed to Mother's guests. I paste on a polite smile as the ladies approach with open arms and cries of welcome.

"Jennifer, sweetheart, how are you doing?"

"Your little boy is *such* a delight. You also have a daughter, right?"

I extend my hand to Bugs, who is threading his way through the milling Hatters. "No, ma'am, I have another son."

"So sorry to hear about your trouble. But I know Queen Snippy loves having you here."

I blink. "Who?"

"Her Royal Highness. Your mother."

How could I forget? The Hatters bestow royal names on one another, and my mom rules this particular chapter with a red velvet glove.

"We're enjoying the queen's hospitality," I say, addressing as many Hatters as I can. "But if you all will excuse me, I think my little boy could use an appointment with the royal bathtub."

I smile and pull Bugs toward the hallway, and at one point I glimpse the queen smiling by the front door. Because she's wearing her hostess face, I doubt any of her guests know how hard these last few days have been for her . . . for all of us.

Mother loves me and my kids, but she's not accustomed to having two young boys and a spring-loaded terrier underfoot. And as grateful as I am for her support, I don't want her to spend her slender retirement income on us. Neither do I want her to become a full-time babysitter.

"If you ladies will excuse me . . ." I tighten my grip on Bugs's hand and push him out of the kitchen. Skeeter, who has let himself in through the doggy door, dances at my son's side.

When we enter the quiet hallway that leads to the bedrooms, Bugs grins up at me. "We got busted!"

"And whose fault was that? You didn't have to take some of everything on the table." I sigh as some still-functioning part of my brain raises a mandatory maternal warning. "You shouldn't eat so many sweets before dinner. You'll ruin your appetite."

"I won't."

"You will. And you need a bath."

"Can't I wait until after dinner?"

I lean against the wall and close my eyes. It'd be so easy to give in—seems like the thing I do best these days is surrender to the men in my life.

I look down at him. "All right, but you have to wash your hands before you eat those snacks. And you head into the tub first thing after dinner without arguing. Okay?"

"'Kay."

Bugs and Skeeter scamper away and turn into the first doorway on the right—Mother's sewing room, now serving as a bedroom for Bugs and Clay. Since quiet reigns in this hallway, I know Clay is either shooting hoops at the park or riding his bike. At thirteen, he's smart enough to leave as soon as he spots a red hat.

I grip my purse and trudge toward Mother's guest room. The flowered, lace-trimmed bedspread isn't my taste nor are the decoupage doilies on the walls. Mom said I could hang some of my pictures, but as long as I don't unpack our furnishings, I can believe this situation is only temporary.

I sink to the edge of the bed and kick off my shoes, then pull my purse toward me. The real estate agent's check now lies in the fold of my wallet, so I take it out and stare at the number in the box: forty thousand dollars.

I can't help feeling like a contestant on some kind of cheesy game show. If offered the choice of a luxury car, the down payment on a town house, or a year in a nice apartment complex, which should I choose? All three are decent prizes, but none of them come with a guarantee.

A cackle creeps down the hall and slides beneath my closed door; one of the Red Hatters is chortling her way into the hallway bathroom. I close my eyes against the sound and topple sideways onto my pillow.

I need a relaxing hour in the tub, but I don't dare commandeer the bathroom until the last Hatter has gathered her leftovers and gone. I need a good soak and a good night's sleep, because tomorrow I have to get up, get dressed, and go out to look for a job. Again.

Finding new employment would be easier if I hadn't been married to Captain Gregarious. Thomas, a legislative assistant for Virginia's *other* senator, is known and liked by almost everyone on Capitol Hill. The notion of hiring his ex-wife is proving to be about as popular as New Coke.

While I'm out suffering through perfunctory interviews, the boys and Skeeter will stay with Mom. Though she insists she doesn't mind watching them this summer, I know better. Clay is at that awkward age, and Bugs's dramatics would try the patience of a plow horse. Mom loves my little guys, but she hasn't been a full-time parent since I left home more than twenty years ago. Come to think of it, *I* haven't been a full-time mom since I came off maternity leave after Bugs was born.

I snort at the irony: if I hadn't been so particular as I screened potential nannies, my family might still be complete.

My thoughts keep whirling as my body relaxes into numbness. By the time I'm fifty, my boys will be sixteen and twenty-four. Old enough to have survived whatever trauma their father and I have inflicted upon them. Old enough, I hope, to forgive us our mistakes.

Maybe by then I'll be able to put on a red hat and take my silliness seriously.

An unexpected clattering jerks me back to wakefulness. I didn't mean to doze off, but it sounds like World War III erupted during my twenty-minute nap. Skeeter is barking, Clay and Bugs are shouting at each other, and my mother is singing "Peace in the Valley" at the top of her lungs—probably as an exercise in wishful thinking.

The boys must be ravenous. I force my legs to the side of the bed and blink the room into focus, then patter to the kitchen in my bare feet. Mom is standing at the freezer, peering into its crowded depths, while Clay eats peanut-butter-and-cheese crackers at the bar. Skeeter sits at Clay's feet, hoping for a dropped morsel.

Bugs rummages through pots and pans in an open cupboard. "How about spaghetti?" He pulls a huge pot into his lap. "You have straw noodles in the pantry, Grandma. I saw 'em."

Mom shakes her head. "No sauce."

"How about noodles and butter?"

My mother makes a face. "Is that what that horrible nanny used to feed you?"

Not the nanny—me. I step into the kitchen before Bugs can reveal my culinary inadequacies. "Let me call and order something." I move toward the cupboard where Mom keeps the yellow pages. "Maybe Chinese or Italian. I could go for a grilled chicken salad."

"Nonsense." Mom closes the freezer and opens the refrigerator door. "Why order out when we have food right here?"

Because it's easier, I want to say, but Mom grew up in an era when easy didn't matter and women cooked three-course meals every night. She doesn't often criticize me in front of the boys, but sometimes I can feel her disapproval like a pair of sharp eyes pricking at the nape of my neck. *Mothers should stay home with their kids. Mothers should cook dinner for their children. Mothers should monitor the television and encourage their sons to read. . . .*

"I'm ordering pizza," I announce, ending the debate. "I know you don't feel like cooking after your big shindig. Pizza's quick and easy."

"No olives." Clay frowns from the end of the bar. "I hate olives."

"Noted," I answer, as if this is news.

I turn to the phone on the wall and punch the buttons, only a little embarrassed that I've already memorized the number. I can't see Mother shaking her head, but my internal radar registers radiating waves of disapproval.

"How many times have we had pizza?" she asks, an artificial note of brightness in her voice. "Three times in the last week?"

"Four," Clay answers, quick to supply the enemy with ammunition. "Wednesday, Friday, Saturday, and today. And that's not counting leftovers."

"Pizza's good for you." I fold one arm across my chest as I wait for someone to pick up. "It's got all the food groups: protein, starch, dairy, fat—even fruit, if we get the one with pineapple."

Bugs crinkles his nose. "I hate pine yapple."

I cross Bugs off my list of allies.

A man with a thick accent—Indian or something—comes on the line. I order a large sausage pizza and a large Hawaiian. "By the way, do you have salads?"

"Yes."

"Two salads, please. With grilled chicken."

"No."

"No what? No chicken, no salad, or no, you don't want to take my order?"

"No salad for delivery. Dine-in service only."

I exhale a sigh. "Two large pizzas, then. For delivery. As soon as possible."

I rattle off Mom's address and listen as the order taker repeats it back. When he finally gets it right, he tells me our dinner will cost thirty dollars and arrive in an hour.

Great. My boys will have eaten every cracker in the pantry by the time the pizza gets here.

When I hang up, Mom's expression has softened. "Let me fix you a glass of tea," she says. "Sit down, Jen. You boys take those snacks and go watch TV. Let your mama rest awhile, okay?"

Clay grabs the box of crackers and heads toward the living room; Bugs and Skeeter follow, both anxious for a handout.

I sink to a barstool at the counter and rest my head on my hand.

Mom fills a glass with ice. "How'd the job hunt go today?"

"I've had interest from several offices on the Hill, but once they find out I was married to Thomas . . ." I shrug. "No one wants a chief of staff who's likely to butt heads with one of Senator Barron's top aides. Until the gossip about our divorce dies down, I don't think I'm going to find work in the Capitol."

Mother doesn't reply, but the way she presses her lips together speaks volumes. She doesn't like Thomas much these days. I'm not sure she ever did.

But right now I can't afford to tiptoe around people's feelings—I need a job. Yet while thousands of people work in and around Capitol Hill, public service is like the proverbial goldfish bowl. The story whispered around the coffeepot is usually broadcast from the rotunda by five o'clock.

Even if by some miracle I find a job in an office that rarely deals with Senator Barron's staff, I doubt I'll ever escape the rumors and questioning glances. I'd be willing to leave Washington for a while, but northeast Virginia has been my home for years.

If I were president, I'd issue a proclamation: men who insist on their right to a midlife crisis must pack up and move away until the mood has passed. I'm sure we could find a suitable cooling-off place for them. Maybe Mars.

"It's your hair," Mom says, pouring tea into two ice-filled glasses. "That no-style style you have. You should put your hair up. Maybe try a French twist. You need to look more professional when you interview."

I swivel my gaze toward the dining room window and try to ignore the remark. I'm sure Mom means her comment as a suggestion, but from here it feels like criticism. "My hair is fine," I say, my voice flat.

"Your hair has always been fine," she answers, completely missing my point. "Maybe some mousse would give it a little extra body. If you want, I can ask Baroness Barbara Bee if she can recommend something."

I know I ought to change the subject, but I can't resist. "Who?"

"The baroness—one of our Hatters is a hairdresser; didn't you know? Barb's had her own shop for years."

This time I *do* change the subject as Mom sets two glasses of iced tea on the table. "I'm sure I'll find something. It's going to take a while, though. In the meantime, at least I have the equity from the house for living expenses." I take a sip of the tea and try not to gag. Mom's tea is like honey.

"You know the Lord will provide. He always does."

Leave it to Mom to hand me another useless bromide. I get up and walk around the counter, keeping my back to her so she won't see the frustration on my face. I love my mother and I love the Lord, but sometimes I think Mom would charge hell with a bucket of platitudes and a handful of gospel tracts. She's never been divorced, and she was married to a man who dedicated his heart to his family and his body to the army. The woman has no idea what I'm going through.

I walk to the sink and quietly add a little water to my iced tea glass, then force a laugh. "At least the boys are on summer vacation. I won't have to worry about settling them into a new school for a few weeks."

"You know I'll watch the boys anytime you need me," Mom says, but when I turn around, she's set her jaw as if bracing herself for the task.

The jut of her chin becomes more pronounced when Clay sprints through the kitchen with the crackers, followed by Bugs and Skeeter.

The battered inner bag has ripped, and bits of salty orange squares trickle to the floor with every step.

Obviously Bugs and Skeeter care more about catching Clay than cleaning up his trail of crumbs.

I apprehend my oldest son the second time he lopes through the dining room. "See this?" I point to the streak of orange on the floor. "You'll find a line all through the kitchen, the dining room, and probably the living room, too. I suggest you get busy with the broom and dustpan."

Clay screws up his face. "But, Mom! Bugs keeps trying to get—"

"Bugs can hold the dustpan while you sweep. But both of you need to start cleaning."

While the boys grumble and Skeeter licks crumbs from the tile, I step back to the counter and rest my hand on my mother's arm. "You've done more than enough for us, Mom. I know the boys are a handful, so—"

"So nothing. I love looking after my grandsons, and I'll do it until . . . well, until school starts."

I pat her arm, noticing for the first time that her skin feels like crepe paper. "You've raised your kid, Mom; I won't ask you to raise mine. If you have a meeting or want to have lunch with your friends, let me know so I can work something out. We don't want to tie you down."

She opens her mouth, about to protest again, but I shake my head. "That's it for now. I'm too worn-out to argue with you."

※ ※ ※

After dinner, I leave Mom and the boys in front of the television while I go to the boys' room and sit at Mom's sewing table. Since the sewing machine has been temporarily moved to the closet, the table serves as a repository for my paperwork—the divorce decree, bills, real estate contracts, and a dozen change-of-address cards lacking only our new address.

My to-do list lies next to the bills, its numbered lines scrawled with reminders about the boys' dental appointments, required back-to-school checkups, and a list of questions to keep in mind when I find a rental and am able to investigate schools. Bugs should start kindergarten this fall, and not knowing where he'll pass this milestone galls me. I suppose I can do my best to make his first day special wherever we are, but I can't stop a huge knot of mother guilt from rising in my throat whenever I think about the uncertainty of our future.

My guilt sharpens into resentment, however, when my thoughts shift to Thomas. I asked for custody and got it, but even with Thomas paying child support, the arrangement hardly seems fair. In late summer, when I'll be trying to find a job and get the boys ready for school, my ex-husband and his girlfriend will be enjoying the five-week congressional recess. He'll probably head for the Bahamas or someplace even more exotic. . . .

I push those thoughts aside. I will drive myself crazy if I fixate on a man who has temporarily lost his mind. What's done is done. Thomas ran away with our nanny; he divorced me. Now I have to keep placing one foot in front of the other. I do what I can for my boys. I pray and remind myself to breathe.

Day after day, I play Wonder Woman, a role I didn't ask for and don't like. But when the world tilts on its axis, you do what you have to do until the planet rights itself again.

I open the bills that the U.S. Postal Service has, in its infinite wisdom, chosen to forward to me instead of my ex-husband. I need to make a payment on the Visa card, but I shove the bill for Thomas's life insurance back into the envelope. He can pay for his own insurance. As long as he remains away, he can do whatever he likes.

At nine o'clock, I slip into the living room and find Bugs and Skeeter asleep on the floor. Clay sits in the recliner, his gaze glued to the TV screen, and Mother snores softly on the sofa.

I ruffle Clay's hair. "You doing okay?"

He nods without turning his head. "Mom?"

"Hmm?"

"I really want that Madden game. For my Nintendo DS."

I draw a deep breath. "Is it expensive?"

"Well . . . yeah."

"And have you been saving your allowance?"

His skinny throat bobs as he swallows. "I don't have enough."

"When you do, you can get the game, okay? Now I have to get Bugs to bed." I bend and scoop my youngest into my arms, amazed as always that this gangly male creature came from my body.

He wakes as I carry him through the hall and immediately asks to be put down.

Reluctantly, I lower him to the tile.

"Was I asleep?" he asks, taking my hand.

"Yes."

"I'm not tired."

"I think maybe you are."

"Is Clay still up?"

"Not for much longer."

We reach the bed, where I've already turned back the blankets. Bugs hops onto the clean sheets and squirms beneath the covers. "Want me to pray tonight, Mom?"

"That'd be nice."

Bugs presses his palms together and closes his eyes so tightly that his golden lashes nearly disappear. "Dear Jesus, thank you for Grandma and Mom and Clay and Skeeter and Bubba Bagels. Thank you for Dad, even though he doesn't live with us anymore. Thank you for TV and pizza and video games. Forgive me for my sins. Amen."

By some miracle, I'm able to smile as he settles under the thick comforter. "Who's Bubba Bagels?"

The dimple in his left cheek winks at me. "Jesse's dog. He's humongous."

"Who's Jesse?"

"He lives next door . . . I think. Maybe he just visits his grandma, like we do."

"Is this big dog nice?"

"*Really* nice. 'Cause I know I'm not supposed to talk to strange dogs."

"That's right, kiddo." I press a kiss to my son's cheek and smooth the comforter over his chest. "I'll see you in the morning."

"Is tomorrow going to be a great day?"

I close my eyes, wishing he hadn't asked. The question comes from something Thomas used to say whenever he put the boys to bed. "Yes." The word sounds strangled as it passes through my tight throat. "A great day."

Those three little words hold more hope than my entire heart.

Joella sits at the kitchen table, her fingertips tapping the side of a cold coffee mug. The quiet hour before bedtime is usually her favorite part of the day, but she can't feel tranquil or reflective when a screeching car chase is reverberating off the walls of the living room.

She draws a deep breath and consciously expands her lungs until she feels the stretch of her rib cage. Stress is her enemy; it raises her blood pressure and makes her heart work harder. She needs peace and quiet, but her family's needs come first.

She grimaces as Clay belches loud enough to be heard above a climactic car crash. Has Jen completely forgotten to teach her boys manners? Of course she's been through a lot in recent months, but Clay should have been taught proper etiquette years ago. Young women today, though, have so many other things on their minds . . . especially Jen. Especially now.

Joella closes her eyes. The sink behind her is overflowing with dishes, the leftover pizza needs to be tossed out or refrigerated, and she'll need to disinfect the spots where the dog licked the floor. These days she cleans from morning until night. No sooner has she set one room to rights than someone traipses through and messes it up again.

Jen and the boys don't mean to be a bother. They're people, that's all, and people are sometimes hard to have around, especially when you've become accustomed to living alone.

Joella never thought she'd admit that she *likes* the solitary life. Living alone, she can stay in bed as late as she wants or get up at 3 a.m. if she can't sleep. She can eat a bowl of Special K for supper or not eat at all. She can wear her pajamas in the garden or leave them on all day because her schedule doesn't revolve around anyone else's. The best part of living alone is cleaning her house and knowing that it will stay clean until after the Hatter get-together or the Sunday school tea or until *she* decides to mess things up.

Still . . . when your only child needs you, how can you not help? Jennifer had no place to go when Thomas demanded she sell the house, and what kind of grandmother would insist on her right to a tidy kitchen while her grandkids live in a motel or some dreadful rental apartment? Bad enough that those dear boys will have to deal with a divorce. Maybe their memories of this awful time will be eased by the happiness they enjoyed while living at her house.

Oh, Lord, let me be a bright spot in this murky year. . . .

"Grandma?"

The shout comes from the living room, but Joella doesn't answer shouts. A moment later Clay appears in the kitchen, bare chested, tousle haired, and heavy lidded. "Do we have any more milk?"

Now that he's asked politely, she smiles. "Why don't you look in the refrigerator and see?"

He scratches his side and moves toward the fridge. She waits, expecting to hear the milk jug slide from the shelf, but after a while she feels a breath of cold air against the backs of her bare legs.

She turns in her chair. Clay stands before the open door, still scratching at his side, his eyes wide and unfocused. What is the child doing?

"Clay, did you want milk?"

He nods.

"Then take out the jug, close the door, and pour yourself a glass."

She bites back her exasperation as the boy pours himself a drink in slow motion. What is *with* these children? Are they so accustomed to having everything done for them that they can't do anything for themselves?

She stands and moves to the counter, stepping around Clay as he leans against the fridge and sips his milk. In the sink, four dirty plates slant against one another atop at least a dozen glasses and cups. You'd think one boy could use one cup for the entire day, but no, Clay and Bugs want a clean cup every time they need to wet their whistle. She used to run the dishwasher once a week; now she runs it once a day. The water bill will be sky-high this month and probably next month, too.

She stops stacking dishes as a stab of guilt pricks at her soul. What is she *thinking*? She'd open her veins for Jen's boys. She'd empty her bank account if it'd help that fractured family make a new start.

That's why they're here. Jennifer isn't herself these days. She needs someone to help her think clearly. Bugs and Clay need a firm hand and consistent reminders. And the good Lord has given Joella everything those three need.

She hums to herself as she bends to open the dishwasher. Having her family here requires certain adjustments, but she's happy to make them.

All in all, it's nice to be needed.

4

*F*riday morning brings a smattering of rain from the west—enough to keep the summer heat at bay and snarl the interstates with fender benders. For the first time in weeks, I'm grateful that I don't have to drive into the District.

I make sure the boys are dressed and fed; then I put on a pair of shorts and an old T-shirt. Today I want to do something to help Mother around the house. I need to show my appreciation for her hospitality in some tangible way.

Since Mom can't get up and down as easily as she used to, I'm outside weeding the flower bed when she opens the front door and extends the cordless phone. "Some lawyer is looking for Jennifer Graham. That'd be you."

I wipe my muddy hands on my shorts before taking the phone. "Did he give his name?"

Still in her housecoat, Mom retreats behind the screen door. "He rattled off three or four names, but I didn't catch them. And don't forget to deadhead the geraniums."

I breathe deeply and hold the phone at my waist. In the last six months I've had more dealings with lawyers than in ten years of political work. I thought I was finished with negotiations . . . so what is Thomas up to now?

I blow out a breath and bring the phone to my ear. "Jennifer Graham speaking."

"Ms. Graham, this is Daniel Sladen, of Lawson, Bridges, and Sladen in Mt. Dora. How are you this fine day?"

The casual question catches me off guard because I'm struggling to remember if I've worked with Lawson, Bridges, Sladen, or anyone in Mt. Dora. None of the names are familiar, but if Thomas has hired a new team to confiscate 50 percent of everything I owned during our marriage, tough. He can't have half the silver in my teeth.

I prop one hand on my hip and thank the Lord that my Roth IRA is untouchable. "I'm represented by Andi Pettigrew in Falls Church. I suggest you take this matter up with her."

"Um . . . I thought it might be nice if we talked first. We usually speak to the heirs before we involve their lawyers."

The unexpected word strikes my ear like a jolt of electricity. "Did you say *heirs?*"

"Yes, ma'am. Ned Norris passed away last month, and we've been working hard to settle his estate. Tracking you down has proven to be a challenge."

"Ned Norris?" I look at Mother, still lingering behind the screen door. "I'm sorry, but I don't recognize the name."

"I believe he was your father's uncle . . . so he'd be your great-uncle. Mr. Norris had no children, and his wife predeceased him by several years. So he's left his entire estate to you."

Mother steps out from behind the screen, her forehead knitting in a frown. "What's this about Uncle Ned?"

I cup my hand over the phone. "Deceased."

The lines on her forehead deepen. "I knew he passed on, but we haven't heard from him in years. Seems like—"

I lift a hand to silence Mother because I can't follow two conversations at once, and I'd rather listen to the lawyer. Beneath my sweaty T-shirt, a kernel of hope sprouts, sending tendrils of optimism through my heart.

An estate. That usually means dozens of boxes for the nearest thrift shop, but it could also mean money, a house, even commercial property.

"Mr. Sladen—" I turn to escape Mother's curious gaze—"when you say *estate*, you mean . . ."

"His business, naturally," the lawyer answers, "comprised of the building, the land, and all necessary equipment. The place has been closed since Ned had his stroke, but a caretaker has lived on the premises to take care of the structure and the equipment. People in Mt. Dora have been giving their business to the folks in Eustis or Tavares, but it shouldn't take much if you want to get the operation running again."

My mind fills with images of cozy restaurants, quirky retail shops, perhaps a small town real estate office. I'm a natural organizer, so with good help I could probably handle any of those businesses. I want to crawl through the telephone line and *kiss* this lawyer.

"That is incredible." I bite my lower lip and look at Mother. "What sort of business is it?"

Mr. Sladen releases a short, embarrassed laugh. "I'm sorry. I thought you knew."

"No."

"Then it's about time you became acquainted with your uncle's legacy. Ned Norris served the Mt. Dora community over fifty years; there's scarcely a family in town he hasn't helped at one time or another. Our mayor spoke at Ned's funeral, said Ned was the kind of man you'd call when nobody else could help."

For some reason, I envision a saintly-looking man at a desk with an adding machine. Could Uncle Ned have been a tax preparer?

"Please," I say, realizing that something about my uncle's career has made the lawyer uncomfortable, "if you could tell me the name of my uncle's company . . ."

"Fairlawn," Mr. Sladen replies. "Your uncle has left you the Fairlawn Funeral Home."

※※ ※※ ※※

A whiff of dust rises from the old photograph album as Mother lifts the cover. Black-and-white photographs clutter the crumbling pages, barely held in place by folded paper corners that have long since lost their adhesive.

The dust tickles my nose and makes me sneeze.

"Bless you." Mom points to a photo of a tall, thin man with a crew cut. "That's Ned. That little boy next to him? That's your father."

The little boy in the photo is wearing a cotton sunsuit, his legs like plump sausages beneath the elastic casings. I chuckle, a little boggled by the thought of Brigadier General Nolan Norris as a chubby toddler. "Did you know Ned well?"

Mom sighs. "I wish I had. He and your grandfather went their separate ways after their parents died. They were the only two children in the family, you know, Ned and Vane. Ned and Marjorie ended up in Florida, while Vane and Vera married and settled in Virginia. Ned and Marjorie never had any children, and Vane and Vera only had your father."

Her smile quirks with a memory. "Papa Vane used to say they wanted ten kids, but your father wore the *want* right out of them. Nolan thought that was the most hilarious thing he'd ever heard."

As always, we fall silent at the mention of my dad. He's been gone six years, but Mother still gets weepy when she mentions him.

When Mom swipes a tear from her lashes, I figure it's time to move the discussion along. "So . . . when's the last time you heard from Uncle Ned?"

She snorts a laugh. "I guess that'd be when I heard he was dead. His friend called, Gerald or Gary somebody or other. Said Ned passed away in his sleep at the nursing home. I figure that's a good way to go when you're eighty-nine. Much better than what your father endured."

For a moment neither of us can speak. It's as if my dad's illness has invaded the room, bringing with it the scents of medicine and decay and disinfectant. In the silence I can almost hear the labored rasp of Dad's breathing, a sound that grated on our nerves until we begged God to make it stop. . . .

And one day he did.

I stare out the window until Mom turns the page and looks at another picture, a photo with no obvious emotions attached. I follow her gaze, but I still have questions.

"Did you know—" I edge up to the topic—"that Ned was a mortician?"

"Heavens, no. If I'd known, I'd have sent a bigger spray of flowers to the funeral home."

"Surely he wasn't still running the place." I frown at the thought of an octogenarian lifting corpses. "I can understand why he wouldn't want to leave his home, but he had to have help with the business."

"I don't know what he was doing, Jen. We lost touch after Papa Vane passed, and the army moved us around so much. . . ." Mother flips through the rest of the photograph album, but Uncle Ned doesn't surface again.

I leave the album on Mom's knees and go to the bedroom for my laptop. Mother doesn't have a computer, so I have no choice but to use dial-up to access the Internet.

Back in the living room, I plug in the phone cord and power up the machine.

Mom watches over my shoulder as the laptop connects with the usual buzz and burble. "What are you going to do with that?"

"Look him up."

"Who?"

"Ned Norris."

She laughs. "Honey, I'd bet my bottom dollar that he wasn't into computers."

"Mom, these days almost *every* business is on the Internet. Give me a minute and I'll show you." I cross my arms while the computer finishes its hookup. Then I click on Google and type *Fairlawn Funeral Home* in the search window.

After what feels like an interminable interval, a window opens. If this site can be trusted, the Fairlawn Funeral Home is a sprawling pink, white, and gray Victorian—a mansion, really, with a wrap-around front porch, hundreds of decorative spindles, and a towering turret.

"Oh my." Mom's voice is almost reverent. "Looks like Ned did right well for himself."

"The place could be mortgaged to the hilt."

"I doubt that. Both Ned and your grandfather were funny about loans—they hated being in debt."

I scan the Web site, but the page offers little information other than the business name, address, and the number of a telephone that has probably been disconnected.

Mom squeezes my shoulder, obviously impressed. "Just think—you own that house."

I stare at the picture in disbelief. The house is the type of grand old Painted Lady I would have given my right arm to own when I was younger, but now I can't get past the function behind the facade. "I own . . . a funeral home."

"Doesn't matter what you call it—that's a gorgeous house. I told you the Lord would work things out."

I squint at the photograph and count windows. How many bedrooms are in a house that size?

"Here you are," Mother rattles on, "wondering how you and the boys are going to survive, and God drops this beautiful place into your lap."

"It's not in my lap. It's in Florida."

"So? Florida property is valuable. You'll make a fortune when you sell it."

"I'll be lucky if I can afford the inheritance taxes."

"Let the lawyers sort that out. You shouldn't worry."

I lean back and sort through the few facts I know. Mr. Sladen didn't mention any monetary figures, so I don't want to get my hopes up. A house as old as this might be free of encumbrances, but who knows how much it's worth? And though I could never see us living in Florida, I can't help wondering if that diamond-shaped window in the turret belongs to a third-story room or if it's merely decorative.

I turn to my mother. "So, do you want to come with us?"

"What?"

"I might as well go down and look the place over. I think the boys and I deserve a Florida vacation."

A frown line settles between Mother's brows. "Why don't you just let the lawyer sell it?"

"Why shouldn't I go? It's perfect timing—the boys have nothing special to do this summer, I'm unemployed, and we haven't taken a family trip since before Bugs was born. It might be fun for all of us . . . if you want to come."

Mom bends to look at the computer screen again. "I suppose it would be foolish to sell the place without checking things out. After all, that house could be crammed full of antiques."

"Or junk."

"Or worse. I read about this funeral director who took people's money and never buried them. He let the dead bodies stack up like cordwood."

I give her a get-real look. "You think Uncle Ned would do that?"

"No. Ned was a good man. I know that much."

I close my eyes to envision my nearly blank calendar. I have a couple of appointments next week, but they are routine interviews, nothing promising. I could easily cancel.

I have no reason to spend the summer in Virginia. Thomas hasn't asked to see the boys lately, and who knows? If I take off without asking his opinion or checking his schedule, maybe he'll see a new side of me, an aspect more unstructured and fun. After all, he said he *loved* Nanny Fiona's spontaneity.

Mom looks thoughtfully at the computer. "Do you suppose this house is close to Disney World?"

"That'd be nice," I answer, disconnecting the phone line. "Because unless I bribe them first, there's no way my boys will want to visit a funeral home."

$\mathcal{M}_y$ favorite Internet map site tells me it should take thirteen hours to drive from Mother's house in Fairfax to Fairlawn in Mt. Dora. But I'd bet Mr. MapQuest has never driven 840 miles with a Red Hatter, two active boys, and a high-powered terrier.

I am just settling into cruising speed on I-95 when Mother announces that she needs a rest stop.

"Try not to think about your bladder," I tell her. "Close your eyes and relax. I don't mind if you sleep."

"I don't need to sleep," she insists. "I need to potty."

This, of course, elicits a flood of giggles from the backseat. The boys can't believe Grandma is talking like a two-year-old, and frankly I can't either.

I slant the van toward the nearest exit, and we park at a gas station while Mother hurries off to the restroom, her purse swinging from one arm. I glance at the gas gauge, thinking I might as well fill up, but we haven't used even an eighth of a tank. Clay focuses on the racks of candy in the station windows while Bugs stares at a cement mixer parked outside.

"Well, guys—" I turn to smile at my sons—"are you excited about the trip?"

Clay looks at his new video game with the bored nonchalance of a thirteen-year-old. "I guess."

"Mom," Bugs asks, still staring at the concrete mixer, "where are we goin' again?"

"Disney World," I tell him, "after we visit this little town called Mt. Dora."

"Will there be kids in that place?"

"I'm sure there are lots of kids."

"And what is it we won?"

I have tried to explain the situation, but Bugs seems to think an inheritance is akin to winning the lottery.

"We've inherited a house—a big one. It's ours, but we're not going to keep it. We're going to go down, look it over, and get it ready to sell. When someone agrees to buy it, we'll have enough money to buy a house of our own in Virginia."

"So we won't have to live with Grandma," Clay adds, elbowing his brother, "and I can have my own room again."

"Right. Maybe. I'm not sure what's going to happen, but I know everything is going to be okay. Sit back and relax, Son; it's going to be a long trip."

Bugs settles in his seat and calls for the dog. Skeeter jumps up and noses Bugs in the ribs, which sets the boy to giggling. I don't mind the noise, but apparently my youngest can't maintain control of his bodily functions while he giggles, because the relative calm is blown apart when a staccato sound erupts from Bugs's corner.

"Oh, man!" Clay unbuckles his seat belt and reaches for the door. "I can't breathe!"

"Stay in the van, Clay."

I give the order in my firmest voice, but Clay keeps fumbling with the handle. "Mom, I can't stay in here. Not with that."

Bugs laughs even harder, releasing spasmodic squeaks as he curls on the seat. Skeeter spins in a canine dance of delight.

"It'll be okay," I tell Clay. "Sit still."

"But the air is full of fart particles! You can't expect me to breathe—"

"Don't move, either of you." I unbuckle my seat belt and turn as far as the driver's seat will allow. "You are going to stay in this van and wait for Grandma." I shift my attention to Bugs. "And you, young man, will kindly refrain from—"

"I couldn't help it, Mom! Skeeter—"

"Don't blame the dog." I look toward the restroom and silently urge Mother to hurry. If she takes much longer, I might jump out to buy rope and duct tape.

When Mom finally comes out of the restroom, Skeeter is panting, Clay is pouting, and Bugs's giggles have subsided to random hiccups. But instead of walking to the van, Mother heads toward the station's convenience store. I have an idea what she's up to, and my hunch is confirmed when she reappears with a bulging brown paper bag.

"I've got munchies," she announces as she slides into her seat. "Cokes and candy and peanuts. Bugs, you like Yoo-hoo, don't you?"

She doles out junk food while I rap my knuckles against the steering wheel and stare out my window. No sense in protesting, and how can I forbid the boys a treat when Mother plans on eating in front of them? She's bought four twenty-ounce drinks, which means we'll be pulling off the highway for another snack run/bathroom break in an hour or two.

In the rearview mirror, I see Bugs dangling a gummy worm in front of Skeeter.

"No candy for the dog," I warn, starting the van. "Doggy biscuits only."

While I watch the reflection, Skeeter springs up and snips the multi-colored night crawler from Bugs's fingers. Bugs presses a finger to his lips, sealing the child-dog conspiracy.

I growl deep in my throat. "I saw that, Bradley Graham. I can see you in my mirror."

"But, Mom—" Bugs grins as the dog gives the worm a vigorous shake—"Skeeter *took* it from me."

I look to Mother, expecting an expression of commiseration, but she gives me that can't-you-make-him-obey? look.

I put the van in gear and head toward the highway. This is going to be a long, long drive.

❈ ❈ ❈

"I *hate* breathing truck exhaust."

Joella holds her breath as Jen zips up to the bumper of a belching semi, then cuts sharply into the left lane. She's now almost on *top* of some little foreign car, but she doesn't seem to notice that she's close enough to count the longish hairs on the back of Mr. Sports Car's neck.

Joella silently presses her foot to the floor, willing the van to slow down, but Mr. Sports Car glimpses Jen in his mirror and stomps on the gas.

At Joella's right, the semi driver honks as Jen edges past him. Joella looks out her window, wondering if the truck driver can read the desperation in her face. *Help, I'm being held prisoner by my crazy-driving daughter.*

Jen would get upset, of course, if Joella said anything about her driving. She'd try to laugh off Joella's concern, and if pressed, she'd say something about being an experienced driver who knows what she's doing. By the time the conversation ended, Joella would feel like a fool for bringing the matter up.

But isn't a mother *supposed* to correct her child?

She sucks in a breath as Jen cuts in front of the semi to let another speed demon zoom through the left lane.

"These people!" Jen glances at her exterior mirror. "Where's the fire?"

"I was about to ask you the same thing." Joella's words hang in the space between them, breezy and ponderous at the same time, and after a moment she wishes she could scoop them up and stuff them back down her throat.

"Mom." A heavy line of reproach underscores that word. "I'm a good driver. I'm used to driving in the District."

"I know you are, honey."

"I've never even gotten a ticket. The only accident I've ever had is the time I slid down that ice-covered hill, and that wasn't my fault."

"I know, dear."

"I just want you to relax." Jen settles her arm on the driver's door, leaving only one hand on the steering wheel.

Joella's nerves tense. Doesn't Jen realize how dangerous one-handed driving is? For the greatest maneuverability, a driver's hands are supposed to be in the ten-and-two position. Why, if someone were to swerve into their lane right now, there's no way Jen would be able to keep this van on the highway.

Joella glances at the backseat, where both boys are quiet. Bugs is sleeping with Skeeter in his lap while Clay plays a new game on his handheld Nintendo gizmo. He nearly drove her crazy moping about Madden, so before they left she gave him the thirty dollars he needed to buy it at Target. Jen might not approve, but at least it's keeping the boy occupied.

So this is as good a time as any.

Joella draws a deep breath. "I'm not sure you realize—" she lowers her voice—"that high-speed driving is extremely dangerous. If something happens, you have less time to make a correction and—"

"Mom."

"—you never know if the guy in front of you is going to drift or if a tire is going to blow—"

"Mom."

"—and *you have your children* in the car. So you need to keep both hands on the steering wheel." Joella crosses her arms, pleased that she's made her point without making a scene. Jennifer's no fool; she won't have to be reminded again. Joella glances to the left and is relieved to see that her daughter has lowered her free hand to the proper place on the wheel.

Cheered by this small but satisfying victory, Joella pulls her knitting from the bag at her feet. Might as well get some work done on this long drive. She takes out the half-finished project, wraps a strand of yarn around her index finger, and examines the stitches on the needle. She's making a scarf for Bugs in blue and gray, the official colors of Fairfax High, located only three miles from her house. The boy will need a scarf this fall when he goes to kindergarten, and he might as well have one in Fairfax colors.

She hums along with the radio as Lulu sings "To Sir, with Love." The song always strums a chord of memory.

"Did I ever tell you," she says, settling into the clicking rhythm of her knitting, "that this song was playing when you were born? Or at least it was playing before they knocked me out. When I woke up, I wanted to hear it again so I could hand you to your father and sing, 'To sir, with love. . . .'"

She glances at her daughter, expecting to see a smile, but Jen's expression has hardened into the scowl Joella has seen over breakfast bowls and in department stores, after curfew at the front door and beside dented bumpers.

She lowers her needles and braces for what is sure to come. Jen's not the type to let something fester. Like her father, she's likely to come right out with what's on her mind.

But sometimes you have to lance a boil.

"Okay." Joella turns in her seat. "What'd I say?"

Her daughter's chest rises and falls as her gaze darts to the rearview mirror. "I never knew," she says, her voice blistering, "that you think I'm a lousy mother."

Joella doesn't move. "Wh-what?"

"I have *children in the car*," Jen says, mincing her syllables. "You implied that I don't care about my kids."

"Why, I never—"

"I drive badly because I don't care—isn't that what you meant? Maybe you think I want to hurt them? to hurt myself?"

Joella groans and pinches the bridge of her nose. How can Jen bring that up with Clay awake in the backseat? "Honey, we don't have to—"

"That was a mistake, Mom, a mistake. I'd had dental work, and I lost track of time because I was in so much pain."

"And I believe you. But the doctors had to be sure, so when they asked me—"

"You should have told them I'd had a root canal. But instead you told them that my marriage was falling apart."

Jen's voice has that jittery tone, an edge Joella hasn't heard since those awful months right after Thomas left. She leans forward, checks to be sure her grandsons haven't noticed, then reaches across the chasm and squeezes her daughter's arm. "I'm sorry. I didn't mean to make things difficult back then, and I didn't mean to hurt your feelings a minute ago."

"Things are tough right now, but I'm doing the best I can. I'd give my life for my kids. You should know that."

Joella can barely draw breath. "I never meant to imply that you weren't a good mother."

Jen swipes at the tear trickling down her cheek. "That's what you said."

"Honey." In spite of her efforts to remain calm, Joella's lower lip wobbles. "You're a *wonderful* mother. You are. I can imagine what you've been going through—"

"No, you can't." Another tear, another angry swipe.

Because this conversation is heading toward dangerous waters, Joella lifts her hands in surrender. "I'm sorry. I think you're doing a fine job, and I'm sorry if I hurt you. I'm sorry I'm your mother. I'm sorry about everything I've ever done to ruin your life."

Jen's hand clenches on the steering wheel. "Take it down a notch, Norma Desmond."

"I will if you will."

Jen dips her chin in the briefest acknowledgment and punches the radio to another station.

Joella stares at the road and presses her palm to the window as they zoom by one of the speeding roadsters that passed them earlier.

Maybe the best way to keep peace on this trip is simply to close her eyes and zip her lip.

6

$\mathcal{S}$ated with a Cracker Barrel breakfast, on day two of our trek Mom and Bugs fall asleep somewhere south of Savannah. I assume Clay is dozing too, but after a few miles he leans forward to tap my shoulder.

"Mom—" he keeps his voice low—"tell me again what kind of place we're going to see."

I shift my gaze toward the grassy median and search for the right words. When I first told the boys about our trip, I deliberately avoided describing Fairlawn as a funeral home. I wasn't sure they'd know what a mortuary was, so why risk alarming them?

"It's a house, Clay. A pink house called Fairlawn."

"Who names their house?"

"Well . . . some people do. If the house is big enough or special."

Mom lifts her head. "Fairlawn is more than a house," she murmurs in a thick voice. "It's a business. A family business."

I exhale in a steady stream. Why does she have to be such a light sleeper?

Clay scoots forward and rests his elbows on the backs of our seats. "What kind of business is it?"

I would give Mom a warning glance, but I have to pull to the left to avoid being trapped behind a slower driver.

Before I can settle into the left lane, Mom answers Clay's question.

"Fairlawn is a funeral home. A place where they hold services for people who have passed on."

Okay, at least that was a tactful answer. In the rearview mirror I can see Clay watching the road with a furrowed brow. "That sounds creepy."

I grab hold of the conversation before it veers out of control. "I saw a picture on the Internet. Fairlawn is a beautiful house with a wide porch and a gorgeous turret."

Clay's lip curls exactly like Thomas's. "Why would anyone want a turnip in their house?"

"A *turret*—it's like a tower. Anyway, the house has a wide lawn where you and Bugs can play football."

"We're not thinking about *staying* there, are we?"

I force a laugh. "No way. But the property officially belongs to us, so I have to check it out and make arrangements to sell it. Our uncle was in a nursing home before he died, so the place probably needs a good cleaning and a few repairs."

"Seat belt," Mom says absently, and for an instant I'm not sure if she's reminding me or Clay.

Clay settles back into his seat and clicks his belt. When he speaks again, his voice wavers. "Are there dead people in the house now?"

"No, honey. The business hasn't been in operation for a while."

"Do you think it has . . . ghosts?"

"Sweetheart." Before Mother can give me a why-haven't-you-taught-him-better? look, I lacquer my voice with reproof. "You know there are no such things."

"This kid in my science class saw a ghost once. And Madison Carmichael said she heard one laughing in the house where her grandmother died."

"Uncle Ned didn't die in this house; he passed away in the nursing home." I lift my foot from the gas as the bubble of a highway patrol car comes into view. "You don't have to worry about anything, Son. We're going to have a nice visit, I'm going to take care of a few business details, and then we're going to Disney World."

"After that, we're going home?"

Where *is* home?

When I falter, Mom steps in with the answer. "After that, we're going back to my house."

When Clay picks up his iPod, I hope the matter is settled. Because Bugs is still at an impressionable age, we have to act like visiting a funeral home is no big deal. Now that I've addressed Clay's fears, he will play the cool older brother. I shouldn't have to worry about either child when we actually arrive at the mortuary.

And yet . . . in the silence of the van, I can't help dredging up my own misgivings. In all my thirty-nine years, I've been to exactly two funerals: my dad's and Deborah Mitchell's. My dad's funeral was an awful experience, and two years ago I slipped in and out of Deborah's only because she was a member of my Sunday school class and once brought me a cherry pie when I had the flu. But that had been a hectic day. Senator Franklin had been rushing to a vote on the Hill, and Deborah's funeral could not have come at a more inconvenient time.

Bottom line? I know nothing about the funeral industry and have absolutely no desire to learn.

Good thing I won't have to. Fairlawn is a lovely Victorian that should appeal to anyone who wants to live in a small town. We ought to be able to sell the property in a snap.

If all goes well and the market holds, I should make a good return on anything we have to invest in the house. Within a few days, Lord willing, the boys and I can return to Virginia and set about the work of rebuilding the home Thomas abandoned.

In time, maybe the Lord will lead him back to us. Maybe by then I'll be able to look at the man without wanting to crown him with a cast-iron skillet.

※ ※ ※

We pull into Mt. Dora at four o'clock. The van smells of dog and French fries, and I'm sure I do too. But as I drive through what appears to be the center of town, I'm delighted to be minutes from an opportunity to stretch my legs and relieve this seat's suction grip on my thighs.

Mom sits up and plucks at her curls as we drive through the center of town. "Charming." She peers at the storefronts. "It's picturesque."

Old-fashioned is the adjective I'd use, but I'm not going to argue. An unspoken cease-fire has held since Jacksonville, and I won't risk another skirmish.

Dozens of antique shops line the main road, and nearly everyone on the sidewalk carries a shopping bag—a sign of a healthy economy. We pass a diner, a dentist, and a doll shop, and for some reason the alliteration delights me.

I grab my cell phone from the seat pocket and press a number I've already programmed. The secretary answers on the first ring and patches me through to Daniel Sladen's office.

I hope Uncle Ned's lawyer is not one of those men who leaves the office early, but it's hard to imagine anyone working late in a place that looks like Mayberry.

"Mr. Sladen, Jennifer Graham." I greet him in my most professional voice. "We've just arrived, and we'd like to see the house. Should we stop by your office for the key?"

Sladen's laugh rumbles in my ear. "No need, Ms. Graham. I'll meet you there."

"I don't want to trouble you—"

"No trouble at all. I should be at the house in five minutes."

I drop the phone into my purse and glance at Mother. "The lawyer's going to meet us at Fairlawn."

"Probably wants to check you out and report back to the local rumor mill."

I give her a disapproving look and brake for an unexpected stop sign. A gaggle of pedestrians streams through the crosswalk, and I can't help being impressed. "This downtown looks healthy enough. Unusual to see so many people active in a town center."

"Unless the town center is all there is." Mom cocks a finger at the road, silently informing me that the crosswalk has emptied. "Downtowns don't die unless people move out to the suburbs. I don't think this place *has* any suburbs."

I drive through the crosswalk and tug on the map at my side. After a glance, I take the next left onto West Eleventh. We drive almost a mile; then I turn left and spot my inheritance beyond the railroad tracks. The Fairlawn Funeral Home stands at the crest of a hill . . . and looks *nothing* like the photograph on the Web site.

That's unfair; there is a *slight* resemblance. The house still has two peaked gables with a turret in between. The windows on either side of the turret sag like aging eyes, and half the decorative spindles lean to the right or left like broken teeth. The diamond-shaped window still adorns the tower, and the porch continues to hug the house on two sides and a corner, but the pretty pink of the photo is now a peeling shade of Pepto-Bismol, and the gray on the upper story looks more like grime than paint. Yellow dandelions have conquered the wide lawn, and the painted sign out front is cracked and fading.

Mom lifts her sun visor and groans. "Can you give it back?"

"Oh, man!" Clay slides to the edge of the bench and stares out the window. "It *is* a haunted house!"

Clay's assessment couldn't be more accurate. The Munsters, the Addams Family, and Norman Bates would feel right at home in this place.

In a quavering voice, Bugs asks, "Is it still going to be a great day?"

"Sure it is, honey." Like Sigourney Weaver in a host of *Alien* movies, I stare at the hulking monster beyond and wonder if I should flee or fight.

I grip the steering wheel. Thomas is always telling me that I limit my leadership by not delegating enough. I always counter that if you want something done right, you have to do it yourself.

If we had argued about *this*, Thomas would have won the debate. Why didn't I ask Mr. Sladen to sell this pathetic pink palace and send me a check?

Sometimes I am my own worst enemy.

I muster a smile and turn off the road, then point the van up the driveway and pull into the gravel parking lot at the side of the building. "Doesn't this place look . . . interesting?"

"It's a mess," Mom says, her voice flat. "Poor Ned must not have been able to afford a decent caretaker."

I put the van in park and sit in silence, eyeing the monstrosity that fills my windshield. If Ned couldn't afford to maintain the house while the business was operating, how am I supposed to get the property ready to sell with no income at all? I have an untouchable retirement fund and the equity from the sale of the house, but we're going to need money for living expenses.

The thought has barely slipped through my brain when a black BMW pulls into the parking lot, a cloud of dust rising in its wake. This has to be Mr. Sladen.

I jerk my thumb at the other car. "At least the lawyers do all right in this town."

Mom turns to look. "He's probably hoping you'll sue somebody for saddling you with this eyesore."

Any other day I would have chided her for making that kind of comment in front of the boys, but since the divorce I've been worn out by lawyers. The woman who represented me did a decent job, but at certain points during the negotiations I thought she was more ticked at Thomas than I was. I was furious, yes, but she couldn't seem to understand that I didn't want to burn any bridges with the father of my children. I'd even be willing to reconcile someday . . . as long as he suffers like a gut-shot desperado between now and then.

A silver-haired man in a long-sleeved dress shirt steps out of the car. He's carrying his coat over his shoulder as if he knows good manners demand that he wear a suit, but no man in his right mind would wear a jacket in this blistering heat.

Mom whistles. "What an attractive head of hair."

"Calm down, Delilah."

"Oh, he's too young for me. But you—"

"Enough, Mother." I open the door and hop out of the van, leaving Mom to handle the boys and the dog. "Mr. Sladen?"

"Ms. Graham." He strides toward me, hand extended, and I can't help but notice that the man *does* have nice hair. "So happy to meet you. I trust you and your family had a good trip?"

I force a smile, willing to bet my last dollar that this man has never traveled with children. "Fine, thanks. I hope we didn't pull you away from some important business."

"You are my important business today."

The line feels canned, but his eyes gleam as he smiles and gestures toward the front door. "Shall we go in?"

"Sure . . . but let me check on my family first." I glance over my shoulder and see that the boys have already scrambled out and are running across the dandelion lawn. Skeeter is baptizing a bush while Mom dangles from her seat as if reluctant to step into the scorching sunlight.

Mr. Sladen points to a stand of trees in the distance. "There's a park just past the fence at that tree line. Some swings, a ball field, a couple of basketball hoops on a court by the lake. It's a safe area, if you'd like to let your sons work off some steam."

"I heard that," Mom calls. "I'll keep the boys busy." She slides out of her seat, slams the door, and comes over to shake Mr. Sladen's hand. "Joella Norris, Jennifer's mother. A pleasure to meet you."

"The pleasure's mine. You were Ned's . . . niece?"

Mom smiles. "My husband was Ned's nephew. Anyway, let me take these boys and keep them out of your way. We'll come back up in a bit."

"Keep them out of the water, okay?" I turn to watch three-fifths of my family troop down the hill. The sun is so strong that I can almost hear the skin cells on my exposed shoulders sizzling like bacon. "Scorching," I say without thinking.

"You get used to it," the lawyer answers.

I have no intention of getting used to it, but neither do I want to insult this man. "I'm sure you do," I murmur, following Mr. Sladen onto the front porch.

My first impression of Fairlawn's interior is . . . *stifling.* I step into a shadowed foyer and inhale the odors of dampness, mildew, and dust.

I must have made a face, because Mr. Sladen gives me an apologetic smile. "Sorry about the heat. A couple of the bedrooms have window air conditioners, and the unit that services the workroom is fine. The other units need to be replaced."

"Oh. Okay." Not knowing what else to say, I fan the heavy air away from my face and look around. At my right and left the dark-paneled foyer opens to two spacious rooms. Straight ahead, a tall staircase leads up and away from the doorway.

I step to the side and peek into the sunlit room at my right.

"The south chapel," Mr. Sladen explains. "There've been times when Ned conducted two services within a couple of days. The double chapels allowed him to leave the casket and flowers set up for visiting hours and the funeral service."

The word *casket* raises gooseflesh on my arms. "Did Uncle Ned actually *live* here?"

The lawyer blinks. "Oh yes, I thought you knew that. Forgive me; I should have realized you'd want to see the living quarters first. They're upstairs, so if you'll come with me . . ."

I follow Mr. Sladen up the carpeted wooden staircase, uncomfortably aware of the heat. Though I wanted to look nice for this meeting,

I wish I'd worn shorts. The lining of my dress pants keeps sticking to my thighs, and the back of my neck is damp under my hair.

"This split staircase is a nice feature." I flap my hand at the steps we're climbing. "This landing must have shielded Uncle Ned's wife from all the goings-on downstairs."

Mr. Sladen smiles. "I never thought of that. I doubt Marjorie would have thought of it either, as involved as she was in Ned's work. She often did hair and makeup for Ned and usually sang at the services."

"How convenient."

We turn at a midpoint landing and continue to the second story, where the air feels thinner and even hotter.

The staircase opens to a wide landing furnished with an old television, a dilapidated sofa, and a pair of mismatched chairs. I grimace when I notice the curved wall and realize that this glorified TV room is, in fact, the turret. The diamond-shaped window that caught my imagination is embedded in the wall high above my head, its glass dulled by a layer of grime.

"The living room." Mr. Sladen gestures to the space.

I stand back to take it in. The air here feels like it has been breathed too many times, and the color of the carpet has polarized to a nondescript shade of gray. One of the windowsills features a little fly cemetery, and the sight of a half-completed jigsaw puzzle on a low coffee table gives me the heebie-jeebies. Did Ned have his stroke halfway through this Norman Rockwell picture? The way random pieces are scattered about, it looks as though he stepped away only a few minutes ago.

Mr. Sladen notices the puzzle too. "Looks like Gerald has found something to occupy his time."

"Who?"

"Gerald Huffman, Ned's right-hand man. Gerald's always referred to himself as the caretaker, though he's actually a licensed embalmer. When Ned was unable to manage by himself—all that lifting and turning, you know—Gerald took up the slack. He lives in a suite at the side of the house. Over there."

When Mr. Sladen points to an archway at the edge of the landing,

I lean forward to take a look. The kitchen area beyond is barely big enough to hold a table, counter, stove, and fridge. Beyond that lies a single closed door. Though technically I own the building, I'm not sure I have the right to approach that room . . . and I'm not sure I'm thrilled with the idea of a strange man living here.

"Does Gerald come with the house?"

Mr. Sladen laughs. "Not legally, though I'm sure he'd love to stay. As executor, I've kept him on but only until you decide what you want to do with the place. Gerald is a wonderful man, but he's no spring chicken. He may be hoping to retire."

I hope he is.

The lawyer might have said more, but at that moment the door opens and an old man emerges. His snowy brows lift at the sight of us; then he hurries forward, reaching a hand out in welcome. "You must be Jennifer."

Mr. Sladen steps forward and shakes Gerald's hand. "Gerald, let me introduce Jennifer Graham, your new landlady."

"Nice to meet you, Mr. Huffman." Feeling duty-bound to spare him any unnecessary exertion, I walk toward him and am surprised by the strength of his grip.

His hand holds mine as we take each other's measure. His eyes probe mine like searchlights, and in a flash I realize that he's probably looking for some hint of my intentions.

I glance at the lawyer, hoping he'll tell the caretaker that it's time to move on, but Mr. Sladen has chosen this moment to examine a book on top of the TV. I smile at Gerald, eager to express my gratitude for his service to my great-uncle, but the man stands in front of me with the air of one who will not be moved. Maybe it's the jigsaw puzzle spread over the coffee table or the fact that he's wearing plaid house slippers, but I can't shake the feeling that Gerald Huffman belongs to Fairlawn in a way Fairlawn will never belong to me.

And he *likes* living here?

He grins at Mr. Sladen. "Pretty thing, isn't she? Doesn't look a bit like Ned."

For some reason I find myself blushing. No man, young or old, has flirted with me in . . . well, I can't remember the last time a man said I was pretty. But I'm sure it was many years and several pounds ago.

"I'm delighted to meet you, my dear." The older man's eyes glitter behind a pair of wire-rimmed glasses. "By george, maybe she *does* look like Ned. She has his nose."

I'm searching for the proper way to respond to that comment when Gerald offers to bring in my suitcases.

"Please don't trouble yourself. We're going to look for a hotel—"

"Aren't but two hotels in Mt. Dora. And why would you stay there when you own the largest house in town?"

Before I can protest again, Gerald turns on the lawyer. "Shame on you, Daniel, for not bringing her bags up the stairs with you. Could have saved me a trip." The old man walks away, his shoulders twitching as he assumes responsibility for our luggage—whether I want him to or not.

His comment, however, has piqued my curiosity. I turn to Mr. Sladen. "Is this really the biggest house in town?"

"The Lakeside Inn is larger, but I suppose it'd be accurate to say Fairlawn is the largest private house in Mt. Dora."

I congratulate myself on uncovering a unique selling point and lean over the stair railing. "Please don't bother with the suitcases, Mr. Huffman. We'll go to a hotel."

"I doubt you'll be able to get a room." Mr. Sladen places his hand on the wooden rail. "Don't put yourself out, Gerald. I'll get her bags."

"No—no, really, we're not staying here. Surely we can find a room at that inn."

The lawyer gives me a smooth smile. "I checked. The Lakeside Inn has no vacancies—something about a wedding this weekend—and the hotels fill up quickly in the summer. One of the B and Bs might have a room, but they're expensive. If you insist, I could have my secretary make some calls—"

"How expensive?"

He pulls a handkerchief from his pocket and wipes a sheen of perspiration from his upper lip. "They start at a hundred dollars a night. You'll need at least two rooms, because they're not really set up for families. The bed-and-breakfasts are geared more for honeymooners and couples who want to splurge on a romantic weekend."

I turn away. Thomas and I used to enjoy the occasional romantic weekend, but divorce has turned those memories into a history best forgotten . . . until my heart toughens.

I walk to a bookcase and run my fingertips along the dusty edge. The top shelf is filled with paperbacks, mostly private eye mysteries by Raymond Chandler and Conan tales by Robert E. Howard. Old books by yesterday's writers.

As I assured Clay earlier, I haven't planned on spending a single night in this way station for the dead. But though I'm officially a property owner, I'm cash-poor, and I can't afford to spend two hundred dollars a night while we investigate the options for this house.

And not many B and Bs are pet friendly.

"We *could* stay here," I say, "but it's bound to be awkward with all of us intruding into Mr. Huffman's space. My boys can get rowdy."

"Gerald won't mind; he's the nicest man you could ever meet. A deacon in our church."

"Still—" I hesitate. How does one tactfully explain that no modern mother should trust a stranger with her little boys? I look directly into Mr. Sladen's eyes. "Would you leave your kids with him?"

The lawyer slips his hands into his pockets. "If it'll make you feel any better, I know that Lydia Windsor, your closest neighbor, used to leave her son with Gerald whenever things got hectic at the shop. Lydia wouldn't go out with Joe the grocer until he passed a polygraph, but she always felt comfortable leaving Brett with Gerald."

I blow out a breath and look down the hallway leading away from the turret living room. "I assume the other rooms are down there?"

Daniel Sladen brightens. "Of course. It really is a lovely area. Ned's wife had a gift for decorating. I think you'll find the living quarters quite comfortable . . . once we open a few windows and let in the breeze. There are four large bedrooms and two baths in that wing."

I trudge behind him as he leads the way. Two doors open off each side of the hallway, and another stands at the end of the hall. The first door on the right leads to a bathroom with an old sink, an antique toilet, and a claw-footed tub. Bugs will love the tub because he hates the way a shower sprays water in his eyes. Clay will think the tub is for sissies.

When Mr. Sladen opens the other doors, I murmur quietly and move on. Ned's wife may have had a gift for decorating, but the woman's sense of style passed away twenty years ago. The four bedrooms are done in shades of blue and purple, with floral wallpaper on only three of the four walls in each room. Each space contains a double bed, a dresser, a standing mirror, and a shallow closet that looks as if it might hold only a sleeveless blouse, a miniskirt, and a pair of skinny jeans.

I point to the wallpaper in the third bedroom. "I think my mother had a dress that would match that pattern."

A smile plays at the lawyer's mouth. "I think my mother had those flowers on her dishes."

The bedroom at the end of the hallway features a particularly awful paper of purple flowers with foil petals, but I'm able to overlook the atrocity on the walls when I spot the wide windows that open to views of the yellow-dotted lawn and the trees beyond.

"Gerald's suite overlooks the parking lot," Mr. Sladen says, struggling with a stubborn window sash. "This was Ned and Marjorie's room, and it's the best view in the house. I'm sure it could use updating, but it's an attractive space, don't you think?"

Is the man blind or completely bereft of good taste? I step farther into the master bedroom and run my hand over the oak grain on the dresser. I'm no expert, but I have a feeling almost every piece in this house is antique. On the other hand, with the exception of Daniel Sladen and a few shoppers on Main Street, I don't think I've seen anything in Mt. Dora less than a hundred years old. Even Gerald looks about twenty years past his prime.

"The place has potential," I admit. I walk to the bed and push on the mattress, half expecting the frame to collapse beneath the pressure.

"Gerald has a woman come in once a week to clean," he explains as he moves to the second window. "He told me she worked extra hard this past week because she knew you were coming. The beds have clean sheets, and I think Gerald stocked extra groceries in case your kids want a snack. We want you to be comfortable until you've made arrangements for your move."

For a moment his words don't register; then they clatter into my consciousness. "My what?"

Mr. Sladen's eyes cloud with confusion. "After speaking to your mother, I assumed you were coming to stay."

I sink to the edge of the bed as my knees buckle. Though this isn't the most professional place to hold a conversation with one's lawyer, the stifling heat has sapped my strength.

"Mr. Sladen—" I look toward the doorway, where I almost expect to find Mom fluttering like some overprotective guardian angel— "when did you talk to my mother?"

He leans against the wall and crosses his arms. "A day or two after you and I spoke, I called to see when we might expect you. You weren't in, so your mother and I chatted a few minutes."

"And she told you I wanted to *move* here?"

"Actually, no." I am somewhat gratified when a flush creeps up his cheeks. "She told me about your divorce and said that you and your boys were living with her until you could find a place of your own. Naturally, I—"

"You *assumed* I'd want to live here. Maybe begin a new life in Mt. Dora?" I force myself to chuckle. "I'm sorry, Mr. Sladen, but I don't think I could live in Florida. It's too hot."

"Virginia's hot too."

"Not year-round."

His mouth curls in a wry smile. "I'd be a lousy lawyer if I got into an argument with my own client, so let me just say that I'll help you in any way I can for as long as you're here." He straightens and uncrosses his arms. "How long *are* you staying?"

"Only as long as it takes to sell the house. I know we have a lot of work to do, so I thought we'd spend some time here. Surely it won't take more than a few days to get the house ready for the market." I frown as another thought strikes. "By the way, is there anything wrong with the structure? I know the exterior could use a coat of paint and the interior could use new carpet and wallpaper, but if Fairlawn needs more than cosmetic work—"

"We had an inspector come through." Mr. Sladen pulls his hands from his pockets to count on his fingers. "The roof's about gone. The electricity in the living area hasn't been brought up to code. The attic is underinsulated, so the power bills have to be high—when the air conditioner is working, that is. I've already mentioned that two AC units need to be replaced, and there's evidence of termite damage at the rear of the building. You'll have to see to those things before you even think about selling . . . unless you want to let it go as a fixer-upper."

I draw a deep breath. I've watched enough of those home improvement shows to know that fixer-uppers bring in far less than a home's market value. "If I sold it as is . . . any idea how much I could get for it?"

The lawyer's mouth clamps tight for a moment, and his Adam's apple bobs as he swallows. "A house like this in Eustis sold at auction the other day."

"For how much?"

"Well . . . ten."

"Only ten thousand?"

"Ten dollars. A woman bought the place to tear it down. After paying the back taxes and hiring a demolition company, she realized she didn't get much of a bargain."

I press my hand over my face and resist the urge to groan. I'd happily tear this place down if I thought I could sell the land, but this property is probably too far from the city center to be prime real estate.

If I repair the place, though—if I slap on a coat of paint and rip off this awful wallpaper—there's a good chance I could sell it for top dollar.

Suddenly I wish I'd gone into general contracting instead of politics. "Mr. Sladen—"

"Please call me Daniel. We're small-town folks around here."

"All right." I give him a tentative smile. "Daniel, is there any money left in the estate? anything we can use to fix up this place?"

"Now that you mention it, yes."

"How much?"

He gives me a quick look, then drops his gaze to the floor. "After the funeral expenses, taxes, and nursing home costs . . . remaining cash assets are, I believe, $563.72." He clears his throat. "Or it might be $536.27. I have a touch of dyslexia."

I blow out a breath. "Okay. Anything else?"

"No other assets. But Gerald says he could use some new equipment down in the prep room. Whether you replace those items will depend, of course, on whether you decide to sell the house as a residence or—"

I cut him off with an uplifted hand. "What is the prep room?"

"The place where he prepares the bodies. Where Gerald does the embalming."

I shake my head, having already heard more than enough.

$\mathscr{G}$erald tugs on his belt, pulling his trousers more firmly about his hips, and checks the dusty minivan's tires. Looks like the woman came all the way from Virginia on at least one underinflated tire, so it's a good thing she didn't have a flat on the interstate. The woman he met had nice fingernails and a fresh coat of lipstick, though, so she cares about details. She's not mechanical, obviously, and she's been too busy to have a mechanic take a proper look at this vehicle.

He peers through the window and spies a crumpled McDonald's bag lying in the corner of the floor along with two crushed soft drink cups.

Ned's niece has been busy with those boys. And Daniel did mention a recent divorce.

You're doing it again.

A smile quirks the corner of his mouth. Even after twenty years, Evelyn's voice rings in his memory. She used to hate his habit of looking out over the congregation and summing up his church members' personalities after observing a few telling details. "But you only hated it," he says, looking at the sky as if he could catch a glimpse of heaven, "because I was almost always right."

He tests the rear hatch of the vehicle. It's unlocked, so he lifts the door and steps back as a backpack, a basketball, a plastic container of dog biscuits, and a half dozen comic books tumble onto the ground.

"Sir? Sir! Let me help you with that."

He turns to find a mature woman striding toward him, her face flushed in the heat. A compact mass of white curls caps her head, and her arms move like pistons beside a body as solid and straight as a pillar.

He scoops up the basketball before it can roll away. "You must be Jennifer's mother."

She extends her hand—short fingernails, unpolished, a no-nonsense grip. "Joella Norris. And you are?"

"Gerald Huffman. Ned's assistant."

"Gerald." She cocks her head like a curious bird. "Glad to know you. Nolan and I didn't hear much from Uncle Ned after he moved down here, but I'm grateful he remembered Jennifer. This inheritance . . . well, it came at the perfect time. I know it's going to do her good."

"Ned would be glad to hear that. Now, how can I help you? Do all these bags need to be brought into the house?"

"We're staying here?" Her eyes widen for a moment before a quick smile crosses her face. "All righty, then. I suppose everything goes inside, but let me call the boys to give us a hand."

Gerald smiles at the woman's take-charge attitude, then pulls the largest suitcase from the back of the van and sets it on the ground. The leather case is well made and seems at odds with the rest of the bags, but Daniel said Ned's niece used to work for some Washington hotshot. Maybe all Washington bigwigs travel with leather luggage.

He takes a floral suitcase from the stack, figuring it belongs to the mother. With the two largest bags in hand, he lurches toward the front steps, where he meets the younger woman and the lawyer.

Daniel hurries down the stairs. "Let me take those inside for you."

"I can manage," Gerald insists, taking his time. "But there are other bags in the trunk."

Daniel hesitates, then follows the young woman to the van.

Gerald continues his upward climb, pausing to inhale on each step, and finally enters the shade at the top of the porch.

He sets the luggage down and digs in his pocket for his handkerchief. He turns as he mops his brow and can't help noticing that

Jennifer has pulled her mother aside. Daniel is busy at the open hatch, probably sorting through comic books and backpacks, while Jennifer paces before her mother, her posture erect and her jaw set as she delivers . . . what? A lecture?

Gerald wipes his brow a final time and stuffs his damp handkerchief back in his pocket.

Fairlawn has been too quiet for too long, but it looks as though the old house is about to be visited by a whirlwind. "Yessiree," he says, heading toward the door. "Things are about to get interestin'."

⁂ ⁂ ⁂

An hour after our arrival, Mom, Bugs, Clay, and I have dropped our suitcases into vacant rooms and staked out temporary territory. Skeeter has sniffed at each piece of furniture and vacuumed up every loose crumb on the kitchen floor. Bugs has climbed in and out of the claw-footed tub, flushed the antique toilet eight times, and determined that his bed is *not* as springy as a trampoline. Clay has expressed shocked dismay because the old television doesn't have the proper ports or whatever he needs to connect to his Xbox.

Together Gerald and I have walked through the upstairs and opened every window, even chipping off old paint when necessary to lift the sashes. Some of the stubborn windows have to be propped open with yardsticks and books. The place still isn't what I'd call comfortable, but at least there's a bit of cross-ventilation.

My eldest son is flabbergasted when Gerald tells him Fairlawn doesn't have cable. "Only six channels?" Clay wails. "What do people *do* around here?"

Mom wanders through the house with wide eyes, trying to find evidence of the family history in the furniture, the china, even the few pots and pans. "See this piece?" she says, handing me an iron skillet she pulled from a cupboard. "I have one just like it, and I think it came from Nolan's mother. This one must have been Vera's too and somehow found its way to Marjorie. Now it's come all the way round to you. . . . Imagine that."

57

I'd like to, but I'm trying to keep a tight rein on my imagination. Other than the two chapel rooms and the foyer, I haven't seen anything of the downstairs, and that's fine with me. If there are preparation rooms and caskets and a minimorgue down there, Gerald is welcome to cloak them in secrecy. I know I'll have to examine those areas eventually, but first I need to get my family settled.

Now my great-uncle's assistant is mixing a pitcher of frozen lemonade in the kitchen while the boys and I gather around the chrome-and-vinyl dinette set. Mom stands beside Gerald, pulling mismatched glasses from a cupboard. Clay elbows me and grins at what he interprets as Mom's flirtatiousness, but she's not flirting—she's taking over. Though Gerald has lived here since shortly after Noah's flood, Mom will be in charge of the kitchen by tomorrow afternoon.

If Gerald doesn't send us packing before then, that is. He seems like a nice old man, but even a saint's patience has limits. If one of us has to go, I'll volunteer and take my crew with me. Staying here with a virtual stranger is just too weird.

"So," Gerald says, stirring the frozen concentrate into a pitcher of water, "when does the truck pull in?"

Mom wrinkles a brow. "What truck?"

"The truck—you know, the moving van. Even though the house is furnished, I'm sure the boys have toys and things they want to bring from Virginia. You girls probably have boxes of clothes."

His comment makes Mom stammer, but at least I understand why he's confused. "Gerald . . ." I hesitate, not sure how to tell him we haven't come to stay. When I sell the place, Fairlawn's new owners might not want to employ an elderly mortician/caretaker. They may not even intend to use this place as a funeral home. Fairlawn could easily serve as a private residence, an art gallery, or an antique shop.

I shoo the boys toward the television and tell Skeeter to keep them company. When the three of them have settled on the rug, I turn back to Gerald. "Actually—," I begin.

But the old man keeps talking as if he didn't hear me. "Let me tell you a story," he says, pouring lemonade into glasses. "Before Ned had his stroke, back when he was in good health, he started praying about how to change his will. He and Margie had no kids, but Marjorie had a slew of nieces and nephews, any one of whom would have been happy to get their paws on this place. But he knew that lot, knew 'em better than Marjorie did, and he didn't want to see Fairlawn torn down or turned into a boardinghouse for strangers. So one night he lay in bed prayin' on the problem, and he woke up with the answer."

He pauses to hand Mother a glass, and his reference to my uncle's simple piety makes me wince. I've been a Christian since childhood, but for the last six months I couldn't help feeling that a wall of hurt stands between me and the Lord.

Why didn't God do something to prevent my husband's betrayal?

"So Ned," Gerald continues, "walks into this very kitchen the next morning and says, 'It came to me in a dream. Fairlawn is to go to Nolan's daughter. It'll be a great home for her and her kids while the Lord uses the place to minister to his children.'"

Gerald sets a glass of lemonade before me and nods as if his story conclusively settles the matter. "So you see, Miss Jen, I knew you'd come even before you did. Seein' you standing on the porch with your boys was like watchin' Ned's vision come to life."

I look at Mother, hoping Queen Snippy will come up with a diplomatic solution to this dilemma, but she looks as dumbfounded as I feel.

"Well—" I swallow hard and lift my lemonade—"thank you for sharing that story. I don't know that I place a lot of stock in dreams, but it's a comfort to know Uncle Ned was thinking of us."

He lifts his glass and touches it to mine. "I don't know that Ned knew much about you in particular, missy. But he was a great one for seeking the Lord. When he prayed, God answered. Why, I could tell you stories—"

"I think," Mom interrupts, catching my eye, "that I'd like you both to take your glasses and move into the TV area. If I'm going to make dinner, I'd like to be able to maneuver without stepping on someone's toes."

"Mom, you don't have to—"

Gerald thumps his glass to the table. "Miss Joella, I won't hear of you cooking after a long trip like that. You must be plumb worn-out."

"Nonsense. Cooking relaxes me. I just need a chicken." She looks at Gerald. "You *do* have a chicken in the freezer, don't you?"

Gerald shakes his head. "Sorry."

"Ground beef?"

"Nope."

"Cheese? Eggs?"

"No, ma'am. For dinner I usually ride my bike down to the diner or eat a Hungry-Man in front of the TV."

Mother props her hands on her hips and gives me a determined smile. "We'll talk later. Right now these children need food, so I think I'll find a phone book and order up a pizza."

I smother a grin as I look toward my boys. We've traveled hundreds of miles to a new town and a strange house, but some things never change.

❈ ❈ ❈

I'm reading the home inspector's report in the master bedroom when daylight blinks off like a burned-out lightbulb. On my way to the lamp, I pause by a window and watch as the outside air transforms from blue to black. Now that the day has officially ended, I'll have better odds at prying the boys from the TV show they're watching with Mother.

As I walk through the gloom of the hallway, I see Gerald standing in the kitchen. A wary expression flickers across his features as he studies Bugs and Clay. What is *that* about? I know he's probably not used to children, but my boys are generally well behaved. And we're not going to be a permanent problem.

I step into the living room and point the boys toward the bathroom so they can brush their teeth and get to bed. The sooner we establish a routine in this place, the better off we'll be.

We need stability. Even here.

I am herding Bugs from the bathroom when he asks if he and

Skeeter can sleep with Clay. I expect Clay to protest, but he limits his reaction to a melodramatic sigh. Bugs may be too young to understand what kind of house this is, but Clay knows . . . and he's a little nervous.

Maybe we all are. About the town, the old man down the hall, and the strangeness of this creaking house.

"I'm hot, Mom," Bugs complains as he walks toward the bed.

"That's the thing about nighttime, you know—things cool down after dark. Let me see if that ceiling fan has a high speed."

After yanking the rusty chain three or four times, the ceiling fan whirs to life, fluttering Skeeter's fur and bringing a smile to Bugs's face.

I pray with the boys, tuck Bugs into the big antique bed, and call Skeeter up onto the mattress. I make Clay promise not to stay up too late. He's sitting in a chair in the corner, his eyes glued to his Nintendo. He's been playing Madden so long I'm surprised the game still holds any challenge for him.

Clay closes his eyes as I kiss the top of his head, but his gaze swings toward me when my hand reaches for the lamp.

"Why don't I leave the light on for your game," I say, knowing full well that Clay often plays in the dark. "You can turn it off whenever you're ready. Everything's going to be fine, boys; we're going to have a lot of fun while we're here."

Clay nods, but my maternal instinct assures me that this lamp will burn all night.

Once the boys are settled, I return to the living room at the top of the stairs. Mom and Gerald are watching TV, but as soon as I sink into the sofa, Gerald straightens his recliner, gives me a jaunty salute, and announces that he's heading off to bed.

I glance at my watch—the man goes to sleep at nine?

After he leaves, I hear the muted sound of a radio coming through the wall. I can't be sure, but I suspect he went to bed early so Mom and I can talk.

Queen Snippy sits on the opposite end of the couch with her arms crossed and her gaze on the television. When the studio audience erupts in laughter and she doesn't even crack a smile, I know she's not watching.

I click off the power and toss the remote into the center of the sofa. "So. Are we going to talk about it?"

Mom's head rotates toward me. "Seems to me you've already had your say. You pretty much dumped every thought in your head this afternoon."

"I was upset, Mom. Your telling Mr. Sladen about the divorce makes me sound like some kind of pitiful person when I—"

"I certainly did *not* make you sound pitiful. I have never said anything to give anyone that impression of you."

"You didn't have to tell him about my personal life. That man is an estate lawyer; he can't give you advice about my divorce. You shouldn't have said a word."

She draws a deep breath, her chest rising and falling in the lamplight. "I don't know what to say anymore. He was a nice man. I enjoyed talking to him. You've never seemed to mind when I tell the Hatters about you and your kids—"

"That's different! They're old women, and I don't even *know* them. I have to interact with this lawyer on a professional basis."

"Well, excuuuse me." Mother displays her teeth in an expression that is not at all photogenic. "Forgive me for not being *professional* in my *home*. I take people as I find them. I don't have class A colleagues and class B friends—"

"That's not what I meant."

"You don't even know what you mean. Your problem, dear, is that you're so busy trying to be professional that you've forgotten how to be . . . to be . . ."

"What?"

"To be nice!"

"Nice?" Heaven help me, I'm shrieking at my mother. I close my eyes, count to five, and try to take deep breaths. Mom has no idea what I'm going through; she has no clue how weary I am. She came along to help me, but right now I'm wishing she'd stayed in Virginia.

I wish I'd been a test-tube baby.

"You know," Mom says, apparently on a roll, "you need to make a list, tell that lawyer what needs to be done, and get your kids out of here. This place isn't safe. I don't know how people live in this wilderness."

The sudden change in topic leaves me breathless. "What are you talking about?"

"Mosquitoes." She dips her head in an emphatic nod. "Did you see that lake behind the trees? Mosquitoes breed in bodies of water, you know. They carry the West Nile virus, and people die from that. And these lakes are filled with alligators. I asked Gerald about them. He said you can't find a body of fresh water without at least one gator in it, and I don't think you want one of the boys or their little dog being hauled off by a twelve-foot monster."

The possibility hadn't even occurred to me. "Gators get that big?"

Mom presses her hands to her forehead as if I'm giving her a headache. "Don't you read the paper? The gators are running *amok* down here—amok! The news was all over CNN a few weeks ago."

I stare at the blank television. "I don't remember hearing any reports about alligators."

"That's because you don't care about anything but politics. Listen to me, Jen." She leans toward me, her expression earnest and intent. "We've come, we've seen the place, and it's a mess. God bless Uncle Ned for thinking of you, but this inheritance isn't an asset—it's a liability. The building is decrepit, the business isn't functional, and for months people here have been taking their funerals elsewhere. You know nothing about undertaking, so maybe we should pack up in the morning and head off to Disney World."

Overcome by a sudden sense of weariness, I prop my head on my hand and study my mother. What motives could possibly lie behind this sudden suggestion?

Maybe she heard me tucking the boys into bed. She may be thinking I actually *meant* everything I said about having fun while we're here.

I lower my hand and meet her gaze head-on. "You do realize, don't you, that I'm not moving to Florida."

"I never said you were. No matter what that lawyer thinks."

"But this place could be a godsend if we invest a little time and energy. If this house sells for what I think it's worth, the boys and I could buy a nice place in a really good neighborhood."

"In Fairfax?"

"Maybe. Someplace close, anyway."

She gives me a smile of pure relief and pushes herself up from the sofa. "Good night, sweetheart. Don't stay up too late."

"Did you know," I call after her, "that Fairlawn is the biggest private house in Mt. Dora?"

Without hesitating, she tosses a reply over her shoulder: "That only means you'll have to buy more paint than anyone else in town."

My mother . . . always looking for the cloud behind the silver lining.

I wait until she reaches the end of the hallway, and then I turn out the lamp. Darkness swims up from the first floor and engulfs the cozy sitting area. Despite the heat, a shiver ripples along my spinal column.

Clay's not the only one feeling nervous tonight.

I turn the lamp back on and hurry to my room.

9

*W*hile the boys munch on bowls of Cap'n Crunch cereal, Gerald comes out of his room and pulls his suspenders to his shoulders. "Mornin'," he calls, beelining to the coffeepot. "Everybody sleep okay?"

I look at the boys, who are bright-eyed with curiosity. I don't know if they actually slept through the night, but neither of them came to wake me.

Skeeter trots to Gerald's feet and looks up, probably hoping for a treat.

"Ignore the dog." I lift my coffee mug. "He'll sit up and beg in a minute, but you don't have to feed him. He gets plenty to eat."

"I used to have a little dog like that," Gerald says, spooning sugar into his cup. "Cute as a button 'til the snapping turtle got him."

Across the table, Mom chokes on her buttered toast.

"Um, Gerald—" I hurry to change the subject—"is there a drug-store or grocery nearby? We need to pick up a few supplies."

"Sure, yeah, everything you need is either downtown or on the main highway." Gerald sips his coffee, then smacks his lips. "Matter of fact, I imagine you ladies would like to drive out and take a look around. If that's so, I'd be more than happy to find someone to watch the young'uns while you're gone."

I can't help noticing that Gerald doesn't volunteer *his* services. Is he afraid he'll miss an exciting installment of *Dialing for Dollars* or whatever they show on morning TV around here?

I cup my hand around my coffee mug. "Thanks, but maybe we'd better take the boys with us. I'm not sure I'd want to leave them with someone I've never met."

"Really, Jen." Mother makes a face and lowers her voice to a whisper. "I love these boys, but it's hard to get any shopping done when they're along. You go to the store. I'll stay here."

"But don't you want to go?"

She stares at the tabletop and sighs. "I'll be fine. I'll just sit in this sweatbox and watch the wallpaper curl. Maybe I'll drop a couple of pounds . . . from excessive perspiration."

That does it. I *have* to take Mom with me or I'll never hear the end of it. I look to Gerald for help, but he's studying the top of Bugs's head as if he expects a pair of horns to sprout at any moment. "Gerald?"

"Hmm?"

"I'm in a bit of a bind. I'm sure you have a lot of work to do, but—"

"Miss Jen, there's not been any real work since Ned passed, just a little upkeep. Nobody's dyin' to get into my prep room, if you know what I mean."

I manage a lame laugh, and even Mother smiles.

The man hesitates, then nods as if he's come to a decision. "I guess I could watch the boys for you. They could play at the park, and after lunch we could rustle up a couple of fishin' poles and go dangle a line in the lake."

"Sweet!" Bugs lights up like a lantern, and even Clay looks interested.

When I look to Mom for assurance, she lifts a triumphant brow.

I'm not exactly thrilled about leaving the boys, but Gerald seems harmless. Daniel Sladen likes him and so does my nearest neighbor, whoever she is.

If you can't trust your great-uncle's embalmer to watch two boys for a couple of hours, who can you trust?

I look at Mom and mouth the word *Realtor*. Then I smile at Gerald. "Sounds like a plan."

❈❈❈ ❈❈❈ ❈❈❈

Mt. Dora looks like the sort of place Mayberry's Aunt Bee would visit for a night on the town. Now that my eyes aren't bleary from highway driving, I have to admit the town has a certain chocolate-box charm. According to a map I snagged at a gas station, the town centers around Lake Dora, an elongated body of water that looks a bit like three stomachs linked together. Two other bodies of water, Lakes Beauclair and Carlton, occupy low-lying acres in the south of town, while Lake Ola snuggles up to the edge of Highway 441, Mt. Dora's link to surrounding cities.

On our sightseeing tour, I drive past all that water and think of alligators and snapping turtles and virus-bearing mosquitoes. Why *do* people live here?

I scan the horizon for signs of a mountain, but if Mt. Dora *did* exist, it's been leveled or pushed into a lake. Still, the land is hillier than most of central Florida, giving the area a gentle, rounded look. Sedate white houses nestle among full-canopied oaks that border quiet streets. Overhead, scribbles of clouds drift in a sky the color of Bugs's eyes. I'm charmed . . . until the sun bursts out from behind one of those oaks and threatens to fry my nose.

"What do you think?" I ask as I pull the van into a parking spot. "Could we find someone who'll want to buy Fairlawn and move here?"

Mom squints at the sky. "I'd say that depends on whether they visit in summer or winter."

Not everyone shares her pessimism. The area is considered so lovely, the red-haired waitress at the Coffee House tells us, that Tavares, Eustis, and Mt. Dora make up what locals call the Golden Triangle, a section of Florida known for high elevation, pristine lakes, and majestic oak groves.

"The only problem—" the waitress rubs her nose with the back of her hand—"is that I'm allergic to oaks, so I sneeze from the end of February straight through June. Other than that, living here is a downright pleasure."

I lift a brow as I look at Mother. Does everyone in town think I want to live in this burg?

The waitress catches my look and laughs. "I'm not trying to snoop, but I know you're the lady who inherited Fairlawn. I'm Annie Watson. Daniel told us about you last night when he stopped by for dessert. Said you looked right at home in the place."

This news makes Mother drop her cinnamon bun. She dives under the table to retrieve it while I introduce myself and struggle to maintain a neutral expression. "We like the house well enough," I answer, taking pains to keep my voice smooth. No sense in letting everyone in town know we're bailing as soon as we can unload our pink elephant.

Mother emerges from beneath the table, tosses the remaining piece of bun onto her plate, and presses her lips together in a vain attempt to suppress a smile. "Is Mr. Sladen always so free with his opinions?"

The waitress cock-a-doodles a laugh. "Oh, honey, don't mind our gossipin'. We get a lot of people through here with the antique dealers and all, but we locals like to know who our neighbors are. So Daniel told us all about you and your boys." She smiles at me. "I have a son too. Justin's in fifth grade. Maybe our boys will be in school together."

I'm about to murmur a polite denial when Mother clears her throat. "I don't suppose," she says, her voice dry, "that *Mrs.* Sladen voiced an opinion about Fairlawn?"

"There is no Mrs. Sladen." The waitress's hazel eyes sparkle as she tops off Mom's coffee. "Not for the last ten years or so."

Mom makes a tsking sound. "I'm sorry. Did she pass in an accident?"

"Left town in a Jag. Met some salesman up at the country club and took off with him. Daniel didn't contest the divorce, but some folks around here think he should have. Doesn't seem right, an attractive man like that left to spoil on the vine."

Mother opens her mouth as if she would like to continue the discussion, but I cut her off with a stern glance. Waitress Annie does not need to hear the details of my personal life even though it has been encouraging to hear I'm not the only one whose spouse took off during a midlife crisis.

I clear my throat. "Um, Annie—"

"Yes?"

I'm about to ask if she could recommend a real estate office, but I wave the question away. This coffeehouse appears to be a major stem of the gossip grapevine, and there's no reason to tip my hand until I know exactly when I'll have Fairlawn ready for the market.

"Never mind." I drop a couple of dollars on the table. "Thanks for the coffee," I tell her. "The cinnamon buns were wonderful."

"The best," Mom adds. "And we especially appreciate the air-conditioning."

Annie gives us a quizzical look, but I shrug and shake my head. Then Mother and I tuck our maps into our purses and reluctantly step out into the devastating sunshine.

❁❁ ❁❁ ❁❁

Now that the park swing has slowed, Bugs slides off the seat. He wants to land on his feet like Clay always does, but he loses his balance and topples forward, his hands smacking the soft, black sand.

Ouch. Even the dirt in this place is hot.

He glances at the basketball court to make sure Clay didn't see him fall. His brother's head is still bent over the ball he keeps bouncing, slamming it with one hand and then the other. There's no shade over the basketball court, so Clay's dark T-shirt is wet with sweat.

Skeeter prances at Bugs's side, eager to move on. The dog has already checked out the dock, the picnic tables, and a couple of trash cans near the water. "In a minute, boy. We have to wait on Clay."

Bugs wipes his hands on his shorts and watches as his brother bends his knees and launches the ball toward the hoop. It hits the backboard, rolls around the rim, and falls to the side. No good.

Clay goes after the ball, then catches it and stops dribbling. Bugs wipes a trickle of sweat from his forehead and stares as a boy comes through the break in the chain-link fence—a big boy, probably old enough to drive.

No wonder Clay stopped dribbling.

"Hey." The kid nods at Clay and bounces his own basketball on the asphalt. "Wanna shoot?"

Bugs bites his lip as his brother rolls his ball from one hip to the other. "I was just about to leave."

The kid shoots from the middle of the court and grins as the ball swishes through the net.

Sweet.

"You must be one of the kids from Fairlawn," the boy says, waiting while Clay catches the bouncing ball. "My mom told me about you guys."

Bugs walks forward as Clay slaps the big kid's ball across the court.

The kid catches it and rests it on his hip as he grins at Bugs. "Hey, little dude." He glances at Clay. "You know this one?"

Clay nods. "That's Bugs."

"For real?" The kid's grin widens. "Hey, Bugs, I'm Brett. I think we're neighbors."

Bugs wipes his hands on his shorts again, not sure what he's supposed to do next. Maybe he's just supposed to stand around and watch.

Brett jerks his chin at Skeeter, who is circling the players on the court. "That your dog?"

Clay shrugs. "He's ours. But mostly he hangs out with Bugs."

"Better keep an eye on him. There's folks around here who'll feed poison to a strange dog."

Bugs calls Skeeter to his side as Brett dribbles the ball a couple of times, sends it through his legs, and spins around to catch it. The kid is smooth. Like a milk shake.

"So," Brett says, holding the ball again. He looks at Clay. "How d'ya like living at the dead shed?"

Clay shoots a worried glance at Bugs. "'Sokay."

"Did ya hear any ghosts last night? anything bumping around in the tomb room?"

Bugs looks at Clay, but his brother's face has gone blank.

"It's just an old house," Clay finally says. "I didn't hear anything."

"You must be hanging out in the wrong part of the house." Brett bounces the ball again and winks at Clay. "I hear that old man Huffman keeps heads sitting on a table in the room where he empties out all the blood and stuff. There's a window you can peek through, if you've got the guts. You can actually see 'em."

Dead heads? Bugs waves at his brother, but Clay doesn't notice. He's grinning at the older kid as if this is all some kind of joke.

"Oh yeah?" Clay bounces his ball too, just like Brett, then catches it with one hand and hugs it to his hip. "I think I'd like to see that. The heads, I mean."

Brett's grin widens. "Come on, then. I'll show ya exactly where they are. But we gotta be quiet. Mr. Huffman doesn't like people hanging around the evisceration station."

Bugs doesn't know what Brett means, but the place he's talking about sounds bad. Really bad.

"Clay?" Bugs hurries after his brother, who is already following Brett toward the gate. "Clay, what's a tomb room?"

His brother doesn't answer but catches up to Brett. They are whispering to each other, laughing, and taking such big steps Bugs can barely keep up.

He follows the older boys through the narrow stand of trees but stops in the shadows when Brett leans against a pine and points to the back of the pink house. Bugs sees a garage, a sidewalk, and a small porch.

"See that door?" Brett says, pointing to a door Bugs has never noticed before. "That's where they bring in the dead people."

"That's not true." Bugs lifts his chin. "There aren't any dead people in our house. Mom would have said something."

"She wouldn't tell *you*, squirt. People always hide stuff like that from kids." Brett jerks his chin toward the corner of the house. "You can find out about the dead heads for yourself. See that little window next to the porch?"

Bugs creeps forward and peers through a stand of bushes. The window is set high in the wall, but there's some kind of metal box beneath it.

"Your brother and I are tall enough to look through the window," Brett says. "We could give you a boost so you could see inside . . . but I don't know. Maybe you're not old enough to handle it."

Bugs looks from Clay to Brett and sees them exchange a glance.

Clay shakes his head. "I don't think Bugs ought to look. But I'm good. Let's go."

"Okay. But be quiet."

Clay and Brett hunch their shoulders and run forward in a crouch, pausing by the bushes next to the big metal box. Skeeter trots off with them.

Bugs hesitates, then sprints after the others. He doesn't want to look in the window, but he doesn't want to be left alone in the shadowy woods either.

Clay is grinning when Bugs catches up to them. "So you came," he says, standing with his back pressed to the wall of the house. "Don't tell Mom what we're doing, okay?"

Bugs takes a step back as the big metal box begins to vibrate and roar. "What is that thing?"

"It's part of the air conditioner." Brett lifts his voice to be heard above the machine. "This is a good time to look, because Mr. Huffman won't hear you if you scream. Ready?"

Clay grins as both boys turn to the window. "I can't see anything," Clay says. "A curtain's in the way."

"Easy enough to fix." Moving as carefully as a robber, Brett lifts the bottom half of the window and slides it up. Then he and Clay step closer and peer into the mysterious room.

"That is too cool," Clay says, sounding more okay than he ought to.

"Isn't it?" Brett points into the space beyond the fluttering curtain. "See that head over there? I think I knew that girl from school."

Clay rises on tiptoe. "She musta been pretty . . . when she was alive."

Bugs stares up at his big brother, unable to believe what he's hearing. This can't be right. There's no such thing as a tomb room or a table with heads on it . . . is there?

"I wanna see." Bugs draws himself up to his full height and squeezes into the space between the other two boys. "Gimme a boost, will ya? I wanna look too."

"I don't know, Bugsy." Clay turns from the window and gives Bugs a sad look. "It's kinda creepy in there."

"It'll give you nightmares." Brett lowers his arms from the windowsill. "Maybe we should just go before Mr. Huffman shows up."

Bugs puffs out his chest. "If you don't give me a boost, I'm gonna tell Mom and Mr. Gerald that you were out here peekin' at girls' heads."

Brett runs a hand through his short hair. "You know . . . maybe we should help him take a peek."

Clay crosses his arms. "I dunno. He might get scared."

"I won't!" Bugs glares at his brother. "I didn't keep the light on all night—you did!"

Clay's eyes harden, and then he smiles at Brett. "Okay, let's lift him. You take one leg and I'll take the other. We'll let him look but only for a second—"

"That'll be long enough."

The older boys bend and lace their fingers together.

Bugs slips his left foot into his brother's hands. "You aren't gonna tell on me, are you?"

Brett snorts. "Why would we do that when we were peekin' too?"

Satisfied with the big kid's answer, Bugs braces himself on Clay's shoulder and slips his other foot into Brett's hands. Together they lift him, but all Bugs can see is the edge of the white curtain.

"You're gonna have to push that thing outta the way," Clay says, his breath coming in odd little gasps. "Here, we'll lift you higher so you can see better."

"Wait, Clay. I can't—"

Before he can say anything else, Brett and Clay push him onto the windowsill and through the open window. Bugs closes his eyes, afraid of what he'll see; then he hears the slam of a door . . . and footsteps.

Can a dead head *walk*?

Kicking at empty air, he teeters on the sill, unable to slide backward without losing his balance and falling. He snatches a breath, and his head fills with a smell unlike anything he's ever breathed before. He screams, the air filling with a screeching sound that ends only when arms as strong as iron wrap him in a monstrous embrace—

That's when he feels a warm wetness between his legs . . . and begins to cry.

"Calm down, boy! What in the world?"

Because the voice sounds familiar, Bugs opens one eye. Mr. Gerald has him. The old man sets him on the floor and steps away, his hands slipping into his back pockets. "Are you okay, son?"

Bugs hiccups and lowers his head. The wet spot has darkened his shorts, and a yellow puddle is spreading over the floor.

Mr. Gerald clears his throat. "Oh . . . hmm. Let me see what I have around to clean you—that—up. You just wait there, and don't worry."

As the old man shuffles away, Bugs sniffs and wipes his nose with the back of his hand. There are no dead heads in this room, only a lot of cabinets and a couple of tall tables the color of a bathtub. There's a faucet at the head of one of those tables and some strange tubes.

But no heads.

Mr. Gerald comes shuffling back, a wad of paper towels in his hand. Something inside the old man cracks when he kneels in front of Bugs, but he doesn't complain as he wipes Bugs's wet legs with the paper towels. "You got clean clothes upstairs?"

Bugs nods.

"You go up and get 'em on. Bring these shorts back down and I'll toss 'em in the wash."

Bugs takes a step toward the door, then turns and looks at Mr. Gerald.

"Don't worry," the old man says, wiping up the puddle on the floor. "I won't tell a soul."

10

Fortunately for us tourists, most Mt. Dora businesses are situated in the downtown district. Mother and I don't have to walk more than two blocks before we spot a real estate agent's office.

Feeling a little like a spy, I slip through the doorway and pick up a free catalog of available listings. I want to get a feel for the Mt. Dora market and size up my possible competition. I need to gather a few facts before I'll know if I should advertise Fairlawn as a residence or a business and how much improvement and/or repair I'll be expected to do in either case.

Mom, who is never at a loss for words, makes small talk with the agent on duty while I scan a bulletin board filled with pictures of available properties. After skimming a few listings, I settle into a sense of relief. This little part of the world is an upmarket area, and that's a good thing. Property is expensive in northeastern Virginia, too, so the more profit I can clear from Fairlawn, the better off we'll be.

If my ex-husband hadn't been in a hurry to sell our house in Falls Church, we would have made a more substantial profit. But Thomas wanted his half of the equity, and I didn't want to stay in the home where my heart broke into a thousand pieces. We'll get another house, a place where we can start fresh.

A photograph of another Victorian catches my eye. Like Fairlawn, it has a steeply pitched gable roof, stained glass, a sprawling front porch, and gingerbread trim.

"This house—" I turn to the real estate agent and point to the photo—"is it for sale?"

The woman, a brunette who's wearing a skirt she probably needs axle grease to enter and exit, follows my finger and laughs. "Heavens, no. That's the Donnelly House, one of our historic landmarks. Built in 1893 by the man who became Mt. Dora's first mayor."

"Oh."

When I give her a disappointed smile, the agent zooms in like a press photographer on a politician. "Are you interested in an older home? We have several on the market and many within walking distance of the downtown district."

"I'm not interested in buying an older home. . . . Actually I'm interested in selling one." I catch Mom's eye and relay a silent message: *Might as well come out and admit it.*

"Really?" The woman moves closer, all business now. She extends her hand. "I'm Sharon Gilbert. And you are?"

"Jennifer Graham." I shake her hand, eager to get the formalities out of the way. "I'm from Virginia, but I've recently inherited a house here. Since I've no plans to relocate, I thought I might explore my options in selling the place."

When Ms. Gilbert cocks her head, I can almost see her mentally reviewing recent obituaries. "You can't be the Whitsons' daughter. She lives in Nebraska—"

"Ned Norris was my great-uncle. I'm interested in selling Fairlawn."

Obviously that's not the answer she's expecting. Her lips part, her eyes widen, and for an instant I can't tell if she's delighted or horrified by the prospect. Then she tips her head back and releases a peal of laughter. "You want to list the funeral home? Ohmigoodness, the very thought—"

"It's a lovely property," I remind the agent as she clings to the edge of her desk in mild hysterics. "I think it has tons of potential."

"Oh my." Ms. Gilbert wipes tears of mirth from the corners of her eyes, then leans on her desk and smiles. "I'm sorry, but I've never been asked to list a . . . well, you know."

"Funeral homes *do* change hands. I'm sure it happens every day."

"Not around here." Ms. Gilbert inhales an audible breath and smooths the wrinkles from her jacket. "I suppose we could take Fairlawn as a commercial listing. But even before Ned had his stroke, most folks were taking their, um, loved ones to the mortuary in Eustis. I'm not sure Fairlawn could even compete in today's funeral industry. It's so outdated."

I glance at Mother, who is probably feeling as clueless as I am. "How can a mortuary be outdated? They've been embalming people since ancient Egypt."

"Well, it doesn't have a crematory, for one thing. A lot of people these days don't want the fuss of a burial. They want to burn and blow, you know?"

I can't believe I'm feeling defensive. "I suppose the facilities could certainly be updated. And competition is healthy, Ms. Gilbert. I'm sure people around here would like to have a choice in mortuaries." I pull my purse onto my shoulder and turn toward the door. "As a matter of fact, perhaps there's another real estate agent who would appreciate the opportunity to sell a lovely Victorian home that happens to be the largest privately owned home in Mt. Dora."

"Wait." The Realtor glances at my mother, adjusts her expression, and adopts a more businesslike tone. "You don't know this area, do you?"

"I fail to see why that should matter."

"It matters because Mt. Dora is comprised of just over fourteen thousand people, most of whom live in an area of less than five square miles. Our average resident is forty-six years old. Since the construction of new mortuaries in Eustis and Tavares, I can't imagine that we would have enough business to support another funeral home in Lake County."

I look at Mother, unwillingly impressed. This woman knows the people of this area, and she's done her research. If she says the Fairlawn Funeral Home can no longer function as a profitable business, she's probably right.

I smile and approach the problem from another direction. "Maybe we shouldn't market the property as a mortuary. The house would make a lovely bed-and-breakfast, don't you think?"

Ms. Gilbert's mouth spreads into a wide smile. "Mt. Dora needs another B and B like we need another lake."

"Then why not sell it as a private residence? Fairlawn is every bit as lovely as that Donnelly House you're so proud of."

Ms. Gilbert presses her lips together. "Not now it's not. And no one is going to want to live in a former funeral home. Not when there are so many other choices available."

"Fairlawn could be an art gallery. An antique store. A museum."

She shakes her head. "Too far out of the downtown district. There's no foot traffic out that way."

"Well . . . perhaps the land is valuable. It's near the lake and the park; it's a huge lot. Someone could move the house and build on the land. It's a beautiful site, up on that hill. . . ."

"What you're suggesting would be impossible. Fairlawn was built in 1885, and it was Mt. Dora's first funeral home. It's been added to our historic register, so it'd take an act of the city council to rescind the designation."

Always ready to pinch-hit, Mother steps up to the plate. "That's fine. We'll take our case to the city council and—"

"I wouldn't count on a favorable response." Ms. Gilbert laces her talon-tipped fingers. "Mt. Dora is known for being a historic community. Our council members are more likely to declare Spanish the official language than they are to remove any of our historic homes from the registry."

Mother lifts a brow, probably wondering if it'd be worth her while to enlist a few local Red Hatters in her stand against the city council, but I'm reasonably sure not even Queen Snippy could sway these people. Even without looking at the official demographics, I can tell this city is mostly white, traditional, and conservative. Whether I like it or not, Ms. Gilbert has given me a fair evaluation of my property's sales potential.

I push a stubborn hank of hair behind my ear and turn to look at the photos on the bulletin board. "Suppose I give you the listing. Suppose you put it in the MLS and we work together to sell the place."

The woman's eyes narrow. "The last time I was up there, I could tell the house needs a lot of work. I doubt it will show very well."

"I'll make you a deal, Ms. Gilbert. I'll stay in Mt. Dora over the summer—" I ignore the strangled sound coming from Mother's throat—"and do my best to get the place spruced up. I can afford to invest in a few repairs, and I can paint, wallpaper, and maybe plant some flowers to enhance the property's curb appeal. In return, I'd like you to treat Fairlawn like the lovely historical home it is. Do your best to sell it, and I'll work hard to make the place shine."

The agent crosses her arms and chews on her bottom lip. "For an albatross like that, I'd have to earn a full 7 percent commission."

"Two would be better. I've seen the average selling price of properties in the area, and Fairlawn is a lot of house on an oversize lot. It will still net you a handsome profit at 2 percent."

"Four. I'll have to pull out all the stops to even get people out there."

"Three. I won't exactly be eating bonbons while waiting for you to arrange showings."

A smile twitches at the corner of Ms. Gilbert's mouth as she extends her hand. "Three it is. I always did enjoy a challenge."

❧ ❧ ❧

My mother is about as flexible as a brick wall. She gets out of the van, slams the door, and glares at me through the window. "I can't *believe* you promised to spend the summer here."

I grab my purse and two plastic bags, then slide out of the driver's seat. Mom has been singing the same chorus and verse ever since we left the grocery store. "It'll take me that long to get the house fixed up. When it sells, we'll leave."

She hurries around the front of the vehicle to cut me off. "But some houses sit on the market for over a year! This is not a cute little bungalow—it's *The Money Pit* meets the *House on Haunted Hill*. No one in their right mind is going to touch it."

"It's a challenge—that's all. And I'm ready for a challenge." I look up at the pink and gray monster looming in front of us. "Besides, it's not like I had anything to do in Virginia."

"You were looking for a job."

"And I've found one. The Lord sent me this house, so I'm going to restore it and sell it. I saw the selling price of a few older homes. If we get this place spruced up, we could get seven hundred thousand for it."

"But how much will you have to put into this behemoth?"

I look up at the diamond window in the turret. "I have some money to invest. With a lot of elbow grease and a little bit of a miracle, the payoff will be worth it."

Annoyance struggles with affection on Mom's face as she stares at me; then she jerks her collar away from her glistening throat. "I hope you're not expecting *me* to stay here all summer. I'll melt away in this heat."

"You can go home anytime you please . . . but the boys and I would love it if you stayed." I offer her a smile of truce. "Shall we go in and see what the kids are up to?"

The house is dense with quiet when Mother and I make our way up the groaning stairs. Mom heads off to her room, and I find my sons sitting at the kitchen table. Gerald has heated bowls of soup for the kids, and apparently he's entertained them as well.

"Did you really *eat* them?"

Bugs's question stops me dead in my tracks.

"Sure," Gerald replies, his attention focused on the dishes he's washing. "What's the sense of giggin' frogs if you aren't planning to eat them? We'd bring 'em back, slice off the legs, skin 'em, and fry 'em up in flour. With salt, pepper, and a squirt of lemon juice, you can't ask for better eatin'."

"Hi, guys." My greeting sounds strained as it passes my lips. "And what are we having for lunch?"

A faint smile lifts the corner of Gerald's mouth as he looks at me. "Tomato soup, missy. Campbell's."

"Oh."

I step over Skeeter and slip into an empty chair as Gerald lifts a pot from the stove. "Want some?"

"No, thanks. Mom and I had a big breakfast in town."

I sit in silence as the boys finish their soup. Apparently my presence is a conversation suppressant, for neither the boys nor Gerald says another word about frying frogs, fishing, or whatever they did this morning. Clay is pink in the face, like he's been out in the sun. Bugs is pink too, but he also has dirt under his fingernails and a chalky smear on his cheek.

My youngest slurps the last of his lunch and slides from his chair. He's about to dart down the hall, but I put out my arm and catch him before he can flee.

"Wait a minute, young man," I say, quietly delighting in the soft pressure of his belly against my bare arm. "You need to take your bowl to the sink and thank Mr. Huffman."

Bugs turns to obey while Gerald wipes his hands on a dishcloth. My son mumbles a thank-you, and Gerald responds with a gruff, "You're welcome."

Clay takes his bowl and spoon to the sink, offers perfunctory thanks, and sprints out of the kitchen and down the hallway with Bugs and Skeeter following.

"We didn't go fishing because your boys met Brett Windsor today," Gerald says. "I'm pretty sure I heard them goofin' around at the back of the house."

My maternal alarm clangs. "How old is this Brett?"

"He's seventeen, but you don't need to worry; he's a nice kid. Mischievous, like most young'uns, but not the sort to get into real trouble. He and his mother live in the house at the end of our drive."

His phrasing catches my attention. "And his father?"

"California, I think. Brett spends the summers with his mom."

That's odd . . . but maybe the kid prefers California. I stand and move to Gerald's side, where I can look through the kitchen window over the sink. From here I can see the gravel driveway and a small house nearly obscured by trees. A metal sign of some sort swings in the lawn. "Is that Lydia's house?"

"Oh—have you met her?"

"No. Daniel mentioned her."

Gerald pours the leftover soup into a Tupperware bowl. "I saw you lookin' at the little guy's hands. I probably should have made him wash up."

"I hope they didn't cause any trouble for you."

"Nothing I couldn't handle. Boys will be boys, I guess."

I'm not sure what he means by that, but he doesn't look upset. He places the Tupperware bowl in the fridge, then sets the soup pot in the soapy water.

I sit down again and wish Mother would come out of her room. This man promised to keep an eye on my kids, but they look like they've been roaming through the woods all morning.

"The creek out back is a great place for boys to play," Gerald says, sliding a sponge around the pot. "All kinds of bugs, minnows, frogs— you never know what you'll find down there."

I straighten and try to see out the window. "Are you sure it's not dangerous? Bugs isn't a strong swimmer, so I don't want the boys anywhere near that lake without an adult to watch them."

Gerald chuckles. "That creek out back's no deeper than my ankle. It can flow pretty fast after a sudden storm, but most of the time it's just a trickle. Bubbles up from a spring somewhere in the woods and flows down into the lake."

I prop my elbow on the table and bite my thumbnail. Should I slather the boys in antibacterial lotion before letting them out of the house? Should I make Bugs wear those inflatable doughnuts on his arms?

Gerald glances my way as he rinses the pot. "Relax, missy. Generations of Mt. Dora boys have played in that creek, and not one of 'em's come to harm."

Slowly, I slump in my seat. Maybe he's right. I'm probably feeling overprotective because Thomas isn't around. I used to imagine myself and Thomas as an umbrella sheltering our children. Now, because my husband has stepped out of the picture for a while, I can't help feeling that I'm all that stands between the boys and disaster.

But Gerald ought to know what's safe . . . shouldn't he?

I tilt my head and listen for sounds of life from the boys' rooms. I hear a ball bouncing, the scratch and click of Skeeter's nails, Clay's muffled groans as he plays his video game.

They're fine.

I suppose I ought to be grateful that the boys have found a way to occupy themselves while I talk to Uncle Ned's assistant. I've been dreading this conversation ever since leaving the real estate office, but I'm not one to put off unpleasant tasks. One thing I've learned from working in politics is that you need to deal with dreaded duties as soon as they arise.

"Mr. Huffman—"

"Please. Call me Gerald."

I swallow hard. "Gerald, would you mind sitting down? I need to talk to you about something important."

"I'll be right there."

I study his lined face as he wipes the counter with a dish towel. If he's guessed what I'm about to say, he doesn't seem too distressed.

Finally he drops into a chair and folds his hands over the soft paunch at his waist. "What's on your mind?"

"It's like this." I press my palms to the table and stare at my fingernails. "I don't know a thing about the mortuary business, and I don't think I'd be any good at running a funeral home. I'm grateful Uncle Ned left me this place, but I've decided to sell it because my family needs the money. This morning I listed the property with a real estate agent, so I'll need you to make a list of everything that needs repairing in the house."

My words, which poured out in a solid string, are followed by the thick silence of concentration. Gerald stares at me like a man faced with a complex algebra problem; then his pupils constrict to pinpoints. "You can't mean it."

"I do. I'm not equipped—"

"I know this place is a lot to drop in a woman's lap, but you can't sell Fairlawn. It's a family business. *Your* family business."

The prohibition rankles. No one—except maybe my mother—tells me what to do. Not even this old man who, as I understand it, is *not* family.

"Gerald—" I firm my voice—"I don't think you appreciate the challenge that lies ahead of us. The real estate agent laughed when I told her what I had in mind, but I'm willing to stay here over the summer and do whatever I must to get this place in decent shape. You'll have all that time to make plans of your own. When Fairlawn sells, the boys and I will go back to Virginia, and you'll be free to do . . . well, whatever you want to do."

I let my gaze drift to a section of peeling wallpaper, and for a long moment neither of us speaks. When I finally find the courage to look at Gerald again, his chin has lowered to his chest. He's staring at the table, apparently focusing on some thought or memory I can't even imagine.

"I suppose," he finally says, "that sometimes the good Lord leads us down paths we don't expect."

Don't I know it. I nod to encourage his train of thought. "Change comes to all of us sooner or later, but change can be a good thing. . . . At least that's what I keep telling myself."

He sighs and drums his fingertips on the table.

"Do you have children?" I ask, trying to encourage him to raise his sights past Fairlawn.

"A daughter. In Atlanta."

"Well then." I fold my hands. "Maybe you could go visit her. Atlanta's a great place. The winters are mild and the land is—"

"Too crowded." He dips his head in an abrupt nod and turns sideways in his chair. "I guess I'd better get started on that list."

"I'd appreciate that."

He begins to push himself up but hesitates. "I do have one suggestion for you."

I smile, happy to placate him. He's being far more reasonable than I'd expected. "I'd be glad to hear it."

"While you're fixing things up, let me open Fairlawn for business again. I think it'd do this town a world of good to see the place back in operation. Might even help you sell the place."

For an instant I'm so startled I can't speak; then objections pile on top of each other in their rush to get out of my mouth. "We can't do that. I'm not qualified to run a mortuary. We don't have a license. There aren't enough old people in Mt. Dora, and the Realtor told me—"

"I can run the business. Our license is still valid. And old people aren't the only ones who die."

I sputter and think of my impressionable sons. "I have two young boys, Gerald. I'm not sure I want them exposed to death."

"Missy—" his voice gentles as he reaches across the table for my hand—"death is a part of life; don't you know that? But if it concerns you, I'll make sure the boys stay out of the preparation room."

I shake my head. "Opening the business will only confuse things. Besides, I need to do some major redecorating and cleaning. You can't be holding funerals while I'm painting windowsills and stripping floors—"

"We'll manage." Gerald pats my hand. "It's not like we have funerals every day. Besides, we have a lot of supplies. It'd be good for us to use 'em up."

I stare at him as a shiver climbs the staircase of my spine. "What kind of supplies?"

"Eye caps, chemicals, makeup, caskets. I could take care of three or four clients without having to order a single thing."

"We have *caskets*? In the house?" I shudder. "I don't even want to know what an eye cap is."

"It's a—"

"Stop." I put up my hand. "Tell me where the caskets are so I can keep the boys away."

"They're downstairs. We've got six or seven in the display room. Everything from fabric-covered particle board to a fancy copper model with an innerspring mattress."

Apparently I haven't seen the display room . . . and I don't think I want to. "Couldn't you sell those to another funeral home?"

Gerald laughs as though I've just suggested he stand and do the funky chicken. "Why would they buy from us when they could buy direct from the manufacturer?"

"Um . . . maybe to save on shipping?"

"Miss Jen—" again with the hand patting—"let me put a notice in the paper. Some of our older folks were counting on saying their final farewells in the Fairlawn chapel. Some of 'em even prearranged their funerals. We owe them. I'd feel a heap better about your plans if you'd let me do this."

What can I say? This man, who has taken care of my great-uncle and fed my boys, has presented his case with clarity and logic; plus, he's promised to work with me.

I'll just have to beg God to shower good health and long life on everyone in Mt. Dora for the next three months.

"All right." I take Gerald's hand and squeeze it to prevent him from patting me again. "If it'll make you feel better, post the notice."

❧ ❧ ❧

After taking a shower and blowing three fuses in an attempt to dry my hair, I curl up in the middle of my bed with paper, a pen, a copy of the home inspector's report, and the Mt. Dora yellow pages. Gerald has also given me his list of suggested repairs, but it's far from complete.

My list, however, is growing like a kudzu vine.

Crucial repairs calling for professional help

    1. Repair / replace central air-conditioning units.

    2. Upgrade electric for second floor.

    3. Treat house for termites.

    4. Hire carpenter to repair termite damage on back porch.

    5. Add insulation in attic.

    6. Inspect roof—repair or replace?

    7. Is water heater really about to blow?

Crucial cosmetic work

    1. Strip outdated wallpaper.

    2. Repaper or paint stripped walls.

3. *Replace carpet in public areas.*

4. *Clean carpet in living areas.*

5. *Paint entire house exterior.*

6. *Repaint front porch.*

7. *Sew new curtains for all windows.*

8. *Spray lawn for weeds and plant annuals in flower beds.*

Optional

1. *Upgrade kitchen countertops and appliances.*

2. *Replace tile in kitchen and bathrooms.*

3. *Replace bathroom fixtures.*

I study my list and place check marks next to the tasks Mother and I can accomplish. We could never paint the entire house—too many gables and too much gingerbread—but we could sand and paint the front porch, and that'll do a lot to enhance the building's appeal. We can sew curtains and throw away the faded rugs currently collecting dust in every upstairs room. We can strip the wallpaper and put up something more contemporary; if we can't manage that, we can slap fresh paint on the walls.

I'm going to make a clean copy of my list and post it on the refrigerator door. We'll all be able to see it there, and we'll be able to track our progress. The work won't be easy and it won't happen overnight, but as long as we're moving forward, Sharon Gilbert will be able to show the property and assure any prospective buyer that the house has incredible potential.

I have to believe it does. Because this house is our God-given ticket back to Virginia, back to our old neighborhood, back to the life we left.

Perhaps even back to Thomas. Though something in me will doubt him every time he says he loves us, my sons need their father, and I believe God can put our marriage back together. The hurt of betrayal will stay with me awhile, but if God gives me strength, I'm willing to forgive the man.

If he's willing to ask for forgiveness.

And who knows? Thomas has always admired successful women, so if I show him how much I can accomplish without his help, maybe he'll realize we work best as a team.

I open the yellow pages and search for the most important professional on my list: an air-conditioning repairman.

※ ※ ※

Bugs waits in the bathroom, toothbrush in hand, until he hears his mother's step on the wooden floor. He hurries to the sink and brushes with all his might until Mom leans against the doorframe and smiles. "That's a great job, kiddo. Ready for bed?"

He spits into the sink and blinks as she leans forward to run her thumb along the side of his mouth. "You still got some suds there, baby."

He scrubs his face with a towel and follows his mom into the hall. The room he's supposed to sleep in is right in front of him, but—

"Mom?"

"Yes?"

"You think Clay would mind if I slept with him tonight?"

Mom rests her hand on the top of his head. "I don't think he's ready for bed yet."

"That's okay. I can wait."

Mom tilts her head and gives him a funny look; then she places her hand at the back of his neck and nudges him into his room. "Why don't I sit with you for a while?"

"Can Skeeter sleep with me?"

"I think he'd like that. You can keep him company."

Bugs calls the dog, who comes clicking into the room, his head cocked. "Up here, boy."

Skeeter leaps onto the big bed while Bugs sticks his legs under the sheet. Mom puffs up a couple of pillows, and then Bugs says his prayers.

"Dear God, thank you for this day and our food and for Clay and Skeeter. Thank you for Mr. Gerald and the creek, and bless Brett and Mom and Grandma and Dad, wherever he is. Bless all the poor people in the world and the sick people, too. In Jesus' name, amen."

He opens his eyes and finds Mom watching him with worried eyes. "This boy, Brett—do you like him?"

Bugs pets Skeeter as he thinks. It wasn't nice of Brett and Clay to push him through the window and run, but if he complains, Mom might not let him and Clay hang out with Brett anymore. Clay'd be mad about that.

Bugs looks at his mother. "Brett's okay. He's old."

"So I hear."

"But Clay likes him a lot."

Mom nods and tucks the covers around Bugs's waist. "Are you okay if Clay doesn't want to sleep with you tonight? I'm just down the hall, you know, and so is Grandma."

Bugs touches his tongue to the front of his teeth. This house is very dark at night, and he doesn't know where everything is. All he's seen of the downstairs is that tomb room and the hallway.

At least there were no dead people in that place. Unless they're hidden in a drawer or a closet.

"Mom?"

"Hmm?"

"Does Mr. Gerald keep dead heads downstairs?"

Mom pulls away, her face twisting in a funny look. "Did Clay tell you that?"

"Brett said Mr. Gerald keeps dead people's heads in a big room. I didn't believe him, but maybe they're somewhere else—"

"Honey." Mom rubs his arm and smiles. "Your great-great-uncle and Mr. Gerald used to run a business downstairs—a mortuary. Do you know what that is?"

Bugs shakes his head.

"Well, do you remember last summer when our lawn at home filled with dandelions like those out front?"

"The fuzz balls?"

"Exactly. Remember how you and Clay used to pick the fuzz balls and blow on them? The fuzzy parts would fly away while the ball and stem remained in your hand. Remember how Skeeter used to try and catch the fuzzies?"

Bugs laughs. "They flew too high for him."

"That's right, Bugsy. When people die, the invisible soul flies away just like the fuzzy bits of a dandelion. All that's left is the body, like the empty ball and stem. Because people are created in the image of God, we need to treat their bodies with respect. So they are taken to a mortuary, where workers fix them up and put them in a fancy box for burial. That's what Fairlawn used to be—one of the fix-up places, sometimes called a funeral home."

Bugs remembers the bottles and tables and hoses he saw. "Do they sometimes give the bodies a shower?"

"I suppose they do."

"But they don't keep the heads."

"No, they don't."

Bugs thinks a moment more. "And the fuzzy bits—they fly away, right? They don't hang around like ghosts?"

"No, Bugsy, they don't. Nobody's in this house but you, me, Clay, Grandma, Mr. Gerald, and Skeeter."

"And Jesus?"

"Yes." Mom smiles. "Jesus will never leave you."

Bugs counts the names on his fingers. Five people, one dog, and Jesus. No one else.

He wants to believe, but his mother's been awful jumpy lately. And she can't know everything about this place. They haven't been here long enough for her to know everything about funeral houses.

What will happen if he wakes in the middle of the night and finds a dead head on the end of his bed? His Sunday school teacher has never talked about *that*.

Just thinking about it makes his eyes sting. He looks away, trying to hide his watery eyes.

But his mom is too quick for him. "Bugs, baby, are you scared?"

He shakes his head. He can't admit the truth or his brother will call him a baby. The word doesn't sound nice when Clay says it.

"I miss Daddy," he says, knowing that sometimes even Clay still cries about Dad when he thinks no one is looking.

Mom pulls Bugs close and rocks him slowly. "You're going to be all right, sweetie. Everything's going to be fine. Your dad just needs a little time."

Bugs nods, then closes his eyes as Mom releases him and tucks him into bed. "Is tomorrow going to be a great day?"

"You bet it is. A great day."

He turns toward the wall and runs his fingers over Skeeter's soft side. It's nice to know Jesus is always around, but it's also nice to have someone to touch in the night.

11

$\mathcal{J}$oella fastens the last button on her blouse, then smooths her cotton slacks and creeps to her bedroom door. After listening for sounds of activity, she steps into the hallway.

The house is unusually quiet for a Saturday morning. Bugs, usually the first one up, is sleeping late; Clay hasn't stirred from his room; and Jen will probably sleep another hour. That leaves only Gerald, who could pop out at any moment.

She tiptoes down the hall and stops at the landing to peer into the kitchen. The coffeepot is still empty, the overhead lights off. Gerald must be sleeping late too.

Grateful for an opportunity to look around without an escort, Joella places her hand on the wide, wooden banister and descends the stairs. Gerald hasn't actually *forbidden* them to look around the business half of the house, but he seemed relieved when Jen said she didn't even want to see the lower floor.

Could the man be hiding something?

Like her father, Jennifer sometimes suffers from tunnel vision. She's always been happy to narrow her focus to a few tasks and ignore other important details. As a brigadier general, Nolan had a slew of officers to back him up. Jen has only her mother.

Joella turns at the bend in the stairs and moves more slowly down the lower section of the staircase. The foyer, at least, is familiar; she and the boys have already crossed the threshold a dozen times. They have peeked into the chapels and noticed nothing unusual apart from the aged pews and the faint aroma of flowers that lingers in the curtains and carpeting.

But no one in her family has explored the rest of the first floor. As a responsible property owner, Jen ought to check out the contents of these rooms. A prospective buyer might ask a question, and she'll need to answer.

Joella pauses in the foyer and glances at the summer sunshine outside the windows. A pity, really, that this house has been haunted by the specter of death. Fairlawn is the sort of place the Astors might have designed as a winter home. Without the pews, this sunny south chapel could be a lovely drawing room, the west chapel a billiards room for the gentlemen.

Someone, however, had other plans.

She turns and follows the hallway that runs parallel to the staircase. She shivers in an unexpected draft—this section of the house isn't currently air-conditioned, but it's noticeably cooler than the second floor. Of course, one would expect the dead to be stored in a cool place.

The layout before her is simple enough—two rooms on the right, two on the left, the large prep room at the back.

A sign hangs on the farthest door.

> # STOP
> It is a violation of Florida law to enter
> this room without authorization.

She snorts a laugh. Why would anyone *want* to go into the preparation room?

The first door on the left opens to reveal a dingy bathroom—of course, even a funeral home needs a restroom for visitors. Joella frowns at the rusty stain around the toilet bowl. Jen will probably need to replace this commode and sink, but perhaps the hardware can be salvaged. Those faucets could be antique.

The first door on the right leads to a sparsely furnished office. A desk sits beyond the doorway, and a bookcase against the wall overflows with leather-bound volumes, stacks of periodicals, and over a dozen bulging notebooks. Joella thumbs through the magazines: *Fishing, Reader's Digest, Mortuary Management.* Ned and Gerald must have saved every magazine they read.

She pulls one of the binders from the bookcase and flips through white and yellow copies of receipts, contracts, and letters. Apparently neither Ned nor Gerald ever felt the need to transfer their records to a computer.

She slides the binder back onto its shelf and slaps dust from her hands. Nothing unusual here; no evidence of buried secrets. Daniel Sladen must have examined the books when he evaluated the estate, so apparently everything passed muster.

She steps back and regards the space with a critical eye. The room could serve as a study for some fortunate buyer, but the new homeowner would definitely want to rip out or paint this depressing dark paneling. She could suggest that Jen paint the walls a warm beige or tan. . . .

An unexpected creak strums a shiver from her. She turns, her nerves at a full stretch, and watches as the door swings forward on its hinges . . . and something dangles from a hook on the back of the door.

For an instant her blood chills with memories of slumber party stories about hook-handed serial killers, but her eyes mist when she recognizes the dark object as a man's coat and slacks. Ned must have kept his funeral suit here, where he could easily pull it on for services or viewings.

She reaches out to caress the soft wool of the jacket. How many families did Ned console while he worked at Fairlawn? The lawyer told Jennifer that Ned had ministered to nearly every family in Mt. Dora at one time or another. He might have worn this suit in each of those situations.

Joella presses her hands against a fold in the slacks. Is this shiny spot the result of kneeling in prayer for those families? The worn area is at the knees, and there's a matching spot on the other pants leg.

She closes her eyes as a flood of regrets overwhelms her thoughts. Ned seemed like the kind of man who might have had a positive influence on her late husband, but Nolan had little contact with his uncle after Ned and Marjorie moved to Florida. Nolan took after his father, Vane, a charming fellow who was more glitter than gold.

Nolan glittered too, even in army camouflage. He still sparkles in Jen's memory, and that's okay. A girl should think well of her father.

Joella blinks a sudden wetness from her eyes and leaves the room. Only three doors left, and she doesn't care to visit the preparation area. But there's a mystery room across the hall from the office.

The hum of machinery reveals the nature and purpose of the space before she turns on the light. After flipping the switch, she sees two dusty air-conditioning units with silver arms that snake into the ceiling. The wall in front of the hulking units is lined with a washing machine, a dryer, and a laundry tub.

When a roach scurries away from the light and disappears beneath the dryer, Joella exhales in relief. At least she and Jen won't have to frequent a Laundromat while they're here. A stack of folded men's underwear waits on the washer, so that machine, at least, must be operational. And this room isn't too creepy, as long as one doesn't mind sharing the space with a few roaches.

She knows roaches. Early in her marriage, she and Nolan lived in army housing and became well acquainted with vermin of all sorts. She learned how to bait the pests with boric acid, which might not be a bad idea for this place.

She steps into the hall and looks at the remaining unexplored area, the room next to the office. Gathering her courage, she swings the door into a dark space. A fringe of sunlight seeps from beneath a pair of drapes over a window at the back of the room, providing the only light until Joella fumbles for a switch. She finds it and gasps at what the narrow room reveals: caskets, at least a half dozen. Wooden, metal, and fabric-covered, they stand along the walls like silent sentinels. One, a tiny pink box not more than two feet long, rests on the floor near the windows.

She shivers as countless scenes from vampire movies flash through her mind. She knows she's being silly, but there's no denying the hush that pervades this room, a solemnity that has nothing to do with the deep scarlet carpet or the dark-paneled walls. The air feels thicker here, harder to breathe, as if it's permeated with the sorrow of a hundred farewells.

She turns off the light and backs out of the room, closing the door firmly behind her. Obviously this is the place where Gerald brings a family member when it's time to pick out a coffin. It's not a place she wants to linger.

꙰ ꙰ ꙰

When the bedsprings creak, I wake from sleep as if slapped. I am curled into a ball and clinging to my pillow as though it's a life preserver, but even the curtain of hair across my eyes can't disguise my mother's stern presence at the side of the bed.

"Jen." She leans toward me and speaks in that no-nonsense tone that spells trouble. "We have to talk."

"I'm awake." To prove my point, I release my desperate grip on the pillow and push myself into a sitting position. Mom isn't frantic, so no one's dying, but she's obviously upset about something.

I brush my hair out of my eyes and check the clock. How can she be so worked up before eight in the morning? "What's wrong?"

She looks away as if she can't bear to give me bad news directly. "Have you looked around downstairs?"

"I've seen the chapels."

"I'm talking about the rest of the downstairs."

I hate to admit it, but she's surprised me. "You went into Gerald's *workroom*?"

"Good grief, no. I went into those other rooms."

"What other rooms?"

She draws a deep breath. "There are four rooms along the hallway that leads to that prep room. One is a bathroom—"

"That's certainly logical."

"—one is an office, one a utility room, and the other . . ."

I brace for the big revelation and try to fill in the blank. What else could be down there? A holding room for flowers? A babies' crying room? A storage space?

Mom's face has become a pale knot of worry.

Please, Lord, don't let Gerald be hoarding unclaimed bodies in a freezer. "Mom—" I lower my voice—"what did you see?"

She shivers and rubs her arms. "Coffins. All standing up like they're waiting for Dracula to take them for a test drive."

I blink at her in amused wonder. "Isn't this where you're supposed to remind me that this is a funeral home?"

She straightens her spine. "It's not a funeral home now. What if Bugs or Clay stumbles into that room? They could be scarred for life!"

"You think this is news to me?"

"Caskets!" She shudders as if the word itself has the power to terrify. "That room was unlocked, Jen, and you know how the boys are. They're curious, and they're going to find that room before long. They'll be playing hide-and-seek or something—"

"Kids don't play hide-and-seek anymore. They play video games."

Mom draws herself up another inch. "You don't know what they're doing because you're always working. Before the divorce, you were always at the office; here, you're always thinking about that stupid list. Most of the time you don't even know where your boys are."

She's angry because I'm not freaking about the caskets, but she's forgotten that I'm not at my best in the morning. I have little patience with her tirades *after* I've had my caffeine, and today I haven't yet had a chance to even *smell* my coffee.

I roll to the other side of the bed. "Let it go, Mom. Maybe we need to toughen up. Maybe we shouldn't turn the kids into paranoid wimps who freak out at the sight of a casket. I also refuse to go on this little guilt trip you've arranged, so hush. I'm working hard on that to-do list so I can create a good home for my boys—a home even Thomas might enjoy. Clay and Bugs are my responsibility, mine and my husband's, so I'd appreciate it if you'd just back off."

When she rears back, for half a second I wonder if I've gone too far.

I've been harsh, but so has she. If we're going to live together, we have to be honest with each other.

"Well." With an offended expression, she stands and smooths her hair. "Forgive me for waking you."

"I needed to get up anyway."

"To start work on your *list*?"

"To get breakfast for the boys and *then* to get started on my list. I'm going to work on the front porch, and I thought I'd ask the boys to help me sand and paint." I force a smile. "It could be a fun family project."

An invitation to join us is clearly implied, but Mom doesn't pick up on it. Instead she lifts her head and stomps out of my room, her steps rattling the brass lamp on the nightstand.

12

Joella pulls the last of her clothing from the drawer and drops it into the open suitcase on her bed. Paint the front porch? What kind of way is that for young boys to spend a summer Saturday? It's a stupid way, but Jen won't see that. Just like she doesn't see that Thomas is gone forever and they're better off with him out of their lives.

Joella steps across the hall into the bathroom and removes her toothbrush and toothpaste from the holder. Her toiletries bag sits on the back of the toilet; she picks it up and tosses her toothbrush inside, then glances around to be sure she's not leaving anything important behind.

Nothing . . . except her only daughter and her grandchildren. But they don't want her. They don't need her. Jen would rather chase a rainbow than exercise a little common sense. Joella has given up her summer to help them, to make sure they can sell this place and move back to Virginia, but Jen has so much more in mind. Like an alcoholic who clings to his bottle, she wants to believe that Thomas will come back.

Well, she can have him. She can do whatever she likes.

Clutching the toiletries bag to her chest, Joella reenters her bedroom and drops her bag into the suitcase. A quick look in the closet shows that she's left nothing behind but a couple of sprained hangers.

She walks to the bed and zips her suitcase. *"A home even Thomas might enjoy."* What is Jen thinking? And calling him her *husband* after all he's put her through—the floozy nanny, the divorce, the way he hinted that she should quit her job instead of him quitting his. They were both employed by Virginia senators. Thomas could have left his job as easily as Jen. But no, it's always easier for the *woman* to start over. It's always the *mother's* job to muddle through until the husband settles down.

She used to think Jen was a modern woman, but sometimes the girl is so blind she just won't see.

She's too much like her father.

Joella drags her suitcase off the bed and winces as its weight thuds on the floor. The bag feels heavier than it did when they left Virginia. . . . Either that or her muscles have turned to jelly at the thought of leaving her grandsons.

She sits on the edge of the bed. Why shouldn't she leave? She's doing no good here. Jen isn't listening to a thing she says. Jen will always plunge right in and do whatever she thinks is right; trying to guide that girl is like trying to lasso the wind. Nolan was like that too, as implacable as stone.

Joella lifts her gaze to the window and presses her lips together, stopping a fountain of tears. She won't cry this time; never again will she cry over Nolan.

All she needs is a quick hug from the boys and a ride. Then she'll be on her way to Virginia, where life is calm and predictable.

She steps into the hall and listens for the sounds of the house. The pipes are humming in the wall adjacent to Jen's bathroom, so she's probably in the shower. The TV is blasting cartoons, so Bugs must be awake and in front of the television.

Joella pastes a smile on her face and walks through the hallway and into the living area.

Bugs glances up, then focuses on her feet. "Why are you wearing shoes, Grandma?"

"Because I'm going out." She peers past him into the kitchen. "Is Mr. Gerald up yet?"

"He's getting dressed. He came out to plug in the coffee."

Joella moves past Bugs and stands in the kitchen. The space feels more crowded than usual, the cupboards slightly yellow in the pale light of morning. A faint chemical scent lingers beneath the fragrant aroma of coffee—probably the roach killer Gerald sprayed under the sink last night.

She pulls a pair of mugs from the cupboard. She might as well pour a couple of cups while she waits, but she'd like to be out of the house before Jen comes out of the shower. No sense in lingering; no sense in waiting for the bubble to burst. Jen's plan has disaster written all over it, but she'll never realize the truth.

"Mornin'."

She startles, then gives Gerald a flustered smile. "I'm glad you're up. I wonder if you could do me a favor."

He heads to the coffeemaker and lifts the decanter. "Name it."

"I need a ride to the bus station. I'm going back to Virginia."

If he's surprised, he doesn't show it. He gestures for her to extend one of the mugs in her hand. "I thought you were staying over the summer."

She shrugs as he pours coffee. "Jen doesn't need me here."

Gerald's mouth shifts just enough to bristle the whiskers on his cheek. "I think she needs you more than she knows. And you don't seem the type to run when the going gets tough."

"I'm not—at least I didn't used to be. But lately . . . I don't know. I get so frustrated with that girl." Joella sinks into a kitchen chair and inhales the rich fragrance from the steaming mug. Aware of Bugs's presence in the next room, she lowers her voice. "I try to guide her, to give her the benefit of my experience, but she doesn't listen. She doesn't even want to hear what I say. I can see that she's heading for a collision, but she doesn't want to hear bad news." She forces a chuckle. "Believe me, I've thought about jumping up and down and waving my arms, but Jen would probably have me committed."

Gerald grins as he sits in the chair across from her. "Kinda makes you appreciate all that God goes through when we insist on doing things our way, doesn't it?"

"Hmm." Joella sips her coffee as his words resonate in the quiet space. The man has made a good point, but he doesn't know Jennifer very well. He hasn't watched her grow from a skinny girl with braids to a woman who seems bent on repeating every mistake Joella's ever made. She meets Gerald's eye. "I'm a believer, but I'm not God. I don't have his patience."

"Actually, you do." He stirs sugar into his cup. "You just have to exercise it."

He stands to pull the cream from the refrigerator as understanding seeps through Joella's frustration. *Exercise patience*: two little words—only two—urging her to do something that ought to be easy when dealing with those she loves. She's patient with Bugs. She's patient with Clay. She's even patient with that squirrelly dog because she knows the boys love him.

Being patient with them is easy because they don't test her like Jen does, like Nolan did. By the time Nolan died, Joella thought she was finished with exercising patience, but apparently God has more to teach her . . . because she hasn't learned very well.

What sort of woman runs when she's tested? The sort who has little endurance, shallow character, and weak faith. The sort who would set a bad example for her family.

She exhales a long sigh, then lifts her mug. "You make a powerful pot of coffee, Gerald Huffman."

❈ ❈ ❈

Bugs sits on the front porch step and watches a pair of crows wading through the lawn. The birds are big and black, some of the biggest he's ever seen, and they don't look happy. One of them has mean eyes, and that bird focused on him just before it chased a blue jay from the tall grass.

Skeeter is missing, and Bugs wonders if a mean crow could have frightened the dog away. Skeeter could probably bite a crow, but a crow as mean as that one might be able to peck at a dog. The bird could have attacked Skeeter, and now the dog might be afraid to come back.

Bugs would be afraid. He wants to go home, but Grandma says

they have to stay while Mom fixes the house. Mr. Gerald is nice, but Clay has stopped talking to Bugs since he met Brett, and Brett no longer wants to do the things Bugs likes to do. Clay wants to spend all his time with Brett, so Bugs and Skeeter get left at the house with a TV that gets only six channels and a kitchen so small you can barely turn around without bumping into someone.

And no matter what Mom says, this house is the dead shed. Everyone says so, even other kids at the park. They laughed when Bugs said he lived in the pink house, and they ran away before he could ask if he could swing with them.

He doesn't want to live in a big pink house. His other house was brick, like Grandma's, and Daddy lived in it too. But they don't have that house anymore, and he hasn't seen Daddy in a long time.

What if he never sees Daddy *or* Skeeter again?

❀❀ ❀❀ ❀❀

I'm on my way to the van when I spot Bugs bouncing Skeeter's ball on the porch steps. He looks as morose as he did the day the "redheads" descended on Mom's house, but today there's not a Hatter in sight.

I stuff my shopping list into my purse and sink onto the step beside him. Mom's rebuke keeps whirling in my head, so there's no way I'm going to The Home Depot and Wal-Mart without taking the time to talk to my little guy.

"Hey, dude." I drop my knee until it nudges his. "Whatcha doin'?"

He shrugs. "Waiting for Skeeter to come home."

"Oh yeah?" I look out across the lawn, but I don't see any sign of the dog. "Where'd he go?"

"I don't know. I think the crows scared him away."

I search the trees at the side of the property, but apparently the crows have gone into hiding along with the dog. "I don't think crows could do that. Skeeter is a brave dog, and you know he likes to explore." I nudge Bugs again. "Want to go shopping? I thought I'd pick up a few shorts and T-shirts—something cool for us to wear in this sweatbox of a house."

He lowers his chin onto his palm. "I hafta wait on Skeeter."

"I'm also going to Home Depot—you could look at toilets with me."

For some odd reason, Bugs has always loved looking at the bathroom and kitchen displays. He also loves paint chips, so I'm hoping he's destined to become a contractor.

But not even the promise of shiny plumbing appeals to my sad son. "I need to wait for Skeeter."

I sit with him and watch the wind scissor the grass. Gerald really ought to mow the lawn before we attract snakes and rats and whatever else prowls in the woods around here. It'd be nice if we had a fence for the dog, but I'm not spending that kind of money on a house I'm trying to sell.

I slip my arm around Bugs's shoulder. "You look sad, kiddo. Are you still missing Daddy?"

For a moment he looks at me with a question in his eyes; then he returns his gaze to the lawn. "I dunno."

"You don't have to be sad. You'll see your daddy again before you know it. We'll go back to Virginia as soon as this place sells. I know we haven't seen your dad in a while, but he's not gone forever. And I promise you this—when you see Daddy again, it'll seem like no time at all has passed. Okay?"

Finally I'm rewarded with a small smile. "Yeah."

I kiss the top of his head and grab my purse. "Are you sure you don't want to go to the Depot? You can pick out some paint chips."

"I wanna go around back and look for Skeeter."

"All right then. But stay away from the lake, okay?"

A lump rises in my throat as I watch Bugs stand up, race to the end of the porch, and jump off. Despite the time I've taken to sit with him, guilt lies heavy on my shoulders.

What can I do about it? I'm a woman with responsibilities, more now than ever.

13

The boys and I spend Sunday morning preparing lost-dog posters for the neighborhood. Bugs cried himself to sleep last night, and I'm beginning to worry about the dog. Skeeter is always running off to chase rabbits and birds, but he's never stayed away overnight. Could he have been grabbed by a gator? Mom's made me paranoid, plus I've heard rumors about dogfighting rings and researchers who snatch pets off the street and use them in awful experiments.

After Gerald comes home from church, he and Bugs walk to the end of the road with a stack of posters and a stapler. They return a half hour later, tired, sweaty, and empty-handed. Mom cups Bugs's face in her hands and tells him to exercise patience, but her words do little to comfort him.

I'm sanding windowsills and railings on the front porch when a woman and a teenage boy walk up the drive. The boy is leading Skeeter on a leash. I yell for Clay and Bugs, who tumble through the doorway and hurry to greet our guests.

Only then do I turn my attention to the woman. Because it's Sunday afternoon and she's carrying a rectangular pan, I suspect she's playing Welcome Wagon hostess . . . and may even think we've come to stay.

I glance at my pale legs and wish I'd put on something more presentable than elastic-waist shorts and a T-shirt. I drop my sandpaper and wipe my dusty hands on my shorts.

My visitor is wearing a summer dress and sandals, probably what she wore to church—a habit we've set aside since coming to Mt. Dora. I thought about church this morning when I saw Gerald leaving the house with his Bible, but I don't want to face a hundred questions about who we are, why we're in Florida, and what happened to my husband.

Right now I'd rather fill out a tax return than a church visitor's card.

I am swiping dust from my forearms when I hear Clay greet the teenage boy. So this is Brett, the young man who has so impressed my sons. The woman must be his mother.

I try on a practice smile. The woman notices and releases one side of the pan long enough to wave.

"Thank heaven someone found that dog."

I flinch as Mom's voice filters through the window screen. I have no idea how long she's been standing behind the open window, but my mother doesn't miss much.

"This must be Lydia," I say, keeping my voice low. "How old do you think she is?"

"About your age, probably." Mom leans on the windowsill and rests her chin in her hand. "Maybe a little older. She looks nice."

The woman striding up our sidewalk wears a short, modern haircut, but her hair is a steely shade of gray and streaked with silver. Her face is as smooth as a baby's, so she could be anywhere from forty to sixty.

"Is it true?" she calls, coming up the steps. "I saw the notice in the paper, so I was hoping to catch you at home. I'm Lydia Windsor."

"Jennifer Graham." Obeying an old instinct, I extend my hand, but Lydia doesn't shake it. Instead she offers me the rectangular pan, which I almost drop before recovering from the unexpected gesture.

"A housewarming gift," she announces. "Pineapple right-side-up cake. I was going to bake it upside down, but I didn't have a tray to flip it onto. So I left it in the pan and figured it'd taste the same no matter which side you eat first."

"That's . . . wonderful. Thank you. And thank you for bringing Skeeter back. My sons missed him something awful."

"Brett recognized him right away, but he didn't see the dog until I'd tried five or six times to shoo the little varmint out of my tomato patch. He kept plucking the fruit from the plants and bringing them up to the house." She tilts her head. "Did you teach him to do that?"

"Eat tomatoes?"

"He didn't eat them. He stripped those plants clean, though, all but a couple of baby buds." She isn't angry with me, at least not yet, but clearly she isn't happy about what Skeeter has done to her garden.

"I'm sorry." I shift the heavy cake pan from one arm to the other. "We've never had tomato plants, so I really don't know what would make him do that sort of thing. If you want, I could—"

I'm interrupted by Clay's shout: "Fetch, Skeeter!" He throws the dog's ball across the yard, and the boys watch as Skeeter zips across the lawn, rippling the grass as he runs.

Lydia laughs. "Well, don't that beat all. I'll bet he thought he was bringing me his little red ball."

"But dogs are color-blind."

"Most of the tomatoes he plucked were green." She smiles, clearly waiting for me to invite her in, serve coffee, or perform some other neighborly act of goodwill, but I haven't time for such things today.

"So," she says when I hesitate, "is it true?"

"Excuse me?"

"The newspaper ad said Fairlawn is back in business. Is that right?"

I stifle a groan. I'd been hoping no one would read Gerald's newspaper notice.

"Gerald only wants to honor some presold contracts." I glance over my shoulder. "Mom? Could you come take this?"

Almost instantly Mother steps onto the porch, introduces herself to Lydia, and relieves me of the heavy cake pan. "Mmm, that smells wonderful," she says, radiating goodwill. "Won't you come in for a glass of lemonade?"

I suppress a smile. The *last* thing I want to do is stop working to chitchat with a neighbor I'll probably never see again, but if Mom plays Lady Bountiful, I'll be relieved of the role. At least one of us needs to maintain a good reputation. After all, no one will want to buy Fairlawn from an inhospitable family with a tomato-stealing terrier.

"Thank you, but I need to get home." Lydia's smile broadens when she sees my barely disguised look of relief. "You have a lot of work to do, don't you?"

I bend to pick up my sandpaper. "We're getting the place ready to sell. Sharon Gilbert's coming by later to put the sign in the yard."

"I'm sorry to hear that." Lydia's regretful expression seems genuine. "Brett and I loved Ned, but I was hoping we could welcome a woman to the neighborhood. When I heard you had two boys, I thought Fairlawn would be ideal for them."

"Virginia will always be home to us. We don't know a soul in Florida."

A faint light twinkles in the depths of Lydia's dark eyes. "You do now."

"Well, a mortuary isn't my idea of the ideal home, if you know what I mean. It seems so . . . creepy." I pull my hair off my sweaty neck. "Doesn't it bother you to live so close to this place?"

"Oh, I've never minded living next door to Fairlawn. One thing's for sure—I couldn't have asked for quieter neighbors." She smiles at Bugs and Skeeter. "I'll be sorry to see you go. How long do you think you'll be here?"

"Not long. I need to have the boys back in Virginia by the time school starts in the fall."

"I understand. Brett will be a junior this year, but his school's in California. He'll have to leave in early August."

She's just handed me the perfect opening to ask about Brett's father and their custody situation, but I don't want to hear the marital history of a woman I may never see again. So I opt for the easy comment. "My boys like Brett a lot."

"He likes them, too. By the way, if you need anything, we live in the white house just to the right of your driveway. It's tucked behind the trees, but it's a nice long lot that runs right up to the park at the lake. I run Twice Loved Treasures from my home, so stop in sometime. "

"Twice Loved . . . what?"

"I take other people's junk and make something beautiful from it. It's my gift."

I shade my eyes with my hand and make a token attempt to look down the hill, but I'm not really interested in trash, treasures, or trading recipes.

Lydia smiles at Clay, who's come over to return her leash. "Brett has to mow the lawn this afternoon, but when he's done, maybe you guys could go to the ballpark. There's a citywide softball game this afternoon. If you don't want to play, it's still fun to watch."

Clay looks at me, eagerness shining in his eyes. "Could I go, Mom?"

He put in a full hour of sanding before he gave out, so how can I deny him the opportunity to have a little fun?

"I don't see why not." I smile at Lydia. "If Brett still wants to go after all that lawn mowing, could he swing by and knock on the door?"

"I'll remind him. And I'll let you get back to your work, but remember this: Gerald's a dear man, but he wouldn't know about a lot of things that concern us single mothers. So don't hesitate to call if you need anything."

She turns and walks away, leaving me to wonder what she meant by that last comment. Was she talking about hairdressers? gynecologists? alimony?

I'm still wondering when she pauses at the end of the sidewalk to twiddle her fingers in a final wave.

14

"So you see, Ms. Graham, you're gonna need a TXV and an EER higher than twelve—I'd recommend at least a sixteen for this house. You'll be replacing two units—one to service the first floor, one for the second, with an air cleaner on the unit for the upstairs. That's where you spend most of your time, right?"

I nod as if I've understood every word. Charley Gansky, of Gansky's Get Great Air, is a rotund man with a round face and a sweaty clump of thinning blond hair.

His brown eyes narrow. "You know about SEER ratings, right?"

I nod again.

"Good. The Lennox units I have in mind have a SEER rating of 16.5, and they'll do a good job for you. I'll be giving you a bid on two three-ton units. That'll include variable-speed air handlers, of course, and we'll check that all the ducts are sealed and insulated. I'm tossing in the air cleaner to welcome you to the neighborhood." Gansky's broad face splits into a grin. "You're fortunate that Ned put in central air, or you'd be looking at a complete ventilation system, ducts, the works."

"The works?" I echo. "Yes, I am fortunate."

My head aches with information overload, and the faint pounding at my temple quickens when a black BMW pulls into the parking lot. For a moment I'm afraid a rival air-conditioning installer has shown up early for his appointment; then I remember the car . . . and the lawyer who drives it.

I give Charley Gansky a pained smile. "Do you need anything else from me?"

"No, ma'am."

"Thanks for coming out, then. The sooner you can get that bid to me, the more we'll appreciate it."

I leave him scribbling notes on his clipboard as I walk toward Daniel Sladen. The lawyer has stepped out of his car and is looking at the house with an appraising eye. . . . At least I *think* he is. Hard to tell what he's doing behind those sunglasses.

He smiles, though, when he sees me walking toward him. "Ms. Graham! How are things coming along out here?"

"Fine," I tell him, wishing I didn't look quite so disheveled. "This place feels like contractor central. I think I've talked to every painter, electrician, and exterminator in Lake County."

Daniel rests his arms on the top of his car and nods toward Gansky's white van. "I see Charley's doing some work for you."

"He's giving me a bid. I like to get at least three before deciding anything. I usually ask for recommendations, but—"

"Charley's a good guy." The warmth of Sladen's voice reflects in his smile. "He'll treat you right."

"Thanks, but I doubt you came out here just to give Charley a reference." I wave toward the porch. "Do you mind if we talk over there? I'm about to broil in this sun."

"Lead on." He closes his car door and follows me up the sidewalk. Once we reach the porch, he removes his sunglasses, and I find myself relaxing. Under all that great hair, Daniel Sladen has nice eyes . . . for a lawyer.

I gesture to the rockers. "I'd invite you in, but until we get the air conditioners replaced, it's more miserable inside than out."

"I like porches," Sladen says, settling into a rocker. "Where is everyone?"

I sit in the chair next to his. "The boys took Skeeter down to the creek. Mom's at the grocery store, and Gerald's probably down in his dungeon—it's the only cool space in the house."

Sladen laughs and rubs his hand over his chin. "Actually, Gerald's one reason I came out today. I saw his newspaper notice about Fairlawn. Are you really reopening the mortuary?"

My hand tenses on the armrest. "Has our license expired or something?"

"Nothing like that. I was only curious. Last time we talked, you weren't excited about Fairlawn's funereal, um, aspect."

I turn and hug one knee to my chest. "Truthfully? I'm still not thrilled about it. But Gerald says we have a ton of supplies and some outstanding contracts—not to mention a roomful of caskets. He convinced me that we ought to go back into business for a while at least."

"For how long?"

"As long as it takes to get the house sold. The new owners can use the place for whatever they like."

He nods and looks out over the lawn.

I'm tempted to follow his gaze, but I'd rather study Daniel Sladen. How can he sit outside in a long-sleeved dress shirt and tie without sweating?

The man must have ice in his veins.

"This certainly is a pretty place," he says, patting the arm of his rocker. "I'd hate to see it fall into the wrong hands."

"Anybody who has the courage and the money to buy this old house will *be* the right hands—and they'll have their work cut out for them. Gerald says old houses are like old people—something's always wearing out."

Daniel grins. "Better not let your mother hear you say that."

"Why not? She's always complaining about getting older. But I'm not far behind her. These days I can barely read the newspaper without my glasses."

"Tell me about it." He taps the front of his shirt, and for the first time I notice a pair of folded readers in the pocket. "Well—" he rubs the arms of his rocker again—"I thought I'd come out to see how you folks were getting on. But it looks like you have everything under control."

"Is that all? You said Gerald's notice was just one reason for coming out here—"

"Oh! Almost forgot." He pulls a folded slip from his pocket and presents it to me. "As promised, the balance of your uncle's estate—$563.72."

I study the numbers on the check. "Thanks. This will help."

"Wish it could be more."

"That's all right. I'm grateful for every penny these days." I stand to see him off. "Thank you for coming. If you have any recommendations for contractors . . ."

"Looks like you're doing fine," he says, grinning over his shoulder as he walks away.

❈ ❈ ❈

I'm standing before a pineapple right-side-up cake, and the only knife I can find is a scalpel. Some part of my brain accepts this as perfectly normal, considering that I'm standing in an embalmer's kitchen, but when I slip on rubber gloves and slice into the cake, blood oozes from the cut and an alarm shatters the quiet—

I sit up to the trilling of my alarm clock. No, my clock *beeps*, so I must be hearing the old phone in the kitchen. It's ringing . . . at 4 a.m.

My thoughts swerve immediately toward my loved ones. Mom, Bugs, and Clay are safe in the house with me, so no one could be calling with bad news about them. My father's already passed on, so—

Good heavens, could something have happened to Thomas?

I fling back the covers and stumble down the hall, my feet thumping heavily on the wooden floor. In the light of the lamp by the sofa, I see Gerald standing in the kitchen, the phone in his hand. I hesitate in the doorway, my palm pressed to my pounding heart.

"All right," he says, scribbling a note on a pad. "I'll see you soon." He hangs up and looks at me. "Everything all right, missy?"

My finger trembles as I point to the phone. "Who . . . what happened?"

He tears the top page from the notepad, then folds it and slips it into his pocket. "I have a pickup."

"A what?"

116

"Lulabelle Withers passed. Over on Highland Street."

My nightmare of scalpels and oozing cakes returns in a rush of reality. I brace myself against the doorframe and take a deep breath. "I was afraid someone died."

"Someone did."

"I mean . . . someone I know."

"Stick around long enough and you'll know everyone who comes through our back door. You needn't sorrow for Mrs. Withers, though; she was ready to go. She celebrated her centennial birthday last year, and that TV reporter announced her name on the morning news. She got cards from all over the state."

"So . . . she's, um, coming here?"

He chuckles. "Not on her own. I have to go pick her up."

For a moment I chew on the foot I have planted in my mouth. I never thought much about how the dead *arrive* at funeral home. Never occurred to me that someone has to go get them.

Especially at four in the morning.

In the train of that thought, another question rises. "How do you . . . ?"

"Hmm?"

"Do you pick them up in your Plymouth?"

A smile lifts his lined cheeks. "You haven't been out to the garage, have you?"

I've been parking the minivan out front, next to Gerald's tanklike sedan. "I didn't know there was a garage."

"It's at the back of the property. That's where we keep the call car and the hearse."

I step back, aware that I've stumbled into an alien world. I may have mingled with movers and shakers on Capitol Hill, but at Fairlawn, I'm an outsider.

Gerald shuffles into his bedroom and closes the door. I watch light bloom at the threshold and hear the sounds of a man getting dressed.

I walk to the counter, knowing I should do something to help.

For a few weeks at least, I am his partner in this venture. Maybe he'd appreciate a cup of coffee.

Dark liquid has just begun to trickle into the decanter when Gerald's bedroom door opens. He walks into the kitchen wearing black pants, a white shirt, and a black string tie.

Mt. Dora's version of 4 a.m. formal wear.

He pulls his favorite cardigan sweater from a wall hook and checks his hair in the chrome toaster.

I give him a smile. "You look nice. Mrs. Withers's family will be impressed."

"They won't be looking at me." Gerald licks the tip of his index finger and smooths a piece of hair sticking out from above his ear. "During the pickup, most people are too upset to even notice me. I'm spiffin' up for Lulabelle. That lady deserves a little extra attention."

"So—" my brain has gone into overdrive, juggling my to-do list, the Realtor's suggestion that we have an open house, and the electricians who have yet to give me bids on updating the wiring—"we'll be having a funeral, right? Within the next couple of days?"

He nods. "Probably Sunday afternoon."

That's not good. People go house hunting on Sunday afternoons, and nobody's going to want to tour Fairlawn in the middle of a funeral.

"Couldn't we have the service on Saturday night or Sunday morning? Maybe Lulabelle would want a quiet affair."

"Funerals are for the living, not the dead. Folks will want to come pay their respects, so we'll need to plan on a full house."

"But I wanted to have an open house, and the Realtor said Sunday afternoon's the best time." I know I sound like a whining child, but at four in the morning, whining comes naturally to me.

Gerald walks to the archway and pauses as his cheek curves in a smile. "What's the problem? Lulabelle was a grand lady; she'll fill the house with no trouble at all."

With brittle dignity he moves toward the staircase, leaving me alone to mull over his unconventional suggestion.

I wake just before nine, feeling both guilty and grateful that Mom has taken care of the kids while I slept. When I haven't heard any boy noise by the time the clock finishes striking, I roll out of bed and head toward the kitchen, looking for coffee and maybe a doughnut. An unnatural silence fills the house. . . . Where is everyone?

I find a stranger standing at the sink. My yelp of surprise startles the young man into dropping his mug; then he releases a scream even higher and louder than mine.

We retreat to opposite corners, both of us pale and wary. Before the intruder can move, I snatch a butcher knife from the chopping block and wave it in his direction. "What have you done with my family?"

"Nothing!" He raises his hands over his face and gapes through splayed fingers. "Who *are* you?"

The sound of pounding footsteps only increases my alarm. Does this burglar have an accomplice? I glance toward the landing in time to see Gerald panting his way up the stairs. He's wearing a brown rubber apron, latex gloves, and a look of intense concern.

"What in the name of pete is going on up here?" He frowns at my knife before noticing the broken pottery and spilled coffee. His face falls. "That was my favorite mug."

I point my blade at the interloper. "You know this guy?"

Gerald gives me a look of disbelief. "It's all right, Ryan. This is Jennifer, Ned's niece. She's our landlady."

The slender stranger looks unconvinced. "Tell her to put the knife away."

Gerald turns to me. "Jen, I'd like you to meet Ryan Evans, our hairdresser and makeup artist. I'm sorry I didn't think to warn you, but Ryan's always had the run of the place."

I slide the knife back into its slot in the butcher block as the young man peels himself off the wall. "Sorry." I tug self-consciously on my pajama top and motion toward the mess on the floor. "I'll get a mop and a dustpan."

For once, Gerald doesn't argue with me. By the time I return with a mop from the bathroom closet, Ryan is reenacting an exaggerated version of our encounter.

"She scared the sense right out of me," he says, his hand trembling around a fresh cup of coffee. "She came out of nowhere, and you know how skittish I am in this house."

Gerald acknowledges my presence with a flash of his brows and turns to Ryan. "I've told you a hundred times—there aren't any ghosts here."

"How would you know? You're probably asleep when they come out."

I clear my throat as I lower the mop into the sink. "I'd appreciate it if you didn't talk about ghosts around my boys." I glance out the window. "By the way, Gerald, where *are* the boys?"

"Your mother took them to town for breakfast." He pulls off his gloves, tosses them into the trash, and shuffles to the coffeepot. "Mmm, that smells good. Don't mind if I take a break."

Ryan takes another sip from his mug, then plucks a napkin from the counter and touches it to the side of his mouth. I hate to say it, but his actions are . . . dainty. "How's our patient?" he asks.

"She's settling. You can start to work in another couple of hours."

"Okay. I stopped by because my mom heard the news from Annie Watson. But if you don't need me for a while, I'll head to the salon."

"She'll be ready after lunch. But this time—" Gerald grins at me— "maybe you should come in the back door."

Ryan casts another chilly look in my direction and heads down the stairs.

After the front door slams, I collapse into a kitchen chair. I'm not sure which has unnerved me more—the stranger in the kitchen, the talk of corpses *settling*, or Ryan Evans himself.

I press my hand to my forehead. "He scared me to death, Gerald."

"Apparently the reaction was mutual."

"And . . . I don't know how to say this, but he *still* scares me."

"Ryan? He's harmless."

Has the man no eyes? "Gerald—" I lean forward and peer up at his face—"I don't want that young man around my sons. There's enough gender confusion in this world without guys like Ryan adding to the mix."

Gerald looks at me, his eyes clear and direct, and in that instant I realize he understands *exactly* what I'm trying to say. "You're new in town," he says, his voice cool and inflectionless, "so I don't suppose you could know Ryan as well as I do."

"Of course not, but I know an effeminate man when I see one. My boys aren't going to be seeing much of their father this year and—"

"We haven't really talked about this," he interrupts, "but are you a follower of Christ?"

The question steals my breath away. I stare at him in a paroxysm of wonder, shame, and indignation. "I . . . of course I am."

He lifts a brow. "That's good. Then you should know that Ryan is one of your spiritual brothers. He's a Christian too."

"That doesn't mean—"

"He lives in an apartment in the Biddle House. Because he loves the Lord, Ryan lives as chaste a life as Miss Biddle herself, and that's saying something."

"I'm not implying that he—would—could—" Because my words are tumbling over each other, I pause and draw a deep breath. I'm so confused I don't know what I'm saying or not saying.

I wish I hadn't said anything at all. I wish Gerald hadn't felt it necessary to ask about my spiritual life.

I wish I didn't feel so far away from the Lord.

I prop my elbow on the table and drop my throbbing head to my hand. "I'm sorry."

"Apology accepted . . . on Ryan's behalf."

Gerald sips his coffee as I scoop up the pieces of the broken mug, toss them into the trash, and attack the coffee spill with the mop.

I'm *so* glad we won't have to stay here. How could I expect my boys to form a proper masculine self-image if they shared a house with two women, an old man, a male makeup artist, and the occasional corpse?

We need to get back to Virginia. Clay and Bugs need their dad, and I need . . . normalcy.

I'm sure Mom is also eager to go home. We've had our disagreements since we've been in Mt. Dora, but most of the time she's a real trouper, helping with the boys and even my fix-up projects. She's cooked dinner for us several times, refilled the pantry with staples and necessities, and brought a much-needed touch of domesticity to the house. The fresh flowers on the foyer table are Mother's doing, as is the lemony scent of furniture polish in areas that used to smell of dust and mold. Even the fly cemetery has vanished from the windowsill.

If we sell this house anytime soon, Mom will deserve most of the credit. I've been busy dealing with repairmen, but she's done a lot to make this place look homey.

"We're back!" The front door slams. Bugs runs up the stairs, sprints into the kitchen, and hugs my knees as Skeeter bounds after him. "What's for lunch?" he asks.

I laugh and tousle his hair. "It's only nine-thirty, kiddo. Lunch won't be ready for a while yet."

"What's for snack, then?"

"Didn't you just eat?" I look around, helpless.

Gerald opens a brown bag on the counter and pulls out a banana. "Here you go, sonny. That'll hit the spot."

I stand back, mystified. I've never been able to get Bugs to eat bananas—he doesn't like something about the texture. But here he is, peeling the fruit like a monkey.

Mother trails Bugs into the kitchen, her cheeks flushed and a shopping bag dangling from her arm. "Guess what?"

I'm not in the mood for games. "Why don't you tell me?"

"I'm going to lunch with the Hatters."

"But—"

"But what?"

But you're not supposed to get involved down here. You're not supposed to get attached. These are the thoughts I want to communicate, but instead I find myself croaking, "But you don't have your red hat."

"Not a problem." She opens the shopping bag and pulls out a wide-brimmed millinery creation. The straw is a bit bedraggled and uneven, but a rose the size of a dinner plate adorns the brim.

Mom beams at us. "I found it at Twice Loved Treasures. Isn't it unique?"

I mumble something insanely supportive and turn back to the sink. As water streams over the coffee-stained mop, I find myself muttering a prayer: "Lord, the sooner you can get us out of here, the better off we'll be."

15

"I hear Lulabelle Withers is over at Fairlawn now."

"That's right." Joella smiles across the table at Alyce Baker, aka Her Royal Seamstress. The veil on Alyce's red straw hat keeps getting in the way of her Grizzly burger.

Ginger Sue Wilkerson, aka the Duchess of Dolls, points to the offending lace. "Why don't you just stick that thing up on your brim?"

Alyce shakes her head. "They say a veil makes a woman appear more mysterious."

Edna Nance, aka Dame Tootz, snorts. "I have enough lace on my face. A veil would be redundant."

Joella laughs and leans closer to Ginger Sue, who invited her to this get-together at Shoney's. "I must say, you all do have a good turnout."

Ginger Sue lifts her iced tea glass in a mock salute. "You'll never find us passing by an opportunity to party, Queen Snippy. So . . . why don't you tell us about your chapter up there in Virginia?"

Joella leans back, pleased by their interest. "We have a great group—about forty of us, usually—and we often meet at my house."

Ginger Sue's eyes widen. "Your house is big enough to hold a meeting?"

"Hatters don't have meetings," Alyce and Edna chorus in unison. "We have *fun*."

"We have *get-togethers*," Joella reminds Ginger Sue. "You haven't been a Hatter very long, have you?"

Ginger smiles and pushes a strand of bleached hair away from her brow. "I'm only fifty-five. Barely eligible."

"That's halfway to one hundred and ten," Alyce replies, wrapping her hands around her burger. "And nobody around here has made it to one hundred and ten."

"Which reminds me . . ." Edna shifts her gaze to Joella. "We saw the notice in the paper. Is Gerald serious about cranking things up to full speed at Fairlawn?"

Joella smooths the napkin in her lap. "He wants to feel useful, I think, like we all do. My daughter is still trying to sort her priorities. There's a lot of work to be done on the house, and there's no way she can afford to do everything."

Edna folds her hands. "I hear there's no husband around."

"Divorce." Joella looks around the table. "It happens to lots of young couples these days, doesn't it?"

"Even Queen Elizabeth," Ginger Sue says. "Four children and three divorces among her kids. Not to mention more scandals than you can count."

Edna makes a face. "That toe-sucking thing got to me. Imagine being the queen of England's daughter-in-law and letting some man nibble on your feet."

"I feel sorry for the queen," Alyce echoes. "Even with all that money and power, she can't smooth things out for her kids. Some couples are going to have problems, and I don't think there's anything we can do about it."

Edna snaps her fingers at the waitress and points to the empty water glasses on the table.

The frazzled girl nods and rushes off to take an order to the kitchen.

The waitress's frantic expression reminds Joella of Jennifer—her daughter never looks relaxed anymore. At the end of the day, when she ought to be enjoying her kids, she is always fretting about something on that silly to-do list.

"I try to be helpful," she says, thinking aloud. "But kids today don't want our help."

Alyce nods. "You gotta let them make their own mistakes."

"But you still have to look out for them—that's what mothers are for." Joella shakes her head. "You ask me, I think the blame mostly lies with men. I knew Jen's husband was a loser from the moment she brought him home, but her father absolutely loved Thomas. Couldn't say enough good about the guy."

"She married him, didn't she?" Edna asks.

Ginger Sue waves her fork in Joella's direction. "You can't blame men. As I recall, it wasn't Prince Andrew getting his toes licked. Women have to carry their share of the blame."

She lifts the ketchup bottle and squirts a thick puddle on her plate. "Take my son, for instance. He was living with a girl in Eustis, fixing up her home, being a daddy to her children. He put in a new kitchen for her, spent every free minute for nearly a year working on her place. When he finished, the girl kicked him out. He could have had a good savings account, but he put every extra cent into that girl's house. Now he's in a funk."

"Jen's not in a funk." Joella raises her chin. "She was upset when Thomas took off, but she's doing pretty well, considering he left her with two young sons."

Alyce lifts the edge of her veil. "The divorce—his doing or hers?"

"His," Joella states flatly. "Jen let him go, but I think she'd take him back if he came crawling home. And that's a pity."

Ginger Sue clucks in sympathy. "I had my son's little tramp pegged the moment I met her. Any girl who'd let a guy move in without a marriage license . . . well, he was a fool, and I told him so from the first. But when truth hurts, it isn't always welcome."

Joella tilts her head. "What does your son do?"

"He's a carpenter." Ginger Sue dunks a thick French fry into the ketchup. "He's good, too. Hasn't had a single complaint about his work, but it's hard getting jobs when you're first starting out."

Joella lifts her glass of iced tea as her thoughts whirl. Ginger Sue's son would probably be grateful for an opportunity . . . and heaven knows that Jen needs a carpenter. That back porch is so riddled with termites it's a wonder Gerald hasn't crashed through the planks.

"My daughter needs a carpenter." She slants a brow at Ginger Sue. "A small porch at the back of the house is about to collapse. I know Jen would like the thing replaced."

The woman's eyes light up. "Mitch—that's my son—would do good work; I promise. He's busy at a construction site in Tavares now, but he'll be done in a few days. He'd give your daughter a good price."

"Well, tell him to come around as soon as he can. Jen would love to talk to him." Joella smiles as the waitress brings the water pitcher. "Anybody have a son who's an electrician?"

16

On our second Friday at Fairlawn, I stand in the doorway and watch rain bounce off the roof of Floyd Fontenetta's pickup. Fontenetta is the twelfth professional and third electrician I have interviewed this week. He's spent the last two hours examining Fairlawn's walls, fuse box, and sockets. Now he's out in his truck, writing up his official and undoubtedly mind-boggling estimate.

Seems fitting that he should do it in one of the worst storms we've had since arriving in Florida.

Gerald says I should get used to afternoon thunderstorms because they roll across the state almost every summer day. The first time a storm swept over us, I thought we'd been caught in a hurricane. I told the boys to run for the basement, but Gerald laughed and said Fairlawn didn't have one. He laughed so hard, he nearly popped the button on his work pants.

I think Gerald actually *likes* storms. When they rumble in, he stands by the kitchen window sipping coffee or lemonade. As they toss spears of lightning from cloud to cloud, he sits in the TV room and watches the light show through the windows. When the rain passes, he takes his drink to the front porch, where he sits on a towel in his favorite rocker and hums old hymns until dinnertime.

I close the door, tired of breathing air so hot and wet it might have risen from a steaming washcloth. I have to open the door again, though, when I peek through the sidelight and see Fontenetta pull the collar of his jacket around his neck. Here he comes.

The electrician sprints through a murk that goes nova when a bolt of lightning zigzags through the heavy cloud cover and crashes with a booming roar. He ducks and runs faster, then leaps up the steps and looks at me with a grin on his wet face. "Thought that bolt had my name on it for sure."

He's joking—I think—and I manage a weak smile as I cross my arms and join him on the porch.

Fontenetta hands me a damp sheet of yellow paper. "Here it is— everything you'll need to bring the upstairs up to code."

"This will keep us from blowing a fuse every time we plug in a hair dryer?"

He grins. "You could even plug in a curling iron with this setup. I have a wife and two daughters, so I know about these things."

I hold the damp paper by its edge, thank him for his time, and go back into the house. After closing the door, I hold the rain-spattered page up to the light and search for the grand total: twelve thousand dollars.

For wires.

I blink away the image of dancing dollar signs and begin to climb the stairs. This estimate will join all the others waiting inside the notebook on my bed. Next week, if I can find the courage, I will bid farewell to my nest egg and begin to support several Mt. Dora families.

Mom lifts her head as I walk through the TV area, where she and the boys are watching the weather report. "Good news?" she asks.

I groan and plod past her.

Once I reach my bedroom, I close the door, sit on the edge of the mattress, and pull the calculator toward me. Like any good business-woman, I've gathered several bids on each project, even though it meant waiting at the house for carpenters, exterminators, painters, and electricians who rarely showed up at the designated hour.

Fontenetta was my last appointment . . . and I hope this is the last bid I have to get.

I pick up my notepad and pencil in the electrician's estimate, then punch the number into the calculator.

My to-do list has evolved.

Phase One: Crucial repairs calling for professional help

1. *Repair/replace central air-conditioning units: lowest bid—$11,545.50.*
2. *Upgrade electric for second floor: $12,000.*
3. *Treat house for termites: $3,000.*
4. *Hire carpenter to repair termite damage on back porch: $3,000-$4,000.*
5. *New insulation in attic (not priority).*
6. *Inspect roof—repair or replace? Replace: $20,000. Repair: $15,000.*
7. *Is water heater really about to blow? (Let's hope not.)*
8. *Professional house painting: $23,000.*

The termite treatment is mandatory; I can't sell the house without it. Ditto for the roof repair and air conditioner replacement. I wouldn't buy a house with substandard electrical circuits, so that's a must-complete project too.

Grand total of crucial items on my short list: $72,545. And fifty cents.

Income? Zilch, unless you count the child support payments that trickle in once a month.

Cash assets? Five hundred sixty-three dollars and seventy-two cents from Uncle Ned's estate plus my half of the equity, which is now less than forty thousand, minus our living expenses for the next several weeks. I have a retirement fund, but I can't touch it without paying penalties and possibly impoverishing my retirement years.

There's no way I can afford to do everything I need to do. I could take out a loan and use Fairlawn as collateral, but I don't think an unemployed single mother of two children would be a good credit risk.

So . . . I'm stuck. But I refuse to be defeated. Despite the fact that I haven't been a particularly attentive daughter, my heavenly Father has given us this house, led us here, and taken care of us along the way.

I'm no theologian, but I know God loves his children even when they're outraged and hurt. I know he wants families to be whole. He knows my boys need their daddy. He knows that beneath my anger, some part of me still loves Thomas.

So I'm grateful, and until Thomas comes to his senses, I'll keep working. As long as I have breath and a brain, I'll figure out some way to make this place provide for us.

Even if it takes longer than I expected.

I look at my window, still sheeted with rain. Those sun-bleached curtains may have to hang there for a while.

❧ ❧ ❧

Joella crosses her arms and waits for the click of Jen's door. The girl has barricaded herself in her bedroom again, trying to sort out her problems while her mother waits outside, ready to help.

Didn't she express interest when Jen walked past? Didn't she convey helpfulness without butting in? She's been careful not to cross the line, but Jen scarcely seems to notice. Talk about blind . . .

Desperate for fresh air, Joella goes downstairs. Rain is still tapping against the windows, but the overhanging clouds match her mood.

She steps onto the front porch and looks up and out, beyond the wide soffit. A sliver of blue sky has appeared in the west, so the storm is passing.

That's good news. This chapter in their lives is passing too, day by excruciating day.

She crosses the porch and sinks into a rocker, not caring that raindrops are darkening her slacks. Why should she care? This place, these people . . . she might as well be in a foreign country. Even the Hatters here, women with whom she shares many life experiences, move at a different pace from the women in Virginia. Yesterday Ginger Sue promised to have her son contact Jen about the porch, but Mitch hasn't called or stopped by. Joella practically offered the boy a job, but how does he respond? He ignores her.

She gets enough of the silent treatment from her daughter. She certainly doesn't need it from Ginger Sue's son.

The only person who hasn't given her the silent treatment is Gerald, but she'd be happier if he left her alone. She understands why the man might be lonely for female companionship, but he's not at all her type. The Hatters twittered when they asked her about him, and Edna blushed whenever Gerald's name came up. They all seem to think he is a fine catch, but he's far too country for Joella. And he's a *mortician*! What in the world would they ever find to talk about?

The door latch clicks behind her. Someone is coming out to the porch, maybe Clay or Bugs. Maybe even Jen, finally ready to ask for a bit of advice.

"Joella?" Gerald drawls. "I wondered if maybe you wanted to go into town for some ice cream."

She stares at the gravel parking lot, steaming after the rain. Is he asking her *out*?

She stops rocking but does not turn to meet his eyes. "Gerald, I am not unaware that half the women in town think you a fine catch, but I'm not interested in going into town with you today or any other day. I'm not interested in ice cream socials, afternoon matinees, or Sunday suppers. I am here to help my daughter unload this pink monstrosity, and soon we'll be going back to Virginia, our real home."

Behind her, a floorboard creaks as the door closes. For an instant she's sure he's gone back inside, but then he chuckles. "I'll be sure to put that bulletin on the evening news. In the meantime, if you see your grandboys, will you tell 'em I went to get the ice cream they wanted?"

Joella's cheeks heat to burning. Was this only about the *boys*? "Oh, good grief." She pushes herself out of the rocker and turns to face him. "The darlings want ice cream? Let's go get a half dozen gallons."

Gerald's mouth creases into a grin. "There you are," he says, his eyes sinking into maps of wrinkles. "I knew there had to be a girl beneath all that starch."

❧❧❧ ❧❧❧ ❧❧❧

On Saturday afternoon, I decide to strip the faded wallpaper in the foyer, thinking that the job won't be too strenuous. The air conditioner is still on the fritz, but the heavy cloud cover makes the house feel a bit cooler than usual—maybe 98 degrees instead of 102. Within a few minutes, though, sweat is rolling down my backbone.

I am reaching for a long strip when Clay springs onto the porch and thrusts his face against the window screen. "Mom?" He jerks his thumb over his shoulder. "I think Gerald has a customer coming up the walk."

"That's *client*," I say, moving toward the doorway.

Clay sprints off the porch and disappears into the stand of trees at the edge of the property. I'm not sure what he and Brett are up to out there, but if they aren't building a tree house or pretending to be Tom Sawyer, I don't want to know.

My eyes widen when I open the door and see an elderly woman shuffling up the walk. She wears a flowered dress that reaches well past her knees, low-heeled shoes, and despite the heat, a white cardigan. She walks with a careful, small step, supporting herself with a silver cane tipped in white rubber. A dowager's hump has curved her spine, but the woman looks up at me as she inches down the sidewalk.

"Be there in a minute," she calls, her voice surprisingly cheery for a woman visiting a funeral home. "I'm making good time."

Now that I've been spotted, I have no choice but to step onto the porch and await our visitor. At the rate she's progressing, I could have finished stripping the south wall and gotten a good start on the west.

When she finally pauses at the bottom of the stairs, I reach down. "Can I lend you a hand?"

"Why, thank you; that'd be nice."

Her skin is as dry as tissue paper against mine, but her grip is surprisingly tenacious. I help her up the steps, accepting her slight weight with each upward motion.

When we finally reach the porch, she grins like we've just scaled Everest. "That's a good walk," she says, tapping her way toward a rocker. "I'm ready to set a spell."

"Um—" I gesture toward the front door—"would you like to go inside? It's not much cooler in there, but . . ." *If you want to lie down or have me call an ambulance . . .*

"Land sakes, sweetie, we can visit as well out here as in there." She reaches the chair and carefully turns around. "Right now I don't think I can talk these legs of mine into taking another step."

I hesitate again, not certain why she's come. It's Saturday, so is she paying Gerald a social call? I think he's taking a nap, but I'd rather wake him than send her back down the sidewalk in this heat.

I tug down the hem of my ragged shorts and wish she hadn't caught me in my work clothes. "Ma'am, is there something I can help you with? Or have you come to see Gerald?"

She straightens and leans hard on her cane. "I've come to see Lulabelle Withers."

Ick. For two days I've been trying to ignore the fact that Gerald's working on a body downstairs. "Mrs. Withers isn't, uh, ready. The service is tomorrow at one."

The woman blinks. "I have a prearranged contract too. I wouldn't expect you to know that, seein' as you're new in town."

I can't help noticing that people around here don't expect a lot from newcomers. I force a smile. "Why don't you sit down? Can I get you a glass of iced tea?"

She drops into the rocker and sighs as if the weight of the world has just rolled off her shoulders. "If you have sweet tea, I'd be beholden to you. If you don't, I'd just as soon take a glass of water while we have our talk."

I excuse myself and trot upstairs to the kitchen. I'm pretty sure Mom has made a pitcher of sweet tea, so this lady is in luck.

When I return with two glasses on a tray, my guest has relaxed enough to close her eyes and let her age-spotted hands dangle over the arms of the rocker. She rouses at the sound of my footsteps and lifts a glass with genteel grace. "My name," she says before taking a sip, "is Mavis Biddle. I live in the Biddle House on Baker Street."

From the way she announces this, I know I'm supposed to be impressed. Still, it takes me a minute to place the name.

"Ryan, the young man who helps Gerald." I give her a careful smile. "He rents from you?"

"My second-floor tenant." Her features soften with approval. "He's a good boy."

"I met him a couple of days ago. He seems very . . . talented. I'm not sure I could do what he does."

"No one can do what Ryan does. Mr. Norris depended on him. Gerald does too."

I set the tray on the small table between us. "How can we help you today?"

Her blue eyes drift away from mine. "Every year," she says, "I update the directions for my funeral and bring a copy to Mr. Norris. Since he's passed on, I figured you'd know what to do with my letter."

I clasp my hands. "I'd be happy to give your letter to Mr. Huffman. He's handling all the Fairlawn business until—for now."

"But I heard a woman owned the place."

"That's true. I do. But I don't know anything about the business, so—"

"I suppose you'll have to do." Careful not to spill her drink, she takes a white envelope from her straw purse and hands it to me. "You can read it later. I just want your promise that you'll follow my instructions and let me have a Red Hat funeral."

I wince. "Did you say *Red Hat*?"

"Yes'm. I'm the queen of our local chapter, and my service wouldn't be complete without my sister Hatters. I still want the preacher, of course, and my friend Ruby will play the organ. When it comes time for people to speak, I'd like my sisters to have a say. And I want the kazoos when the pallbearers carry me out."

I sit back and cover my mouth with my hand, not sure if I should humor Ms. Biddle or call her next of kin. Is the woman delusional?

My mother is a serious Hatter, but not even she would ask for kazoos at a funeral service.

When I'm fairly certain I can look at my guest without smirking, I lower my hand. "Ms. Biddle, don't you think an organ benediction might be more appropriate than kazoos?"

"The kazoo—" she lifts her chin and boldly meets my eyes—"is an equal-opportunity instrument. Anyone can afford one; all the girls can blow one. When I roll out the door, I want everyone to hear the Hatters playing 'When the Saints Go Marching In.'"

I tap her letter on my lap. With any luck, this woman has a completely rational next of kin who will give Gerald the liberty to ignore any inappropriate last requests. "I assume you've written out all your wishes? They're in your letter?"

"Of course they are, honey." Her eyes twinkle over the rim of the glass as she sips her tea. "Mmm, that's good. You must be from the South."

"Virginia—right outside DC."

"That's right. I met your mother at the Hatter luncheon. I can tell you come from good stock. One Southern gal can always recognize another, don't you think?"

"I suppose." I lift my glass too, and for a moment we sip and rock to the rhythm of the wind rustling in the pines at the property line.

I'm remembering what Gerald said about funerals being for the living, not the dearly departed. As crazy as Ms. Biddle is for her Red Hat friends, surely she has a son or daughter who would faint at the thought of a kazoo recessional.

"Ms. Biddle—," I begin.

"It's Miss," she says, her birdlike eyes training on me. "Never married. Oh, I had my chances, but never could find a man who could do more for me than I could do for myself."

I mentally bid farewell to the notion of counting on her children for help. "Do you have family members who'll be attending the event?"

Her laugh is surprisingly youthful. "Not much chance of that, hon. I've outlived my parents, three sisters, and six cats. I don't think I'll discover any other family in the time I have left."

"But surely you have someone—a cousin, perhaps? Nieces or nephews?"

A frown appears in the fair skin between her brows. "I suppose an Alabama cousin or two might show up . . . but only if they think I'm mentioning them in the will." Her eyes dart from left to right; then she bends toward me. "I expect they're all anxious to get their hands on the Biddle House, but I'm leaving that to the Red Hat Society—with the condition that they allow Ryan to stay on as long as he likes. We'll be the first chapter in Florida to have a permanent meeting place."

"Well, I'm impressed."

She dips her chin in a determined nod. "'Tis a fine gesture, I think. Someone needs to do something for us older ladies. Most folks want us to roll off in a corner and knit booties, but I've never been the knitting type. I'm not giving up my home, either, not until the good Lord calls me to glory." She clutches the handles of her purse. "If there's nothing else, young lady, I think I'll be going. Thank you kindly for the tea. If there's anything in my letter Gerald doesn't understand, you have him give me a call. He has my number."

As she fumbles for her cane, I reach out and touch her hand. "Miss Biddle?"

"Call me Mavis, hon."

"Mavis . . . do you mind me asking how old you are?"

I thought the question might offend her, but her lined lips crinkle into a smile. "I'll be eighty-six next Thursday. Old enough to be ready to go, young enough to be in no hurry. And a sight younger than Lulabelle Withers."

I stand with her, silently offering my hand for support, but she leans on her cane instead. She does grip my arm as we make our way down the three porch steps; then she gives me a final grin and begins her cautious journey over the sidewalk.

I find myself studying the cracked concrete and wondering if Gerald could find a way to patch the uneven spots. A smooth sidewalk might add to Fairlawn's resale value, but more than that, I don't want my walkway to be the cause of an injury that might dispatch a woman like Mavis Biddle before her time.

After lunch, I stuff the last of the torn wallpaper strips into trash bags and haul them out to the garbage cans by the garage. Somehow I summon enough courage to open the door, and sure enough, the sight of the long, black hearse gives me the willies.

I brush the last of the wallpaper dust from my hands and walk toward the back porch, where I left Lydia's cake pan before gathering the garbage. I've kept the pan nearly a week, so it's about time I did the neighborly thing and returned it.

I reach Lydia's house in less than five minutes, but I'm sweating like an old cheese by the time I join a couple of shoppers browsing the whirligigs on her lawn. I smile and nod at them as if I'm interested in the twirly birds and garden angels; then I head toward the stepping stones that lead to her front door. The house is open, but I hesitate at the screen door, not sure of the proper etiquette. "Hello? Anybody home?"

A shadowed figure approaches, and Lydia's husky voice welcomes me in. "Jennifer! Come on inside."

I step into the cool shade of what looks like the living room of a serious kitsch collector. Behind the sofa stands a bookcase, its shelves filled with dolls made of spools and yarn, crocheted angel toilet paper covers, and tissue box holders made of tree bark. A triangular piece of polished wood snags my attention, and I am unable to guess its purpose.

"Like that?" Lydia purrs. "It's for your reading glasses."

I tilt my head. "I don't get it."

"It's a nose." She pulls her specs from her pocket and lets them fall onto the triangle. "See? Your glasses wait on *this* nose until you need them on yours."

I have to admit it's cute, but I'm not here to shop. "I wanted to return this," I say, handing her the rectangular pan. "Your cake was delicious. I'm sorry I kept this for so long, but we've been busy—"

"Come on in—have a seat. I've been hoping we'd have a chance to get to know one another."

I cast a longing glance at the door, but Lydia has already snaked an arm around my waist and is leading me toward a formless sofa draped in purple velvet.

"I can only stay a moment." I sink into the sofa and gulp when my rear settles at a point about a foot below my knees. What is this thing, an elongated beanbag?

Across the aisle, Lydia sits on an inflatable pink armchair and crosses her legs. She pushes a rebellious strand of hair from her face and leans toward me, her eyes alive with curiosity. "So, how do you like Fairlawn? Is the roof still leaking? I hear your mother's getting to know the Red Hatters. Are you and Gerald getting along? I couldn't help but notice Mavis Biddle passing by earlier today. Was she bringing her annual letter?"

I pick a couple of random questions off the top. "Yes, Miss Biddle brought her letter, and we like the house. We're probably going to spend most of the summer working on the place because we'd like to find a buyer as soon as possible."

"Still planning on heading back to Virginia, then."

"That's right."

She leans back and picks up a pencil from a side table, then taps it against her chin and slowly exhales. Though she's not looking at me, she must feel the pressure of my eyes, because the corner of her mouth twists in a wry smile. "Don't mind me. Ten years ago, I couldn't get out of bed without having a cigarette. Brett finally convinced me to quit, but my hands miss having something to play with, you know? So I always try to keep a pencil handy."

"Well . . . at least you're not trying to smoke it."

She laughs, louder and longer than is reasonable, then leans toward me again, the pencil dangling from between her fingertips. "Gerald's a good man, you know. I imagine it feels weird, staying in a house with a stranger, but I can vouch for him. He and Ned have acted as ministers to this town on many occasions when the professional preachers didn't know what to do. That summer the Brown triplets died . . ." She shudders as if the memory is too much to bear.

But she's piqued my curiosity. "What happened?"

She lifts the hand with the pencil and points it in my direction. "No one living here will ever forget it. Mitzy Brown had triplets in '86—made all the papers. She named them John, Paul, and George, and when people asked what happened to Ringo, she'd always say she planned to have him later. Those boys were the darlings of the town but as spoiled as two-week-old potato salad. The summer they turned ten, they sneaked away from a community picnic one afternoon and untied a boat at the dock. Mitzy about lost her mind when she couldn't find them, and the entire town fanned out to search.

"Finally someone spotted the rowboat, empty. The sheriff came out to drag the lake, and Mitzy nearly had a nervous breakdown when they brought the first boy up three days later. Found all three of them right next to each other at the bottom of the lake. I always thought that was ironic, like they were back in the womb again." She brings the pencil to her mouth and touches the silver-tipped end to her teeth, probably taking another draw on her imaginary cigarette.

I close my eyes. I don't even want to *think* about the scene she's describing.

"Anyway—" Lydia's voice grows huskier—"Ned and Gerald made it possible for Mitzy and Steve to have a proper viewing—you know, with open caskets. I was surprised; you don't often see that with drowning victims, but Gerald's a near genius when it comes to fixing folks up. Mitzy was grateful; she said she didn't want to put her boys away until she'd had a chance to kiss 'em good-bye."

She falls silent as sorrow creeps through the room like a fog. We are both mothers, Lydia and I, and no matter how different our personalities, we can well imagine what Mitzy Brown suffered.

After a long moment, my neighbor swivels her gaze toward me and attempts a smile. "Maybe that's why I've never minded living next to a funeral home. In their own way, Ned and Gerald were in the business of healing people. Most everybody needs some kind of healing today, don't you think?"

As a flash of loneliness stabs at me, I murmur something about needing to get back to work.

17

On Sunday morning I wake to the sound of rain and snuggle back under the covers, exhaling in pure relief. No one could expect me to get the boys ready for church when it's raining like a biblical plague. Besides, we have a busy day planned, with the open house and the funeral. . . .

I'm about to reenter my dreamworld when I become aware of a distant pinging sound. I shake off my drowsiness and sit up. Last week I had inspectors crawling all over the roof to look for damage beneath the shingles. Did they secure the shingles they lifted? Has one of our minor leaks become a deluge?

I throw a light robe over my camisole and pajama bottoms and creep down the hallway, scanning the ceiling as I go. Several old stains mar the tiles in this part of the house, but I don't see any wet spots. Yet the ping persists.

My heart sinks when I walk through the TV area and hear a steady tap beating beneath the higher-pitched ping. I step into the kitchen and flip on the lights. In the center of the ceiling, a gray circle is spreading over the tiles and sending a steady drip onto the kitchen floor. Another spot over the sink is dropping water into an empty saucepan. *Ping.*

I growl and fling open a cupboard. Gerald's kitchen has exactly three cooking containers—an iron skillet, a spaghetti pot, and a small saucepan.

The leak over the sink will not be a problem unless the noise drives us nuts. I slide the spaghetti pot under the largest drip and pray the ceiling doesn't sprout a new leak before the storm stops.

I'm sitting cross-legged on the floor, my gaze fixed on the tiles over-head, when Gerald comes out of his room. He pulls a suspender over his T-shirt and grimaces at the ceiling.

"There's a bit of flashing in a gully up there," he says, pointing to invisible things I can't even imagine. "When it stops raining, I'll get out the ladder and try to spread a little tar around—"

"You are *not* getting up on that slippery roof." The firmness in my voice catches both of us by surprise.

"But, missy—"

"I've seen the pitch on those eaves, Gerald, and I don't want you up there, especially if it's wet. I'll call a roofer tomorrow morning. We'll let him handle it. Besides—" I soften my smile—"you have a service today, right? You don't have time to climb around on the roof."

My reminder lights a spark in Gerald's eye, and in that moment, it hits me—the man *enjoys* funeral services. Maybe they represent the culmination of all the work he's done in his preparation room, or maybe he enjoys being a public figure, if even for an hour. But he has reminded me of the service several times, broadly hinting that I should keep the boys busy and refrain from painting or stripping wallpaper when the mourners arrive.

For Gerald's sake, I hope it stops raining.

※ ※ ※

Fortunately, the rain slows to a drizzle by midmorning. Mom takes the boys to Shoney's for brunch, and I realize that I can get a little paint-ing done before the funeral guests begin to arrive. So I pull on a pair of old shorts and a T-shirt, then trot down the stairs.

Because the southern side of the house is exposed to strong sun-light all day, the paint on that section of the porch railing has almost completely flaked away. The roof has kept the railing dry, so I figure

I can apply at least a coat of primer before I have to disappear for the funeral service.

I also have to keep an eye out for Sharon Gilbert, who has promised to bring an open house sign at twelve-thirty. She will stand quietly in the foyer before and after the funeral, available to show the house if anyone's interested in a tour.

Mother insists that an "open house funeral" is tacky, but Gerald is stubborn and I am desperate. To keep the peace, Sharon promised that this will be a dignified open house—no balloons, no door prizes, and no pop music playing on the radio. Yet she did whisper that she plans to bake cookies so the house will smell "homey."

The primer goes on easily. I'm finished with that step by eleven, so I pop the lid off the can of enamel and start applying the first coat of paint. At the store I was stymied by so many shades of white, but the salesman assured me that Victorian Snow would be perfect for Fairlawn.

I'd been impressed that he knew the name of my house until I realized he probably knew *my* name too. The local grapevine is so efficient that I don't know why people in this area bother to read the newspaper.

I have finished the top railing and am beginning to paint the spindles when I hear the crunch of tires on gravel. I stand and push hair from my eyes with the back of my wrist, then feel a drop of paint slide down my nose.

Great.

The car is a familiar black BMW. Daniel Sladen's.

I lay the paintbrush across the open can, pick up a rag, and swipe at my face.

The lawyer gets out of the car and looks up at the porch. "Jennifer? You missing something?"

"What?"

He opens the back door and out bounds Skeeter. The dog prances at Mr. Sladen's feet for a moment, then sprints up the porch steps.

"Skeeter! How did you get out?" I ruffle the dog's wet fur and try to remember when I last saw him. He was with us this morning, because Bugs fed him. He must have slipped out when Mom and the boys left.

I open the front door and shoo the dog inside the house. "Thanks for bringing him back."

"No problem," he calls. "Actually, I was hoping to catch you. Do you have a minute to talk?"

Do I? I glance at my wrist, but I didn't put my watch on this morning. Something tells me I probably need to clean up the porch, but first I have to deal with this lawyer.

"Come on up." As he approaches, I swipe at my nose and glance at my reflection in a windowpane. I check my palm for wet paint, then walk over and extend my hand. "Good to see you again, Mr. Sladen."

Daniel Sladen is wearing nice belted pants, a dress shirt, and a tie—good heavens, he's in his funeral clothes. What time *is* it?

"It's Daniel, remember?"

"Right. Daniel."

After he shakes my hand, he steps back and surveys the place. "You've been busy. This porch is looking nice."

I shrug the compliment away, though I'm pleased he noticed. "We've done a little sanding and painting, and I spent last week getting bids on all the major projects. The air-conditioning and the roof are my top priorities. We have a leak over the kitchen, and Gerald tells me we sometimes get water in the attic. Of course, water never makes it all the way to the first floor, which is a good thing, I suppose." When I realize I'm babbling, I clamp my mouth shut.

Daniel grins.

"Something funny about a leaky roof?"

"No, but you're saying *we*. Does this mean you're thinking about staying on?"

"Not at all." I waggle my finger like a scolding schoolteacher. "It means we're all pitching in to get this house ready for the market. See? Sharon Gilbert's already listed the house in the Multiple Listing Service."

He turns to look at the realty sign in the lawn. "Ah. I hadn't noticed."

"So." I hook my thumbs into my pockets. "Is there some way I can help you, or have you come by to take advantage of Gerald's casket clearance?"

He cracks another smile and pulls a folder from under his arm. "Actually, I came early to the funeral because I need your signature on a couple of documents. You know how it is—we have to cover all the bases in triplicate before the job is finished."

"I know. I've worked with more than my fair share of lawyers." Mindful of the passing time, I wipe my hands on my paint rag and accept the papers. "Do you have a pen?"

He takes one from his pocket and offers it to me.

I look around, but I've moved the plant stands and the little table that usually sits between the rockers. "And something to write on?"

"Here." He turns around. "Use my back."

And so I sign a half dozen pages attesting that I, Jennifer E. Graham, have taken possession of Fairlawn Funeral Home, that I'm not a wanted criminal, and that I don't owe the IRS any back taxes. When I'm finished, I hand Sladen his papers and pen and give him a smile. "I expect you'll be doing this again when we sell the place."

He slides the pages back into the folder. "I don't handle real estate law—that's my partner's area."

"Your specialty is estate planning?"

"That's right. If you need a will, I'm your man."

His last three words hang in the air between us, personal and piquant. I find myself staring into his dark eyes, wondering if he meant to be provocative. . . .

Gerald breaks the silence. He steps onto the porch, his face red and flustered as he tugs on the sleeves of a dark suit coat. "Good grief, missy. The service starts in half an hour."

I tear my gaze from the lawyer. "Service?"

"Lulabelle!"

I bring my hand to my forehead, as embarrassed as an adolescent. How could time slip away from *me*, Miss Organized? I've got wet paint on the south porch rail and rags scattered all over the floor—

"Go," Daniel says. "I'll clean. You run upstairs and wash the paint off your nose."

"I'll do it. I don't have to do anything at the service—"

He catches my hand. "Don't you get it? For however long you stay here, you're the first lady of Fairlawn. Everyone expects you to be at the funeral, and I know they'd appreciate it if you put on a dress and acted as hostess."

I'm *what*? For a moment I am tempted to stamp my foot and argue, but I don't have time for a temper tantrum.

And Daniel Sladen is probably right. If I want to sell this place, I need to show the people of Mt. Dora that I'm a rational, calm woman with whom it'd be a pleasure to do business.

I swallow my objections and stride to the door, leaving the lawyer to clean up my mess. Isn't that what they do best?

※ ※ ※

Thirty minutes later, I'm wearing a simple navy dress and standing next to the guest book at the back of the crowded west chapel. The parking lot has filled, so several cars have had to park on the lawn, which makes me wonder whether these people have come to pay their respects to Lulabelle Withers or to check out the new owner of Fairlawn.

I chase that egotistical thought away. For all I know, Lulabelle could have been a beloved teacher, an actress, or a mayor's wife. Gerald certainly thought a lot of her.

He doesn't think so much of my real estate agent. As promised, Sharon Gilbert stands in the foyer dressed in a professional blazer and black pants, a handful of dignified brochures in one hand. The foyer has filled with the scent of oven-fresh snickerdoodles, which moves several of our funeral guests to tears. (Apparently Lulabelle was fond of baked goods.) Unfortunately, Sharon has to run upstairs and pull her cookies out of the oven every ten minutes or risk filling the house with the odor of *burnt* snickerdoodles.

I haven't been to many funerals, but this one looks as though it will be especially touching. Mrs. Withers's family has placed a series of framed photographs on a long table next to the casket. The hodge-podge collection of frames leads me to suspect that these pictures were taken from mantels, end tables, nightstands, and pianos. The photos feature Lulabelle in several seasons of life—as a child, a young woman, a beaming bride, a proud mother, and a glittering grandmother in an evening gown.

As for Mrs. Withers herself, I have to admit that Gerald and Ryan did a wonderful job. My only basis for comparison is a recent photo, but the woman inside the burnished casket wears a serene smile and lies with her fingers interlaced on a silk pillow. Gerald's capable hands have smoothed the wrinkles from her brow, and Ryan's artistry has restored color to her complexion. Lulabelle looks like she has fallen asleep . . . which, I suppose, is the simple truth.

The minister, a pleasant young man from the First Presbyterian Church, tells the crowd about the time Mrs. Withers defied the women's committee and insisted on wearing pants to a church picnic. He tells several heartwarming stories about the woman and expresses his conviction that Lulabelle is looking down on us from the arms of her Savior. "And you know—" his smile deepens into laughter—"I think she's up in heaven baking cookies!"

When the minister concludes his remarks, Gerald turns up the volume on a CD player. As the strains of "I Love You Truly" fill the chapel, one of Lulabelle's grandsons, a distinguished-looking man of about forty, stands and dances with his teenage daughter.

I blink away unexpected tears as the last note of Lulabelle's favorite song fades into silence. Members of her family, who have been sitting in the first row of the chapel, stand and make their way down the aisle. I pick up a box of tissues, ready to offer them to grieving relatives, but most of them wear soft smiles.

And in that moment I realize what Gerald meant when he said that funerals were for the living. This was a celebration of a life well lived.

I smile silent condolences whenever one of the departing guests catches my eye; then I move to the front door and watch as they get into their cars and follow the hearse to the graveyard. It's not a long drive—Pine Forest Cemetery is less than two miles away. But this is Fairlawn tradition, and it must be observed.

None of the funeral guests have ventured upstairs to tour the house or to sample Sharon's snickerdoodles. But that's okay. This afternoon was meant for something more important.

I close the door, understanding far more than I did a week ago.

※ ※ ※

After dinner, I step onto the front porch to enjoy the relative coolness of a summer evening. Gerald sits in his favorite rocking chair, his face turned toward the spot where the sun is descending in a vibrant splash over the oaks.

I gesture toward an empty rocker. "Mind if I join you?"

"The view's free and so is the company."

We sit in silence, both of us digesting the events of the day. After a while, Gerald begins to hum. Because his voice cracks on the high notes, it takes me a while to recognize "Peace Like a River."

I listen until he hums through a verse and the chorus; then I shift in my chair to face him. "You and Ryan did a beautiful job on Mrs. Withers. I know her family appreciates your care for her." I chuckle. "And I hope I look that good when I'm a hundred years old."

Gerald doesn't answer, but his eyes take on a wet gleam that speaks louder than words.

We rock in companionable silence as the sounds of the house spill through the open windows. I hear Bugs giggling in the bathtub, my mother's stern voice reminding him to wash behind his ears, and Clay complaining that the picture on channel eleven is distorted with wavy lines. Even Skeeter adds to the friendly bedlam as he scratches at the front door, eager to be out on the porch.

And Gerald is a man accustomed to quiet.

I turn back to the darkening horizon. "We've really turned your world upside down, haven't we? I'm sorry about that."

Gerald chuffs softly. "A man who can't change might as well be dead."

"So . . . you don't mind? The noise and the constant commotion?"

He coughs and lifts one shoulder in a shrug. "Tell you the truth, I didn't know what to think when y'all first came. But now I think your boys have taken ten years off my life."

"You feel like you'll die ten years *sooner*?"

"Not what I meant. I feel ten years younger."

Grinning, I let my head fall to the back of the chair and notice that the paint on the ceiling panels is peeling. I'll bet there's a special name for that kind of paneling, and I'd better learn what it is. I'm pretty sure we'll need to replace it soon.

I breathe deeply of the summer night's perfume. "I thought the boys would miss their friends, but they seem to have made new ones."

"I saw Brett and Clay coming back from the park today," Gerald says. "They've hit it off."

"Lydia and I had a nice talk yesterday. I returned her cake pan and got a look at the crafts she sells. We talked for half an hour, and I came home with a birdhouse made of shellacked shoe boxes. A housewarming gift."

Gerald laughs and rubs his chin. "That store of hers makes you look twice at things before you throw 'em out."

I wait, hoping he will fill me in on the story of Brett's absentee father, but apparently I'm sitting with the one person in town who doesn't think of chitchat as an Olympic sport.

I lean back and close my eyes, surrendering to the steady sound of our rockers scraping at the porch paint.

Thomas and I never had time to sit like this in Fairfax. We were always rushing, often not arriving home until after dark. After dismissing the nanny, Thomas would help Clay with his homework while I read to Bugs. When both boys were in bed, Thomas and I would spend at least an hour watching CNN, perusing the *Congressional Record*, or making notes on correspondence we'd brought home from the office. I thought we were good parents, good partners, and good employees. Were we good at anything?

Lately I've had the luxury of free time, and in quiet moments the oddest questions enter my head. What is gravity, and what would happen if it loosened its grip on us for, say, thirty seconds? My mother loves her home, so why did she never complain about moving around so much as an army wife? Why is God allowing my husband to go through a midlife crisis?

Is the Lord as upset with me as I am with him?

As I sit in this rocking chair, for some reason my mind doesn't center on the tasks crowding my to-do list. At this moment I couldn't care less about the leaky roof, the inadequate wiring, and the broken air conditioners.

I keep thinking about Lulabelle Withers and her family, about how they danced to her favorite song and celebrated her heavenly arrival. The west chapel didn't feel at all creepy this afternoon; the place felt more like a living room than a funeral parlor.

Once things slow down a little, I might have time to enjoy my boys. Time to listen to them, sit with them, maybe even take them fishing down at the dock.

If it were me instead of Lulabelle Withers in that casket today, would my sons' photos show me playing with them . . . or consulting a list?

On nights like this, I could almost be convinced to stay in Mt. Dora.

18

I'm studying the nutritional label on a box of Lucky Charms when Clay calls from the living room. "Hey, Mom! Dad's on TV!"

My chair scrapes the linoleum as I push back and hurry to the television. Sure enough, Thomas's handsome face fills the screen.

"Oh no." I grip my throat as a knot forms in the pit of my stomach. Capitol Hill staffers operate under one primary rule: remain anonymous whenever possible. Don't let yourself be quoted, don't give out your boss's position, and don't leak anything—unless, of course, your boss has tasked you with anonymous leaking. Despite those prohibitions, here's Thomas, brazenly addressing the reporter who has thrust a microphone in front of his face.

"Of course Senator Barron has considered the nuclear energy bill," he says, smirking as if the question barely deserves a reply. "And he'll address the matter as soon as he's released from the hospital."

I glance up at Mother, who has materialized at my shoulder, and ask, "Have you heard anything about Barron being in the hospital?"

"That's the first I've heard of it," she says, reaching for the newspaper. "I always said that man works too hard."

I'm still trying to make sense of it all when my cell phone begins to ring. My nerves hum with an adrenaline rush as I reach over the arm of the sofa to fumble for my purse. One ring, two—where's the phone?—three rings. "Hello?"

"Jen? I need you."

I melt against the sofa. "Thomas? What is going on up there?"

"Barron had chest pains last night, nothing serious. They're only keeping him under observation. But tomorrow he's supposed to deliver a position paper on nuclear energy and developing nations. Franklin had you do some work on that issue, didn't he?"

I close my eyes, silently savoring the moment. Thomas called me. He needs my expertise. Barron hasn't done his homework, and when he turned to Thomas, Thomas turned to me.

How sweet it is.

"The information you want is in the Committee on Foreign Relations database."

"We can't find it."

"That's because it's filed under *K*, for Senator Patsy Kincaid. She did a lot of the initial research before Franklin got involved and expanded the paper."

I hear clicking keys, followed by a sigh of relief. "Thanks, hon. I owe you a big one."

Yes, you do.

Bugs and Clay are waiting, as tense as cats, and I realize they haven't spoken to their dad in weeks. "Hey, Thomas, while we have you on the phone—"

"Gotta run, Jen. Take care, and thanks!"

The phone clicks and I'm left with dead air, but I smile even as my heart breaks. "Of course, I understand. Yes, I'll tell them." I place my fingers over the mouthpiece. "Is today going to be a great day?"

"You bet it is!" Bugs shouts. "A great day!"

Clay grins as a flush brightens the freckles across his nose.

I smile at nothing and say good-bye to no one, then look away so the boys won't see my tears.

19

Thomas is not a perfect man, but he's thinking of me. He got into trouble and he called. Me. The man needs me.

Our telephone encounter wasn't perfect, but it was enough to convince me that God hasn't abandoned us and Thomas's first instinct is to reach for me when he needs support.

I sink to the edge of the bed and close my eyes, clasping my hands like a six-year-old uttering her first heartfelt prayer. "Thank you, Lord, for bringing him one step closer to us. Thank you for understanding my anger and my doubts. Thank you for your eternal patience and help me be patient too. . . ."

I feel like celebrating, so I shut the bedroom door and twirl around the room in a pajamas-and-bare-feet ballet that culminates in a breathless swan dive onto the bed.

I turn over and lie still, hand against my heart, feeling the pulse of blood beneath my palm. One of these days, maybe soon, Thomas's heart will beat in this spot, when we are again joined as man and wife, the way we once were, the way we were meant to be.

One of these days Thomas will wake up and realize that he's traded a loving wife and two wonderful boys for a blonde floozy, a deceptive heart, and four pounds of silicone.

Until that day, I have to carry on. Persevere. Hold down the fort and all that military jargon my dad loved to use.

I have work to do.

I push myself up and head for the shower.

An hour later, dressed and refreshed, I eye the lists, estimates, calculator, and notes that clutter the bedspread. This is the week I begin my repair-and-renovation project, but how do I jump in? Should I flip a coin or close my eyes and point?

We're desperate for air-conditioning, but that's one of the more expensive items on my list. Perhaps we'd be more likely to attract potential buyers if I contacted the housepainters first. Then again, what if the housepainters are busy and make us wait several weeks? I'd be better off putting our money into the air-conditioning so we could at least wait in relative comfort.

I'm sitting cross-legged on the bed, trying to decide which professional to call, when a thought strikes: *I'm living in the largest private house in Mt. Dora.* The fact means nothing at first, but it twirls in my head like one of the whirligig lawn ornaments for sale at Twice Loved Treasures.

I lie back and consider the thought further. I'm living in the city's largest private house, *and* I need more time and money to get Fairlawn in shape for a decent sale. How do other people with big, old houses earn a living? In historic areas of the country, they open them to the public. In Mt. Dora, they turn them into bed-and-breakfasts.

The thought of hosting overnight guests at Fairlawn is so wacky that I begin to laugh, though I feel a long way from genuine humor. In order to operate Fairlawn as a B and B, I'd have to repair the air-conditioning, redecorate the common rooms, and kick at least one of my family members out of a bedroom. Since I have the largest bedroom and an attached bath, the displaced person will most likely be me.

Well . . . why not? Redecorating is one of the least expensive items on my to-do list. I'd enjoy the work, and Mother could help. Painting, sewing curtains, baking a batch of muffins, and frying up a skillet of eggs and sausage on the days we have guests—what could be so hard about that?

I need to replace the air-conditioning units anyway, and freshened bedrooms would go a long way toward selling this house. I could start with the master suite, and I can bunk with Mother when we have guests. If I can get another room in decent shape—probably Bugs's, since it's right across the hall from the other bathroom—he could sleep with Clay when we have *two* sets of guests.

Furnishings? No problem. I own a house filled with glorious antiques. And while Fairlawn's decor is sorely outdated, I have boxes of decorator items in storage. All I have to do is phone Lisa, my friend from Virginia. She'll call a moving company and oversee the emptying of the storage unit that holds my few remaining possessions.

I sigh, thinking of all the precious things I've packed away. My favorite artwork, vases, and china. My photograph albums and linens. And my books, stacks and stacks of novels, many of which are still new and unread.

Mom and I could work on the public rooms one by one. We could begin with the smaller west chapel and turn it into a grand dining room. A steady stream of guests would bring in an extra two or three hundred dollars a day . . . and that kind of money will buy a lot of shingles.

I gather my thoughts and move through the living room, where the boys are absorbed in a wrestling video we picked up at Wal-Mart. In the kitchen, Mom has made a batch of egg salad, and Gerald is helping her spread the salad on bread for sandwiches.

I slide into a chair at the table and stare at the old wallpaper with a smile tugging at my lips.

Mom is about to pull a bag of potato chips from the cupboard, but she halts when she sees me. "What canary did *you* swallow?"

I transfer my gaze to Gerald. How will he feel about this proposal? If he wants to leave, we'd have an extra room for guests, but any B and B could use a live-in handyman. It's hard to imagine Fairlawn without him.

"I have an idea." I am careful to look at both of them, not wanting either to feel left out. "Since there's no way I can afford to do everything that needs to be done to the house, I thought we could let Fairlawn make a bit of money for us."

Gerald's brows rise. "We could push prepaid burials and bring in some new contracts. You want to me to place an ad in the *Orlando Sentinel*? It's a much larger paper, and if we run a special, maybe a two-for-one—"

"Good grief, no." I resist the urge to roll my eyes and look at Mom. "I was thinking that we could use Fairlawn as a bed-and-breakfast for a few months. If we get the AC fixed and spruce up a couple of rooms, we could bring in a steady income while we tackle the bigger projects. In five or six months, a year at the most, we could complete all the repairs and sell Fairlawn for what this house is really worth."

Mom tosses the bag of chips onto the table. "But Sharon Gilbert says there are already too many B and Bs in Mt. Dora."

"There are several, I know. But there are none as grand as Fairlawn, and none have its colorful history. Haven't you seen ads for those haunted house tours in New Orleans and Charleston? People love that kind of thing."

Gerald makes a moue of distaste. "You want to tell people Fairlawn is *haunted*?"

"We don't have to say it's haunted because people are naturally skittish about funeral homes. We simply tell the truth and let people's imaginations do the rest."

Gerald sinks into a chair. "I don't like it."

I press my lips together, refusing to utter the reply that springs to my tongue: *And I own the place.*

"You can continue your work," I point out. "Nothing has to change until the house sells. The bed-and-breakfast shouldn't interfere with your operation, but we might need to use the west chapel for a dining room. This kitchen is too cramped to seat guests."

Mother is no happier with the idea. "You want us to stay here another *year*?" Her brows draw together in an agonized expression. "I didn't sign on for that, Jen. I have responsibilities at home. Our Red Hatters' fall festival is coming up. I always help with the Christmas program at church, and my house is always featured on the Fairfax Ladies' Tea and Tour—"

"You don't have to stay." I reach out and touch her hand so she won't think I'm chasing her away. "You can go back to Virginia whenever you like, but you're also welcome here. If this thing takes off, I know I could use your help."

A tremor touches her pink mouth. "I just don't like it," she says, crossing her arms. "I don't like it one bit."

Dismayed, I watch as Mother turns and stalks to her bedroom. She's had strong reactions to my ideas before, but I can't understand why this idea should upset her so.

What, exactly, doesn't she like?

❉❉ ❉❉ ❉❉

Joella slams the bedroom door more forcefully than she intended to. Why do children insist on breaking your heart? Jennifer has a good head on her shoulders, but sometimes Joella wonders if there's a spreadsheet where her daughter's heart ought to be.

"*You can go back to Virginia whenever you like. . . .*"

Obviously Joella's presence here doesn't matter. Come or go, Jen says; suit yourself. Because she's going to do what she wants to do no matter what Joella thinks.

How in the world did she raise such a stubborn daughter?

Joella lies on the mattress and stares at the slow-spinning ceiling fan overhead. Maybe Jen is simply obeying old behavior patterns. She's accustomed to looking out for Thomas and the boys; she's not used to considering Joella's needs or desires.

Yet with all they've been through in the last month, you'd think she'd have learned to adjust. You'd think she'd notice how the boys have come to depend on their grandmother and how said grandmother has taken up the slack without being asked. You'd think Jen would realize how many meals her mother has cooked and how many loads of laundry she's done. Jen should appreciate all the times Joella has urged the boys to be quiet because their hardworking mother is asleep.

But Jen has been caught up in her lists and her phone calls. She's been thinking more about selling this stupid house than about her family. Joella has been praying that God would use the divorce to

159

strengthen her relationship with her daughter, but Jen has little time these days for anything but her grand plan to be ready for Thomas's return.

Why can't she see that Thomas Graham is nothing more than a worthless sack of skin? He's a homing pigeon who never wants to go home, a star athlete who never learned the meaning of the word *team*.

He's just like Jen's father.

Joella rubs her temple as the realization unfurls in her consciousness. Nolan Norris and Thomas Graham—two men never looked more different, but they were formed from the same character mold. Spontaneous, charming, fun-loving . . . no wonder Jen fell in love with Thomas. He entranced her the same way Nolan enchanted Joella, holding her in awe of his charms while he hid his considerable shortcomings.

Maybe this is all Joella's fault. If she hadn't been so careful to white-wash the truth when Jen was growing up, maybe Jen wouldn't have fallen for a man like her father. If Jen had been a little more intuitive, she might have sensed the tension in the air, but most kids never see their parents as people. Joella certainly never did, and Jen was always running off to student government meetings, ballet practice, and church youth group. When things got rough, Joella was grateful that Jen kept herself busy, but maybe all that activity wasn't such a good thing.

When someone raps on the door, Joella dashes wetness from her eyes. "Come in."

Jen moves into the doorway, a woebegone look on her face. "I'm sorry you're upset, Mom, but I don't understand why. You're going to have to fill me in."

Joella pushes herself up. "I'm fine."

"No, you're not." Jen steps into the room and eases onto the foot of the bed. "You know I can be thickheaded. If I've done something, tell me so I can try to make things right."

Joella blows the hair out of her eyes and looks toward the window. How can she correct something that went wrong over forty years ago? She can't change the past, but maybe she can affect the future.

"Jen—" she draws a shaky breath—"I watched you when Thomas called. You lit up like a Christmas tree, and . . . well, you broke my heart."

Jen runs her finger over the pattern on the chenille bedspread. "I know you don't like him—for a long time I didn't, either. But he's my husband."

"Not anymore."

"He'll always be the father of my children. Clay and Bugs need their dad, so when Thomas is ready for me to forgive him, I will. It won't be easy, but I'm willing to try."

"I believe in forgiveness, honey. The Lord knows I forgave your father more times than I could count. But Thomas is . . ."

"What?" A muscle clenches at Jen's jawline.

Joella lowers her gaze. "He's so much like your father. I hate to see you pin your hopes on a man who might not change."

"But he might." Jen's voice softens. "I remember hearing you and Dad argue sometimes, but you always worked things out. You stuck together, didn't you?"

Reluctantly, Joella nods.

"I'm glad you did. But we were always moving around, and that was hard for me. I want my boys to have stability, and that's what Thomas can give them. So when he calls, I'm going to answer. When he gets tired of his fling, I'm going to be waiting with the boys, ready to welcome him home. I think it's the right thing to do."

Joella knows it's useless to argue. She has taught her daughter to be patient, kind, and loyal . . . to a man who doesn't deserve her.

"Mom, don't be hurt." Jen squeezes Joella's bent knee. "The boys and I have to go where the Lord leads us, and though I don't know why, he's led us down here. He's given us this house. I'm trying to be responsible with the things he's given us because I believe this is all part of a plan . . . for reconciliation."

Joella runs her hand over the bedspread and gives her daughter a tight-lipped smile. "You're not actually looking forward to staying in Mt. Dora, are you?"

Honest surprise shines in Jen's eyes. "You think I'm happy about being here with the gators and mosquitoes and scorching heat? Have you lost your *mind?*"

Joella returns her daughter's smile. "I guess . . . if you are serious about this bed-and-breakfast idea, I'll help for a while. I want to enjoy my grandsons while I can."

"Mom." Jennifer reaches out and wraps her arms around Joella's neck. "I have every confidence that we're going back to Virginia when the time is right. Everything's going to work out. You'll see."

Joella returns the embrace, though she doesn't share Jennifer's confidence. She once knew a leopard who couldn't change his spots. . . .

XX XX XX

As soon as the kitchen empties out after lunch, I grab the Gilbert Realty magnet from the refrigerator and dial Sharon's number. When the agent comes on the line, I clear my throat. "Sharon? Jennifer Graham here."

"Jennifer! I was just thinking about you."

"Listen—" I pause as the ice maker drops ice into the bin with a satisfying chunkalunk—"I wondered if you've had any interest in Fairlawn. Has anyone called?"

"These things take time," Sharon replies, her voice as smooth as cream. "The property went in the MLS last week, so you never know when we'll get a call. If you can give me another date for an open house, that's sure to spark interest—"

"I don't think I want to have another open house. It's just too hard to guarantee that we won't be having a funeral at the same time. I did want you to know, though, that it's okay if you put Fairlawn on the back burner. We've decided to stay awhile."

"*What?*" I think the woman drops the phone. After a few seconds of thumping and bumping, I hear her ragged breathing in my ear. "What did you say?"

"I don't want to take a below-value offer, and I can't afford to complete all the repairs Fairlawn needs without additional income. So I've decided to let the house pay for its own renovation."

Silence rolls over the line; then the agent chuckles. "And how is Fairlawn going to do that?"

Impossible to miss the sarcasm in her voice, but I lean against the refrigerator and think of Mrs. Withers's grandson dancing with his daughter in the chapel. I'm not sure I'll ever grow accustomed to caskets and chemicals, but a funeral home like Fairlawn deserves to keep its doors open.

"Gerald is going to keep running the mortuary, and I'll keep working on the renovations. While we're working, Fairlawn is going to become one of Mt. Dora's fabled bed-and-breakfasts."

"You're going to run a B and B?"

"I thought we might try it. How hard can it be?"

From the way she clicks her tongue, I'm not sure Sharon approves of my idea, but she's not going to argue with a client. "Good luck, then. And if I get a call from someone who wants to see the place?"

"Bring them over. We'll do our best to make the house shine."

20

"Charley Gansky's coming by for a check," Jen calls from her seat in the van. "It's downstairs on the foyer table."

"Don't worry," Joella answers from her upstairs window. "I'll take care of it."

A flutter of worry crosses Jen's face as she puts the van in reverse and drives away.

Joella waves good-bye and retreats from the window, fanning her damp chest with her blouse. Barely ten o'clock in the morning, and already the upstairs is like a furnace. That air-conditioning repairman can't come soon enough.

Jen is on her way to the fabric store in Eustis. At first she planned to go alone, but Joella reminded her that the boys might enjoy the air-conditioned store . . . and they could bring their electronic gizmos to occupy themselves while they waited. The boys were unexcited until Joella casually mentioned that they could grab a pizza for lunch; then both boys clamored to go with their mother.

Joella is glad the house is empty—or almost empty. Gerald is puttering around downstairs, but he keeps to himself most of the time.

A feeling of contented relief sweeps over her as she moves into the hall and stoops to pick up an orphaned sock. With the boys out and Jen occupied with her never-ending to-do list, Joella can almost pretend she's back in her tidy empty nest.

She strides into Clay's room, picks his pajama bottoms off the floor, and moves to his bed. He forgot to make it, and Jen forgot to check it. The good habits Joella was working so hard to instill are falling by the wayside here, but maybe Jen will be able to regain her focus once Fairlawn is a bed-and-breakfast. The boys can't be leaving messes all over the house if this place is open to the public.

Joella drops the pajama bottoms and sock into the hallway, then turns back the covers and sweeps candy wrappers from under the sheets. That boy will lose his teeth if he keeps eating candy in bed. With all that sugar fermenting in his mouth, it's a miracle he doesn't have a cavity in every tooth.

Joella makes a mental note to speak to Clay about his candy as she makes the bed and sets the pillow at the top of the comforter.

Bugs's room is even more of a mess than Clay's. The bed is completely rumpled and covered with dog hair. She makes a face and squeals when a pattern on the sheet *moves*. Stepping closer, Joella discovers a rippling trail of ants that leads from the foot of the bed to the windowsill. Backtracking, she finds a cookie smashed between the end of the mattress and the footboard. She grimaces as she knocks the cookie out of the crevice and wipes the trail of tiny ants away with a wet washcloth.

After scooping the leftover cookie into her hand, she holds the ant-covered cloth by a corner and carries it into the kitchen, where she drops cookie and cloth into the covered garbage can. She doesn't like bug spray, doesn't want to use poison in the boys' rooms, but if those kids don't stop eating in bed, this house will be so infested with creepy crawlies that nobody will want to stay here.

She wipes her hands on her shorts and glances at the dog-eared phone book on the kitchen counter. Jen has practically worn that book out in her quest for subcontractors. She's been working so hard on restoring the building that she's had little time to consider how to run a bed-and-breakfast. Joella has no idea how to run one either, but she does know how to get started.

She hums to herself and settles into a chair at the table. While Jen concentrates on curtains and decorating the first guest room, Joella will help in another way. Like Diane Keaton in *Baby Boom*, she will do research. She will call the other local bed-and-breakfasts and see how they do things. She'll make careful notes, so all Jen will have to do is look through the material and decide how she wants to run Fairlawn.

Simple as tic-tac-toe.

She opens the phone book, flips to the yellow pages, and skims the listings under bed-and-breakfasts. She clicks her tongue against her teeth when she realizes Sharon Gilbert did not exaggerate—Mt. Dora has seven fully functioning B and Bs within the city limits.

Still, maybe Jen has a point. None of the other inns doubles as a funeral home.

She jots the names and phone numbers on a tablet and sets the book aside. What does she need to ask these people? How many guest rooms they have, for starters. How much they charge per night. If they have seasonal rates and what kind of breakfast they serve. Jen might also benefit from knowing if her competitors have extras like hot tubs or swimming pools.

Joella chuckles softly. For sure, none of the others will have a casket room.

She picks up the phone and prepares to dial the Magnolia Inn, then hesitates. How should she handle this call? Should she pretend to be a potential customer, or should she play it straight?

She glances at the window over the sink, where a slight breeze is ruffling the dingy curtains. If Jen and the boys are going to live here several more months, she might as well be up-front with their new neighbors. The other innkeepers are going to learn about Fairlawn's new status eventually, so why not today?

She punches in the first number and smiles into the phone. "Hello? I'm Joella Norris over at Fairlawn, and we had a few questions about your establishment. Would you mind taking a moment to talk to me?"

❧ ❧ ❧

"It makes no sense, I tell you." Gerald slams the door on a cabinet and looks at the terrier sitting calmly at his side. Hard to tell whether the animal is offering understanding or looking for a snack.

Gerald moves to the next cabinet and opens the door. "Bad enough that she doesn't understand the mortuary business, but to run a B and B? Until yesterday I thought she was a smart girl. A little closed-minded, maybe, but still a smart girl."

He sighs and removes a carton of rubber gloves, boxes of cotton, and several rubber blocks from the shelves. These are the large rubber blocks used to hold bodies in place during the embalming process, but he knows he has smaller blocks stored someplace. . . .

They'll show up. He's going through every cupboard and drawer, so he'll find them.

This inventory was his idea, though Jennifer certainly should have thought of it. If she is serious about turning this place into a glorified sleep-'n'-snack, it'll only be a matter of time before she starts making noises about selling off the mortuary equipment.

He looks at the photo on the counter: a picture of himself and Ned snapped at the last funeral directors' convention in Orlando. Away from Mt. Dora and folks' expectations, they and three hundred other morticians spent the entire weekend grinning like crazy men.

Gerald focuses on Ned's lean face. "Oh yeah, she said I could keep running things, just like you wanted. But you and I both know yuppies and funerals don't mix. The first time one of her guests stumbles into a viewing when they're looking for breakfast, well, that'll be the last Fairlawn funeral, mark my words."

He writes *positioning blocks, eight large* on his legal pad, then jots a note about the cotton and rubber gloves. No one will want to buy these small items; whoever cleans out the prep room will probably toss these things into the garbage.

"But I have never—" he bends to look at the dog—"been willing to throw out a thing that can still be used. You got that?"

The dog cocks his head and lifts a paw, probably wanting a treat.

Gerald shakes his head and returns to the cabinet. He sets the blocks into the cupboard and spies an extra arterial hook at the back of the shelf. Better make a note of that, too.

He moves to the next cupboard and counts bottles of arterial fluid, then makes a note about the drawer of miscellaneous cosmetics. Somebody will pitch those but not him. Most of them are way past their expiration dates, though Ryan has never complained. And the results are as good as anything that ever walked out of a Merle Norman studio.

A wry smile lifts the corner of Gerald's mouth. Maybe that's the problem—he's past *his* expiration date. He should have retired when Ned died, moved to one of those assisted living places where old people wear velour jumpsuits and play checkers and watch soap operas. Surely one of those places has a front porch with a rocker. Or maybe Jennifer wouldn't mind if he took one of the Fairlawn rockers with him.

He shivers as his mind wanders back to the first time he pulled up in front of the rambling pink house. Ned, an old friend from seminary, had invited him to come to Fairlawn to "rest up and heal." The people of Mt. Dora assumed he came to heal from grief; apparently Ned had spread the word about Evelyn's passing from breast cancer.

The calm surroundings were restful and healing, but Gerald had never been the type to sit and do nothing. He saw Ned comfort those who were sorrowing, and he watched as his friend's skillful hands lovingly restored the appearance of life to the dead.

Before long, he was helping Ned with the embalming. At Marjorie's suggestion, he applied at the local community college, and eighteen months later he received his diploma in mortuary science. After a few years he knew nearly as many tricks as Ned, and in the work he found relief from his grief.

When Marjorie died, Gerald helped Ned prepare his beloved wife for the viewing. As he watched Ned brush Marjorie's silver hair, he found himself wishing he'd been able to care for Evelyn in the same way. They had been close, he and his wife, despite everything. Life tried its best to separate them, but only death succeeded.

Until Ned had his stroke, Gerald almost believed that God would allow them to work together indefinitely, two aging gargoyles united in a common purpose. But a blood vessel in Ned's brain exploded, and after a few months, God called Gerald's dear friend home.

How shortsighted he'd been to think things would never change.

When he first heard that Ned's great-niece had inherited the property, he hoped she would allow him to run Fairlawn as an investment property. Then he learned about her divorce, her two young children, and her desperation.

He hadn't realized that Fairlawn might be as much of a lifeline for her as it had been for him.

So if she needs to turn the place into some kind of fancy inn . . . well, a young woman is entitled to her mistakes. If she wants his room, he will leave quietly. Maybe he'll see if the funeral home in Eustis could use an assistant or scan the classifieds in *Mortuary Management* for a cemetery in need of a caretaker.

He's ready to slow down. He's lived a full life, owned up to his share of mistakes, and done a fair amount of ministry in the Lord's name.

Maybe he ought to just stretch out in one of the caskets and roll down the hill with the rest of the equipment when it's time to go.

21

*O*ur morning at the fabric store is completely unproductive. I had hoped to walk in and be swept off my feet by some stunning pattern that would dictate the colors and style of the entire guest suite, but my mind is boggled by so many choices. A glorious gold, red, and green print catches my eye and reminds me of a Tuscan landscape, but is that too bright for a south-facing bedroom? I find a beautiful blue and green print that's as soothing as a warm bath, but is it too boring?

While I fret over fabrics, Bugs sprints through the store, hiding behind rolls of materials and skipping through the aisles of silk flowers. Clay pretends not to know Bugs when anyone looks in his direction, but he's the cause of Bugs's mad dashes and startling appearances amid the yard goods. I try to ignore both boys, but finally a clerk comes up and asks if I am aware that two kids keep digging for gumball change in my purse.

Yes, I admit. I am.

Lunch at the pizzeria isn't much better. Clay wants pepperoni, but Bugs, my health-minded son, wants mushroom. I order a large pizza with half pepperoni and half mushroom, but somewhere between our table and the kitchen, the waitress botches our order. The pizza she delivers half an hour later is completely spotted with pepperoni *and* mushrooms, which forces Clay to spend the rest of our lunch picking off mushrooms while Bugs does the same with the pepperoni.

My temper has been simmering for almost an hour by the time we return to Fairlawn. The boys, probably sensing an imminent eruption, scramble out of the van and run for the front door. I take advantage of the quiet and lower my head to my hands on the steering wheel.

Do mothers ever run away? I could start the engine and back out of the drive right now. With a little luck, no one would miss me until dinnertime. The boys would be safe with Mother, and Gerald would hold the line if Mom starts panicking about gators and lethal mosquitoes.

But wait . . . mothers can't run away when fathers already have. My boys are counting on me to be their stability. No matter how unsteady I feel, I have to play Rock of Gibraltar.

I grab my purse and slide out of the air-conditioned van, then take shallow breaths of the superheated outside air. People keep telling me I'll get used to the heat, but I don't see how any warm-blooded creature could.

The boys are squabbling in front of the TV as I come up the stairs. Mother isn't fussing at them, so she must be reading or taking a nap in her room. Gerald isn't in sight either, so he's hiding in his room or napping downstairs.

Which leaves me alone with my rambunctious offspring. "Clay—" I'm about to tell him to pick up the jigsaw puzzle pieces he's just knocked onto the floor when the phone rings. I hurry into the kitchen to answer it, turning my back on the small riot in the living room. "Hello?"

"Jennifer Graham?"

"Speaking."

"This is Carol Conrad, owner of the Wordsworth Inn."

I sink into a chair, curious. "Have we met?"

"I want to know," she says, her tone as hard as steel, "what gives you the right to grill my daughter. If you want to run a bed-and-breakfast, that's fine, but don't go around interrogating our staff for trade secrets."

I blink at the clock on the wall. "I beg your pardon?"

"If you want to know our rates, look 'em up like everyone else does. And if you think we're going to give you the recipe for our secret strawberry muffins, you're insane. Find your own specialties, and don't call here again!"

The phone clicks and I stare at the receiver. Who was that woman, and why did she call me? I haven't interrogated anyone, and I don't even *like* strawberries.

"Mom?" Bugs tugs on my sleeve. "I don't feel so good. I think I ate a pepperloni."

Half-convinced that someone has slipped mind-altering drugs into the community's water supply, I turn to look at my son. Bugs has gone pale, he is holding his stomach, and pearls of sweat cling to the skin above his lip.

"Bugsy—"

Without warning, he vomits. I close my eyes as warm murk splashes my blouse and spatters my pants. In the distance, Clay howls with laughter.

Tears tremble on Bugs's lashes. "Mom?"

"Just a minute, honey." I grab a dish towel and swipe away as much of the mess as possible; then I grab Bugs's wrist and lead him to the bathroom. After washing his face and hands, I tell him to lie down on his tummy. If he's not feeling better by dinnertime, we'll go see a doctor.

After he trudges to his room, I close the door, turn on the water in the bath, and add a dash of bath salts. Five minutes later, I'm resting my spine against the curve of the antique tub.

I have a sick son.

The owner of the Wordsworth Inn thinks I'm sabotaging her business.

And I still have dozens of tasks on my to-do list. Among them is a call I need to make. If we're going to make Fairlawn our temporary home, Lisa will need to ensure that all our storage boxes are loaded onto a moving van and shipped to Mt. Dora.

But am I up to this? If I can't complete a mission to buy fabric, how am I supposed to run a bed-and-breakfast?

Until this moment, I have never really doubted myself. Growing up, I watched my father face challenges with a military can-do attitude, and that same attitude always served me well. The senator used to joke that he never worried about anything he'd asked me to do because he knew I'd do it or die trying.

Right now I feel about half dead. Maybe that's appropriate, considering where I'm living.

The sweet scent of bath salts wafts from the bubbles rising in the tub. Mom always says that things look different on the other side of a hot bath. Of course, Mom says a lot of things that aren't strictly true—at least not from my perspective.

About the bath, though, I hope she's right.

※ ※ ※

Joella opens her eyes, blinks rapidly, and realizes that the book she was reading is now facedown on her chest. She snorts softly, sets the book aside, and pushes herself into a sitting position on the bed. Jen and the boys are back; she can hear the TV and the sound of slamming cupboards—probably Clay in search of a snack.

She gets up and walks down the hall, pausing outside Bugs's room. Her grandson is lying on his tummy, his head burrowed into his pillow. She frowns and considers checking on him, but if he's asleep, she doesn't want to wake him.

Better to ask Jen or Clay about the poor child.

She continues to Jen's room, expecting to find the bed covered in fabric samples. The bed, however, hasn't changed since morning, and Jen is nowhere in sight.

She's halfway to the living room when the phone rings. Joella hurries to pick up the extension and nearly bumps into Jen, who comes out of the bathroom wet haired and wrapped in a towel. "Good grief, you scared me." Joella inhales the scent of bath salts. "Why are you bathing in the middle of the day?"

Jen rolls her eyes and sidles past her. "Bugs has an upset stomach. He lost his lunch . . . all over me."

Joella shakes her head. "Poor baby."

Jen picks up the phone, says hello, and listens, a frown line settling between her brows. Then she hangs up.

That can't be a good thing. Joella leans against the doorframe. "Who was that?"

"A crank call. I've been getting them all afternoon."

"Who from?"

"If I knew that, it wouldn't be a crank call."

"Don't they have caller ID in this town?"

"Maybe, but not on Gerald's phones. I think that one's a 1970s princess model."

Jen moves into the small bathroom off the master suite. "By the way, that 'poor baby' a minute ago—was that sympathy for me or for Bugs?"

"Maybe it's for both of you." Joella sinks onto the edge of the bed. "Did you find any material?"

"Ha! Do you know how much stuff those stores carry now? Art supplies, crafts, silk flowers, bakeware. All that, and I still had too many fabric choices."

Jen steps out, wrapped in her robe. The wet ends of her hair have separated into hanks that lie on her shoulders like black ribbons on snow.

Joella stretches out on her side and props her head on her hand. "I had an interesting morning."

Jen sits across from her mother and tugs a comb through her damp hair. "Did Charley Gansky come for his check?"

"Consider it delivered. But that's not the interesting thing. I thought I'd help you get started on this B and B idea, so I made a list of all the bed-and-breakfast establishments in town. Then I made a chart so we could compare their features, rates, and special amenities." She can't stop a blush of pleasure from warming her cheeks. "I thought you could use a head start with a little demographic research."

Jen's eyes narrow as she lowers her comb. "Did you call the Wordsworth Inn and ask about their strawberry muffins?"

"Why, yes. The girl who answered said it was their specialty, so I asked what made them so special. Apparently she'd never actually *made* the recipe, so she said she'd check and get back to me—"

Jen groans. "Mother, how could you? I'll bet half the town is furious with me right now. That's probably why we're getting those hang-up calls."

Joella stares, unnerved by the change in Jen's demeanor. "What did I do?"

"You called without asking me first; you stuck your hand into my business and violated not only my privacy but the privacy of those other people."

"I did no such thing. I simply called and asked a few questions. Some of the people were more chatty than others, but—"

"I didn't ask you to do that, Mother. This is going to be my business, and I want to proceed carefully. You don't know a *thing* about running an inn—"

"Neither do you."

"But at least I've managed an office! I've had enough experience to realize that you can't go snooping into people's affairs without thinking things through. If you'd waited, I could have announced Fairlawn's new status diplomatically, maybe at a civic function. I could have arranged it so the town would support us. Now we'll be lucky if the other innkeepers don't band together and run us out of Mt. Dora."

Joella watches, disbelieving, as her daughter stands and moves to the window, her hands clenched at her sides. Jen's shoulders are trembling, so she is *really* upset.

"I'm sorry," Joella says, speaking to Jen's back. "If you want me to call those people and apologize, I'd be happy to."

Jen whirls and stares at Joella with burning, reproachful eyes. "I want you to leave me alone!"

Like a wasp's sting, the words hurt at first contact, then slice deep. Joella pushes herself upright. She wants to explain that she didn't mean any harm. She only wants to help, but she can't seem to do anything right these days. "Jen—"

"Don't worry about it." Jennifer brings her hands up to cover her face. "Things always work themselves out eventually, but I can't talk to you right now." She rushes into the bathroom and closes the door.

Silence fills the room like a mist; then Joella hears the sound of muffled weeping from behind the closed door.

She's done it again. Without meaning to, she's made a mess of things.

Her joints crack as she rises and walks toward the hallway. For the first time in a long time, she feels old and tired.

Why do the people we love the most hurt us the most deeply?

❦❦ ❦❦ ❦❦

By dinnertime, Mother and I are speaking again, Bugs has recovered from his upset stomach, and I have personally called and apologized to Carol Conrad at the Wordsworth Inn. My mother was only trying to help, I assure her, and we have no intention of making strawberry muffins. Ever. I would shave my head first.

I also call my friend Lisa, who, after giving me the latest Capitol Hill gossip, agrees to arrange for a moving company to empty our storage unit and ship our belongings to Fairlawn.

"It won't be a huge load," I tell her. "Just a few favorite pieces of furniture, some wardrobe boxes, a few kitchen items, and the boys' toys."

After hanging up, I realize that having familiar things around us might do a lot to make Fairlawn feel more like home. Though we've been here more than two weeks, I still feel like I'm living in someone else's house.

Mom is frying chicken when I come into the kitchen and filch a carrot stick from a vegetable tray. "Have you seen Gerald?"

"No." When she doesn't speculate about where he might be, I can tell she's still smarting from our tiff. I take a bite of the carrot. "I'll look downstairs. I need to know if that carpenter came by to look at the back porch."

I head down the stairs, nerves tightening. I hate to admit it, but even now I get a little creeped out when I have to walk down the hallway that leads to the prep room. I hope to find Gerald in the office, the laundry room, or even the display room, but when he's in none of those places, I knock on the last door.

Gerald opens it, his face flushed. "You don't have to knock. You own the place, remember?" He turns and walks away.

That curt remark is so unlike him that I'm reluctant to follow. I look past him into the large area. The cool air feels wonderful, and I'm tempted to forget what this room is so I can stretch out on one of those tables for a refreshing cooldown.

But there's no denying this room's purpose. The two long tables are slightly concave and adorned with hoses and tubes and drainage holes. Odd bottles line the shelves, and the thick smell of antiseptic hangs in the air.

I cross my arms to fend off a sudden chill. "Sorry to bother you, Gerald, but did you see the carpenter today? He was supposed to stop by and give us an estimate for a new back porch."

He cocks a bushy brow in my direction. "Didn't see him."

"He didn't ring the bell? Maybe leave an estimate under the mat?"

Gerald walks to a counter and writes something on a legal pad, then shakes his head. "Didn't see anybody today."

"Oh. Okay, thanks." I'm about to go, but I can't leave things like this. Mother and I understand each other, but I barely know Gerald. I don't know if his dark mood will blow over or if it's come to stay. "Gerald." I move farther into the room, inwardly cringing with every step. "Are you okay? You don't seem like yourself."

He lifts his finger to count a row of bottles lining the wall, then writes on the legal pad. "I'm fine, thanks."

"I don't think you are."

He takes a side step and squints at another row of bottles, but I reach out and grab his arm. "Gerald—look at me. Please."

Reluctantly, he does.

"Have I done something to upset you?"

He looks at me with frustration on his face; then he takes off his glasses, folds them, and sets them on the counter. "I suppose—" he rubs the bridge of his nose—"that I'm tired. I've been taking inventory all day, making a list so you'll get a fair price when you sell off the equipment."

I look around. "This stuff is valuable?"

His faint smile holds a touch of sadness. "Some of it is, yes. As valuable as the work we did in here."

He speaks in a low rumble that is at once powerful and gentle . . . and in his words I finally understand the cause of the man's melancholy: Gerald loves his job. I knew he enjoyed directing funeral services, but I never imagined that any sane person might find this part of mortuary work enjoyable.

Obviously Gerald does, and he's proud of the care he puts into it. Given my avoidance of this place, the man must think I don't care a whit about a tremendously important part of his life.

"Gerald Huffman—" I soften my voice—"please forgive me for being so thickheaded. As long as I own Fairlawn, I want you to continue your work. When this place sells, we'll sit down and talk. Maybe by then you'll be ready to retire."

He gives me an uncertain smile. "I'm not really sure what I'm supposed to do next. When the time comes, I guess I'll be standin' at a crossroad."

I pat his shoulder. "Don't worry. You won't be alone."

❊ ❊ ❊

Charley Gansky says I need a permit before he can pour a slab for my new air-conditioning systems, so on Wednesday afternoon I head down to Baker Street and Mt. Dora's city hall. The municipal building isn't large, but it takes me a few minutes to locate the proper desk, sign the proper papers, and pay the proper fee.

I'm digging for my keys in the bottom of my purse when I nearly bump into a man on the sidewalk. By the time my brain tells my feet to stop moving, I'm eyeball-to-eyeball with my late uncle's lawyer. I sputter out an apology.

Daniel Sladen grins. "My fault for crowding the sidewalk. I should have been on the lookout for distracted new business owners."

Is he talking about the funeral home or—?

"I heard about your plans for a bed-and-breakfast," he says, correctly interpreting my puzzled expression. "Sounds challenging."

"It could be." I bite my lip. "Is everyone in town upset with me? We've been getting these strange calls. . . ."

He laughs. "More than a couple of folks have a bee in their bonnet, yes. But they'll get over it. If the city wants growth—and folks are always saying they do—they're going to have to accept the consequences." He slides a hand into his pocket and glances behind him. "Are you in a hurry? Would you like to grab a cup of coffee?"

I waver on the sidewalk, torn between wanting to talk to him about my new venture and *not* wanting to sit with Daniel Sladen in the center of town. Gossip doesn't fly around here—it *rockets*. And anyone who sees Daniel with me may think he's consorting with the enemy. . . .

But he invited me, didn't he?

I give him a quick smile. "Where do you want to go?"

"La Cremerie is only a couple of blocks away."

"Lead on."

When he places his hand at my elbow to steer me down the street, I'm suddenly aware that to the shopkeepers at their windows, I'm not only threatening the business of seven B and B families, I'm also spending time with Mt. Dora's most eligible bachelor.

I glance up at him through the fringe of my bangs. "You're going to get me in trouble."

"Why? Are you supposed to avoid caffeine?"

I laugh. "I live on the stuff. When I worked on Capitol Hill, I used to drink four or five cups of coffee a day."

"That must have been an interesting job."

"It was, but I never had time to enjoy it. We were so busy rushing from speech to vote to fund-raiser that we barely took the time to savor the few victories we won."

"The pace of life in Mt. Dora is a lot slower." He smiles with a hint of flirtation in his eyes. "Are you already bored with our little town?"

I look up at the sky, filtered through the branches of a moss-draped live oak. This day is as hot as all the others, but the shade makes it bearable. "I haven't had time to be bored. Once I get the bed-and-breakfast up and running, things might be different. But I hear running an inn is hard work."

"I hope you like laundry—that's what the innkeepers gripe about most. Everything has to be washed after every guest."

"Don't forget the breakfast." I grin up at him. "I hear you have to spread a pretty fantastic breakfast or people will go somewhere else. Mother is hinting that we need to put a hot tub out back, but I don't know. A hot tub on a Victorian porch? I can't see it."

"Trust your instincts." Daniel stops, and I'm surprised to see that we've already reached La Cremerie. We walk inside, and though he's mentioned coffee, my gaze drifts toward the ice cream. Nothing would taste better on a hot summer afternoon.

"Two single scoops in sugar cones," Daniel says, rapping his knuckles on the metal countertop. "Whatever flavor the lady wants."

I smile at him, grateful for his flexibility, and ask for vanilla. Because the day is advancing and we both have things to do, we walk back to Baker Street, where my van is parked. On the way we talk of people, work, and ways to beat the heat.

As Daniel Sladen leaves me by my vehicle, he leans on the hood and looks at me. "So . . . does this bed-and-breakfast plan mean you're staying in Mt. Dora?"

I search his face as a battle rages within me. This is a nice man, a *kind* man, and if I were free, I could easily be attracted to him. But my sons' father lives in Virginia, and I've promised them that we're moving back there.

I've promised myself that I will give Thomas every opportunity to come home.

"We'll stay for a while," I tell Daniel, wanting to be honest. "I'm going to need an income. The boys will need to start school in a few weeks, and I don't want to yank them out in the middle of the term. So, yes, I suppose we'll stick around at least a few more months."

"Good." He slaps my van and smiles, then turns and strides toward his office.

22

I haven't danced the merengue in years, but when Charley Gansky's Get Great Air van pulls into the driveway on Thursday morning, I grab Bugs's hand. "We're getting air," I sing, flipping my hair over one shoulder as I improvise a little heel-toe-heel move in my bare feet. "We're getting *cool* air!"

Grinning, Bugs matches me, flip for flip and step for step. Mom leans against the wall and watches from the hallway, a smile nudging into a corner of her mouth. Clay pokes his head into my room and responds to our merriment with a scowl.

Who can understand a teenage boy?

Bugs and I collapse on the bed, breathless from our hilarity, and Mom appears in the doorway. "Don't work up a sweat too soon," she says, flinging a dish towel in my direction. "He's here, but we don't have air-conditioning yet. Remember: what *can* go wrong *will* go wrong, especially in this house."

I'm too excited to be distracted by her pessimism.

"Mom?" Bugs asks. "Will we have air-conditioning *today*?"

"I don't see why not." I lace my fingers across my stomach and smile at the stippled pattern on the plastered ceiling. "You might even get out of the tub tonight and feel a chill. You might need to sleep under a blanket."

"Wow."

I glance at him, searching for signs of sarcasm, but Bugs is still too young for such things. I tousle his hair and sit up. "I'd better go downstairs to see if Mr. Gansky needs me."

My feet have scarcely touched the floor when my cell phone rings. I glance at it, half afraid Mom's dire prediction has come true. Has the bank been robbed and all our money stolen? Is Charley Gansky burying a dead body beneath my new concrete slab?

A glance at the caller ID reveals that Sharon Gilbert is calling. "Hello?"

"Jennifer? Great news. You're not going to believe this, but I have some folks here from out of town, and they want to see Fairlawn."

My heart lurches against my rib cage. "When?"

"How about ten-thirty? I know that's not much warning, but they're in Mt. Dora only for the day."

"That's okay. Bring them over." I click off the phone and stare at Bugs.

"You look funny, Mom. Whassa matter?"

"It's time to call out the troops, Son. We've got to get this house spotless in less than half an hour."

When I move into the hall and shout for help, Mom, Gerald, and Bugs leap to answer my call. Clay stays in his room, but I am content to let him remain sequestered. If he's in a melancholy mood, we'll all be happier if he's out of sight.

I stride into the kitchen and pull my emergency house-showing list from the top of the refrigerator. "Gerald, will you sweep the porch, wipe off the rails, and set fresh pillows in the rockers?"

"Sure thing."

"Mom, can you clear the kitchen counters, put potpourri on to boil, and remove all the toiletries from the bathrooms? Check to be sure there are clean towels on the racks."

"I can do that."

"Bugs?" I bend to look him in the eye. "Can you tidy up your bed, put Skeeter in his new crate, and make sure he has his bone to keep him happy? Spray a little air freshener in your room, okay?"

I check the list for unassigned duties. "I'm going to throw open all the windows, put easy listening on the radio, and make sure Charley Gansky leaves room for those folks to inspect the new air-conditioning units. Am I forgetting anything?"

I look from Gerald to Mom to Bugs.

"The lamps." Mom points toward the living room. "It always looks nice to have a few lamps burning."

"I'll turn on the lights downstairs." Gerald hitches up his pants and grins. "And don't worry. The prep room is clean and clear. No need to fret about anything down there."

"Okay." I glance at the clock. "When you're done, meet me on the front porch. We have exactly twenty-two minutes, so let's get moving."

We race off to do our chores, and for the next few minutes I'm aware of little but the adrenaline racing in my bloodstream. I make sure all the windows are open—not a difficult task, since they've pretty much remained open since we arrived—and peek into Clay's room for a fast surveillance.

He glances up from his Nintendo. "What's happening?"

"Some people are coming to look at the house." I check his floor, his closet, his bed. "Toss those dirty clothes into the hamper, will you, and come downstairs. We're all going to leave the house so these people can look around in peace."

I hurry on to my next task, trusting that Clay will recognize my no-nonsense tone and realize that this is serious business. I flip on the lights in the hallway, click on my bedside lamp, and adjust the small floor fan so it blows a gentle breeze throughout the master bedroom. I scoop my pajamas from the floor and stuff them under my pillow. The only missing detail is fresh flowers for the bedside table, but some things can't be helped.

On a quick pass through the living room, I turn on two lamps, switch off the TV, and tune the radio to an easy-listening station. I take the stairs two at a time, land on both feet in the foyer, and speed into the laundry room, where I find Charley Gansky kneeling in front of the old air-conditioning unit.

"How's it coming, Charley?" The perspiring man opens his mouth to answer, but I don't give him time. "The thing is, Charley, we have people coming to look at the house—prospective buyers, you know. Would you and your guys mind going for a cup of coffee at ten-thirty? You don't have to stay away long; a half hour should be plenty of time for them to take a look."

Charley studies the dismembered units at his feet. "You want I should take these old units out?"

"Sure, if you can do it in about fifteen minutes. It'd open up this space beautifully."

I glance at the washing machine and dryer to be sure we don't have dirty clothes protruding from any of the openings. Two camisoles dangle from a hanger at the end of a shelf, so I pull those down and stuff them into the dryer, out of sight.

"Thanks, Charley," I call, twiddling my fingers over my shoulder. "Let me know if you need any help."

❦❦ ❦❦ ❦❦

Mom, Gerald, Bugs, and I are sitting in rockers on the front porch when Sharon Gilbert pulls up in her Lexus. I do a quick head count, then hesitate.

"Skeeter's in his crate?" I speak between my clenched teeth, not wanting our guests to see anything but a smile.

Bugs nods. "He's okay."

"Anybody seen Clay?" I tear my smiling gaze from Sharon long enough to look at Mom and Gerald. "Did either of you see Clay leave his room?"

"I did." Mom gives Sharon and company a regal wave. "I heard him go down the stairs."

"He's probably out in the woods," Gerald adds. "I wouldn't worry none."

As Sharon and her prospects come up the walk, we stand to greet them. The man and woman with Sharon are probably in their middle forties, and both have a well-preserved look. The man wears khakis and a polo shirt. The woman is wearing black-on-white polka-dot capris topped by a white-on-black polka-dot shirt with black-on-white polka-dot high-heeled sandals.

I swallow a rising wave of bile.

"Jennifer," Sharon says, all smiles, "I'd like you to meet Dr. and Mrs. Jim Shepard. Dr. Shepard is thinking about setting up a practice in Mt. Dora."

I'm tempted to say the house will be perfect for him, but some instinct warns me that it'd be better for the doctor to decide this for himself. I thrust out my hand. "So nice to meet you."

After shaking both of the Shepards' hands, I herd my family toward the front porch steps. "We were just on our way to get some ice cream. Have a nice look around, and if you have any questions, you know where to reach me."

Sharon thanks me with a smile, and we trudge toward the minivan.

"That woman isn't going to like the house," Mom says, heading toward the passenger door. "Did you see how she was dressed? She's modern, so she's not going to like all those antiques."

"She's not buying the furniture. She's interested in the house," I answer. "Maybe she will be able to see the potential in it."

Mom opens her door and steps back to let a wave of superheated air roll out of the van. "You'd better hope so."

"He ought to appreciate the place," Gerald says, following Bugs to the side door. "There's room for an office, even an examination room if he should want to operate from the house. Might be a nice touch, having an old-fashioned family practice in Mt. Dora."

We pile into the van and I turn the key. For a long moment we sit there, hot and perspiring, while the auto air-conditioning struggles to bring the temperature down to double digits.

"So," Bugs pipes up, "where are we gonna go?"

I look at Mom. "Too soon for ice cream?"

She snorts.

Gerald stretches his legs into the empty space at the side of the van. "Maybe we could go for coffee?"

I glance at my purse, which I've dropped into the empty space at my right, and realize that I don't have my wallet. Yesterday Gerald suggested that I move all my paperwork to the office, so I did. I was paying bills there last night . . . and my wallet is on the desk, right where I left it.

I look at Mom. "Did you bring your purse?"

Her eyebrows lift. "Was I supposed to?"

I catch Gerald's gaze in the mirror. "Gerald, do you have any money?"

His mouth curls in a one-sided smile. "Sorry, missy. I ran out in such a hurry. I plumb forgot my billfold."

Without thinking, I look at Bugs, who lifts two empty hands.

I sigh and drop my forearms to the steering wheel. "I guess we can't go anywhere. Not only do I not have any money, I don't even have my driver's license."

"You'd better drive somewhere," Mother urges. "If we sit out here with the motor running, those people will think we're nuts."

When no one suggests a better idea, I put the van in reverse and pull out of the parking lot. We drive to the end of the driveway, do a three-point turn in front of Lydia's house, and drive back up to Fairlawn. With the engine running at idle speed, we inch to the far north side of the parking lot, then back up and creep to the southern edge.

Mom keeps an eye trained on the house. "No signs of them," she says, gesturing toward the steering wheel. "Keep driving."

I point the van toward Lydia's house. "Look, Bugs." I shift my right leg so he can see that I'm not pressing the gas pedal. "See how the van can drive itself?"

Bugs leans forward to humor me. "That's cool, I guess."

We might have idled up and down the driveway all day, but finally the front door of the house swings open. Like a doused cat, Mrs. Shepard hurries over the porch and down the steps, followed by her husband. They make a beeline for Sharon's car while the real estate agent huffs behind them, her lips pursed and her cheeks flaming.

I drive up to the house, put the van in park, and hop out.

Sharon stops in midflight long enough to give me an I'll-talk-to-you-later look, then gets into her car and pulls away.

Speechless, I turn and regard the occupants of my van. "Okay," I say, mentally reviewing every possibility for disaster, "which one of you was the last to see Clay?"

※ ※ ※

Murphy's Law variant #105: Whoever can mess it up *will* mess it up.

We find Clay in the foyer, shirtless and shoeless, with a bedsheet in hand. For about sixty seconds he tries to play the wide-eyed innocent, but between the heat of my stare and the evidence on his face, he realizes he's busted.

"I couldn't resist," he says, grinning at Bugs. "When you all went outside, I climbed up on Gerald's table and covered myself with the sheet. I put some food coloring on my face so it'd look like blood."

That explains the red trickle at the corner of his mouth.

"It was hilarious," he says, looking at Gerald. "They came in and were talking, and then one of the ladies said something about the body on the table. The man was trying to act all macho, so he lifted the sheet. When he did I made a face—" Clay demonstrates by twisting his face into the most demented grimace I've ever seen—"and one of the women started to scream. The man ran after her and so did the other woman—"

"Clay Edward Graham," I say, my attention drifting away on a tide of exasperation, "get up to your room. I haven't the energy to deal with you right now."

Realizing, no doubt, that three's a crowd in such a teachable mother-and-son moment, Mother and Gerald slip away. Gerald heads down the hall to his prep room; Mother takes Bugs's hand and leads him upstairs.

Clay, however, doesn't budge. Neither does he take his eyes from my face. "I don't want to go to my room," he says, his eyes insolent and accusing. "You can't tell me what to do."

"I can't?" My weariness flees, replaced by a tide of irritation. "I'm your mother and you will obey me."

"I won't. You think you can drag us down here, ruin our summer, and take us from our friends, but you can't. I'm tired of obeying you. I'm tired of *you*."

"Maybe the feeling's mutual, kid." The words have no sooner left my lips than I realize I'm behaving as childishly as Clay. But I'm too tired to know what to do, too worn-out from dealing with the house and contractors and real estate agents.

Clay drops his arms to his sides as his hands clench. "I don't have to do what you say because you're not my father."

"Really? Well, your father's not here, so you're stuck with me. Get upstairs, and don't come out of your room until you're ready to apologize for this crazy stunt and the attitude you've been displaying—" I break off my tirade as a small voice rises from the staircase.

"Don't blame Clay, Mom." Bugs stands on the first step, his arm wrapped around the newel.

"What?"

"It was Brett's idea. I heard him telling Clay that he thought it'd be fun to play dead if people came over. So it isn't Clay's fault."

"Bugs!" Clay's eyes narrow into slits.

"It's true, Clay. I heard him."

"It may have been Brett's idea," I say, speaking in a calmer tone, "but it was Clay's doing. So, Clay, I still want you to go upstairs and wait in your room until you can apologize. And when you come out, I don't think you should hang around Brett anymore."

Clay's mouth tightens with mutiny, but he races up the stairs and out of sight. Yet his anger continues to resonate in the quiet foyer.

Bugs looks at me, his eyes wet. "You're not mad at Clay, are you?"

I blow out a breath and draw my youngest son close. "I'm angry right now, yes. But I won't stay angry with your brother. I love him, and we're going to work this out."

Bugs leans against me. "I hope Clay works things out with me, too. He's going to be mad 'cause I told you about Brett."

I take his hand and lead him toward the stairs. "Clay's your brother, honey. I promise he won't stay mad at you forever."

23

I am sleeping, snug in a blanket of exhaustion, when the sound of pounding wakes me. I lie flat on my back, my hands pressed to the mattress, and try to remember what day it is. Thursday? No, Friday. Do I have workmen coming today? None that I know of. Charley Gansky and his crew were here yesterday, but just when they were ready to finish up the job, one of Charley's workmen discovered that they'd lost both new thermostats somewhere between Fairlawn and the Coffee House, where they'd gone to lie low while we tried to show the house to prospective buyers.

Though Charley's crew retraced their steps, they never found the thermostats, and the air conditioners won't run without them. So Charley had to order new thermostats, which, he assures me, will arrive soon . . . maybe after the holiday.

I'm not expecting workers today, so why does it sound like someone is trying to rip the house from its foundation?

I throw on a robe and flip my hair from beneath the collar, then hurry down the stairs. A glance out the front door reveals a battered blue pickup but no workmen.

But now I can tell the noise is coming from the back of the house. I sweep down the first-floor hallway and through the preparation room, barely looking at Gerald's tools and bottles. The back door of this room opens onto the termite-damaged deck that occupies a low position on my to-do list. The strange screech and rip is now hurting my ears, so either the termites have developed industrial-strength jaws or someone has decided to rid me of my pathetic porch before Gerald puts a foot through a floorboard. . . .

I fling open the door. A young man stands beside the porch, shirtless and sweating though it's only seven-thirty. A foam coffee cup sits on the edge of the deck and vibrates next to a clump of geraniums as the stranger uses a claw hammer to rip a section of railing away from the house.

I throw up a hand and move into his line of vision. "What do you think you're doing?"

He grins at me and releases the railing. "You must be Ms. Graham."

I stare at him, trying to recall if I've talked to this man on the phone. "And you are?"

"Mitch Wilkerson, Ginger Sue's son. Sure hope I didn't wake you up."

I can't place either name. "I'm sorry, but I don't remember you. Have we talked?"

"Don't think so." He hooks his thumb through a loop on his denim shorts. "Your mom talked to my mom. I woulda come sooner, but I had to finish the trim work on a house over in Tavares."

"Wait a minute . . . our mothers set this up?"

"Right."

"Well . . . don't you think it would have been nice if you'd talked to *me*? I mean—" I point to the grass, where one complete railing and several floorboards have been tossed like firewood—"you've started on work I didn't authorize."

"I thought it was a done deal." He sucks at the inside of his cheek for a minute. "I have an estimate here, but I didn't want to wake you. I thought you could sign it after you got up, you know, and had your coffee."

I straighten and wrap my robe more tightly around my waist. Is he implying that I'm not fit for company yet?

I put out my hand. "May I see the estimate?"

"Sure thing." He reaches into a back pocket, takes out a folded paper, and hands it to me.

I can read the word *estimate* and see several sentences in the center of the page. Of the two lines at the bottom, one has been filled with a scrawled signature (obviously Mitch's), and the other is blank.

It's an estimate, signed and delivered. But without my reading glasses, it's all a blur.

"Mom told me to give you a good deal." He gestures to the paper in my hand. "So I did. I'll rip out this old porch, haul away the debris, and build you a new deck of pressure-treated lumber that should last fifty years. I'll put extra concrete around the footers to guarantee stability. All the construction will be up to code, and I've already pulled the permit."

"Sounds like you've thought of everything."

"I try to." His grin widens. "You know, I heard you have a teenager, but that can't be right. You're too young to have a kid that old."

Well, since he's already done so much . . . I fan myself with the folded paper and try to think things through. This guy is young, so maybe he needs the work. If I hire him, word will surely get around town that I'm doing my part to support Mt. Dora's young entrepreneurs.

I pat the empty pocket of my robe. "I need to get a pen."

He pulls one from his shorts. "Here you go."

I scribble my signature and hand the paper back to him. "I expect you'll want a deposit."

"Tell you what—" he folds the estimate and slips it into his pocket—"since our moms sort of sprung this on you, why don't you pay me when the work is done? I figure this job'll take me two, three days, tops. And I promise you'll be pleased."

The arrangement is unconventional, but the porch isn't large. The cost of concrete and a few pieces of lumber isn't likely to make him miss a rent payment.

"Okay." I give the porch one final glance and go back into the house. Hidden behind the sheer prep room curtain, I study Mitch Wilkerson. The guy is younger than the other men I interviewed, but he handles that hammer like he knows what he's doing. He's brought a couple of sawhorses, and he has a truck for hauling his supplies. What else could he need?

Please, Lord, let this guy be okay. I close my eyes and lift a fervent plea. *And give me the grace to bear my mother's good intentions.*

❧❧ ❧❧ ❧❧

Mom is slack-jawed and snoring on her pillow when I stride into her room. "Joella Norris—" I plop on the edge of her bed and jostle the mattress—"what in the world have you done?"

Her eyes spring open. "What? Who?"

"Wake up." I wait, giving her a moment to reenter reality. "Mom, who is Mitch Wilkerson?"

She blinks at me. "I have no idea."

"I think you do. Mitch Wilkerson is downstairs. He says you set the whole thing up."

"What?" She rolls onto her side, supporting herself on one elbow as she pinches the bridge of her nose. "Mitch—oh! Ginger Sue's boy."

"Sounds right. Is Ginger one of your Hatter friends?"

Mom drops back on her pillow. "Finally! She remembered to have him stop by."

"He didn't stop by, Mom. He started to work. He's got half the back porch scattered all over the lawn."

Her smile vanishes. "He wasn't supposed to *work*. He was supposed to come talk to you."

I lift my gaze to the ceiling. *Lord?*

Mom kicks her way out of the covers, then sets her feet on the floor and moves toward the closet. "I'll go down there and talk to him. He wasn't supposed to start work. Ginger Sue must have misunderstood—"

"Forget it. He's already pulled the permit, so I signed his estimate. But the back porch was at the bottom of my priority list. None of our B and B guests would even see that rickety old thing."

"But a prospective buyer would. And you never know when someone is going to want to see the house."

Grudgingly, I admit she's right.

Mom fluffs her hair and turns to face me. "Did he give you a good price?"

"I couldn't read the paper without my glasses. But the lowest bid I got was three thousand, so I hope he's less than that."

"I'm *sure* he will be. Ginger Sue said he'd give you a break because he really needs the work."

Mom looks so earnest, so guilty, that I'm tempted to drop the matter and leave her alone. But this isn't the first time she's caused trouble for me. Unless I make her understand, it won't be the last.

"Mom." I stand to look her in the eye. "You can't keep meddling in my business. This is my house, my inheritance, and you have to trust me to handle it. If you want to help me take care of the boys, you're more than welcome to stay, but you can't keep interfering. You're making things difficult."

Mom stares at me for an instant, her face blank; then she manages a tremulous smile. "I didn't mean to meddle. I'm sorry."

"Sorry doesn't pay the bills, Mother, and it doesn't keep strangers from tearing up my house without permission. So if any of your other Hatter friends want to help, send them straight to me, okay?"

Mom nods, but from the telltale quiver of her chin I know that tears are bubbling beneath the surface of her smile.

I leave her alone to have a good cry. If I didn't expect the boys to wake at any moment, I'd indulge in one too.

Joella rocks on the front porch, her mood as dark as the thunder-cloud on the western horizon. The carpenter didn't show up this morning. Jen doesn't care because it's Saturday, but Joella hoped Mitch was as desperate for work as Ginger Sue implied. Jen would be impressed if he was such a go-getter that he finished the porch in only a couple of days.

But he isn't working on Saturday, so there's no way he'll show up tomorrow. Maybe he'll come Monday, but Tuesday is the Fourth, and Joella's sure the carpenter will spend that day eating hot dogs and ham-burgers at Ginger Sue's while he watches fireworks from his mother's beautiful, termite-free porch.

In the meantime, the folks at Fairlawn have nothing—literally. Yes-terday Mitch managed to completely rip out the old porch—no small feat, Joella has to admit—but he's left them without even a frame to step across. If poor Gerald wants to go out to the garage, he'll have to open the back door, hop to the ground two feet below, and wade across several yards of heaped black sand.

No, accepting Ginger Sue's offer wasn't the smartest thing Joella's ever done. Whoever said no good deed goes unpunished certainly nailed that truth.

She leans forward in her chair as Brett Windsor comes into view. He's carrying a jug in one hand and some kind of wand in the other, pointing at patches of dandelions.

"Brett?" She waves when he lifts his head. "What are you up to?"

He waves the wand in her direction. "Hey, Mrs. Norris. Gerald asked me to spray the dandelions." He jiggles the jug. "Got a gallon of weed killer in here."

"Ah." She sighs, wondering if Brett knows that Clay and Jen are still on the outs over a stunt the older boy suggested. Lydia's son certainly doesn't seem to be a troublemaker. He's probably just mischievous.

She blinks as another teenager comes around the corner of the house, a pretty blonde with a matching jug in her hand.

"Brett?" Joella calls again. "Did you know you have a shadow?"

He glances over his shoulder and grins. "That's Jessica. Jessica, that's Mrs. Norris."

The girl tips her face toward the porch. "Hello."

"Nice to meet you." Joella folds her hands across her lap. Such a fine-looking girl—pretty in a wholesome way and not all painted up and dressed in stretchy bits of fabric.

She stands and moves to the porch railing. "Would you young people like some lemonade? It's a scorcher out there."

Jessica looks at Brett, who looks at the lawn. "Can we take that break when we're done here?" he says. "We only have this one strip to spray; then we'll be finished."

"That's a good idea. You'll need to wash your hands after handling that stuff."

Joella goes inside and climbs the stairs (a nuisance that has proved to be a blessing, since her legs feel stronger than they ever did in Virginia) to the kitchen. She takes two glasses from the cupboard, opens the fridge, and frowns. Gerald, who drinks lemonade like it's water, has let the pitcher run dry. Either that or one of the boys put the empty container back in the fridge.

She tsks under her breath and retrieves the pitcher from the shelf. After rinsing it out, she finds a packet of presweetened lemonade mix and dumps it into the container. She's running water over the mix and a handful of ice cubes when she hears the front door open and foot-steps on the stairs.

"Come on up," she calls, glad that Jen and the boys have gone to the grocery store. She can't help feeling that she's inviting the enemy into the camp. "Everything is almost ready."

Brett lopes into the kitchen, drops into a chair, and unfolds his long legs until they protrude into the narrow aisle between the table and the cabinets. Jessica is more reserved, hesitating in the doorway until Joella suggests that she sit.

The girl has good manners.

When the phone on the wall rings, Brett looks at Joella. "Want me to grab that for you?"

"Ignore it," she tells him. "It rings all the time these days. If it's important, the people will leave a message."

Brett gives her a quizzical look, but as Joella predicted, the caller hangs up just as the answering machine clicks on.

"See what I mean?"

The teens accept their drinks with thanks. Brett guzzles his in one long swallow, then drops the cup back to the table, thumps his chest, and exhales through his open mouth. "Man, that hits the spot."

Joella lifts the pitcher. "Let me pour you another. You can get dehydrated so easily when you're working in the heat."

After refilling his glass, she sits at the end of the table and searches for a way to bring up a touchy subject. Brett needs to know that he has gotten Clay into trouble, but she doesn't want to embarrass him in front of Jessica.

"I don't think I've seen you around these parts." She smiles at Jessica. "Have you known Brett long?"

Joella catches the quick look the teens give each other.

"Yes, ma'am," Jessica says. "But we've been hanging out only for a couple of months. I only get to see him in the summer."

"Young people ought to hang out." Joella looks at Brett and smiles her approval. "I know that my grandson Clay enjoys hanging out with Brett."

The tips of Brett's ears go pink. "He's a nice kid."

"He certainly thinks the world of you. I think you could tell him to jump off a cliff and he'd do it." She lifts the pitcher again. "More lemonade?"

"No, ma'am, I'm good." Brett takes another sip of his drink. "I guess we should be getting out of your way."

"In fact," Joella continues, idly tracing her initial on the table-top, "the other day Clay pulled a really silly stunt that got him into a lot of trouble with his mom. Bugs told Jen that it was all your idea."

Brett's mouth opens. "What'd he do?"

"We had people coming to look at the house," Joella says. "We all waited outside so they could look around without being bothered, but Clay climbed onto the table in the preparation room, covered himself with a sheet, and pretended to be a dead body. When someone pulled the sheet back, he made a face and nearly scared a poor woman into a heart attack."

Jessica gasps, and Brett's eyes appear to be in danger of dropping right out of his face. "He didn't!"

Joella presses her hand to the tabletop and lowers her voice to a conspiratorial whisper. "Was that your idea?"

"Why . . . I never . . . it was just . . ." He looks at Jessica before dropping his head into his hands. "Man, I never dreamed he'd do it! We were jokin' around about the tomb room, and I said wouldn't it be funny to pull a stunt like that. I didn't tell him to *do* it. Honestly, I didn't think the kid had the guts to do something like that."

Joella leans back, satisfied with his answer. "I know you didn't. But Clay admires you, and with his dad gone . . . well, he's trying his best to impress *someone*, and I'm afraid he did that to impress you. He and his mom aren't seeing eye to eye right now, so you may not see much of him for a few days."

Brett lowers his hands, but he's still shaking his head. "He must be in big trouble."

"You could say that." Joella stands and reaches for her purse on the counter. "What did Gerald promise to pay you for the weeding? He's not here right now, but I can pay you—"

"No thanks, Mrs. Norris; that's all right. I feel terrible about what happened. Should I—?"

"You're fine, Brett; it wasn't your fault. I'll get things sorted out with Jen."

Brett pushes up from the table. "We ought to go, Mrs. Norris. Thanks for the lemonade."

Joella watches the pair move down the stairs, one dark head, one blonde, bent together in hushed whispers.

Young love. She'd almost forgotten how sweet it could be.

***

I park the van and turn the key, reluctant to leave this air-conditioned space. Charley Gansky keeps assuring me that our thermostats will come any day, but we are still living in a breezy sweatbox.

The boys scramble out of the van, but I call them back and ask them to take at least two grocery bags into the house. Gerald helps too, grabbing four bags, and I find that I have nothing left to carry.

While the boys mutter and complain, I head for the mailbox, where I'm hoping for good news. Maybe a letter from Virginia, maybe a catalog with autumnal sweaters or pumpkins on the cover. Though the thought of sweaters makes me perspire, the sight of a nice, round pumpkin might help me forget that it's July and ninety-nine degrees in the shade. . . .

The mailbox contains the electric bill, the water bill, two real estate ads, and Gerald's copy of *Mortuary Management*. The magazine cover features a photograph of Arlington National Cemetery, where rows and rows of graves have been adorned with simple American flags.

Must be a mortician's concept of a memorable Fourth.

I flip through the glossy pages as I climb the hill. The magazine features include an article on preselling plots, a colorful report on a new line of hand-painted caskets, and editorials on the pros and cons of "green burials"—apparently a new movement involving corpses that are wrapped in shrouds and buried without benefit of embalming or casketing. Unlike cemeteries, where the land is set apart for long-term use, once a "green" burial ground is filled, the land is available to be used for something else—even, say, a convenience store.

I shiver as I imagine a backhoe unearthing someone's skull. Ick. I resolve to ask Gerald about the legality of such things; then I turn to the classifieds in the back of the magazine. There, in bold print, I see the ad.

FOR SALE: FAIRLAWN
Located in scenic Mt. Dora, Florida,
charming funeral home completely equipped.
Long-established clientele waits to welcome you to our fair city.
Call 352-555-3857 for appointment and terms.

Gripped by the paralysis of astonishment, I stop and stare at the magazine. Who could have placed this ad? Not Mother. She wouldn't even know how to contact *Mortuary Management*. If Sharon Gilbert placed the ad, she would have listed her agency's information, but this is the Fairlawn number, the phone that rings for . . . Gerald.

Gerald must have called the advertising department right after I told him I wanted to operate Fairlawn as a bed-and-breakfast.

Why would he do this behind my back? Does he think I'm so desperate for money that I'll take the first offer to come in? Is he trying to get rid of us?

I curl the magazine in my hand and look up at the turret. Behind that wall, Gerald is probably watching TV with my boys.

The man is practically part of our family now, so how could he do this? Gerald built me up with that story about Uncle Ned's vision; he made me feel that Fairlawn might be part of my destiny. Though I really didn't believe it, *he* seemed to . . . until now.

Obviously he was trying to get me to stick around just so he wouldn't have to move. When I mentioned the bed-and-breakfast, he placed this ad.

I push at my sweaty bangs and wonder if I'm jumping to conclusions. Could this be a misunderstanding? No, the proof is here, in black and white. Despite all his pep talks and fatherly encouragement, Gerald wants me to sell.

He doesn't believe in me. He doesn't want me to own this place at all.

Well. Now I know how he really feels about things.

With a heart too heavy for words, I continue my climb up the hill.

25

Joella pushes away from the table as Jen enters the kitchen, her hair askew and her robe untied. Her eyes widen, though, when she sees that Joella is wearing a dress. "Oh my. Did I miss something?"

Joella stands, takes her empty cereal bowl to the sink, and turns. "I figured it was time someone in this family got back into the habit of church on Sunday mornings. I'm going with Gerald. Bugs said he wants to come with us."

Jen sinks into a chair as a guilty shadow moves through her eyes. For a moment Joella is afraid her daughter will argue, but she only rests her chin in her hand. "Okay."

"Do you think Clay will want to go?"

"I doubt it. But you can ask him."

"Maybe *you* should ask him."

"I would, but I don't think he's speaking to me yet."

Joella hesitates. "I talked to Brett yesterday. He didn't tell Clay to pull that stunt in the prep room. They were just joking around, like boys do."

"I know, Mom."

"And he admires Brett so much."

"I know."

"So . . . don't you think you could let him hang out with Brett again? The boy is the only real friend Clay's made down here."

Jen sets her jaw in the stubborn line Joella knows only too well. "I'd be happy to let him hang out with Brett, but first Clay owes me an apology. After I get that, we'll talk."

Joella lifts her hands, knowing not to push further. Jen has a point, of course; the boy should apologize. But if this standoff continues much longer, those two are going to forget why they were upset with each other in the first place.

Joella picks up her purse, slides it over her arm, and raps on Gerald's door. "I'm ready," she calls, "whenever you are."

"Five minutes," comes the muffled answer. "I'll be down directly."

Joella turns to face her daughter. Jen is staring at the floor, her face dark with misery.

"Why don't you come with us?" Joella suggests. "We'll wait."

"I don't want to get involved." Jen shakes her head. "We won't be here that long, and . . . church is so couple oriented. I'll feel like a third wheel."

"Churches have singles groups, you know. You might enjoy meeting some new people."

"Let it go, Mom." Jen rakes her hand through her hair and exhales in a rush. "I'll go to church when we get back to Virginia. When Thomas comes home, we'll pick up where we left off." She glances up. "He called the other morning. Did I tell you?"

"About a dozen times."

"Well, you can't blame me for feeling encouraged." Jen shrugs. "We're his family. We're supposed to be together."

Joella takes a step forward and sets her purse on the table. "Sweetheart, not all families stay together. Sometimes people aren't able to work things out. Your father and I, for instance, disagreed on a lot of things—"

"But you stayed together." Jen looks up as dewy moisture fills her blue eyes. "That's my prayer for us, Mom. That God will reunite us."

Joella draws a breath and clamps her lips together. How can she argue with prayer . . . and hope?

❀❀ ❀❀ ❀❀

For two days I debate whether or not I should confront Gerald about the ad in *Mortuary Management*. I can't let it rest, so on Monday afternoon, when Mom takes the boys to search for an air-conditioned superstore, I grab the magazine from beneath my pillow and charge down the stairs to speak to him.

I find Gerald sitting at an empty prep table, a catalog open in front of him. His brows arch when I come in, but he welcomes me with a smile. "Missy! What brings you down here?"

I advance and drop the magazine on the table.

"Oh, good. I was wondering where that was."

I cross my arms. "I saw the ad, Gerald. The ad for Fairlawn." I wait, but his face remains locked in neutral. "Why did you place an ad without telling me?"

A change comes over his features, a sudden shock of realization. "Did you . . . oh my. You thought I was trying to hide something from you? I thought I was helping. You *do* want to sell the place, don't you?"

"Well . . . yes."

"So what better way to sell a funeral home than through a trade magazine?"

I sink onto the empty stool next to him. "This isn't how it's done, Gerald. I signed a contract; *Sharon Gilbert* is supposed to sell the place. When I saw this, I thought you were trying to . . . I don't know, undercut me or something. Bad enough that Mom is constantly messing things up—"

"Hold on now." He gives me the kind of smile you'd give a slow-witted child. "Don't you know that God is in control even of this place? The right person for the job is going to come along in the Lord's perfect timing. You don't have to worry about a thing."

"If you're not worried, why did you advertise?"

"Because—" Gerald's eyes twinkle—"the Lord's not in this alone, you know. We're supposed to do everything we can . . . and wait on him to do the rest. I thought you knew that."

I stare at him for a moment, then slide the magazine toward him. "Sorry I bothered you."

"Come down anytime you need a break from the heat."

I head toward the stairs. Not even the stifling heat of the second floor can entice me to spend a moment more than necessary in that room.

I'm in the foyer, ready to climb the stairs, when I hear the sound of slamming car doors. A quick peek through the sidelights assures me that my family has returned, but Bugs's frantic rush up the steps gives me pause. I open the door just in time for him to crash against my knees.

"Mom," he gulps.

"What is it, honey?"

"It's Skeeter. We had him on the leash, but he backed out of his collar and ran away. We chased him through the park, but he kept running and we lost him."

I look at Mother. Distress is written all over her face, etched deep in the lines beside her mouth and eyes. "We tried to chase him, Jen. We called the dog until we were hoarse. Finally we came home."

I look at Clay, who seems to be wearing his face like a mask. He pushes past me without a word and stomps up the steps.

Bugs is crying now, clinging to my knees. "We gotta find him, Mom. He won't know the way home, will he? And what if a gator gets him?"

His questions pile up with all the other unknowns in my brain, dozens of uncertainties for which I do not have answers.

$\mathscr{A}$fter living so many years in the vicinity of Washington, DC, I am convinced that Mt. Dora's Fourth of July celebration can only be a disappointment. Thomas and I used to take the boys to the Independence Day Parade along Constitution Avenue, and it's hard to imagine anything that can compare to the bands, floats, and celebrities that gather to celebrate the holiday in the nation's capital.

On the morning of the Fourth, however, Gerald assures me that Mt. Dora has its own traditions. "Lots of the downtown stores stay open," he tells me over breakfast, "but if you don't want to shop, you could take a walk down the nature trail. As the sun starts to set, we usually grab lawn chairs and go down to the picnic pavilion at the lake to watch the fireworks over in Eustis. When those are done, the mayor lights our own fireworks; then we go home to bed."

I force a smile and stir my cereal. "Sounds like fun." Truthfully, the day sounds like one long, sweaty encounter with mosquitoes, because my boys won't want to shop, hike, or sit in a lawn chair by the lake. Furthermore, unless Skeeter comes trotting up the driveway soon, Bugs and Clay are likely to stay in a deep funk. They won't want to celebrate anything.

Last night when I listened to Bugs's prayers, he asked God to bring Skeeter home. I said amen and lifted my head, thinking Bugs had finished, but my son remained perfectly still, his hands pressed together, his eyes closed.

"What are you doing, hon?" I whispered.

He peered at me from beneath one half-lifted eyelid. "Waiting."

If I waited like that, I'd have spent the last several months on my knees.

I carry my cereal bowl to the sink. "Do we still have one of those lost-dog posters? I could take it to the library and get some copies made."

"The library won't be open today," Gerald says. "But I'll help Bugs make up some more posters. Not much else to do on a holiday, is there?"

He's right about that. Charley Gansky certainly isn't going to come fix our air-conditioning today, nor is Mitch coming to finish the porch. A week ago I called the roofer, Bob McKee, but I've yet to see a single shingle.

If Gerald helps Bugs with the posters, maybe I could do some sewing or cleaning. The area around Skeeter's crate hasn't been vacuumed lately, so the hair on the baseboard is probably half an inch thick.

I whirl around to face Gerald. "You don't think anyone would set out poison, do you?"

The man's snowy brows knit together. "Poison for what?"

"I don't know, for rats or cats or raccoons. Maybe Skeeter got into it."

"Aw, missy, why do you want to go and worry about a thing like that? That little dog is fine."

"But what if he's not?" I drop into the chair across from Gerald. "It's the not knowing that kills me. I don't know what to tell Bugs, and he expects me to have the answers."

Gerald looks at me with a bland half smile. "Does the Lord always give you answers right away?"

What a question. "Of course not."

"Then let your little guy learn to wait."

I stand and reach for the broom in the narrow space between the wall and the refrigerator. Before my fingers close around the broomstick, though, I hear the sound of angry voices coming from Clay's room. It's not even eight o'clock, and already he's arguing with my mother.

What is it this time?

I leave the broom and head toward the hallway. Bugs's door is still closed, though he can't possibly be sleeping through the storm raging in Clay's room. That door is ajar, and through the opening I see Mother standing with her hands on her hips while Clay sits on the rug with his arms crossed.

"You are behaving like a spoiled child," Mom says, pointing to a pile of clothes on the floor. "You should appreciate your mother's hard work and give her a hand."

"What does she do for me?"

"Why, she does everything for you! And what she doesn't do, I do. We clean your room and cook your meals, and I even gave you the thirty dollars you needed for that stupid game you're always playing—"

"Yeah? Well, I hate my mother and I hate you, too!"

Oh, boy. I stride into the room and look down at my son, whose eyes are as shiny and hard as cobalt. "Clay Edward Graham," I say, barely mastering the anger that quavers my voice, "you will put those clothes in the hamper this instant. After that you will apologize to your grandmother and to me."

Clay looks up at us, twin towers of matriarchal power; then he scrambles to his feet. For an instant I think he's going to pick up the clothes, but instead he kicks them across the room.

"Clay!"

He whirls on me and utters something so vile, so unexpected, that for a moment I wonder if I'm dreaming. But there's no denying the anger in his eyes, the tension in his fists, or the snarl on his mouth.

I draw my hand back and slap his face.

One of his fists comes up, ready to attack, but Mother steps between us. "That's enough," she says, commanding both of us in the same steely tone. "Clay, you will remain in your room. Jen, let's leave him alone to think things over."

After one last withering glare at my son, I leave his room and head to my own. I slam the door behind me, not caring who hears, and sit on the edge of my bed with my face in my hands.

What have I done? I haven't had to spank Clay in years, and I've *never* slapped his face. But he has never said such a thing to me, and I've never been so angry. I used to let Thomas handle these situations. He always managed to smooth things over without shouting or slapping. . . .

I hear a knock at the door before Mom peeks through the opening. "You okay?"

I palm tears from my cheeks. "I'll be fine."

She slips into my room and closes the door behind her. "These things happen, Jen. I never had a son, but all my friends say it's hard raising a boy—"

"Then why don't you leave him alone?" Against my will, fresh rage rises in my chest. "Clay would have been fine, Mom, if you hadn't gone in there and started raggin' on him about the mess in his room. Nobody's coming to see the house, so what does it matter if he makes a mess today?"

Mother's throat works as she stares at me. "So that's what you want me to do? Let him be?"

"Please." I draw a deep breath and look up at the ceiling. "Just leave him alone. He'll be fine."

"But that's his problem, Jen. Don't you see? You've been leaving him alone, and he's feeling neglected. Thomas went off and abandoned him, and now you're doing the same thing. You've been ignoring your kids, especially Clay, and—"

"I am *not* ignoring my kids." The sheer audacity of her statement lights a fuse at my core. "How dare you say such a thing?"

"I dare because I love those boys too. You can't set Clay on a shelf and trust that he'll work things out on his own. You're the parent, for heaven's sake. You're the mother, and you have to help him through this."

"So you want me to be like you? Always hovering, always making suggestions?"

"I want you to look around, Jen. Open your eyes. If you keep ignoring your son, you'll lose him. Sending him to his room is not going to solve his problems. Removing him from your sight will not ease his pain."

"But giving him thirty dollars for a video game will?" I am choking on my words, strangling on my anger. "I wanted him to save his allowance for that game, Mom. I'm trying to teach him how to be responsible, but you ruined all that when you gave him money. He hasn't learned anything . . . except who's the weakest link around here."

Mom flushes to the roots of her hair. "You think *I'm* weak? You don't know anything, Jennifer. You don't know me at all because you're always thinking about yourself."

Her words fall on my face like drops of acid, and I can't take anymore. I step toward her, my hand rising to strike her as if she were a rebellious child, but I can never forget that she's my *mother*, the woman who took me in when the love of my life walked out.

My arm falls limply to my side as Mother's arms wrap around me and her bony chin digs into my shoulder. While I cling to her and sob, she holds me close and murmurs that she understands completely.

By the time my fury is depleted, I am weeping in her arms like the baby I once was. She strokes my hair and urges me to sit on the edge of the mattress.

"I'm sorry," I mumble into her housecoat. "It's just that I don't . . . I don't know what to do. I've never had these problems, and I've never done this alone."

"You're not alone, sweetie." She lifts my chin, then pulls a lock of hair from my cheek and tucks it behind my ear. "As long as you have me and the Lord, you're not alone."

She's right, of course. She's right about so many things.

I curl up on the bed and rest my head in her lap, content to be a child for an hour.

When July 5 dawns, I am more than ready to slide back into our routine. I need to see workmen at the house. I yearn for the sounds of hammers, saws, and delivery trucks. Having people around keeps my family occupied; activity prevents us from wanting to wring each other's necks.

My wish is granted shortly after sunrise. I hear the whine and grind of Mitch Wilkerson's saw before I finish my first cup of coffee, and the UPS truck rumbles up the drive right after I've finished sweeping the kitchen. The delivered package contains three double rolls of wallpaper—enough, I think, to redo the downstairs bathroom. The antique plumbing will have to stay.

After making sure the boys are dressed and fed, I do a quick pickup of their rooms and trot downstairs to the office. I resisted using this space at first because it is dark, depressing, and associated with the mortuary, but Gerald pointed out that the room is quiet and equipped with everything I need.

Now the desktop is covered with estimates, notes, and clippings from magazines. Whenever Mom finds some bit of wallpaper or fabric that might work in one of the rooms, she brings it to the office.

Last weekend she brought in a small bulletin board she'd picked up at Wal-Mart. At first I thought it silly, but now it hangs at my left, blooming with fabric samples and bright corners snipped from various wallpaper books.

Before I can begin papering the bathroom, I have calls to return, a few e-mails to write, and a call to place to the Humane Society. Skeeter didn't come home yesterday, and though Gerald and Bugs walked up and down the street and plastered lost-dog posters throughout the downtown area, we've had no news about our runaway terrier. Bugs cried himself to sleep last night, and Clay has only grown more surly.

Though I am worried about the dog, I'm operating on the principle that no news is good news. As long as Skeeter hasn't been picked up by the dog catcher or a highway cleanup crew, he's probably entertaining strangers or chasing ducks around some lake.

Last night I tucked Bugs into bed and told him that Skeeter would come home when he got tired of roaming. "He knows how good he has it here," I said, wrapping my arm around my son. "And he knows how much you love him. That silly dog will come to his senses soon enough. You'll see."

"I'm not worried," Bugs answered. "I'm waiting for God."

Later, in the privacy of my room, I asked the Lord to keep the dog safe and bring him home quickly. Only a stupid dog would run away from a boy who loved him, and only a selfish animal would stay away while we were all worried sick about him.

I dial the Humane Society and ask if a Jack Russell was brought in overnight. No. I thank the woman for checking and hang up.

I push thoughts of Skeeter from my mind because I need to investigate what sort of household help I'll need to run a B and B. Mom says most of the Mt. Dora inns have only one full-time housekeeper, but I'm thinking of hiring two and having them alternate workdays. The situation might be ideal for a student or a young mother, plus I'd have access to two employees if, heaven forbid, I should get sick or have to leave town.

I'm just about to skim an interesting article in *Innkeeping*, a trade journal for those who operate B and Bs and small inns, when I hear a knock at the front door. I look up and notice that the house has fallen silent—no sawing, no hammering, no yelling children.

I hurry to the foyer, half afraid Mitch has sawn off his arm. But he's standing in front of me, his ball cap in one hand and his estimate in the other.

"All done." He gives me a sweaty smile. "You want to come look?"

"Of course." I slide my bare feet into a pair of sandals by the door and follow him down the porch steps and across the lawn to the back of the house.

I'm impressed. Even in Fairlawn's early days, I doubt the porch looked this good. The new railing is wide and looks sturdy, plus Mitch has replaced the rotting, stick-straight spindles with spiral posts. I walk onto a floor that feels solid and smooth. Mitch has also left a wide opening between the supporting posts, providing more than enough room for Gerald to maneuver whatever he needs to transport into the embalming room.

Mitch is explaining something about footers and concrete when I nod and cut him off. "It looks wonderful. Well done. I'll still have to paint it—"

"I wouldn't use paint on the porch itself. Get a good water-repellent toner or semitransparent stain and put that on as soon as you can. You can paint the rails to match the rest of the house whenever you like."

"Okay." I smile and step back onto the lawn. "If you'll come with me to the office, I'll write you a check."

"Sounds good to me." He grins and hands me the copy of the estimate.

I take it and begin walking back to the front, but on the way I pull my reading glasses from my pocket and search for the bottom line.

What I see stops me dead in my tracks. The other bids I received for replacing the porch ranged from three to four thousand dollars. Mitch—whose mother promised my mother a good price—wants *six* thousand.

The butterfly beat of alarm thrums in my chest. There's no way I would have agreed to six thousand, even with gold-plated spiral spindles. But there's my signature, scrawled beside the word *accepted*.

I choke on something between a shout and a sob.

"Everything all right?" Mitch's concerned expression bobs into my field of vision. "You look a little pale."

I wave the estimate like a fan in front of my face. "This says six thousand, right?"

"Yep. Those posts, that pressure-treated wood—that stuff doesn't come cheap, you know."

"Six thousand dollars. Wow. Why . . . don't you wait on the porch?"

Somehow my feet regain their mobility, enough to drag my shell-shocked frame over the grass, up the porch steps, and into the office. I sit at my desk, take my checkbook from a drawer, and pick up a pen.

My hand trembles as I write in the amount.

※ ※ ※

Joella sets the tuna sandwich on a plate, then slices the bread diagonally and drops a handful of potato chips between the two halves. Jen has been working in the office all morning, too preoccupied to eat. She should appreciate a sandwich about now.

Humming "I Get a Kick out of You," Joella pulls a diet soda from the fridge and pours it over ice in a glass. Jen usually drinks from the can, but there's no telling what germs have been riding around on the top of that can: bird flu, West Nile virus, E. coli. One never knows.

She sets the plate and glass on a tray, then picks it up and heads down the stairs. A heavy silence cloaks the first floor, an almost palpable reverence—probably the emotional residue from so many funerals. Hopefully that stillness will be replaced by laughter and movement once this place becomes a bed-and-breakfast.

She turns at the last step and heads down the hallway. The door to the office is partially open, but no sound issues from the room, not even music from Gerald's old cassette player. Joella sighs. Maybe Jen went out and she's taken all this trouble for nothing.

She prods the door with the tip of her shoe and waits while it creaks open. Jen *is* sitting at the desk, but her head is bowed and her hands cover her face.

Joella winces at an instinctive stab of fear. "Jen?"

Her daughter lifts her head and swipes at a tear.

"Sweetheart, what's happened?"

Jen pushes away from the desk and stands. "Excuse me, Mom. I have to go to the bathroom."

Joella blocks Jen's path. "Did something happen with one of the boys? Is Clay giving you trouble again?"

"I don't want to talk about it. Will you please let me by?"

Joella steps out of the way as Jennifer stalks into the bathroom across the hall. The door locks with a definite click.

What in the world? Joella leans one shoulder against the wall, mystified. Jen was fine this morning at breakfast, so whatever upset her had to have happened between breakfast and lunch. Since the phone hasn't rung all morning, she couldn't have received bad news about Skeeter . . . unless she called and talked to someone. But she wouldn't keep that news to herself.

Joella sets the tray on the desk, moves into the hallway, and peers through the sidelights flanking the front door. No cars in the parking lot. No one's been to the house at all except the UPS man and Mitch Wilkerson, who finished up about an hour ago. Joella went out to peek at the completed project and was grateful that she'd be able to congratulate Ginger Sue on her son's talent and hard work.

So . . . Mitch finished. Jen is either upset because Charley Gansky still hasn't come by to fix the air-conditioning or because Mitch Wilkerson said something stupid. But what on *earth* could he have said? Jennifer isn't easily offended, and she has certainly heard her fair share of nosy comments about this house, her boys, and her divorce.

In search of a clue, Joella returns to the office and steps behind the desk. Several papers lie on the desktop, along with an open magazine and a legal pad scrawled with Jennifer's notes. Joella slides the magazine to the side and spies Mitch's estimate. Unable to read the figure at the bottom of the page, she lifts Jen's reading glasses to the end of her nose . . . and the figure there steals her breath away.

Six thousand dollars. *Six*. And Jen complained because one carpenter came in with a bid of four thousand!

Joella sinks into the chair as a wave of heat rises from her chest. Why, no wonder Jen is upset! Still, she signed the estimate, didn't she?

She did. Which explains why Jen isn't in here screeching to high heaven. She signed the estimate because she trusted Joella. This time, she shouldn't have.

Joella sits for a moment, then reaches out and cautiously lifts the flap on Jen's checkbook. The balance on the page is a fair sight less than it was a few days ago. And why wouldn't it be? Jen has paid deposits to the electrician, the air-conditioning installer, and the roofer. She's bought groceries and clothes and buckets of paint and primer.

And now she's paid the carpenter six thousand dollars.

Oh my. Joella grips the arms of the desk chair and pushes herself up. Only one thing to do, then. No matter how much it hurts.

※ ※ ※

I wait until I hear the sound of Mom's footsteps on the stairs; then I blow my nose one final time and creep out of the bathroom. I was hoping she wouldn't come downstairs until I had my act together, but, like Murphy's Law, where Mom can intrude, she will.

I walk into the office, close the door, and slide behind the desk. My papers are just as I left them, my checkbook undisturbed. At least Mom hasn't made matters worse by snooping.

I pull the legal pad with my to-do list from beneath the carpenter's bill. There's no way I have enough money to accomplish phase one, so I'm going to have to juggle some of my priorities. Maybe I can go with less expensive wallpaper throughout the public rooms and forget about my plan to replace the roof. After all, it'd be cheaper to patch the leaks and replace a few shingles. With any luck, we won't be here when the next major storm rolls through town.

I prop my chin in my hand and wince when I think about Sharon Gilbert. She's not likely to tempt fate by divulging potential problems, but I hope the buyer's agent doesn't ask about the roof's expected life span. I'll have to be honest, and I don't know anyone who'd pay full price for a house with a roof that's been patched together with tar and prayer.

I'm picking up the phone to discuss plan B with the roofer when someone knocks on the door. I set the phone down as Mother comes in.

"Jen—" her face twists in a pained expression—"I'm sorry about Mitch Wilkerson."

"What about him?"

"I saw his bill. I didn't mean to pry, but I couldn't help wondering why you were upset. I also saw your bank balance."

My face floods with heat. "Mother, when are you going to learn that I am not a child? I'm a grown woman, and I'm capable of handling my own affairs."

"But I want to handle this." She pulls her hand from her pocket and hands me a check . . . for six thousand dollars.

I push her hand away. "I can't take your money."

"But you would never have hired Mitch for that amount. You did it because you trusted me."

I tunnel my fingers through my hair and look away. What can I say? Mother has always been able to read me like a book. Maybe that's why I sometimes resent her. She knows me too well. "Mom, take that check back and—"

"No."

"Will you let me finish?" Ready to call a truce, I drop my folded arms on the desktop. "You're on a fixed income, and I won't let you spend your money on Fairlawn. We can split the bill if you want . . . and you can consider your half a contribution to the cause. In return, over the next year I'll try to have a room ready for you whenever you like. Just don't expect the guest suite if we have paying customers in the house."

Mom examines my face for a moment, then places both hands on the edge of the desk and leans toward me. "I know I drive you crazy, and I know you want to be independent," she says, her eyes glittering in the lamplight. "You're like your father; he was always out doing his own thing and leaving me to wonder what he was up to."

Where is she going with this?

She straightens and folds her arms. "I'm not trying to intrude. I'm trying to prevent you from making the same mistakes I've made, the mistakes your father made. He could be so blind at times." She gives me a brief look of helpless appeal. "Maybe I go overboard because I want to be everything you need. Since the divorce, I've been so glad to help, so grateful that you need me, but you are so much your father's daughter. . . ."

"Stubborn?" I whisper. "And blind?"

She smiles. "If I start to meddle, Jen, tell me to back off. But know that I'm meddling because I love you and the boys. That's all."

Suddenly the width of the desk yawns like a chasm between us. I stand and move toward her as she reaches for me. We meet at the corner and embrace.

※ ※ ※

My Fairlawn family is eating spaghetti and meatballs around the kitchen table when the phone rings. For a moment we all freeze, wondering if it could be another irate bed-and-breakfast owner.

Gerald waves a pasta-spun fork in my direction. "Might as well pick it up."

Against my better judgment, I answer the phone. "Fairlawn."

"The funeral home?"

"Yes." I look at Gerald and shrug. "Can I help you?"

The caller explains his purpose, which almost makes me laugh. "One moment please." I cup my hand over the receiver and give Gerald a victorious smile. "You know those caskets you need to get rid of? This young man is from the University of Central Florida chapter of Phi Alpha Delta. They're looking for a casket."

Gerald swallows a bite of meatball. "Somebody die?"

"Apparently not. They'd like to have one when school begins." I lower my voice. "I think it's some sort of initiation thing."

Gerald stabs his fork into the spaghetti and twirls with new vigor. "Absolutely nut. It's disrespectful. No Fairlawn casket is ever going to be trotted out in a parade, an initiation, or any such thing. Ours are reserved for the proper purpose."

Maybe I should remind Gerald that since I own the business, technically those caskets are mine. But he has a point, and my sons are listening. Giving this kid a casket wouldn't be respectful of the funeral industry or of Gerald.

"I'm sorry," I tell the young man on the phone. "Have you tried other funeral homes? . . . You have? Well, I'm sorry about that. But keep us in mind should you really need us."

I hang up as Mother cackles behind her napkin.

28

July 6 is an anniversary for me, but I am determined to ignore it. A shroud of melancholy threatens to engulf me when I wake, but I fend it off and get dressed, focusing instead on the arrival of our air-conditioning guy. Though I have every right to be depressed today, I can't restrain my almost hysterical delight at the prospect of eating, working, and sleeping in cool air.

After Charley Gansky arrives and heads upstairs with a thermostat, I sit in the office and study the *Mortuary Management* calendar on the wall. The photo for the month of July features a star-spangled casket lined with red and white satin.

Am I the only person in this house who finds that picture macabre . . . and significant?

My wedding anniversary has been replaced by three others: the day Thomas left me (July 6), the day he filed for divorce (December 4), and the day the divorce became final (May 15).

I am about to surrender to melancholy when Charley Gansky pops into the office and informs me that the missing thermostats have been installed and both air conditioners are functional. If I close the windows, my house should be as cool as an igloo in an hour or two.

I thank him, write out a five-figure check, and call for help as I hurry up the stairs to lower the windows.

An hour later, I am sitting on the sofa and marveling that the fabric no longer feels damp to my touch. When the phone rings, I find myself hoping it's someone to whom I can crow about *finally* having air-conditioning, but instead I hear a burly voice. The moving van loaded with all our worldly possessions is on its way to Mt. Dora and should arrive at Fairlawn in less than thirty minutes.

I let out a whoop and rush down the hall to tell the boys and rap on Mother's door. Then I hurry to the kitchen to make a fresh pitcher of lemonade. My helpers will be thirsty, and I want to make sure they're hydrated for the job ahead. Another day of progress lies before us, and this one will feel like Christmas.

When the moving van finally rolls down our street, it draws a crowd of curious townspeople in its wake. The driver pulls the big rig into the parking lot and performs a three-point turn, positioning the rear of the van as close as possible to our front door.

I'm impressed.

I skip down the steps to meet him.

"Mrs. Graham?" The blessed man actually winks at me. "You got somebody to help with all this?"

"We don't need much help," I assure him. "It's mostly boxes and a few pieces of furniture."

Bugs, Clay, and Gerald step out of the house. Mom waits on the porch while the boys run to the back of the truck, almost as eager as I am to get the thing unloaded.

The huge door rattles upward, and I see my own blocky handwriting on a big yellow box. Our stuff has been jammed into the van with another family's furniture, but we have no trouble recognizing our boxes.

Gerald adjusts his suspenders as he creaks down the steps. I'm about to tell him not to worry about helping when I spot Brett and Ryan Evans coming up the drive. I'm still a little uncomfortable about having Clay spend too much time with Brett, but it's obvious that the young man has come to help, not incite rebellion. Besides, Brett and Ryan have young backs; they can handle any heavy lifting while Gerald helps us unpack.

An hour later, a train of bright yellow moving boxes outlines the sidewalk. The driver hands me a clipboard and points to the line where I need to sign my name.

"Are you sure that's everything?" I ask Mother.

"It is." She waves my concern away. "Don't worry."

Easy for her to say.

I scribble my name across the bottom of the form and give the clipboard back to the driver. He touches the brim of his baseball cap, then climbs into the cab of his truck and blows the horn for the boys. The huge semi growls as he pulls away, and we begin to sort through our boxes.

I turn and nearly bump into Brett, who is carrying a box to the house. "You go inside, Mrs. Graham," he says, nodding toward the door. "We can handle this stuff."

I watch in amazement as Clay, Ryan, and Brett shoo us women toward the house. "Yeah, you don't have to stay out here in the hot sun," Clay says, sounding almost like his father. "Let us bring the boxes in. You and Grandma can unpack them."

With a small, bewildered smile, I let my son and his friend take charge. Mom and I go upstairs to the kitchen, where boxes have already begun to accumulate.

I rip the tape off the closest box marked *kitchen*. "I can't wait to find my wok. It'll be nice to have some stir-fried veggies." I toss the tape on the floor, lift the box flaps, and pull out a black nightgown.

Mom snorts. "Oh yeah, you need to keep that. Ball up some of that lace and you'd have a dandy pot scrubber."

I let the gown fall to the floor—why do I need it now?—and take out a soup ladle. "What in the world was I thinking when I packed?"

"You *weren't* thinking." Mom attacks another box. "You were upset, and that's okay. Now's your chance to figure out what you want to bring into your new life."

I leave the ladle on the table and step out of the kitchen long enough to look at the boxes piled at the bottom of the stairs. Why not be ruthless? Fairlawn is furnished—not with the furniture I'd choose but furnished nonetheless—and Thomas has had his chance to take anything he wanted from our home. This is my opportunity to get rid of anything that might remind us of heartbreaks and treacherous nannies.

"That's a good idea, Mom." I prop my hands on my hips and turn toward the confusion in the kitchen. "Anything we don't want, we'll put in boxes for the nearest thrift store—or for Lydia, if she thinks she can use the stuff."

"What about this one?" Mom turns the box she's opened, and I see that it's marked *baby clothes*.

My heart twists. There comes a time in every woman's life, I suppose, when she must say good-bye to certain possibilities. I had always thought Thomas and I might have a third child, but I'm thirty-nine, Thomas is still behaving like a middle-aged bad boy, and my baby is five years old. I should be able to surrender that box.

"The thrift store," I say, injecting steel into my voice.

Color me ruthless.

❈ ❈ ❈

"I didn't know you smoked," says Mavis Biddle.

I look up at the Queen of the Southern Sassies, who arrived with a contingent of Red Hatters to help us unpack. For a woman who spends a great deal of time each year outlining the details of her funeral, she is a remarkably hard worker. "I don't smoke."

"Then what's this?" Mavis holds up a flat piece of painted ceramic, but not until she tilts it toward me do I recognize the plaster hand-print Clay made in kindergarten.

"Oh! That's Clay's, so I have to keep that. If you'd put it in the memories box, I'd appreciate it."

She gives the handprint a quizzical look. "How long do you keep a thing like this?"

"As long as you can, I suppose."

She shakes her head and sets it in the box I've reserved for senti-mental objects. "Seems to me that you oughtn't keep things that col-lect dust. After all, if you need an ashtray, the child could make you another one."

My gaze drifts toward the wide window, through which I can see Clay and Brett breaking down boxes on the lawn. "But his hand will never be that small again."

Six hours later, my back aches, my fingers are sore, and our new air cleaner is working overtime to clear all the dust from the air. But we have opened and sorted every single box, and Lydia is ecstatically looking through the cartons we've designated as donations.

Ruby Masters and Gertie Whitehead, members of the Southern Sassies, dust themselves off, hug Mother, and take Miss Biddle home for her afternoon nap.

Even though the majority of our helpers have gone, the house vibrates with a refreshing sense of renewal, and I have to admit that I've never seen a house transform so quickly. Gerald has not uttered a peep of protest at the way we've rearranged things, and he's examined a couple of lamps from the thrift store box as though he might use them in his room. Brett and Ryan used Lydia's pickup to haul the nasty old upstairs couch to the dump; in its place sits my sofa and a matching love seat, both upholstered in a vibrant English chintz. The stiff, carved-back chairs from the foyer are on their way to Gertie's Antiques in the shopping district, and in their spots I've positioned two velveteen wing chairs from my former study. They look lovely flanking the grandfather clock.

Mother dumps two cluttered kitchen drawers into the trash can and refills them with implements from my kitchen. The Fairlawn phone rings a couple of times, but no one leaves a message. Maybe our harassing caller has realized we're going to stick around awhile.

When Lydia's truck hauls away the last empty carton and our neighbors return to their families, I walk into a dignified Victorian mansion that finally feels like home. Photographs of my children adorn the mantel in the south chapel. My favorite art calendar hangs next to the window above the kitchen sink. My bedspread covers the antique bed in the master suite, and tonight Clay will sleep beneath his beloved Star Wars comforter. Bugs will cuddle with his favorite fuzzy blanket, a treasure we had nearly forgotten.

Mom even snagged a few things for her room—pictures of the boys for her dresser and a crystal lamp she gave to me and Thomas as a wedding gift.

The only thing missing is . . . Skeeter. Bugs is afraid one of those unanswered phone calls might be someone with news about the dog, so I try my best to assure him that anyone calling about Skeeter would have left a message. "Besides," I remind him, "you put my cell number on the poster too, and no one has called that phone all day."

By sunset, I'm too tired to care about anything more than finding my bed and crawling into it.

But as I climb the stairs on this first night in a far cozier Fairlawn, I find myself looking forward to the work yet to come. I've never been the sort to loll around and do nothing; something in me will always yearn for a to-do list.

And Fairlawn has such a *long* list: we still have a roof to repair, an attic to insulate, termites to spray, an electrical system to replace, curtains to sew, walls to paint, and a kitchen to update. If we have the time and money, we really ought to replace the carpet in the office and the casket display area.

I chuckle. This place must be growing on me if I can feel at home in those two rooms. The entire Mt. Dora community might grow on me if it weren't for rampant gossip, devastating heat, and possible dog-eating gators.

At the top of the landing, I crouch next to a box of books—I hate getting rid of books, no matter how dilapidated their condition—and the sound of crunching gravel makes me pause. Rarely do people drive out here after dark, so something must be up. . . .

I hear a steady pounding on the door. I am about to stand and go down the stairs, but Gerald catches my arm. "It's for me," he says, and as he moves into the lamplight I see that he's wearing dark pants and a string tie.

I haven't seen him dressed like that on a weeknight since—

My heart tightens. "Who?"

"Mavis Biddle," he says, walking slowly down the steps. "Ryan's going to ride with me in the call car and help me bring her in."

I snatch a breath. "Mavis? But she was just here."

"I know."

I remain by the books, frozen. Mavis? She spent all morning helping me open boxes, and now she's *gone*?

As I watch Gerald descend the stairs, I move past the memory of my morning to the afternoon when I first looked into the woman's blue eyes and felt her fierce determination.

The image sharpens and I remember everything.

A few days ago, Mavis Biddle sat on my front porch and made me promise to give her a Red Hat funeral.

29

The next morning, Mother and I meet at the kitchen table, both of us stiff and sore. I had forgotten how demanding moving is, but my muscles are determined to remind me. For some reason, my feet feel like I've walked thirty miles, yet I haven't left the house in the last couple of days.

I'm about to pour a second cup of coffee when my cell phone rings from the depths of my purse. I can't imagine who would be calling this early, but a glance at the caller ID settles that question: Thomas.

I flip the phone open and shoehorn a smile into my voice. "Hello?"

"Hi, Jen." His voice is bright too. "How are the boys?"

I glance at Mother and shrug. "They're fine."

"Great. Hey, we're on vacation, so if you haven't signed them up for camp or something, I thought I'd spend a couple of days with my kids."

I close my eyes, amazed by the man's blithe ignorance. "Thomas, when do you have to be back at work?"

"Monday, of course."

I look up at the calendar by the sink. Today is the seventh; Monday is the tenth. Not a lot of quality time between those two dates.

"Thomas, do you know where I am?"

He laughs. "Did I catch you out shopping?"

"No, I'm at home."

"So, should I pick the boys up at your mother's?"

"I'm in *Florida*. The boys and I have been in Mt. Dora for a month."

He wouldn't know this, of course. He sends his child support payments to my lawyer, who deposits them in my account. For all I know, the payments are automatically deducted from Thomas's paycheck, so he never has to think about us.

He doesn't answer for a moment. When he does speak again, his voice is chilly. "That took some nerve, moving the boys to Florida without even telling me."

"I have custody; I don't have to tell you anything."

"But still . . . I thought you would want me to spend time with my sons."

"I did. I do. But we've been gone a month, and you never even noticed. In all that time, did you once think about calling the kids?"

"You know how crazy the Hill is. I barely have time to think about eating, let alone calling home."

"Unfortunately, I do know." When I worked on Capitol Hill, there were days I could almost forget I had children. If we hadn't had a dependable nanny, I don't know what we'd have done.

Then again, if we hadn't had an *attractive* nanny, we might not be divorced.

"Thomas—" I soften my voice—"believe it or not, I do understand. But if you want to be the kind of father our boys need, you're going to have to make a point of remembering to call. They miss you. They need you."

He exhales heavily into the phone, then clears his throat. "Why Florida, for heaven's sake?"

"A great-uncle left me his estate—a house called Fairlawn."

"Nice place?"

A wry smile twists my mouth. "It's . . . interesting."

"Okay." His voice becomes brusque and businesslike. "Well, you know the calendar—our summer break begins on August 7. Maybe I can find some time then."

"I'm sure the boys would like that. Let me know."

Mom lowers her coffee mug as I drop the phone into my purse. "Thomas doing well?"

"Okay, I guess."

"Does he want to see the boys?"

"He can't now . . . maybe later this summer. If he can squeeze them in." I don't mean to sound sarcastic, but bitterness bleeds into my voice. Mom understands, though, and the boys aren't around to hear.

I'm about to dive into a pool of self-pity when the Fairlawn phone rings. I make a mental note to call the phone company and ask them to install an additional line. I don't want my family to tie up the business line, nor do I want people calling at all hours to ask me to pick up a body.

Besides, when this place is functioning as a bed-and-breakfast, we'll need a reservations number. Maybe a Web page, too, and a way for people to make reservations online.

Gerald reaches the phone before Mother can grab it. He listens intently, then says, "I'll have to let you know." After hanging up, he looks at me. "Mavis."

I have an idea what he means, but Mother doesn't notice the tight line of his mouth. "Oh, does she want me to call her back?" she asks, getting up from the table. "Did she leave a number?"

"I'm sorry, Joella." Gerald's eyes darken with sympathy. "I thought you knew. Mavis is downstairs. She passed yesterday afternoon."

Mom's mouth goes round, a perfect O. "Mavis is . . . downstairs?"

Gerald takes a hesitant step toward Mother. "She took a nap yesterday afternoon and didn't wake up. Ryan thought it odd when she didn't come out for supper, so he went in to check on her. He called me last night, but this place was so busy. . . . I'm sorry I didn't have a chance to tell you."

In that moment I realize something that has not occurred to me before: if living in a funeral home means being the last family to care for our new friends, I'm not sure I'm up to the task. It's one thing to bury strangers and casual acquaintances. Burying friends is far harder.

And taking their money . . .

Against my will, my mind burns with the memory of the afternoon

I accompanied Mother to the funeral home in Fairfax. Mom was calm, even relieved that Dad's suffering had ended, but I was a nervous wreck. I knew how to handle the ticklish who, where, and when of a clandestine lunch meeting between a senator and his opposition, but I had no idea how to negotiate funeral arrangements.

The funeral director, Mr. Cecil Penny, had been a bald man with a fake smile, a clipboard, and a box of tissues. We sat in the parlor of his small mortuary and looked through a catalog of "resting vessels" for which no prices were indicated—and which, I believed, were being set at whatever level Mr. Penny thought we could afford. The man practically salivated when Mom mentioned that Dad had been a brigadier general and would be buried at Arlington. After that, Penny flipped to the front of the catalog and began to salt his advice with phrases like "worthy of the respect due your husband" and "befitting his position." I sat in complete shock when Mom finally selected a casket that cost nearly as much as a new car.

Mr. Penny must have recognized the look in my eye. He offered me a tissue.

By the time we left that meeting, I felt like I needed a shower. If a funeral director has to be pushy and plastic to make a living in the funeral industry, I don't think I'm cut out for the job.

Maybe I should call the nearest frat house and give all those caskets away.

❁ ❁ ❁

"I have here—" Gerald lifts the envelope I remember from a couple of weeks ago—"Mavis's last wishes for her funeral. You were all very special to her, so she wanted you to be here today."

I look around the circle of ladies who have gathered in the Fairlawn chapel to hear Mavis's funeral plans. Besides me and Mother, there are a half dozen other women, most of whom have come straight from church to attend this meeting. Knowing Mavis, I am sure they are all Hatters, though there's not a red hat in sight.

Gerald nods to a heavyset woman sitting near the door. "Eunice, she wanted you to stand by the guest book. Would you mind handling that responsibility for us?"

Eunice presses her handkerchief to her chest and lowers her head in grave assent. Gerald and I both know that no one needs to stand by the guest book; anyone coming through the door would see the book and know what to do. But everyone who meant anything to Mavis has been honored with a specific responsibility, and guarding the guest book is as dignified a duty as serving as a pallbearer.

"Ruby—" Gerald gestures to another woman—"you'll play the organ as guests arrive, correct? Mavis didn't specify any particular songs, but she did mention that she wants the service to feature happy music."

"Happy?" Ruby's tattered voice mangles the word. "I'll see what I can do."

"Thank you." Gerald glances at his list. "Edna, Irene, Myra, Ginger Sue, Alyce, and Frankie—she wants you to be pallbearers."

The women gasp in unison.

"Of course, you won't actually be *carrying* the casket," Gerald assures them. "It rides on wheels. You'll be guiding it, though, and I'll be right behind you to help. Believe me, if I didn't think you ladies could manage it, I wouldn't even suggest such a thing."

Forehead worry lines unravel as the six women focus their trusting gazes on Gerald.

Edna speaks for them. "We'd be honored to do this for Mavis."

"Mavis's minister will deliver a message," Gerald continues, consulting his notes, "and up to three people will be allowed to stand and speak. But no more than three, Mavis stipulated, and no one should talk for more than five minutes. She didn't want anybody hogging all the attention."

Irene cracks a smile. "I can just hear her saying that, can't you?"

"Oh yes," Ruby answers. "She was always the first to blow the whistle if someone got long-winded at a Hatter get-together."

Ginger Sue begins to giggle. Like a happy infection, her chuckle spreads around the room until even Gerald grins.

"I guess that's it." He folds Mavis's letter and slips it back into its envelope. "She did not want organ music at the recessional, but the kazoos are to play 'When the Saints Go Marching In.' If you think the other ladies can handle that, we're all set for the service."

Mavis's best friends smile and stand, dabbing at the corners of their eyes with tissues and handkerchiefs as they embrace. Their sense of relief is palpable—they've been dreading this brush with mortality, but Mavis has made certain the event will be as painless as possible.

The mourners might even enjoy themselves.

I stand too and prepare to smile them out the door. I've accepted that my part in what remains of this family business will be to serve as hostess when needed, and Mom has pointed out that the work will be good practice for being an innkeeper. Being a hostess at Fairlawn can't be any more demanding than being Senator Franklin's chief of staff.

The ladies file past me, murmuring quiet thanks, but the last woman, Alyce, tugs on my sleeve. When I lower my head to talk to her, she pulls me into a quiet corner of the chapel.

"I didn't want to say anything in front of the others because I didn't want to dishonor the queen's memory. But I saw Mavis right after she came back from your house—you know, the day she and the gals were helping you unpack your boxes."

A needle of guilt pricks at my soul. The doctor said Mavis's death was not unexpected; for years she'd been warned about her hypertension and potential heart trouble. Still, I can't help wondering if I was even a little responsible for her death. I shouldn't have let her come to Fairlawn on unpacking day. I should have made her sit down more often. I should have made her drink more water.

"I'm so sorry," I stammer, unable to meet Alyce's red-rimmed eyes. "I didn't know about her heart condition, so I didn't realize she was wearing herself out—"

"Oh, don't trouble yourself about that." Alyce's hand falls on my arm. "No one could stop Mavis when she made up her mind to do something. No, what I noticed that day wasn't her health." She lowers her voice to a whisper. "I noticed her nails."

"Her . . . fingernails?"

"Mavis was particular about her nails all the time. Wore 'em short and clipped, but she liked to keep them polished with a nice clear coat. She said you could always tell a lady by her nails. That's why I noticed her hands that afternoon. Her nails were dull and looked plumb awful."

Alyce doesn't say so, but the implication is clear—Mavis's nails looked bad because she'd been ripping open boxes and pulling out dust-covered books and knickknacks. Is Alyce trying to tear my heart out?

When I don't respond, Alyce hurries to make the point I'm apparently missing. "Jen, I would appreciate it if you'd make sure Mavis's nails get a nice coat of clear polish before the funeral. I know she'd be grateful."

So . . . this whispered conference isn't about making me feel guilty? I blink at Alyce and give her a relieved smile. "I'll be sure to mention it to Gerald. Thank you for bringing this to my attention."

Alyce squeezes my hand one last time and hurries after the rest of the Red Hat brigade.

By the time I clear away the glasses and napkins from our planning meeting, Gerald has disappeared into the preparation area. Maybe I ought to open the door and walk in, but I've never felt comfortable in that room, especially when a body's on the table.

And I can't forget that huge warning sign on the door.

Honestly, I'd rather that room didn't exist. But it does, and I need to speak to Gerald, so I walk to the end of the hall, knock on the prep room door, and wait. If he comes to me, I can talk to him in the doorway and not have to step in . . . and see Mavis.

"Come in," Gerald yells.

I grit my teeth and prepare to wait him out.

After an interminable interval, Gerald finally comes to the door, his face flushed and his brows arched nearly to his hairline. "Couldn't you hear me?"

"I can't come in." I tap the warning sign on the door. "Wouldn't want to break the law."

He rolls his eyes. "Ned and I put that sign there to prevent people from walking in on an embalming, but you can come in whenever you like. You're the boss."

I ignore this permission and cross my arms. "Alyce told me that Mavis's nails are probably in bad shape. She wants us to polish them before . . . you know. She said Mavis would want them polished before the funeral."

Gerald's mouth dips in a scowl. "I don't do nails. That's cosmetics."

"Will you tell Ryan, then? When he comes in to do her hair, make sure he takes a look at her nails. I think she must have ripped them up while she was unpacking boxes." I shake my head. "I feel like her being here is my fault."

"Are you now in charge of when people die?" Gerald asks, but there's no venom in his voice. He closes the door and leaves me in the hallway, but I don't mind. The smell of formaldehyde is beginning to turn my stomach.

I haven't taken three steps before I hear Gerald bellow, "Jennifer!" Urgency lines his voice.

My mind fills with images of him pinned to the floor beneath a pale, stonelike corpse.

Before common sense overtakes me, I open the door and peer into the room. Gerald is standing by one of the long tables, now covered with a sheet. Beneath the sheet is the unmistakable outline of a human body.

"Jen—" he snags my attention with a wave of his hand—"would you be a dear and bring me a glass of lemonade? My throat's awful scratchy this morning."

Since Gerald has never asked me to fetch him anything from the kitchen, I have a sneaking suspicion this request has more to do with getting me over my dread of the prep room than easing his thirst. But I trudge upstairs, pull the pitcher of lemonade from the fridge, and pour him a glass.

Mother lifts a brow as I walk by. "Thirsty?"

"Humph." I head toward the stairs.

I knock on the door of the preparation room again, and as I expect,

Gerald shouts his answer: "Can you bring it in, please? I'm a little tied up."

I do as he says, though my skin pebbles at the thought of entering the room. The air is cooler here and tinged with several distinct odors. The CD player in the corner is broadcasting a Mozart symphony while Gerald hums along.

Gerald's hands are busy with something near Mavis's neck, but he nods. "You can set the glass on the edge of the counter over there."

I maintain careful custody of my eyes as I walk across the room and place the lemonade on a stone coaster. Apparently it isn't unusual for him to get thirsty. What *is* unusual is his asking for fridge-to-mortuary delivery.

When I turn again, my hands are empty and I have no reason not to look up. But like a stubborn child, I keep my gaze pinned to the floor.

"Miss Jen." Gerald's voice is gentle, softly reproving.

"Hmm?"

"You don't have to be nervous about anything in here. Nothing in this room can bother you."

"I'm . . . being foolish, I know."

I remind myself of the things I know: Mavis is no longer in that body; she's in heaven. Gerald is working on a discarded shell, a worn-out temple.

An empty dandelion stem.

Slowly, I lift my gaze and look at the sheet-covered corpse. Mavis's pale shoulders are exposed, her white hair stands nearly straight up from her forehead, and her thin lips are pressed together. I am surprised; for some reason, I expected her to be gaping.

Two tubes penetrate Mavis's neck. One of them runs to a small tank on a nearby cabinet. The tank hums gently as the tube vibrates.

What in the world?

Gerald smiles at my obvious bewilderment. "This line—" he points to the tube connected to the tank—"pumps embalming fluid in. The second tube carries blood and other fluids out."

My stomach flip-flops at the thought of clotted blood and worse flowing out of Mavis Biddle.

I've seen enough.

"Thanks for the lemonade," Gerald says.

I lift my hand in some semblance of a wave and walk away as fast as my wobbly legs can carry me.

30

After dinner that night, I go to my bedroom and start to whip an inexpensive bolt of muslin into curtains for Clay's and Bugs's bedrooms. These won't be fancy window coverings, but they'll be new and fresh.

I've almost finished hemming the first pair when Clay comes in and topples onto my bed. He lies there, facedown on the comforter, until I stop sewing and look at him. "What's up, Son?"

He rolls onto one elbow and picks at the chenille bedspread. "I'm sorry, Mom. About everything."

My heart softens toward my stubborn firstborn. "I'm sorry too, kiddo. I know this hasn't been an easy summer for you."

He doesn't look at me, but he doesn't need to. I see the quiver in his chin and know he's resisting the urge to cry.

Thirteen-year-old boys don't like to cry.

I pick up my needle and stab it through the fabric. "Everything else going okay for you? Did you get all the stuff out of your boxes?"

"One of the kids at the park was giving me a hard time about living here."

So this is about more than the apology. "What'd he say, Clay?"

"He asked if this place grossed me out . . . and I said why should it? Then he asked if I'd ever seen a dead body, so I said no. He said, 'Why not? There's one in your house right now.' And then he told everyone

I was a chicken-livered pinky dweeb because I hadn't been downstairs to look. I wasn't sure what he meant, but I guess . . ."

"Hmm?"

"I guess I *am* whatever he said, because Miss Biddle is downstairs and I don't want to see her. So maybe I am chicken-livered."

I give Clay a look of gentle reproach. "I'm afraid that you're going to hear those kinds of comments as long as we have to stay here. Yes, we live in a funeral home, but funeral homes provide a really important service. Can you imagine what the world would be like without them? People would have to bury their own dead, and what a mess that would be."

Clay's worried forehead clears. "I guess."

"You can trust me on this. During the Black Death, a lot of people didn't know what to do with the dead, so they piled them up in the street. Germs and bacteria were everywhere, so even more people got sick. And that's just one reason funeral homes do a lot of good."

Clay squints at me, digesting these thoughts, and I wish I could think of a way to explain Gerald's business without resorting to the topics of disease and corpses. But those concepts will mean more to my adolescent son than terms like *closure, respect,* and *bereavement.*

"I saw Miss Biddle today." The words slip from my lips before I can consider the consequences.

Clay's eyes widen. "You saw her . . . dead?"

I nod, feeling nearly as skittish as Clay. "She was lying on that big table, covered by a sheet. Gerald was taking care of her."

"Did she—was she all gross and ugly?"

I pull another length of unhemmed curtain onto my lap. "She looked . . . unreal. Sort of like a statue. Anyway, I could tell I wasn't really looking at Mavis. The still-living part of her is in heaven."

"Did she—did she have fangs and long nails? My friend says that fingernails and teeth keep growing after you're dead."

I laugh. "Mavis is not a vampire, Son. She looked like a little old woman who died in her sleep. I'm sure she's looked better, but I'm also sure that Ryan will make her look beautiful for the service tomorrow."

My heart skips a beat as I think of Mavis's fingernails. I must catch Ryan tomorrow and tell him to apply a coat of nail polish.

I can't forget.

⁂ ⁂ ⁂

In less than a month, I've learned that the dying do not keep office hours or respect weekends. People expire at all hours of the day and night, so Gerald can't predict when the phone will ring. The sooner the embalming begins, the simpler the process, and I never know when the faint fumes of formaldehyde will begin to creep up the stairs.

Somehow I miss Ryan's appointment with Mavis Biddle. He must have come before sunrise on Monday morning, but I know nothing of his plans until I hear the front door slam just before seven. I look out my bedroom window in time to see the hairdresser walking away, his backpack slung over one shoulder.

I groan. I didn't get to tell him about Mavis's nails.

I throw on my robe and hurry to Gerald's room. Though he usually gets up with the sun, he's not in the kitchen, so he must have stayed up late to finish whatever he had to finish. In any case, he simply *has* to do her nails before the funeral, and it's supposed to begin in three hours.

"Gerald?" I rap on his door. "Gerald, are you awake?"

I hear a muffled reply; then he opens the door and looks at me through bleary eyes. "Did we get a call?"

"Nothing like that. Did you remember to leave a note for Ryan? About Mavis's fingernails?"

"You woke me for *that*? You can do her nails."

"Let's call Ryan. I meant to tell him, but he came early—"

"Ryan—" Gerald's voice is heavy and patient—"is mourning the loss of his landlady. He and Mavis were close. It wasn't easy for him to come today, and I don't think he'll want to come back before the service."

"But—"

"She's not casketed yet, so you go on. I'm going back to bed, but I'll be down in time to put her in the box."

245

His door closes with a clear little snick, leaving me in the kitchen with a load of guilt and a full-blown case of the willies. Something in me is ashamed to admit I can be rattled by something as common as death. After all, I'm a grown woman and a professional. I've endured political traumas—including a senatorial scandal and a run-in with the IRS—that would make grown men quake with fear. I've lost a husband, a house, and a nanny, a father and a Jack Russell terrier. . . .

Yet I can't seem to make myself go downstairs and apply a coat of nail polish to a dead woman's fingertips.

Get a grip, woman.

I pull myself up to my full height and try to remember what I told Clay last night. Funeral homes provide a much-needed service to the community. Morticians take care of the dead; they do things no one else wants to do, and they do it out of respect for those who have passed away and their loved ones.

I reach into the fridge and pull a bottle of clear nail polish from the butter compartment, then exchange it for a sheer pink. Pink would look more lifelike, wouldn't it?

Cinching my robe tighter around my waist, I head downstairs to the preparation room. The door is closed but not locked, and I inhale the clean scent of hair spray as I enter the room and turn on the lights.

In the gleam of the overhead fluorescents, Mavis lies on the table, her eyes closed, her lips set in a half-smile, her hair curled and shining like a white cloud. Her arms are bent so that her hands rest at her midsection.

Someone, probably Alyce, brought Mavis's favorite Hatter outfit, so she's wearing a red blouse, a purple skirt, and a matching purple jacket. For an instant I wonder how Gerald managed to maneuver a stiff body into such tailored garments, but then I notice a few telltale red and purple threads—the garments have been cut down the back and fitted around Mavis's form.

All she lacks is her red hat, which waits on the cabinet near the table. Bless Ryan's heart—he probably didn't know how to position a hat so it'd fit within the limited space of a casket.

I grab Gerald's stool from the counter and drag it to the table. I unscrew the nail polish lid. A sudden chill climbs the ladder of my vertebrae, but maybe I'm only feeling the impact of the air-conditioning.

I catch my breath and pick up Mavis's hand. I don't know what I was expecting—the chill of marble, I suppose—but though the skin is cool, it's far from cold. Her hand feels nothing like living material. It reminds me of carved wood—stiff and intricately detailed—but still only a reproduction of living flesh.

Ryan must have filed Mavis's nails, for the edges are straight and clean. I realize that this is enough to satisfy any observer, but I promised polish. So I dab the base of each nail with a drop of liquid, then draw the shiny coating toward the fingertip, covering each nail in three distinct strokes.

As I paint my elderly friend's nails, I can't help thinking about everything these hands accomplished in Mavis's lifetime. I didn't know her well, but I've learned a lot about her from her friends. These hands have comforted babies, sewn caps for orphans, prepared meals for her friends, and gathered food for the poor. These hands once played the piano for Mavis's church, they waved at her various beaus, and they picked strawberries at her uncle's farm in Plant City. These hands have polished furniture, rubbed away aches and pains, and shelved countless library books at the Christian Home and Bible School.

In so many situations, these hands demonstrated God's love for the lost and lonely.

When the last fingernail has been painted, I replace the top on the polish. Then, in an instant of inspiration, I position Mavis's red hat on her stomach and adjust her arms so her hands rest on its brim.

I step back to evaluate the effect. If I hadn't known otherwise, I might have thought that Mavis Biddle came in for a quick nap before her weekly Red Hat get-together.

I am about to go upstairs when the preparation room door creaks. I stand in place, overcome with a feeling of incompetence, but the feeling vanishes when Gerald smiles at me. "Wasn't so bad after all, was it?"

I shake my head.

"I couldn't go back to sleep." His smile broadens when he notices

Mavis's hat. "That's perfect." He jerks his thumb over his shoulder. "Would you mind wheeling in the casket? It's out in the hall."

A thousand protests rise in my mind, but I squeak out only one: "I haven't had my coffee."

"It'll only take a minute." Gerald runs his finger over Mavis's forehead as if checking the makeup application. "And I'll need your help getting her into the box."

How in the world did he function before I came along? Yet that's not a fair question, because Fairlawn had to close after Uncle Ned's stroke. Since I gave Gerald permission to complete his work, I suppose it's only fair that I help him reach the finish line.

I draw a heavy breath and move out into the hall. I stare, speechless, when I see the casket against the wall. I'm not sure anyone would consider a casket pretty, but this one is a lovely shade of purple . . . and someone has painted a vibrant red hat on the lid.

I'm not surprised, but I am curious. This is not one of the caskets from the display room.

I walk to the rear of the casket and give the gurney a tentative push. The metal conveyance moves easily, its rubber wheels rolling over the wooden floor with only an occasional squeak.

I wheel the casket into the preparation room. "Where'd you find this?"

Gerald grins. "Mavis special ordered it a few years back. It's been in storage out in the garage."

He takes the opposite end of the gurney and pulls it toward the left of the embalming table until the casket and Mavis are side by side. I step out of the way as he lifts the casket's upper and lower lids; I watch as he removes a satin sheet that covers a thin mattress. He pulls the mattress up and away, exposing piles of sawdust. I am mystified as Gerald moves the sawdust around, glancing from Mavis to the casket and back, smoothing the material. Finally I understand. This supportive layer will elevate the upper portion of Mavis's body once she is placed inside.

When Gerald is satisfied with his preparation, he returns the mattress and sheet to the casket, then gestures to me. "Put your hands under her legs," he says, miming the gesture, "and lift. We'll lift her on three. Ready?"

I swallow hard and step into position. Mother will have a coronary if she walks in on this.

I move to Mavis's feet, stand between her legs, and get a firm grip on each ankle. Gerald stands at her head, with his arms beneath hers. "One, two, *three*."

I groan as we lift Mavis from the table. I doubt the woman weighed more than ninety pounds in life, but she seems a lot heavier as we position her in the lacquered box.

I back away as Gerald fusses at the side of the casket. Even though the lower lid will be closed, obstructing any view of Mavis's legs and feet, he makes sure the lady's hemline is even before he places her shoes next to her bare feet.

"It's hard to get shoes on an embalmed body," he says. I glance over my shoulder, wondering if Ryan or someone else has come in, but apparently Gerald is talking to me. "If the family cares enough to bring shoes, I think they ought to go in the box."

This is not something I want to know, yet Gerald keeps up a steady stream of conversation as he makes minute adjustments to Mavis's hands and clothing. "Anything the family brings, I include in the presentation. Most folks have no idea what's being buried with the body, but that's okay. The family has a right to their comfort."

When he is finally satisfied with Mavis's appearance and position, Gerald closes the lower lid and places a piece of satin over the edge so it forms a curtain between the body and the bottom of the lid. "The apron," he says, settling the fabric in place. "Wouldn't you know this casket came with a red one?"

After one final tweak to the pillow, Gerald sidles next to me. He strokes his chin and lifts a brow. "So . . . what do you think?"

A week ago, I would have said I didn't care; whatever he wanted to do was fine. But things are different now. I know this woman.

I walk over to the casket, raise the edge of Mavis's red hat an inch so it can be clearly seen, and smile at the sight of her shiny, polished nails. "I think Mavis would be pleased."

31

$\mathcal{F}$lowers for the Biddle service begin to arrive shortly after nine: huge sprays of red and purple carnations, a blanket of red roses for the top of the casket, potted greenhouse lilies, and mounds of daisies—Mavis's favorite flower. Gerald and I position the bouquets around the casket, creating a virtual wall of blossoms in order to discourage people from walking behind the display.

At nine-thirty, Ruby Masters arrives to begin playing the organ. The first mourners arrive minutes later. At Mother's urging, I send the boys to Lydia's house so they can hang out with Brett during the service; then I slip into a simple navy and white dress that appears respectful without indulging in dramatics. Something tells me Mavis wouldn't have wanted her friends decked out in black, but the other mourners might not understand if I wear yellow.

By nine-forty-five, a veritable parade of vehicles is heading our way. The cavalcade pulls into our parking lot and raises a cloud of dust that settles over a sea of red hats as several dozen women and a few men walk up the front porch steps and enter the south chapel.

When I come downstairs, I find Eunice Daniels guarding the guest book, a crumpled tissue in one fist. She greets each guest with a sad smile and motions to the book on the stand. Most of the women hug Eunice, a gesture that evokes tears from those who were dry-eyed.

At ten o'clock, after a signal from Gerald, the organist holds the last chord from "Shall We Gather at the River?" Then she lifts her hands and lets them fall to her lap like a marionette whose strings have been cut.

The priest, taking his cue, stands and greets the assembly. "'I am the resurrection and the life. Anyone who believes in me will live, even after dying.'"

From my seat in the back, I lean forward, interested in the service. Mavis was a staunch Episcopalian, and I've never been to an Episcopalian funeral. In his black suit and white collar, the young priest looks out of place amid so much red and purple, but he sends a spirited smile winging over the crowd. He welcomes the guests and extends his hand, giving those present a chance to offer a eulogy.

I bite my lower lip and look around. Mavis gave us explicit instructions—she didn't want a big to-do, and she didn't want anyone to monopolize the service. But how can we stop anyone who's determined to make a speech?

Lydia Windsor, wearing her pencil behind her ear, is the first to stand and move to the small oak pulpit. "I'd just like to say that we're going to miss Mavis something terrible in the days ahead. In a small town, the loss of one is felt by all, especially when the one is as active as Miss Mavis. We will miss her traditions, her sense of humor, and her care for young and old. Mavis loved Mt. Dora and everyone in it, even the tourists."

A wave of laughter ripples across the group as everyone acknowledges what no one dares say aloud: though the downtown merchants depend upon the tourists to keep their shops alive, they aren't always thrilled about the traffic, litter, and havoc that can result from so many out-of-town visitors.

"Mavis—" Lydia lifts her gaze to the ceiling—"I'll miss you. But I'll see you again, so hold a place for me at the table, will you?"

I breathe a sigh of relief as Lydia takes her seat. If everyone else will only follow her example and deliver a *brief* word or two . . .

Mother groans when an elderly man stands next.

Grateful that at least one of us is up to speed on the town gossip, I lean toward her. "Who's that?"

She rolls her eyes. "That's Emmitt Hick."

Really. I've heard about the troublemaking Mr. Hick, but this threadbare man doesn't appear to have an ounce of spunk left in him. According to rumor, Emmitt Hick, owner of a downtown newsstand, has a chip on his shoulder heavy enough to make him walk with a limp. Apparently Emmitt's newsstand did not do well in the winter of '79, a fact he blames on the owners who closed the Lakeside Inn so a Hollywood director could use the grand old hotel in the filming of *Honky Tonk Freeway*.

"Everyone else in town loved the movie people," Mother told me after her first local Hatter luncheon. "They painted the hotel pink and even brought in an elephant to water-ski on the lake. But Emmitt Hick never got over it."

Now Emmitt walks to the front of the chapel, clears his throat, and grips the pulpit with both hands. "Years ago I asked Miss Mavis to marry me. I figured our two fine families ought to merge, since our ancestors were among the first to settle in these parts, but Mavis turned me down. I've asked her several times over the years, hoping to catch her between men friends, but she never gave me any reason to hope for more than polite friendship. So now, Mavis Biddle, I will ask one final time—will you marry me?"

Several gasps disturb the stillness, and every head turns toward the casket. Has the old man snapped? Does he really think Mavis will sit up and give him an answer?

I perch on the edge of my chair as the foyer clock ticks and wind whistles past the window. A drop of perspiration slides down the priest's temple as Emmitt stares at the woman in the casket. In the front row, Ginger Sue Wilkerson fans herself at top speed, while Ruby Masters looks about ready to topple from the organ bench.

Gerald, God bless him, saves us from disaster. He steps forward, takes hold of Emmitt's arm, and smiles at the crowd. "We all know that Mavis considered Emmitt a special friend," he says, as if this were a commonly accepted fact. "Emmitt, I daresay she considered you more a brother than a suitor, and what woman marries the man she loves like a brother? I'm sure if she were able to speak to us this minute, she'd say, 'Thank you, Emmitt, for this honor, but I'm singing with the angels now, and I don't have time for earthly pursuits. So go in peace, dear brother, and I'll see you on the other side of the river.'"

I exhale in relief as a half dozen Hatters respond with a smattering of applause.

Emmitt looks confused, but he allows Gerald to help him back to his second-row seat.

"We have time for one last speaker," the priest says, wiping his brow with his handkerchief as he looks around. "If anyone else wishes to say anything."

Edna Nance stands and turns, not bothering to walk to the front. "I'll take only a minute," she says, smiling broadly enough to reveal a smear of pink lipstick on her front tooth. "I loved Mavis like a sister, but I'm here to tell you she didn't bake that last prizewinning cake from scratch. I have it on good authority that she used a Betty Crocker mix. Mavis thought she'd take that secret to her grave, but I'm not about to let her." Edna sinks back to her seat with an abrupt thump.

I hold my breath and glance from left to right. To my surprise, the other women don't seem at all bothered by this revelation—either that or Mavis's secret had already been broadcast through town.

A flush rises from the priest's collar as he returns to the pulpit. "'Man, that is born of a woman, hath but a short time to live,'" he says, reading from a small black book, "'and is full of misery. He cometh up, and is cut down like a flower; he fleeth as it were a shadow, and never continueth in one stay. In the midst of life we are in death; of whom may we seek for succor, but of thee, O Lord, who for our sins art justly displeased?'"

I glance around the room. Several of the women are nodding along with the priest; a few others are telegraphing with flashing brows. Apparently I am not the only one who's never heard a traditional Episcopalian service.

"'Yet, O Lord God most holy,'" the priest continues, "'O Lord most mighty, O holy and most merciful Savior, deliver us not into the bitter pains of eternal death.'"

I cringe inwardly. I don't know where this reading comes from, but

I suspect it's far different from the comforting Scripture usually read at Southern funerals. If these people are anything like my mother, they want to hear about heavenly mansions and reunions at the River Jordan. They don't want to hear about bitter pains and eternal death.

"'Thou knowest, Lord, the secrets of our hearts; shut not thy merciful ears to our prayer; but spare us, Lord most holy, O God most mighty, O holy and merciful Savior, thou most worthy Judge eternal, suffer us not, at our last hour, for any pains of death, to fall from thee.'"

The wife of the Pentecostal pastor turns in her seat and gives me a sharp look—occasioned, I suspect, by this talk of falling away from Jesus. Surely she doesn't think the priest is implying that Mavis might not make it into heaven after a long and fruitful walk with the Lord. . . .

Just in time, the priest bows his head and begins the Lord's Prayer.

The flashing brows relax as the mourners recite the beloved phrases in unison.

At the last amen, Gerald steps forward and lifts his hands. "Mavis made a special request for our recessional. If those of you who are Red Hatters would pull out your instruments, Mavis wanted us to exit to the confident strains of 'When the Saints Go Marching In.'"

All thoughts of falling away are forgotten as the assembled mourners bend to search purses and pockets for kazoos. While they are occupied, Gerald tucks the apron inside the casket and closes the lid.

When the kazoos have been located, the players move into position against the wall and begin to hum the old tune. The six red-hatted pallbearers take hold of the casket's brass handles and guide the gurney toward the front door.

Eunice moves from her position by the guest book and clears a path by opening the doors. Despite the kazoos, a solemn air pervades the chapel as everyone stands to watch Mavis Biddle, queen of the Southern Sassies, pass one final time.

Just as the pallbearers turn at the last row, a white-and-black flash sprints through the door and enters the foyer, then darts toward the line of kazoo players. The creature begins to bark, and for a full ten seconds I stand stock-still as ripples of shock spread from an epicenter near my stomach. "Skeeter?"

He's dirty, his fur is matted, and there's some kind of rope dangling from his neck, but there's no denying the familiar bounce and sway of our beloved terrier. At the sound of my voice, he whirls and leaps into my arms, covering my face with kisses.

"Skeeter! Oh!" I try to hold him close and quiet his happy yaps, but the faces that turn to me are wreathed with delighted smiles.

Frankie Johnston even leans toward me in the midst of her pall-bearer duty. "Mavis would have loved that!"

When the last mourner has left the chapel, I send Skeeter up the stairs, step into the foyer, and wipe a tear from my cheek. The Hatters, including my mother, have moved down the porch steps and are getting into cars for the short drive to the cemetery. The somber crowd is relaxed now; Mavis's friends are smiling and laughing.

Not until this moment have I realized Fairlawn's potential to touch lives. The job wouldn't suit me, of course, but it seems a shame to ask Gerald to stop doing what he does so well. He is gentle with people dead and alive, diplomatic and thoughtful. I can't imagine him being plastic or pushy, and he encourages most people to arrange for their funerals well before the need arises. He's good at his job, so it's no wonder he resists the idea of turning Fairlawn into a bed-and-breakfast.

As for me . . . maybe I could manage a funeral home *and* a B and B, maybe not. Mt. Dora already has seven bed-and-breakfasts, two modern hotels, and the huge Lakeside Inn. Why do I want to add to the mix when Fairlawn is already a functioning business?

If I give Gerald my blessing to advertise, the mortuary might prove to be more profitable than a bed-and-breakfast. I've seen the need, and the work would definitely be easier. I wouldn't have to give up my room, cook, or do endless loads of laundry. I could learn how to handle intake interviews, and I would never—*ever*—push anyone to pay for something they don't really need.

I walk onto the front porch and watch as Gerald slides the casket into the back of the stately hearse.

For all its quirks and weaknesses, Fairlawn is a shelter for the bereaved. If Mom and I had gone to a home like this instead of visiting Cecil Penny's place, maybe I would be able to think of my dad's funeral without shuddering. We might have left the place feeling comforted instead of manipulated.

Sure, I used to be a master organizer on Capitol Hill, but I worked ten years in Washington without ever feeling that I'd accomplished anything of eternal significance.

Yet in the space of a single morning, Gerald and I have achieved something that just might qualify. We demonstrated that heavenly homegoings can be a joyous affair. We comforted a community and honored a fine woman with the respect she deserved.

And we kept our word to Mavis Biddle, sending her out the door with a glorious and spectacular Red Hatter kazoo band.

32

Over the next several days, I dust off every copy of *Mortuary Management* I can find. If I'm going to help Gerald run this place until the house sells, I want to understand as much as I can about the funeral trade.

The boys watch me read without offering much comment. They're delighted that Skeeter's home (the consensus seems to be that someone found him and tried to keep him), and they seem to understand that Mt. Dora will be our home for now.

"Fairlawn is a lovely old house," I remind them one night after dinner, "and the funeral business is a worthy occupation. If someone teases you about it, just smile. Don't take their comments personally, because people tend to joke about things that make them nervous."

Mother looks at me with a smile on her lips. "You don't say."

When I'm reasonably certain I can talk about the funeral industry without sounding like a complete imbecile, I ask Mom to keep an eye on the boys so I can invite Gerald downtown. A dart of suspicion enters her eyes, but she agrees.

I park the van in the thick shade of a live oak canopy; then Gerald and I walk awhile and browse the storefronts. Every few minutes a local resident stops us to remark on Mavis's funeral, and all the comments are complimentary.

"It's so nice to see Fairlawn back in business," the mayor's wife says, her eyes turning to slits in her smiling round face. "We've missed going to that homey chapel."

"Mavis would have loved it," another woman tells us. "Even with that high-toned minister, it was a perfectly lovely service."

Gerald thanks her and takes my arm, practically pulling me down the street. "That was quite a compliment, coming from Carol. She's your competition."

"She owns a funeral home?"

"She owns a bed-and-breakfast. But enough talk about work. I'll spring for two ice creams, if you're up for it."

"I'm always up for dessert. Just lead me in the right direction."

He does, and soon we are enjoying vanilla ice cream outside La Cremerie on Alexander Street.

After licking my way around the circumference of my overfilled cone, I smile at Gerald. "I'm glad you agreed to come with me today. I've been meaning to talk to you about Fairlawn and my role in the business."

Gerald's eyes twinkle behind his glasses. "I've been waiting for you to bring up the subject."

"Good." I nibble at the edge of my sugar cone, then hold it carefully in my lap. "I've decided not to turn the house into a bed-and-breakfast. Now I see that the funeral home provides a unique opportunity, and I'd like you to continue your work and feel free to do more than honor the contracts you already have. You can advertise, presell, raffle off post-mortem face-lifts. I'm fine with whatever you want to do as long as it's honest."

Gerald's lined cheeks gather up like curtains as he grins. "I'm glad to hear it. Your uncle Ned would be glad too. The thing is, though, that it'd be hard for us to take in new business with only one embalmer."

"Yes. Well." I nibble at my cone again and wipe my mouth with a paper napkin. "I've been looking at the books, trying to figure out how I can keep you employed and still afford to keep upgrading the house. So I propose that you allow me to take over the office—the ordering, billing, sales, contracts, all the paperwork. Teach me how to handle the intake interviews in a way that's not pushy. You'll keep doing the embalmings, of course, and letting me know what you need, but I think I can handle everything that happens outside the prep room. Together I think we'd make a great team."

Gerald doesn't speak but turns sideways in his chair and continues to lick his ice cream. A group of middle school girls passes with noisy giggles, but still he doesn't respond. Did I say something to offend him? Have I misread his intentions?

Finally he looks at me. "I appreciate the offer, missy. Because, you see, I *do* need an assistant. I'm not a young man, and though Ryan helps me out on occasion, he's not always around when I need an extra pair of hands. Sometimes I have to lift a body or transfer it, and I can't always do those things by myself."

A chill spreads through my stomach—a frosty feeling that has nothing to do with ice cream. "I'm not sure I can work in—"

"Family funeral homes like Fairlawn are pretty much two-man operations," he continues. "The phone can ring at any hour of the day or night. That means one of us has to be on call all the time. If I'm out of the house, you're going to have to be responsible for taking care of things."

"I can do that," I assure him. "I'll keep a notepad by the phone, and I've already talked to the phone company about putting in another line. I'm going to ask the electrician about additional phone jacks throughout the house—"

"There's more to the work than taking a message. If I'm out of town, you're going to have to take the call."

My mind spins with bewilderment until I realize what Gerald is saying. *Taking the call* means driving the call car to the home of the deceased and bringing the body back to Fairlawn in a zippered bag.

I push away from the table. "Gerald, I can't—"

"If you want us to operate at full potential, things might get busy. A mortuary chain might be able to afford someone who simply takes names and numbers, but your uncle and I used to split all the duties. Paperwork and bodywork—they're both part of the mortuary business, and they're both important. Fairlawn needs an apprentice, not an office manager, and I happen to think you'd be a good one. I hope you'll pray about it."

A dozen other options rise to the top of my brain, so I grab one and toss it to him. "I could hire an apprentice to help you. They work cheap, right?"

"You're not going to have much luck finding anyone around here. If you hire someone local and pay him apprentice wages, after a while he's going to want to leave and set up his own shop. You'll end up training your competition."

"What if we don't let him stay in the area? We could put a noncompete clause in his contract."

"I doubt you'd be able to enforce it. In this business, you grow close to your coworkers. I don't know why, exactly, but there's something about the intimacy of the work. The human body is vulnerable enough in life, but it's even more vulnerable after death because cuts don't clot and wounds don't heal. You learn to be gentle in this business, with your clients and your coworkers, and I wouldn't want to part ways with someone after working so closely with him. Would you?"

Thomas's face appears in the back of my mind—the husband with whom I have spent sixteen years and more intimate nights than I can count. With Thomas, I shared the birth of two children, my dreams, my silliest fantasies, my secret thoughts, and my far-from-perfect body. I allowed myself to be vulnerable with him . . . and he walked away.

"No," I whisper. "I wouldn't want to lose a close friend."

Gerald's eyes shimmer with sympathetic understanding. "I won't be around forever. When I'm gone, you're going to need to know how to run the place, to keep the business going. One day *you'll* need an apprentice. You'll want to find someone with a heart for ministry—someone who knows how to treat folks in their most vulnerable hours."

I'm about to argue that Gerald will be around at least as long as I am, but like a searchlight penetrating a fog, understanding illuminates a new and unexpected truth. Over the last few weeks, I've thought I was influencing Gerald's future. All the while, he's been hoping to influence mine. Unfortunately, he doesn't seem to realize that I'm thinking of Fairlawn as a temporary gig.

I give the man an uncertain smile. "You think I'm that kind of person?"

"I know you are. I've watched you with the townsfolk, your mother, and your boys."

"But if I went into this—really committed to it—I'd have to go to school, wouldn't I? And probably meet some kind of state requirements—?"

"You'd have to take classes and pass a state exam. The schoolwork will take about a year and a half. You're bright enough to finish the program in a year."

I look at the ice cream melting on my knee. "That's a long time."

"It's only time, Jen. Time that's going to pass no matter what you do with it." His hand reaches across the table and grips mine. "Women make fine funeral directors, and you'd be one of the best. You're sympathetic, organized, and bright. Promise me you'll pray about this."

Pray about it? I don't know what I'm supposed to do until Thomas comes around, but I know I *don't* want to go to school or become a mortician.

I can't run a funeral home. I get nervous around dead bodies, I hate the smell of chemicals, and I have two young sons to protect. Furthermore, I don't plan on staying in Florida. I want to restore the house, clear as much profit as we can from its sale, and go back to Virginia.

I've been praying plenty over the last few days, but my prayer list has been filled with requests for the boys and for Thomas. How am I supposed to make room on my list for mortician's school?

I would explain all this to Gerald, but I can't give him an immediate answer because he's asked me to pray about his offer. Prayer, if done properly, takes time.

So I nod, thank Gerald for his offer, and finish my ice cream.

33

ℐ carry my conversation with Gerald in my heart for a couple of days. I made the old man a promise, so I *do* pray about my role at Fairlawn. I tell God that I'm sure it's not his will for me to become a mortician, so would he please do something to make Gerald see that I'm not cut out for this business?

After praying, I wonder if my reluctance to fully embrace Gerald's idea is due to simple squeamishness, my reluctance to move here permanently, or something else altogether.

Fortunately, the Fairlawn phone has been quiet—none of our clients have died. Gerald spends every morning prowling the obits and often leaves the newspaper open on the kitchen table. I think it's his way of reminding me that people die every day, and a two-man mortuary could be picking up business that is going to Eustis and Tavares.

When Gerald isn't reading the obituaries, he's scanning the classifieds. I suspect he's looking for an apprentice, but I know he won't contact anyone until I give him an answer.

I can't tell him anything because I'm waiting on the Lord. If God is planning to show Gerald how useless I'd be in the funeral home business, he's taking his sweet time about it.

As the middle weeks of July pass in a sweaty blur, the boys spend most of their time playing video games with Brett or prowling in the wooded area behind the house. Mother spends her days looking through wallpaper books. She's not thinking of Fairlawn anymore; she's focusing on the Biddle House. Now that the Red Hat Society of Mt. Dora owns their own building, the Hatters have decided to redecorate the place from foyer to attic. Ryan Evans is overseeing the project, and Mother assures me that he has impeccable taste.

I'm still working on my to-do list. We have a new back porch and air-conditioning—*truly* an answered prayer—and I have finally heard from Bob McKee, of McKee's No Goofin' Roofin'. Trusting in Gerald's promise that a fully operational mortuary will bring in extra income, I've decided to replace the entire roof rather than patch the leaks. If we don't replace the roof, in hurricane season we may find ourselves relying on prayer and bubble gum.

McKee and his crew arrive on a Tuesday morning, before the sun has reached maximum blaze. I step outside and shade my eyes as I look up at the four shirtless young men spidering around the eaves, prying up the old roof with short, flat shovels. Brown shingles are raining off the turret and dropping into my scorched flower beds.

I am enormously grateful I haven't found the time to landscape the place.

Bob McKee comes over to me, clipboard in hand. He smells of tobacco and spicy cologne. "Mornin', ma'am."

"Good morning to you." I gesture to the roof. "Are they going to be okay up there? That's a pretty steep pitch."

"They're used to it." He mops his brow with a handkerchief and grins from beneath the brim of his baseball cap. "They'll spend most of the morning scraping off the old shingles and tar paper. Then they'll remove and replace any rotten wood—"

"That'll be a job."

"Aw, it'll go faster than you think. When the new wood is on, they'll spread tar and cover it with tar paper. Tomorrow, we'll get the new shingles nailed down."

I lower my hand. "What if it rains tonight?"

"You don't have to worry. It's the tar and paper that actually keep the water out; shingles protect the paper and are mostly for decoration."

"Really."

"No goofin'." He touches the brim of his ball cap. "I leave you in good hands, Mrs. Graham."

I let him go, then turn to watch the men on the roof. One of them, at least, has tied a rope around his waist and secured the other end to the point of the turret, but the others are moving around as if they don't believe they can fall.

I want the mortuary to bring in extra money, but I don't want to earn it by killing off our workers.

I leave the roofers to their work and go into the house, where I pause in the foyer to breathe deeply of the cooled and dehumidified air. After fully appreciating the marvels of modern technology, I climb the stairs and find Mom on the sofa, an open wallpaper book on her lap. The television is tuned to one of the morning talk shows, but Mom is probably only half listening.

I sit at the other end of the sofa. "Mom?"

"Mmm?"

"Can I ask you something?"

"Of course." She lifts her gaze and looks at me with an expectant expression. Maybe she knows what I'm going to ask; she has a knack for picking up undercurrents in the house.

"Gerald and I had a talk the other day. I told him I want to take over the bookkeeping and paperwork for the mortuary, but he said he really needs an apprentice before he can start going after new business. He thinks I could do everything he does, but I'd have to go to school and I'd have to help him work, you know, with the clients. *After* they're dead."

Mom smiles. "Were you hoping to embalm them before they die?"

"I'm not joking. I want Fairlawn to be successful, but I really don't think I'm what Gerald needs."

Mom turns a page in the wallpaper book. "When you were about thirteen, you once told me you'd never have children because you couldn't stand the thought of wiping a baby's behind. Then you grew up and had two boys. I never once heard you complain about diapers."

"That's different."

"Is it?" She taps a pattern on the page. "What do you think about this? Too busy for a kitchen?"

The pattern under her fingertip features dozens of rotund French chefs bearing steaming platters of something. "It's okay."

"I don't know. What if we get tired of it?" She turns another page. "You used to get woozy at the sight of blood, but when Clay was learning to walk and split his chin open, you didn't even flinch. He bled all over your kitchen floor, but you pressed a dish towel to his chin, strapped him in his car seat, and drove him to the emergency room."

"I nearly fainted," I remind her, "once I handed him over to the doctor."

"My point—" Mom looks up from the book—"is that you're adaptable. You learned how to clean baby vomit from a suit coat, so I'm sure you could learn to do whatever a mortician does. And you'd do it very well."

I cross my arms, irritated with my mother's impassive compliments. I thought she'd laugh at the idea of me helping Gerald, and I *know* she wants me to sell this place and go back to Virginia.

"If I *did* pursue this," I continue, "what good is a mortuary degree going to do me in Virginia? When we go home, I could easily find work in politics."

"You weren't having any luck before we came down here."

"That's different. I was only looking for work on the Hill. But I could be a lobbyist or work at one of the embassies. . . ."

In the kitchen, the phone rings. I pause and wait for the sound of Gerald's footsteps, but instead I hear the refrigerator door slam, followed by Clay clearing his throat. "Fairlawn Funeral Home," he sings out, his voice a younger version of Gerald's. "You stab 'em; we slab 'em."

I rise from the sofa as a frisson of horror snakes down my backbone. I'm halfway to the kitchen when Gerald's bedroom door opens.

Clay hands Gerald the phone. "Some woman wants to sell you a newspaper subscription."

When my grinning son walks by, I snag his arm. "Not so fast. What do you think you're doing? That's a horrible way to answer the phone."

Clay's smirk evaporates under the heat of my glare. "The lady thought it was funny."

"She hasn't just lost a family member." I release his arm and exhale slowly through my teeth. "Please, Clay, that's a business line. You have to treat callers—*every* caller—with respect. Understand?"

He nods as the back of his neck heats to red, then hurries away.

When his bedroom door slams, Mother chuckles. "You have to admit that was funny."

"That was awful. What if that had been one of our clients on the phone?"

"It wasn't. But look at you, all worked up. Maybe you're more invested in the family business than you realize."

Of *course* I'm invested in the family business. I'm counting on it to provide the money to fix up this house and get us back home. Back to the life we left . . . if it still exists.

I sink onto the sofa and stare at the television, where a talking gecko in a convertible is babbling about auto insurance. Faint thumps and scrapes come from overhead as Bob McKee's men strip the roof off my aging house.

My roof isn't the only thing being exposed this morning. For some inexplicable reason, I feel vulnerable from head to toe.

I lean forward and catch my mother's eye. "What's up with you? Last week you couldn't wait until we moved back to Virginia."

She shrugs, but I spot the quiver of her lower lip. "Maybe I've had a change of heart."

"Did the Red Hatters elect you queen or something?"

"They most certainly did not. It's just . . ." She lowers her gaze to that blasted wallpaper catalog.

But I'm not letting her off the hook. "Mom, what's going on?"

She closes the big book with one swift movement and folds her hands. "I've been praying ever since we got here," she says, tears sparkling in her eyes, "and a couple of days ago I realized I haven't been really praying at all. Every night I've been worrying on my knees, showing God a to-do list even longer than yours. After Skeeter came home, something occurred to me: in my prayer time I've been doing all the talking, but Bugs simply asked . . . and waited. Isn't that more like what prayer is supposed to be?"

She looks at me, a question in her glittering eyes, and I can't answer. Prayer is talking to God, and that's what she's—what *I've*—been doing. We talk, God listens, and God acts. That's been the pattern ever since I learned "Now I lay me down to sleep."

All this heat has muddled my mother's good sense.

I get up off the couch and move toward the kitchen.

"Jen?" Mom calls, a note of concern in her voice.

"It's okay." I pull out a plastic pitcher from the cupboard. "I'm going to take ice water and some plastic cups outside for the roofers."

If I'm considerate, maybe they'll do an extra-good job for us. Fairlawn deserves a decent roof . . . no matter who lives beneath it.

❧ ❧ ❧

After watching the roofers cut out several sections of rotten plywood and scrape off the last bit of tar paper, I decide that Fairlawn looks particularly vulnerable with her bare beams and attic exposed. Since this operation is far too much like surgery for my taste, I go inside and announce that I'm heading to the library if anyone wants to join me.

Bugs begs to come along, but Clay wants to stay and hang out with Brett. Mom decides to curl up with her wallpaper books.

Fine with me.

Bugs and I hop into the van and drive out to the W.T. Bland Public Library, a low-slung, gray structure on North Donnelly Street. The building looks more like a ranch house than a library, but they have a decent children's section and several computers for Internet users.

I get Bugs settled at a table with a stack of picture books before I slip into one of the computer carrels. After entering a few search terms, I gather and print the information I need.

If I should decide to become Gerald's apprentice, before I can be licensed as a funeral director I will have to pass the national board exam. The state of Florida will also require that I have a high school diploma—check—and a certificate of completion from a mortuary college program with classes in anatomy, chemistry, restorative art, microbiology, embalming, pathology, grief counseling, accounting, and funeral service law and ethics. The local community college offers a mortuary curriculum, but that's a lot of information to process in a short time.

I think about my dwindling bank balance and mentally subtract tuition fees. My half of the equity is evaporating at a steady rate, but if we expand the funeral operation, we could replenish that account. By how much? I have no way of knowing.

I glance over at the reference librarian, a dark-haired woman in glasses and a cardigan sweater. She's reading something at her desk, but I hope she won't mind if I pick her brain. "Excuse me?"

She looks up. "Yes?"

"Hi. I'm Jennifer Graham, and I've recently inherited Fairlawn—"

"I know who you are, Ms. Graham." Her features harden in a look of disapproval. "Can I help you?"

For an instant I wonder what I could possibly have done to offend her; then I give her a thin smile. She must be related to one of the bed-and-breakfast families.

"Every morning—" I hold up my newspaper—"I check the obituaries in the *Daily Commercial*, so I've seen that most people are using funeral homes in Eustis or Tavares. We've been on hiatus, but I'd like to make sure Mt. Dora can support its own mortuary."

The librarian folds her pale hands. "And how, exactly, can I assist you?"

I lean on the desk and read her name tag. "Well, Ms. Prose, I was hoping you could help me understand the mind-set of these people. If there's some way we can appeal to their loyalty—"

"*These people,*" she says, a hair of irritation in her voice, "are no different from people anywhere else. Now, is there some reference book I can get for you?"

I back away from her desk. Obviously Jacqueline Prose is not feeling inclined to help me strategize. I force a smile. "Never mind. By the way, in case you haven't heard, Fairlawn will not be joining the ranks of Mt. Dora's bed-and-breakfast inns."

A flicker of confusion fills her eyes, then cools to disinterest.

I spin on the ball of my foot and walk away, ready to collect Bugs and go home.

At moments like this, I could gather my loved ones and drive back to Virginia without hesitation. I am beginning to appreciate the neighborhood where we didn't know our neighbors and the boys had no reason to play outside. Falls Church had no gators, only occasional mosquitoes, and rain fell from the sky in a steady, predictable stream. Nights there brought a breath of cool air, even in summertime, and winter meant fluffy snowfalls, toasty jackets, and tiny white lights in the evergreens flanking our front steps.

I make sure Bugs buckles his seat belt before I climb into the driver's seat and lower my head to the steering wheel. God brought Skeeter home in answer to our prayers.

So why is he waiting to resolve the more important crises on my prayer list?

*　*　*

When the phone rings after dinner, Bugs is the first to reach it. I brace myself for another goofy greeting, but my youngest has learned a lot from watching Gerald. "Fairlawn," he says, followed by, "Hi, Dad!"

I try to keep my heart calm and still as Bugs chats with his father, but my pulse pounds double time when he hands the phone to me. "He wants to talk to you, Mom."

Surely this is no big deal. Thomas probably needs to set the date for his visit with the boys, so I take the phone and steel my nerves for a conversation with the man who hasn't been out of my thoughts a single day.

I'm grateful when Mom herds Clay and Bugs downstairs and onto the front porch.

"Thomas?"

"Jen, how are you?"

I open my mouth to answer, but he doesn't give me a chance.

"Listen, I need to come see you and the boys. We need to discuss something important."

My heart lurches as my gaze travels to the calendar. It's mid-July, and the congressional break doesn't begin until early August. Thomas must be taking time off, and he never does that unless—

I lower my voice to a whisper. "Are you *sick*?"

He laughs. "Don't worry. This is a good thing; I think you'll be pleased. So, what about next weekend? I was thinking about driving down and staying at a hotel for three or four days, maybe doing Disney with the kids. There *is* a hotel in that tiny town, isn't there?"

"A couple of them. And seven bed-and-breakfasts."

"A hotel will be fine. Tell the boys I'll be there sometime Saturday, and give them a hug from me. I'll see you all in a few days."

After he hangs up, I stare at the phone and wonder if I should pinch myself. What in the world has happened to my ex-husband? The last time we spoke he couldn't find room in his schedule to spend a single day with his kids, and now he wants to spend a long weekend with all of us.

Is this the miracle I've been waiting for?

I place the phone on the hook and stare at the speckled pattern on the old linoleum floor. I'm glad Mom and the kids went outside because I don't want to face their questions now, don't want them to study my face.

I don't want them to get their hopes up.

And yet . . . Thomas is taking time off, something he never does. He's coming here, which means he not only wants to see the boys— he wants to see *me*.

I press my hand to my chest, where a dormant kernel of hope has just cracked through a crusty shell. I shouldn't allow myself to hope for much, but what if the man has finally come to his senses?

My imagination supplies a cynical answer: maybe the nanny dumped him. Fiona must have walked out, taking her designer bags and unconventional attitudes, leaving Thomas sadder but wiser. Now he's realized what he sacrificed on the altar of wanderlust. Now he wants to come home. He'll pull into our driveway with a smile on his face, get out of the car, open his arms, and beg us to take him back.

How I would *love* to refuse him.

But that's my temper talking; I recognize its tight little voice. I'm hurt, I'm angry, and I've been betrayed. The selfish imp that hides in my heart wants Thomas to suffer because he's made me suffer. . . .

Yet *reconciliation* is a lovely word.

Maybe that's why the Lord hasn't given me a clear indication of what I'm supposed to do about Fairlawn. If Thomas and I reconcile, the boys and I will need to go back to Virginia sooner than we expected. We could make the move by the end of summer so the kids won't have to enroll in Florida schools. That'd give Gerald time to find himself a real apprentice. The renovation is coming along, so maybe he could oversee the remaining items on my list.

I have to admit I'll feel a pang of loss if I have to leave Fairlawn now. I've invested a bit of myself in the curtains, the color of the new shingles, the paint on the porch railings. Thomas won't appreciate the house, of course. Fairlawn is not at all his taste. He'll want us to replace this charming old Victorian with something big and brick and close to the Beltway.

Come to think of it, Thomas may not appreciate the differences in *me*. Time changes everything, and I'm not the same woman he left so many months ago. That woman didn't know how to cope with desertion; one night she took too many Tylenol and nearly lost her life. She blamed the incident on oral surgery, but the ache in her jaw was nothing compared to the anguish in her heart.

That was Thomas's doing . . . and he has never apologized for it.

Yes, the man is a scoundrel with lousy timing. He's going to show up right when we're beginning to feel settled in Mt. Dora. But he's the father of my children and the only man I've ever truly loved.

I move through the deepening shadows in the hallway and rummage in the bottom of my underwear drawer until I find the blue satin box. Inside, on a tufted velvet bed, are my wedding band and engagement ring.

I slip both rings on my finger and notice that they are not as loose as they were during the stressful time of the divorce. Fairlawn has been good for us—either that or I'm retaining water.

The round diamond winks in the dim light, reminding me that it has lived in this spot, on a vein traditionally believed to lead to the heart, for sixteen years.

If God is faithful and Thomas is true, this ring will soon be residing there again.

34

Grateful to be out of the house, Joella breathes deep of the morning air and smiles at the lacy canopy of a sprawling ear tree. On the other side of the van, Clay slams the passenger door and scowls. He didn't want to come with her, but Joella insisted she needed his help at the grocery.

"Isn't this nice?" She drops her keys into her purse. "It isn't often you find a tree growing near a parking lot, but it'll help the van stay cool while we're inside."

Clay shoves his hands into his pockets and hunches toward the store, leaving her to follow.

She retrieves the shopping list from her purse and hurries after him. She's not surprised at his bad mood. Everyone has been snappish since Thomas's call. Jen keeps saying his visit is no big deal, but she's been cleaning, polishing, and watching the roofers like a raptor. Joella understands why Jen might want to impress Thomas, but that man isn't going to appreciate the dust-free tables or the new shingles.

The automatic doors of the grocery slide open, baptizing the new arrivals in a wave of cool air. Joella feels her shoulders relax—maybe it's the weather that's made the family so irritable. The new air conditioners are working beautifully, but people still have to go outside.

She consults her shopping list. "Clay, why don't you grab a couple of loaves of that cinnamon raisin bread you like so much? I'll be in the produce section; then I'll head over to the cereal aisle."

"Whatever."

Joella feels the corner of her mouth quirk as Clay slouches away. The boy is thirteen, reason enough to be moody, but he's been in a dark mood for the last couple of days. She's beginning to wonder if he's upset by Thomas's impending visit.

Joella grabs a cart and steers it toward the produce section. The lettuce looks good today as do the greens. The boys don't care much for salad, but Jen could live on it, especially if Joella mixes in bits of baked chicken.

She's about to reach for a head of lettuce when a pair of speakers on the display begins to rumble. She waits, smiling, as thunder cracks and the automatic system sprays a fine mist over the produce.

While her lettuce takes its shower, she leans on the cart and looks around the store. Albertsons is having a special on bakery products—buy one pound cake, get another free. That's a good deal, but neither she nor Jen needs to indulge in cake. Gerald might like it, though, and both Clay and Bugs tend to like plain desserts. . . .

"Mrs. Norris?"

She turns to find Brett Windsor and Jessica Fowler standing behind her. "Why, hello! What brings you two to the grocery store?"

Brett gives her an abashed smile and jerks his thumb toward the pretty girl. "She, um, wants to bake a cake."

"From scratch." Jessica lifts her chin. "My mom says it's not that hard."

Joella smiles. "I'm sure you'll do fine. Is someone having a birthday?"

"Just wanted to show him—" Jessica tilts her blonde head toward Brett—"that I could do it."

"Well, have fun."

"Thanks."

Joella smiles as the two teens walk away. Only in Mt. Dora could anyone find such a sweet and old-fashioned girl. She can't recall Jennifer ever trying to impress her boyfriends by cooking for them— Jen was more likely to debate them to death.

She shakes her head, then spots Clay standing at the end of the bread aisle. He's watching Brett and Jessica as they cross the front of the store . . . and he looks like a boy who's just struck out with bases loaded.

Joella sighs as understanding dawns. The boy hasn't been moping around because Thomas is coming. He's upset because his best friend has been spending a lot of time with someone else.

"Clay," she calls, "come help me pick out a nice head of lettuce, will you?"

He walks over, eyes downcast, and drops two loaves of raisin bread into the cart.

The automatic mister has stopped, so Joella props a finger on her chin and squints at the produce. "What do you think?"

The boy barely lifts his head. "I dunno."

"Want a nice chicken salad sandwich for lunch? I could make it with that mayonnaise you like."

"Okay."

"Do you want a slice of lettuce with that sandwich?"

He rubs one sneakered foot over a black mark on the tiled floor. "I guess."

"That sounds good." She picks up the nearest head of lettuce, drops it into the cart, and looks over the tops of the aisles, searching for Brett's dark head. Maybe she should move toward the checkout to avoid distressing Clay any further, but she needs a jar of mayonnaise. Maybe she can help Clay think of other things as they walk over to that part of the store.

"So—" she keeps her voice light as she leads the way—"are you excited about your father's visit?"

Clay shrugs. "I guess."

"Your mom is glad he's coming—for your sake, I mean. I'm sure he's missed you boys."

She cringes when the sound of Brett's laughter floats over the shelves. "My, that sounds like Brett." She glances at her grandson. "Have you seen him today?"

"He's here," Clay says, his shoes *plop-plopping* on the floor. "He's with that girl."

"I see." Joella slows the cart and squeezes Clay's shoulder. "You haven't seen as much of Brett lately, have you?"

Clay won't look up, and Joella knows why. No young man wants to bare his soul and reveal deep disappointment in the canned goods aisle.

"I know it's hard—" she lowers her voice—"but one day you'll meet a special girl, and you'll want to spend as much time as possible with her. Brett still likes you. But he likes Jessica in a different way."

Clay uses his knuckle to wipe something from the top of his cheek, then tilts his head toward the door. "Can we just get out of here?"

She turns the cart toward the checkout stand. "Of course we can."

The mayonnaise can wait.

❧ ❧ ❧

When Saturday morning arrives, I'm up before the sun. I tiptoe to the kitchen, where I make coffee, scrambled eggs, and Thomas's favorite coffee cake. I'm about to whip up a batch of biscuits and gravy when I hear a car door slam.

I glance at the clock. Thomas couldn't arrive this early, could he? Not unless he is as anxious to see us as we are to see him.

I check my reflection in the mirror, fluff my hair, and hurry down the stairs. Before flinging the door open, I peer through the sidelights beside the front door . . . and gape.

Daniel Sladen is coming up the front porch steps, a package and my newspaper in his hand. I watch, bemused, as he sets both items by the door and turns away.

I step out and catch him in the act of descending the porch steps. "Hey, if that box is a letter bomb, you'll be convicted. I'm onto your nefarious activities."

A sheepish smile sweeps over his face. "I didn't want to wake everyone. I'm volunteering at the Home and Bible School today, but I wanted to drop that off."

I look down and whistle at the silver-wrapped package. "Pretty fancy. What is it, a housewarming gift?"

"Why don't you open it and see?"

Is he joking? I bend to pick up the rectangular object. The silver paper is heavy; the man certainly knows how to wrap a present.

"It's not my birthday." I peel the paper away and smile at the cookbook in my hands. "Are you hinting for a dinner invitation, or is the rumor mill reporting that I can't cook?"

He grins and props one foot on a step. "Look at the tab."

I turn the book and spot the sticky tab attached to one of the pages. Curious, I open to the marked recipe . . . and laugh. "Strawberry muffins?"

"I heard that Carol Conrad was miffed about your attempt to snitch her secret recipe. So I thought I'd supply you with a formula you can call your own."

I can't stop a giggle. "Honestly, I can't believe this town."

"I have it on good authority that Carol's specialties are nothing but honey muffins with red food coloring. But these—" he points to the cookbook—"call for real strawberries. I checked."

I close the book and hug it to my chest. "Thank you. You have been a bright light in a foggy harbor. A lifeline to a drowning family. A voice of reason in a babble of confusion—"

"I can tell you used to work in politics." He turns and moves down the sidewalk. "Have a good weekend."

I watch him, noticing for the first time that he's not wearing his lawyerly dress shirt and pants. He's in khakis and a polo shirt, and the effect is . . . nice. "By the way," I call, "what are you doing at that school?"

"Judging a science fair," he answers over his shoulder. "I hear there's an experiment involving gerbils and algae muffins. Remember to keep those off your bed-and-breakfast menu, will you?"

"There's not going to be any menu." I step to the end of the porch. "Actually, I'm glad you stopped by because I wanted to ask you something."

His eyes rest on me, alight with curiosity. "Ask away."

"Thomas, my ex, is coming in later today. He wants to talk. If things go the way I think they will, we'll be going back to Virginia, and I'll need someone to finish up my renovation projects. Could you—would you—check the work of the last couple of contractors? I still need to hire an electrician and a painter. I'd ask Sharon to do it, but I want her to concentrate on selling the property."

Daniel slips a hand into his pocket. "I suppose I could do that."

"You wouldn't have to do much. Sharon will handle all the showings."

He opens the door of his car. "Just let me know."

Is that a note of disappointment in his voice? I return to the doorway and wait until he puts the car in gear; then I send him away with a final wave.

Joella sits on the porch, her hands supporting the book she's been trying to read for the last two hours. Her eyes keep skimming the page, but the words aren't registering. Her mind is too occupied with worries, too shadowed by the fact that Thomas could arrive at any moment.

Jen says she's excited. She keeps dropping hints about going back to Virginia, but Joella can't convince herself that her daughter is doing the right thing. Despite the heat, the bugs, and the gators, Fairlawn has begun to feel like the sort of place Jen and the boys could call home.

Joella lifts her eyes above the edge of the page. Gerald, Bugs, and Clay are sitting on the front porch steps, where Gerald is showing the kids how to work with some kind of putty. Bugs is thrilled with the stuff, enthusiastically twisting the material in his hands. Clay is watching with what looks like mild interest, but Joella can see a spark in his eyes.

Gerald has been good for the boys. The old man has warmed up to them, as Joella hoped he would. In the last few days, he's been more of a father than Thomas ever was.

She looks up as the front door opens and Jen steps onto the porch. She smiles at Clay and Bugs and drops into the empty rocker at Joella's side. "How's the novel?"

"Pretty dull." Joella abandons her pretense and closes the book. "Did Thomas say what time we should expect him?"

Jen stares out over the parking lot. "Not really. I was even thinking about running over to The Home Depot and picking up some plants for the flower beds."

"Better get something hardy. It's still awfully hot."

"Impatiens?"

"Periwinkle would be better. You'll have to water them in for a while, though."

Jen nods thoughtfully at the yard. "I could do that. We'll be here another month at least."

There she goes again, hinting that Thomas is coming to sweep her up in his arms, but Joella knows about men like Thomas. And she doesn't want her daughter to be hurt again. "You know, I've been thinking."

"You're always thinking, Mom."

"About Thomas."

"And?"

"I know you want to reconcile, but I'm not sure it's the right thing for you. The man's no good, Jen. He's—"

"He's my sons' father. And he's my husband."

"Not anymore. You had reason to divorce him."

"I didn't divorce him. He divorced me. And if he wants to come back, I'll forgive him. Maybe that'd be a good thing for the boys."

"You don't sound very sure."

"It's been a while; that's all. We've changed."

"Thomas needed to change."

"Maybe we both did. Maybe this time we'll be better than we were."

"Or maybe you'll make the same mistakes again." When Jen doesn't respond, Joella presses her advantage. "Look at Clay and Bugs. See how patient Gerald is with them? When's the last time Thomas sat with them like that? He was always at work. Your boys never saw him except on weekends."

"They saw him. And they love him."

"What has he ever done for them?"

"He provided a home."

"*You* did that as much as Thomas."

"He . . . he taught them."

Joella snorts. "What?"

"He taught them . . . how to belch at the dinner table."

For a moment Joella is startled by her daughter's frankness; then she laughs.

Jen rises and moves behind the boys. "What are you all doing?" She kneels beside Bugs and touches the soft lump in his hand. "What is this stuff, Gerald?"

The old man winks at her. "Wax."

"Like car wax?"

"We use it for facial reconstruction. But it's fun to play with."

The meaning of his words goes over Bugs's head but not Joella's. Okay, so maybe a mortician isn't the most well-equipped babysitter, but the kids are having a good time.

Jen extends her hand. "Can I play with that stuff for a minute?"

Joella watches as her daughter presses the wax against her palms, flattening it like a pancake. She tests the material, working it with her fingertips and warming it with her hands.

Jennifer has always been able to adapt. She's strong, even in her denial, and she'll stand up to whatever trouble Thomas brings into town.

But even Jen's strength has its limits. How will she cope if Thomas breaks her heart again?

36

$\mathcal{N}$ot wanting to miss Thomas's arrival, I ask Gerald if he'd mind picking up some bedding plants for me. Mother volunteers to go with him, but as they walk to the Plymouth, I hear her grousing about having to go out in the heat of the day.

As they drive away, I realize that Mom is as anxious about Thomas's arrival as I am. She's made her feelings about him clear, but like me, she is chafing with curiosity about the purpose of his visit.

Mom and Gerald return before Thomas arrives, so I'm on my knees beside the flower beds when my ex-husband's black SUV kicks up dust in the gravel parking lot. The boys spill down the stairs and race to see their father while I stand and tug off my dirt-stained gloves. On the porch, Mom's rocker ceases its regular rhythm, and Gerald turns from the newly planted periwinkle he's been watering.

I drop my gloves on the grass as Thomas picks Bugs up and spins him around. He wraps Clay in a bear hug, then grabs a brown shopping bag from the backseat. With the bag in his hand and a son clinging to each arm, he teeters up the sidewalk.

His eyes finally meet mine. "Hello, Jen."

"Thomas."

"Can we sit and talk somewhere?"

"Let's go inside." I pause to introduce Gerald, whom Thomas greets warmly, and I gesture to Mother, still in her rocker.

She inclines her head in a regal nod. "Thomas."

"Joella. You're looking good."

"Thank you."

I wait for Mother to return his compliment or ask about his trip, but she has wrapped herself in a shroud of disapproval that not even Thomas's smile can penetrate.

I open the front door and wait in the doorway as Clay and Bugs disengage from their father. Freed of their clutches, Thomas embraces me as if he's afraid I might crumble at his touch. I return his hug, careful not to seem desperate or needy. He's wearing a new cologne, and the cheek he presses against mine is soft and freshly shaved.

"You look good," he says.

"I *am* good."

If Thomas has come back to us, I want him to know that we have gotten on with our lives. I've come a long way and made a life for us in this place. I may not have him anymore, but I do have a measure of self-respect.

He enters the foyer and glances into the south chapel. "You have someplace more comfortable?"

"Our living room is upstairs."

"I'll follow you."

Clay, Bugs, and I lead the way into the sitting area. As Thomas and the boys make themselves at home on the sofa, I lower myself into the wing chair. I may end up on the sofa and in my ex-husband's arms, but first I have to let him see a woman of dignity, a woman worthy of his admiration. First I want to hear what miracle has brought him to this moment of rapprochement.

"Well," Thomas says, opening the shopping bag, "let's give out the goodies, shall we?"

Bugs's eyes light with surprise. "We get presents?"

Yes, Son, I want to say, *presents are required for guilt-free partial parenting*, but I keep quiet as Thomas pulls gifts from the shopping bag. Maybe this isn't about guilt. Maybe it's about making peace.

"For you." He hands our oldest son a video game.

"Wow." Clay's voice is flat, and when he flashes the box toward me,

I see that his father has just given him Madden, the Nintendo game Clay has been playing for six weeks.

"Hope you like it, sport." Thomas punches Clay on the shoulder, then reaches into the bag for another box. "And for you, kiddo, I have this." He takes out another video game—this one labeled *preschool* and decorated with dopey-looking ladybugs in primary colors.

Bugs's countenance falls, but he remembers to mumble, "Thanks, Dad."

I smile and give Thomas credit for trying. A year ago I might have bought the wrong things myself.

Thomas—looking better than ever—laces his fingers and looks around our small circle. "So . . . what's new with you guys?"

Bugs begins to jabber about Skeeter's narrow escape from the unnamed dognappers, while Clay simply sits and smiles at his dad.

Thomas makes quiet assenting noises during Bugs's story, but I can tell he's not really listening. The man obviously has something more important on his mind.

"Bugs—" I use my firmest voice—"let's take a break and hear why your father came all this way, okay?"

Thomas flashes me a look of gratitude and inhales a deep breath. "I've driven a long way—" he smiles at Bugs and Clay—"to tell you something very important."

The kids settle into stillness and look at him, naked hope shining in their eyes. I fold my hands and lean on the chair's armrest, trying to maintain my ice princess facade.

"Well." Thomas clears his throat. "I guess there's no easy way to approach this."

"You're with your family." I offer him a peacemaker's smile. "You can say whatever's on your mind."

"Good." He claps his hands on his knees. "First of all, I want you to know that I have four tickets in the car. First thing Monday morning, we're going to Disney World."

I blink as the boys erupt in shouts. I've been promising to take them to the Magic Kingdom ever since our arrival, but somehow we've never found the time.

"That's great, Dad!"

"Super sweet!"

"Monday? That's—" Clay stops to do the math in his head—"forty-eight hours, right?"

"Close enough." Thomas flashes a dazzling grin and looks to me for approval. Clearly he's pleased with their reaction, but I'm not sure it's wise to play Santa Claus in July.

Maybe I'm overreacting. I smile and watch my kids cavort on the rug. Clay is doing his best imitation of a running back who's just scored at the Super Bowl, and all I can do is ask myself why I'm not feeling the same joy.

"And now—" Thomas claps for their attention—"I have something else to ask, and I hope it makes you just as happy."

Clay and Bugs stop jiving and listen, excitement pulsing behind their wide eyes.

"I'm getting married on August 12 . . . and I want you boys to be in the wedding."

I close my eyes as a cry of relief breaks from my lips. Finally! He has realized the truth; he has come back to us. He's picked the date and told the boys, so all we have to do is choose the place and tell Mother. . . .

I open my eyes when I realize the boys aren't dancing. We sit in a quiet so thick the only sound is the tick of the foyer clock. Thomas's face is grim, his mouth set in a pale line, and I feel the truth all at once, like an electric jolt to my spine.

I can't breathe. He didn't say *we're* getting married. He said *he* was getting married.

He didn't mention me at all.

I can't move. I can't speak.

Clay recovers first and asks the obvious question. "You're not getting married to Mom?"

Thomas clears his throat. "I'm marrying Fiona. You remember her, right? You liked her a lot when she was your nanny."

Thomas must not realize that his news has frozen me, because he keeps talking as if he has no idea he's just shattered my future. "The wedding is three weeks from today. Your mom can put you guys on the plane, and I'll pick you up at the airport." He looks at me. "We can ask for that unaccompanied minor arrangement, right? I'll have one of Fiona's friends drive them back to the airport after the reception."

From some corner of my selfish heart, acid is dripping into my smile. In a minute or two it will burn clean through, leaving me lipless and raw, but now I manage to look at my ex-husband and shape my mouth to speak. "You thought this news would make me *happy?*"

Thomas Graham—scoundrel, father, former love of my life— squinches his face into a question mark. "You've always said you don't want the boys visiting as long as Fiona and I are living together. Well, we're getting married. Fiona said that'd make you happy."

I close my eyes, suddenly glad that Mother and Gerald are outside. I am going to explode at any moment, and the resulting mess isn't going to be pretty.

She. Thought. I'd. Be. Pleased.

I narrow my eyes and hold Thomas in a death-ray gaze.

My ex-husband is not blind, nor is he stupid. Warned by what he sees in my face, he pushes himself up from the sofa. "Sorry to disappoint." He backs toward the stairs. "I suppose I miscalculated."

I clench my right hand while Clay looks at me, his eyes dark and questioning. Grateful that I've held it together so far, I give my son a reassuring smile while my nails carve half-moons into my flesh.

I'd like to push Thomas down the stairs, but that clueless charmer is the father of my children. Because he holds that title, I will treat him with civility. I will sit still and smile while he leaves our house. I will bite my tongue while he hugs the boys and declares his intentions to marry the woman who destroyed our family.

"I'll swing by later to pick up the kids for dinner," he calls, moving down the stairs with a careful side step.

I can't resist asking a thorny question: "Did *she* come with you?"

He looks at me, his expression pained. "I wouldn't do that to you. In fact, I wouldn't do any of this. Fiona's the one who keeps insisting we have to get married."

Bugs's internal radar has picked up on the turbulence. His slender throat bobs as he looks at me. "Mom?"

I give him a wavering smile. "Would you like to eat with your dad tonight?"

"Around six o'clock?" Thomas calls. "Is that good for you?"

I'd planned to have Lydia and Brett over for burgers and hot dogs, but I can change our plans.

I reach for Clay's hand. "If you'd like to eat with your father, that's okay. You can tell him about your summer."

Thomas turns when he reaches the landing. "I'll be at the Hampton Inn. If something comes up, call me there or on my cell."

The three of us wait until the front door closes; then Clay looks at me. "Did you know about this, Mom?"

I massage a tender spot at my temple. "Your father has always been full of surprises."

"Sometimes I hate him."

The sight of anger on my impressionable son's face is enough to temper the burning at my core. "Sweetheart." I squeeze his hand. "Your father is not perfect, but he does have good qualities, and he loves you."

"I hate him." Clay's words hang in the silence like noxious gas.

Bugs's gaze darts from my face to Clay's as if he's waiting to see if it's safe to breathe in this highly charged atmosphere.

"When you're older—" I pull Bugs toward me—"you boys will understand that no one is all good or all bad. Wise people ask God to help them overcome their weaknesses. The people who aren't so wise . . . well, sometimes they make a lot of mistakes before they realize how badly they've hurt others. Your father hasn't been very wise lately . . . and neither have I. But I'm trying to learn."

Bugs nestles closer, burrowing into the soft space between my neck and shoulder. "If you want, Mom," he says, "I'll stay home. I don't want to be in a wedding."

I release Clay's hand, give him another smile, and rest my cheek on the top of Bugs's head. "We'll talk about this later."

❊❊ ❊❊ ❊❊

Joella turns in her chair as the door opens and Thomas steps onto the porch, alone. No boys swing from his arms this time, nor is Jen in sight.

Joella feels something relax within her.

Thomas pauses in front of the door to pull his keys from his pocket; then he frowns in a way that makes Joella wonder if he's trying to remember something or trying to forget.

"Did you leave something?" she asks.

He looks at her then, his mouth curling as though he would give anything to spit. "No."

"Will we be seeing you again?"

"I'm coming to get the boys for dinner. And we're doing Disney on Monday."

She shifts her gaze to the horizon. "Oh."

"I never meant to hurt them," he says. His credible attempt at coolness is marred only by the thickness in his voice.

"Of course not," she answers. "Hurt is a by-product. It's what gets dished out on our loved ones when we seek our own way."

A flush of anger darkens his jawline. "You don't know what happened. All you've heard is her side of the story."

"I know men like you, Thomas. I was married to one." She waits, certain he will argue, but after a moment she hears the jingle of his keys and his step on the porch.

As he drives away, Joella knows she will go inside and see fresh pain carved into Jen's face. Clay and Bugs may be excited about the things their father has planned, but they also love their mother. They'll be unsettled because she's upset.

If only she could sweep Jen and the boys away from this misery! If she could, she'd fast-forward through these uncertain days and let time resume its normal speed when Jen's wounds have healed and the boys have passed through the turbulent adolescent years.

But that's not how time operates. One day of life rolls seamlessly into the next, bringing yesterday's sorrows and memories with it.

Those events blend into us, becoming an inextricable part of who we are.

Like indistinguishable waves, today will move into tomorrow, just as mothers remain mothers long after daughters become mothers themselves.

37

Gerald must sense my sorrow, because he comes into the house and invites Bugs and Clay to go with him to the park. From the window I watch the three of them strike out across the lawn; then I walk to my bedroom and sit in the heavy silence. Something in me wants to talk to Mother, but first I have to be alone.

I lie back on the bed and stare at the ceiling, noticing for the first time that fuzzy strands of cobwebs dangle from the blades of the fan. I thought I'd dusted every square inch of this house, but I've never looked at the fan from this perspective.

I press my hand over my mouth in anticipation of a crying jag, but the tears don't come. I've shed bucketsful over the last year, but not even the dying embers of false hope can spark a tear from me now.

In some ways, I think divorce is harder than widowhood. When a husband dies, even unexpectedly, the wife must feel a sense of closure. A soul has returned to the Creator; a body returns to dust. The widow doesn't have to worry about running into her deceased partner at church or the grocery store. She doesn't have to go through the house tagging furniture, knickknacks, and family photographs with *his* or *hers* stickers. The widow grieves, she says good-bye, and she moves on with her life.

I've grieved and said good-bye, yet I can't seem to move past Thomas Graham.

Why can't I let him go? What I feel for him now isn't love—not really—because love is nourished by daily giving and receiving. I wanted to reconcile with Thomas for my sons' sake. I wanted him to come home so Bugs and Clay would have their father. I wanted to be a family again, and I didn't want to keep sleeping alone.

I wanted to stand on the moral high ground and smile as he knelt at my feet and begged me to forgive him.

But do I want *him*? Something in me will always admire Thomas Graham and marvel at the way he works a room. But I don't know what he wants these days. I'm not sure I know who he is. I think he will always be fond of me, maybe even grateful for giving birth to his sons. He will always think of the boys with affection . . . when he stops to think about them.

Maybe Mother's been right all along. Thomas is a crowd pleaser, an expert politician, a fine diplomat. But he's not a good man.

Like the dust strings on the ceiling fan, that thought swirls above me.

Thomas will not reconcile; we will not remarry. The Lord has answered my prayer with a resounding no.

I tilt my head and focus on the tenacious tails of dust. The fan is turning on low speed, and I can barely feel its breath. One day, when I have the energy, I'll climb up on the mattress and wipe those strings away.

But now I have to bury a dream.

It's not the first time I've had to face disappointment. I took ballet for years, dreaming of dancing in the spotlight as a prima ballerina . . . until I grew taller than the few boys in my class. Madame DeFarge tried to convince me to keep dancing, but I knew my frame was too long and lanky to fill a star's slippers.

As a senior in high school, I fell hard for Greg Overstreet. He asked me to marry him when we'd been dating six months, and I was thrilled when he bought me an engagement ring. I brought him in to share the news with my parents, and my hopes turned to dust when Mom and Dad smiled stiffly and said we were too young. They would not give their blessing . . . and I knew I couldn't ask God to bless us if I rebelled against my parents' wishes.

After college, I brought Thomas home to meet the folks. Though Mom didn't care for him, Dad adored him, so Thomas and I were married.

I exhale softly in the silence. Burying a dream ought to be easy since I've had some practice. But it still hurts.

I feel Mother's presence before I hear her voice. "It's okay," I tell her without sitting up. "I'm fine."

I hear the soft pat of her sneakers as she steps into the room. The bed sags as she sits next to me.

"How'd you do it, Mom?" Now, against my will, water rises in my eyes. "How'd you manage to stay married? You're so much like me, but I couldn't pull it off—"

"Don't give me too much credit, Jen. You're right about us being alike. We're so similar that you married a man just like your father. Because he was like your father, I knew Thomas wasn't the type to stick around."

I swallow hard. "Daddy stuck around."

She makes a sound deep in her throat. "I never wanted you to know this, but maybe it's time. I cried at your father's funeral not out of sorrow but out of simple relief. For the first time in years, I knew I wouldn't have to worry about where Nolan was at night. I like knowing he's tucked away up there at Arlington."

I push myself up onto my elbows. "Dad *cheated*?"

"Like a tomcat, until he got sick." She rubs her nose with the back of her hand. "Remember all those secretaries he used to meet for coffee? They weren't secretaries."

"I can't believe you'd put up with that. Why didn't you confront him?"

"I did. But I had you to consider. We moved around so much that I didn't feel like I belonged anywhere. My family was gone, so if I left Nolan, you and I would have been on our own with nothing. After a while, it became easier for me to ignore his infidelities. To accept him. But I swore I'd teach you to never let a man hurt you the way I'd been hurt."

My mother is chockablock with secrets. I look at the woman as if for the first time, seeing in her pale skin and blue eyes a resolve I've never noticed. She has always carried herself like a monarch. I used to think that queenly quality rose from something in the marrow of her bones, but now I think it developed out of necessity.

Regal aloofness protected her from my father's philandering.

Some women cocoon themselves in their husband's love. Our husbands forced Mother and me to brace our spines with independent determination.

I shake my head and drop back to the mattress. "Men. What good are they?"

"Don't say that, honey, not even as a joke. You're raising two precious boys, and they're going to be good men because you'll teach them to be faithful. Look at Gerald—he's a good man; Daniel Sladen is kind, and I think Brett Windsor has the right stuff. There's hope for you and your boys."

I turn my head toward the window, where a stiff breeze has begun to rattle the sash. The breeze is welcome; maybe it will dispel the stifling heat that lies over the ground like a damp blanket. The western sky is dark with the approach of sagging clouds, and this, too, cheers my sore heart.

Rain washes clean.

Clay looks shocked to find me dressed for church the next morning. "We're going?"

"Yes." I stroke a quick application of mascara onto my lashes. "So brush your teeth and get moving."

"But, Mom!"

"No buts, young man, get ready. I'm going to get Bugs dressed, and then we're going to church with Grandma and Gerald."

He disappears, and though I know he's not happy, I have to admit that the time feels right. Mt. Dora has been our home for over a month; it's time we threw out an anchor into the community.

Our reception at the Mt. Dora Community Church is even warmer than I'd expected. I spot several of the Hatters, each of whom comes over to compliment me on Mavis's funeral. Sharon Gilbert waves at me from the other side of the sanctuary, and Annie Watson nearly hugs the breath out of me before I remember that we met at the Coffee House.

Daniel Sladen attends this church too. For a moment I can't place the slender woman who shares his hymnal; then I see her narrow hands and remember: Jacqueline Prose, the chilly reference librarian.

We sing, we smile as Annie Watson's young daughter sings a solo, and we listen to the sermon. Clay sits with folded arms, closed eyes, and a bowed head, but I know his pout will pass.

Though I couldn't repeat a word of the sermon by the time we exit the building, the touch of God's Word has soothed my heart. I'm still numb from Thomas's news, and my future is yet uncertain, but my spirit is encouraged.

※ ※ ※

I pick up a pizza on the way home, and the boys have eaten half of it by the time I've changed into shorts and a T-shirt. As Clay tosses an uneaten crust onto his paper plate, I ask him to finish weeding the flower beds along the south side of the house.

"I need to get the rest of those plants in," I say. "And right now those beds are too weedy to work."

Clay isn't thrilled with his assignment. "But I wanted to hang out with Brett this afternoon."

"You can hang out after the flower beds are weeded. The sooner you get started, the sooner you'll be done."

After cleaning up the kitchen, I pull a few sections of the Sunday paper from the basket near the coffee table and scan the headlines. Amazing how little I care about the world of politics these days. I used to spend Sunday afternoons reading the *Washington Post*, the *Washington Times*, and the *New York Times*; now I'm content with a quick glance at the *Daily Commercial.*

After giving Clay a half hour to make progress on those flower beds, I walk outside and put on my garden gloves. Three flats of periwinkles are waiting on the south side of the porch, but when I peek around the corner, there's no sign of Clay.

Not even a spadeful of overturned earth.

I bite down on my lower lip as irritation tightens my nerves. Did he think I was kidding? Maybe he assumes he can get away with something because his father's in town.

I head for Lydia's. Clay and Brett are probably sitting in the shade of her backyard, drinking Cokes and laughing at whatever teenage boys laugh at. I'll try to be calm when I find him, but I'm going to set him straight when we get home.

Lydia's house is quiet as I approach. Twice Loved Treasures is officially closed on Sunday, though the whirligigs are still twirling and the sign still swings in the breeze. I walk along the side fence until I can peek into the backyard. I spot Lydia's lawn chairs but no boys.

I rub my hand hard through my hair, then realize that I'm wearing dirty gardening gloves. Great. Now I'll have to shampoo again to get the sand off my scalp.

"Jennifer?" Lydia's sun hat rises from the cluster of thick vines along the fence. She laughs when I jump. "Sorry, didn't mean to scare you. I'm pulling weeds."

"Funny you should say that. I was looking for Clay, who's supposed to be doing the same thing at our house."

Lydia scans the backyard, then looks toward the lake. "I haven't seen him. Of course, I haven't seen Brett, either. He took off after lunch and hasn't come back."

"If you spot Clay, will you tell him to come right home?"

Lydia releases a knowing laugh. "I'll tell him you were looking for him. I won't mention the part about you being ready to skin him alive."

"Thanks." I take one last look at those empty lawn chairs and stride back up the hill.

39

I fully expect to find Clay hiding out in his bedroom, but when I slam the door open, the room's empty. I ask Bugs if he's seen his brother, but he looks at me with wide eyes and shakes his head.

I go to the window and look out across the lawn. The sun is still bright, but I can hear thunder growling in the distance, and there's a dark cloud looming in the west. Looks like another summertime deluge is heading our way.

I find Mom reading one of Gerald's detective novels in the living room. "Did Clay say anything to you about where he was going?"

She looks up, distracted, but her eyes clear when she recognizes the concern in my voice. "He's not outside?"

"No."

"Brett's?"

"Not there."

She glances at the telephone. "You don't think he went to the Hampton Inn, do you?"

I've been thinking the same thing, but I didn't want to voice the thought. Clay doesn't drive, so the only way he could get to the hotel would be hitching a ride or something equally irresponsible. . . .

"I'll get my keys."

Mom drops her book. We sweep down the stairs and get into the van. The Hampton isn't far, but I have to pass a couple of Sunday drivers on Highway 441—not a pleasant maneuver when your nerves are strung as tight as a bowstring.

Mom and I hurry into the lobby and make a beeline for the front desk. A girl at the counter points me to the house phone, so I ask the operator to connect me to Thomas's room. The phone rings once, twice, three times. . . .

I'm nearing panic mode when Mom tugs at my sleeve and points toward the pool. If I weren't so worried about my son, I might have lost my lunch.

Thomas is sunning himself on a chaise longue while a young woman I've never met applies sunscreen to his back. He's smiling, she's simpering, and I feel a sudden urge to slap them both.

Somehow I manage to curb my more primitive instincts as I sail out to the pool, my mother in tow. "Thomas—" my voice snaps like a whip—"have you seen Clay?"

He looks up, revealing a pattern of indentations on his cheek that match the ribbed pool chair. "He's missing?"

"He skipped out on some chores, and I thought he might have tried to visit you. Have you seen him?"

"No." He looks at the woman, who has retreated to the safety of her own chaise longue. "Have you seen a boy hanging around, about thirteen?"

She shakes her head and picks up a book, but I don't wait around for the introductions. I spin and move away while Thomas calls, "Can I do anything?"

I'm in danger of grinding my teeth to nubs by the time I reach the van. Can he *do* anything? Not *Should I call the police* or *Let me help you look for him* but *Can I do anything*?

As if he should have to be told what to do.

⚜ ⚜ ⚜

We've nearly reached Fairlawn when my cell phone rings. Mom snatches it out of my purse and answers, then looks at me. "It's Gerald. He thinks he knows where Clay is."

I hesitate at a stop sign, ready to turn the van around if necessary. "Where?"

"Bugs said something about wanting to go to the lake with Clay and Brett. Gerald said that wasn't a good idea, but a few minutes later, Bugs disappeared. Gerald checked the dock—Brett's johnboat is not in its usual place."

I look toward the lake as the first shots of rain strike my window. Clay knows he's not supposed to be out on the water without an adult. But he wasn't supposed to leave the house without weeding the flower bed either.

"Bugs is gone too?"

Mother listens a moment more, then snaps the phone shut. "Bugs slipped out when Gerald wasn't looking."

"Okay." The word comes out hoarse, forced through my tight throat. "We'll go to the lake."

As the heavens open and water thrums on the rooftop, I turn on the lights and squint to peer out the windshield, now streaked with runnels of rain. Of course the boys will be okay. They're probably taking cover under one of the picnic pavilions.

When we reach Lydia's house, I pull the van to the side of the road.

"You take the van and go wait at the house," I tell Mom. "I'm going to check the park."

I jump out of the van and jog over the trail that leads to the lake. Flush with determination, I call through the rain, "Clay! Bugs! Brett! Where are you?"

The wind snatches my voice and flings it up to the trees. I glance at the gyrating live oaks, thinking that the boys might have sheltered beneath their canopies, but I'm all alone out here.

Rain slides a snaking finger down the nape of my neck and teases a shudder from me. I've seen enough of these tropical thunderstorms to develop a legitimate case of nerves; they spring up, rip through the area with gale-force winds, and leave a trail of damage in their wake. Most of them are daggered with lightning, too, a danger Clay isn't likely to consider. Brett should know the risks, but he's such a teenager.

At the bottom of the hill, I duck beneath a nearly horizontal oak branch and walk toward the shore. The shuffleboard players and sunbathers have disappeared, but four small boats by the dock strain at their tethers.

Beside another sprawling oak—*lightning attractor*—stands a small, bare-chested boy with red hair. Bugs.

I fly toward him, not caring that the wind is firing sharp pellets of rain at my bare arms. An intimidating gust threatens to knock me off my feet, but I lower my head and press on, determined to eliminate the distance between me and my baby.

"Bugs!" I kneel to gather my shivering son into my arms.

His teeth chatter. "M-M-Mom? Are you m-m-mad?"

I rub at the gooseflesh on his pale skin. "I'm here, honey. Where's Clay?"

"He . . . don't be mad, Mom."

I swallow and grip Bugs by the shoulders. "I'm not mad. Where's your brother?"

Bugs's wide eyes roll toward the sky. "He and Brett—"

"Where are they?"

"Th-they took Brett's boat onto the lake. I was mad because they wouldn't let me come, so I came anyway. But it started to rain . . ."

I grab Bugs's hand and stand to search the water. A misty curtain of rain blocks my view, but the area near the dock is a study in bobbing boats and rolling whitecaps.

Dear God, help me help them.

I scoop Bugs up and set him on my hip, then hurry toward Lydia's, the nearest house with a lighted window.

※ ※ ※

Lydia flings the door open, draws me in, and listens as I try to explain what's happened.

She walks to the bathroom for dry towels and hands a couple to me and Bugs. "Don't worry," she says, her voice low and soothing. "Brett's always going out in his boat, and he's a good swimmer. They'll be okay."

She offers a cup of coffee, but the last thing I need is caffeine. Lydia settles Bugs in front of the television to watch cartoons, but I can't tear myself from her kitchen window and its view of the lake.

An hour passes; the thunder moves away, leaving us with steady rain. Lydia keeps sucking on a pencil and saying the boys will be fine, but she can't hide the worry line that has crept into the space between her brows.

When the rain slows to a drizzle, we go outside to the picnic pavilion. The three of us sit on a picnic table and focus on the misty gray curtain as if we could will it to part and reveal Brett's small johnboat with two boys aboard.

After ten minutes of relative calm, Lydia pulls her cell phone from her pocket and dials 911. I hear her explain the situation.

She puts her hand over the phone. "They're connecting me to the Lake County sheriff," she says, confidence returning to her voice. "They'll send someone out to pick up the boys." She releases a brittle laugh and stares straight ahead as she listens to someone on the other end of the line. After murmuring, "Okay, okay," she hangs up and returns the phone to her pocket.

"Anytime now—" she gives Bugs a bubbly smile—"we'll see that big sheriff's boat pull up with Brett and Clay aboard. The deputies know this lake like the back of their hands. They'll find them in a little while."

I pat my pockets, searching for my cell phone, then remember that I left it in the van. After borrowing Lydia's phone, I call Fairlawn and tell Mother what's happened. She wants to come down to the lake, but I ask her to wait at the house with Gerald. Clay and Brett might come ashore somewhere else and walk up to Fairlawn wet, happy, and completely unaware that they've sent us into a panic.

We wait. We wait until the minute hand on my watch swings from twelve to six. We wait until the rain stops and the tree frogs begin to sing. Lydia's lips are flecked with orange paint, remnants of the pencil she's been chewing. A pair of shuffleboarders come out to resume their game and send curious glances our way.

The sun slides out from behind the clouds and heats the air around us. Aside from the faint sheen of puddles on the weathered boards of the dock, no trace of the storm remains.

Like helium leaking from a balloon, news of our predicament seeps out of Fairlawn. Gerald comes down with dry clothes for Bugs. Annie Watson arrives from the Coffee House, a box of doughnuts tucked under her arm. Ruby Masters drives in from the drugstore. Edna Nance travels all the way from the Leesburg office of the *Daily Commercial*. The boys who play basketball with Clay and Brett materialize like silent ghosts to join our vigil.

At one point I look up and am honestly surprised to see Thomas in the crowd, his hands in his pockets and worry etched into his features.

The sheriff's boat finally appears, a green-and-white vessel roaring across the silver lake. My throat tightens as I watch the boat draw near, water purling at its bow. Lydia and I hurry forward as the driver cuts the engine. By the time the craft glides up to the dock, I have recognized one boyish figure near the bow—Clay, wrapped in a thick white towel.

Even as my heart fills with relief, part of my brain registers what I'm *not* seeing—Brett.

"Mom?"

I pull Clay to my side as Lydia looks over my shoulder, searching the boat. "Brett's a strong swimmer," she says. "I'm really not worried about him." But her voice is fractured, and her smile tight enough to cut glass. She crosses her arms and turns toward the sheriff.

Clay nestles in my arms, and as I walk him to the shelter, I hear snatches of conversation from the men aboard the boat: "lost the oars," "tow rope," and "caught by the storm." One horrible phrase pierces my heart: "The older boy decided to swim for shore."

Clay shudders in my arms. I draw him close and catch Gerald's eye. "I'm taking the boys to the house."

I can't do any good at the lakefront. Lydia will remain on vigil and so will the neighbors until Brett is found.

I glance at Thomas as we walk by. "Are you coming up to the house?"

He smiles at Clay, murmurs something about how he knew things would be all right, and squeezes our son's elbow. Then he looks at me. "Looks like you've got everything under control. I need to get back; Fiona is expecting me to call."

I press a kiss to Clay's wet head and close my eyes as Thomas walks away.

⚝ ⚝ ⚝

Clay falls asleep right after our dinner of grilled cheese sandwiches and chicken soup. Bugs curls up on the sofa to watch TV with Gerald, and Mother reads in the wing chair.

They have all stilled after the anxiety of the afternoon, but I can't relax, so I go downstairs and pace on the front porch. The hour before twilight is usually filled with frogsong, but man-made noise crackles through this night—shouted voices, the blare of a bullhorn, the churning roar of outboard motors. In the last hour, dozens of volunteers have crowded the shore even though there's not much they can do as night approaches. The sheriff has to know that searching for a missing person in darkness is like trying to find a pearl in a hailstorm, yet he will not abandon Lydia. The others will remain by the water as long as the missing boy's mother does.

From the porch, I can see the sheriff's patrol car parked on the road across from Twice Loved Treasures. Something tells me I ought to go down there . . . and if Clay hadn't been involved in this afternoon's disaster, I would be by Lydia's side. But how can I comfort her when my son is sleeping safely in his bed? Won't she resent my relief?

When the sheriff's cruiser drives away and the other cars begin to disperse, I cross my arms and walk down the hill. The night has turned cool after the storm. It is usually hard to see Lydia's house in the dark, but now her bungalow glows like a lantern. In the light streaming from the windows, I see Edna leading Lydia across the front lawn, the older woman's eyes protective and alert as departing friends and neighbors offer the promise of their prayers.

I can't help but notice two county patrol cars and an ambulance parked on the far side of the house.

I walk around the gate and hesitate as gravel crunches beneath my steps. "Lydia?" I wouldn't have been surprised if Edna motioned me away, but Lydia looks at me and her eyes fill with fresh tears. Wordlessly, I step to her side and wrap my arms around her shoulders.

"Is Clay okay?" Her voice breaks. "He's not hurt?"

"He's fine." I squeeze her shoulder. "He's asleep."

Her damp eyes meet mine. "I keep expecting Brett to come walking up and ask why we're making such a big deal over this. Wouldn't that be just like him?"

I nod.

"But if he *could* come, he'd be here by now. He's not an irresponsible kid. He would never stay out this long without finding a way to reach me. . . ."

I squeeze her hand again, empathizing more than I want to. I have tasted this anxiety, and my limbs are still heavy with the paralysis of fear.

Lydia's face ripples with anguish as she clamps onto my arm. "Jen—" she tightens her grip—"tell me again what Clay said about what happened out there."

I know she's searching for hope, for some hidden clue through which we will discover Brett sitting safe and dry on a picnic table somewhere.

"Clay said—" I glance from Edna to Lydia—"that the storm came up and began to swamp the boat. They tried to row, but Clay lost his oar, and Brett lost his while trying to reach the other one. Finally Brett got in the water and said he'd try to pull the boat in. He towed it for a while; then he said he'd swim to shore and send help. He started swimming, Clay lost sight of him, and the boat sank. Clay caught the ice chest and used it to keep himself afloat."

"Brett always wants to be the hero," Lydia whispers. "Always the big man." She turns in the damp grass and stares in the direction of the lake.

40

When I climb out of bed at sunrise the next morning, I feel as though I've aged twenty years overnight. I sit on the edge of the bed and wonder why I've awakened so early before the events of the previous day come rushing back with dismal clarity.

I knot my robe at my waist and wander to the kitchen, surprised to find a pot of coffee waiting. I pour myself a cup and sip it, then walk to the window and stare out. Nothing stirs outside Lydia's house; no banners hang on her front door. No signs of celebration, but someone has tied a huge yellow ribbon around one of her oaks.

Apparently there's been no news in the night.

I take another sip of coffee and frown as I hear a muffled clang and rattle from the first floor. Gerald's bedroom door is ajar, so he must be downstairs.

What in the world could he be doing at this hour?

Clutching my coffee mug, I creep downstairs and turn at the foyer. Panic nips at the backs of my knees when I see the door to the preparation room standing open. Could the sheriff have come here late last night?

Ghost spiders dance across the nape of my neck as I edge forward. I hold my breath until I see that the embalming table is empty.

Thankfully, Gerald is alone down here.

I lean against the doorframe and take another sip of my coffee.

Gerald stands at the counter, pulling bottles from the cupboard, setting out tubes and instruments. I'm ready to tease him about taking yet another inventory when I realize what he's doing.

He's preparing for a delivery.

He's expecting Brett.

"No, no, no." The words slide out of my mouth before I can think. I turn, about to retreat.

But Gerald's voice stops me. "Missy—" his tone is as firm as steel— "you can't run from situations like this. This is what we do. This is what Fairlawn is."

I whirl around, sloshing coffee onto the sleeve of my robe. "It's one thing to work on someone like Mavis, someone I barely knew. But when someone you know is coming—I don't think I want to be here when Brett arrives."

I close my eyes. I'd almost convinced myself we could stay at Fairlawn, that I could develop a sense of detachment that would allow me to serve as Gerald's apprentice.

But I can't. I'm not strong enough. I can't care enough. Lydia has been a good friend to us, but I didn't even want to meet her when we first arrived. I've deliberately kept her at arm's length. I've kept the entire town at a safe distance, only welcoming those who could do us some good.

My blood runs thick with guilt, but this moment has revealed an undeniable truth: I can't do this because I'm selfish.

"Jennifer, look at me." When I obey, I see Gerald regarding me with a look of unguarded tenderness in his eyes. "How do we show the Lord we love him?"

The question catches me by surprise. "What on earth are you talking about?"

"Humor me and answer the question."

I blow out a breath. "We show the Lord we love him by worshiping him."

Gerald takes a pair of rubber gloves from a box. "What else?"

"We . . . tithe."

"And?"

"We go to church."

"All those are part of the answer," Gerald says, "but those are things we do to keep ourselves connected to the Lord. We show Jesus we love him by loving his people. I show Jesus I love him by performing a service nobody else around here wants to do." His gaze rises to study my face. "Lydia is your friend, right?"

I lower my eyes. "I suppose."

"Then she may be depending on you today. If so, you'll have to be strong for her."

I head to the door. "She won't need my help. I'm sure Brett is fine. He'll show up—"

"Good grief, woman, are you *always* this blind?"

I blink, more startled by Gerald's display of temper than by his question. "What?"

"What are the odds that boy is alive? Brett was swimming through a storm without a life jacket. He was brave to jump into the water, but he was also young, and young men make foolish mistakes. You've got to be there for Lydia when she realizes that her son was courageous and good and foolish and everything a young man should be. And then you're going to have to help her plan Brett's funeral."

My breath catches in my lungs. "I can't. Not that."

"You're her *friend*, Jen. And today, I think, Lydia will need someone to show her that Jesus loves her."

Sadly, slowly, I reach out and pat Gerald's arm. I'm not happy about what I've just realized, but the old man is right.

Lydia doesn't need a Cecil Penny to sell her a casket. She needs a friend to help her prepare.

I've been through dark days in the past few months, and I don't think I'd have survived them if not for someone who took care of me. Mother opened her home, her wallet, and her heart to us. Maybe she did it out of maternal obligation; maybe she did it out of love. But one thing is clear: her hands provided many of the answers to our prayers. In her compassionate touch, the boys and I felt the love of Jesus.

I *am* selfish . . . and scared and queasy and uncertain. But with all that I've been given, how can I refuse to help someone else?

❈ ❈ ❈

Not until I see Bugs standing sleepy eyed in the upstairs hallway do I remember what day it is: Monday. Disney World day.

Bugs pads toward me on bare feet. "Mom?"

"Son?"

"Why are you up so early?"

I draw him close in the silence and decide to let his question rest for a while. Does he not remember anything about yesterday? "You hungry? Come on—let's get some breakfast."

I turn on the television when we walk through the living room so I can listen to the morning news as I pour Bugs's cereal. He sits at the kitchen table, one leg swinging in a steady rhythm, as he stares at nothing. The kid looks pitiful sitting there in his pajama bottoms, but at least he's with me. What must Lydia be feeling this morning?

I set Bugs's Lucky Charms on the table, then rush to the window as a siren splits the quiet. The sound grows louder, and I see an ambulance turn onto the narrow road that leads down to the lakeshore pavilion. Without being told, I know that Lydia must be on her way there as well.

I tousle Bugs's hair. "You feeling okay this morning?"

He scoops up a spoonful of marshmallows and sugarcoated crunchies. "I'm hungry."

"I see that."

I step back to the window and bring my hand to my throat. What should I do now? If they've found Brett, will they take him to the hospital or bring him here? Will they have to involve a coroner? And how do I guard my children from whatever grim reality this day brings?

I tap Bugs's shoulder on my way out of the kitchen. "Be back in a few minutes. I'm going to get dressed."

※ ※ ※

An hour later, an odd stillness fills the house. It's almost as if someone
has planted hidden cameras in the halls, and we're auditioning for the
title of America's most robotic family.

Clay eats breakfast and sets his dishes in the sink without being
told. He brushes his teeth, gets dressed, and goes to his room, where
he holds his Nintendo and monotonously plays his football game.

Bugs sits in the living room and watches *Good Morning America*.
Robin Roberts is reporting on the new fall fashions, and Bugs appears
to hang on every word.

Mother stands in the kitchen drinking coffee, but her gaze keeps
straying to the telephone on the wall. She heard the siren too and saw
where the ambulance turned.

I am dressed—I've even put on my sandals—yet I don't know what
I'm supposed to be doing. We are marking time, waiting to hear from
people outside our walls.

If this were any other summer morning, by this time Clay would be
tearing down the hill to see what Brett had planned for the day while
Bugs begged me for permission to hang out with the older boys. But
ordinary life has declared an unexpected hiatus, and none of us know
how to cope with the break in routine.

I lean my forehead against the wall and try to remember how I felt
when Sydney Barrow, one of my classmates, committed suicide in our
junior year. We were shocked that one of us could embrace death, but
in hindsight I can see that our hysterical grief was tinged with excitement at the unexpected drama. Nothing like that had ever happened
at our school; we relished the experience even as we locked arms and
sobbed our hearts out.

I'm not excited today. Neither are my sons.

When the telephone finally pierces the heavy silence, Mother looks
at me.

I lift my hand, wanting Gerald to take this call, but I remember
that the caller might be Thomas.

Of all days for him to be in town.

315

The phone does not ring again, so Gerald must have caught the call downstairs. I stand at the top of the staircase as his steps echo in the hallway.

"They found Brett," he calls far too loudly. "He's in the hospital."

For a moment my mind stutters. "Is he . . . ?"

Gerald appears at the bottom of the stairs, a relieved smile trembling over his lips. "He's alive. The boy *did* make it to shore, but a falling tree landed on top of him. One of the sheriff's bloodhounds found him right after sunup this morning."

"But he's okay?"

"He has a head injury. Lydia's with him at the hospital, and she wants us to pray."

That I can do.

❧ ❧ ❧

I pray for Brett, for his doctors, and for Lydia. I beg God to show me how I'm supposed to see my children through this near tragedy, and I ask him to help me be the kind of friend Lydia will need in the days ahead. I'm praying so earnestly that I don't hear the doorbell.

"Jen?" Mom opens my bedroom door. "Thomas is here."

I groan. "It's Disney day."

She perches on the edge of my bed. "The boys haven't mentioned it."

"Where are they now?"

"Downstairs with their dad. I let him in, called the boys, and told them to wait for you."

I sink onto the floor and prop my elbow on my bent knee. "I don't know. . . . Today might be a good day for them to get away. That'd leave me free to be with Lydia at the hospital, and they could have fun and get their minds off all this."

"They might have fun," Mom says, "or they might be so worried about Brett that they don't have any fun at all."

I exhale slowly and look at her. "What should I do?"

A slow smile curls over her lips. "It's your call. They're your kids. But maybe you should talk to them and see how they're feeling."

316

I like that idea. I put out my hand; Mom grabs it and pulls me to my feet. I lift my chin and go downstairs to talk to Thomas.

He's standing in the south chapel, his hands in his shorts pockets, rocking back and forth on his heels. Obviously he's ready to take the boys and go, but we've put a kink in his schedule.

Fiona must have called and told him to hurry home.

"Thomas." I force a smile. "We've had a rough weekend. Did the boys tell you?"

He nods. "Too bad about that kid. But he's okay, right?"

"Yes, but he and the boys are close."

"The boys and I are close too." He grins at our children. "So, are you guys ready for some fun at the Magic Kingdom?"

On any other day, both Clay and Bugs would have responded with an enthusiastic yes, but neither boy is in the mood to match Thomas's excitement. They look at me as if waiting for some cue.

I reach out and touch my ex-husband's elbow. "Maybe today's not the best day for Disney. Why don't I take the boys to the hospital and let them see Brett? They'll be in a better frame of mind tomorrow. Right now they're still worried."

Thomas shifts, moving his elbow out of my reach. "I have to head back tomorrow. Besides, I already have the tickets, and they're good today only." He bends at the waist and claps like a football quarterback ready to call a play. "Ready to go? Mickey Mouse is waiting."

Clay turns away, his chin trembling, and Bugs rushes to embrace my knees. I'm as surprised by their reaction as Thomas, but at least I understand it.

Thomas's face fills with hurt, confusion, and something that looks almost like shame. "Apparently they don't want to be with me."

"Thomas, that's not it—"

"Yes, it is. I might as well head back to Virginia."

"Don't." My irritation rises. "Don't run back to her when we're waiting here. We're your *family*."

"Are you? I'd like to think so . . . but then I look around and see that you've made a life for yourselves here—a life that doesn't include me." His abstracted eyes rove over the heads of our sons, but they clear as they focus on me. "All those people who came to the lake yesterday—they came because they cared about you, Jen. You have a new family here, and something tells me I'll be lucky if the boys still think of me as Dad a year from now. I'm sorry for that. I'm sorry for a lot of things."

"Thomas, please." I have waited months to hear this apology, yet I do not feel the victory or the joy I imagined, for Thomas's face has filled with resignation. Though Bugs is still clinging to one of my legs, I step toward Thomas, willing to bridge the gap between us. "You can change your plans. Stay with us a couple of days; take the boys to Disney tomorrow. We have things we want to tell you; we want you to be a part of our lives."

Thomas stares at me, thought working behind his eyes, and then he lifts his hand and brushes my cheek. "I have been a fool," he says simply, "and I will regret it for the rest of my life." Without another word, he turns and walks out the front door, leaving as silently as a sleepwalker.

"Is he coming back?" Bugs looks up at me, his face streaked with tears, but Clay turns and runs up the steps.

I can't answer his question, but hope begins to stir within my broken heart.

41

*L*ike the calm after a storm, another eerie quiet falls over the house. I go to the bathroom and splash cold water on my face, then step out to encourage the troops. I find Bugs coloring pictures at the kitchen table while Mom washes the breakfast dishes. Clay has disappeared again.

Gerald is in the prep room, humming as he puts away the equipment he took out this morning.

"Gerald, have you seen Clay?"

He jerks a thumb toward the back door. "Check out there."

I step to the door and peer through the window. Clay is kneeling by a gallon of white enamel and has popped off the lid. He's spread a drop cloth over the floorboards and set out a couple of paintbrushes.

"I can't believe it," I whisper. "Clay is painting the porch?"

Gerald chuckles. "He was moping around and looking for something to do. I suggested that he might get busy weeding that flower bed he was supposed to finish yesterday; then I thought it might be nicer if he surprised you." He looks over his shoulder. "You *did* want those porch railings painted, didn't you?"

"It's on my list. Project number thirty-five."

I press my hand to the glass pane and watch as Clay dips his brush into the paint and begins to paint the posts on the railing. I *hate* painting spindles, so if Clay wants to tackle them, I'll let him . . . and tell him I appreciate it.

I walk outside, cross my arms, and lean against the back wall, well out of Clay's way. "Beautiful day. A good day for painting, I think."

Clay grunts. "Yeah."

"Thanks, Son. I appreciate you doing this without being asked."

When he doesn't respond, I realize I've probably embarrassed him. But it's important that I tell him what I'm feeling, and if he can't answer, that's okay. Right now he probably feels like a powder keg of emotions. I know I do.

I approach a section of unpainted railing and run my fingers over the smooth surface. Whatever happened to the polished career woman who could defuse explosive situations with a carefully worded card and a box of Godiva chocolates? Her office used to run like a Rolls, and no one had a firmer grip on her emotions.

She wouldn't recognize the woman I've become. Of course, she never had to deal directly with her children, argue with divorce lawyers, or confront an ex-husband. She didn't attend funerals or wrangle with contractors, and she wouldn't be caught dead in elastic-waist shorts. She was disciplined, scheduled, organized . . . and aloof.

I used to imagine myself at the pinnacle of success, but I couldn't have been more wrong. Life—*real* life—waited and roiled outside the senator's office. I never experienced its true depths until I came to Fairlawn.

I lean on the railing and watch a blue jay and crow at war in the canopy of one of the live oaks. The crow is apparently casing the blue jay's nest, and the mama jay isn't happy about it. She's fussing, fluttering from one branch to the next, circling around the bigger and faster crow.

"Has Dad always been such a jerk?"

I focus on the blue jay, wondering how she would answer a curious fledgling. Would she tell him the truth about the nasty nature of crows in general, or would she wait until he's old enough to deal with crows on his own?

This line of reasoning is getting me nowhere. My son is not a baby bird; Thomas is not a crow. He's a nice man who happens to be a lousy husband and absentee dad.

And as much as I'd like to vent my frustration, my son bears the image of his father. If I teach him to despise Thomas, am I not teaching him to despise a large part of himself?

"Clay . . ." I search for words. "Your father isn't always . . . the way he was today. Sometimes he's charming and easy to please. Lots of people love him. I loved him once . . . and in some ways I always will."

I step over the porch and move closer to him, taking care not to get in the way of his painting. "After all, your father gave me you and Bugs. I'll always be grateful for that."

Clay keeps painting, but his stroke slows. "Right now I hate him."

"That's because you're angry, and your father was upset this morning too. But he'll take some time to think and so will you. Then he'll come back. He'll always come back to see you."

From where we're standing, I hear the familiar crunch of a car crossing the gravel. I lift my head and try to look around the corner of the house. "Maybe that's your dad now."

I leave the porch and stride across the side lawn. My steps slow, however, when I see that the car parked in our lot isn't Thomas's SUV. It's the sheriff's cruiser. The uniformed sheriff, whom I recognize from last night, is walking toward the front door while Lydia sits with slumped shoulders in the front of the vehicle.

A cold grue raises gooseflesh on my arms. Did they learn something new about Brett's accident? Did someone purposely hurt that boy?

I break into a run.

The sheriff stops on the porch steps when he sees me. "Mrs. Graham?"

"What's wrong? Did something happen to Brett?" I look toward Lydia, whose hand is half hiding her face. When she sees me, she opens the car door.

I hurry toward her as a thousand questions fill my mind. "Lydia, will you come inside? What's happened?"

She looks paler than she did last night. Nervous energy fueled her movements while we waited to hear about Brett, but now she looks as though her life force has been drained by some kind of emotional vampire.

"Jennifer." Her voice breaks. "I was on my way home from the hospital and—"

"Mrs. Graham." The sheriff steps toward me and stops. "I understand that you are related to Thomas Graham?"

For an instant the words dance in my brain like some kind of quiz show question. What does Thomas have to do with Brett? Surely they don't think he had anything to do with the accident.

"He's my ex-husband." I toss Lydia a distracted glance. "He's staying at the Hampton Inn, and I think he was at the hotel all afternoon yesterday."

"We talked to the desk clerk, ma'am, and we talked to Mr. Graham's lawyer. He told me you were divorced, but he says you're the legal executor. You're the one we need to speak to."

I press my hand to my forehead. "I don't know what you mean."

A sense of déjà vu descends with the word *executor*. The word rings with familiarity because I've dealt with it recently. Daniel Sladen was an executor, but I can't be one because I'm not the one who died. . . .

Who did?

I turn to Lydia, a question on my lips.

"Your ex," she says, her eyes filling with tears. "Was he driving a black Navigator?"

I nod.

"Jen, honey, that car was hit by a truck and totaled on Highway 441 an hour ago. The driver was dead on arrival at the hospital, and the man's identification—"

My knees buckle. The sheriff steps forward, too late, as I fall, hard, to the grass.

Weeping freely now, Lydia tumbles out of the car and kneels beside me, her arms slipping around my neck.

"I'm sorry to be the bearer of bad news—" the sheriff's voice rings with authority—"but Thomas Graham died this morning at 8:55. We spoke to a woman whose number we found on his cell phone, and she confirmed that you are officially listed as the man's next of kin. At your convenience, we need you to come to the hospital and make the final arrangements."

I look at Lydia as the words swirl around me. "Arrangements?"

Her lips tremble as she attempts a smile. "The funeral, hon. The paperwork. They want to know what you want to do with him."

What do I want to do with Thomas? In the past few months I have wanted to ship him to Mars, have him tarred and feathered, and shove him down the stairs. In milder moments I have wanted to welcome him back to my home and bed.

I have never wanted to bury him.

※ ※ ※

I am sitting in the empty chair in front of Uncle Ned's desk while Mother and Lydia flutter around me like a pair of ministering angels. Gerald is keeping the kids busy upstairs, giving me time to get my thoughts together before I tell them the news.

Mom brings down a huge cup of coffee, as if an overdose of caffeine will shock me back to sensibility. I want to tell her that I am fully aware of my surroundings. If she asks, I can even name the president.

I just can't seem to find the words to express how I feel about Thomas's death. Maybe that's because I'm not feeling anything.

Lydia draws a deep breath and looks at Mom, who waves her hands in a helpless gesture and jerks her head toward the hallway. "I'll be upstairs with the boys."

Lydia nods. After a moment's hesitation, she sinks into the only other chair in the room, the one behind the desk.

"I haven't told you about my ex-husband, have I?" Lydia leans back in the chair and props her feet on the edge of the desk. "His name is William, but everyone calls him Bill. A truck driver, based in California. Nice guy and attractive, too. Brett looks a lot like his dad, though I think he has my eyes."

I exhale a slow breath, relieved to be talking about something— *someone*—else. "How long have you been divorced?"

"Long time." She pauses to count on her fingers. "Brett was three when Bill won custody, so it's been fourteen years."

"Wait—your *ex* won custody?"

Something that might be a wry smile flits across Lydia's face. "Not what you expected, huh? Bill won custody in our divorce because I was a lousy mother. I couldn't handle all those lonely days and nights when he was on the road. I fell into a depression after Brett was born, and I started drinking. Heavily. I covered pretty well, mainly because Bill wasn't around to see the signs. But one day he came home and found me passed out and Brett crying on the floor—the poor kid hadn't been fed in two days. Bill quit his job, took Brett, and told me he'd leave me if I didn't go into rehab. I didn't believe him, but Bill kept his word. After divorcing me, he moved Brett out to California."

I am too stunned to do anything more than prop my chin in my hand and stare across the desk. "Why, that's awful. It seems so unfair."

Lydia takes a deep breath and adjusts her smile. "It was hard, but it was the best decision for Brett. I was a wreck, Jen. I would have messed him up if the judge had left him with me."

I study my friend through a lace of confused thoughts. "But . . . you're a good mother. Obviously you worked things out."

She snorts. "I finally wised up and got help. But I didn't see Brett for seven years. By the time I managed to stay sober long enough to convince a judge that I deserved to see my kid, Brett was ten and Bill had remarried. Brett spends his summers with me, but the rest of the year he lives with his dad and stepmom in San Francisco."

Sadness pools in my chest, a heavy grief that feels like nausea. All this talk of divorce makes me think of Thomas, and I don't want to think about him now. The man hurt me, left me, divorced me, and walked away just this morning. To make matters worse, he walked away in front of our boys, so I'll be dealing with their guilt as well as my own.

Why didn't I stop him? I could have urged him to come inside for some breakfast, kept him at the house until that monster truck had passed on the highway.

I smile at Lydia, hoping she'll keep talking so Thomas's last words will stop echoing in my brain: *"I have been a fool . . . and I will regret it for the rest of my life."*

Did he know? Did he feel death's shadow approaching?

One appalling and abhorrent thought insists on rearing its head: did Thomas pull out in front of that truck on *purpose?*

I feel like a pack animal that's been forced to its knees under a heavy burden, but the taskmaster keeps piling on more weight.

Tears trickle down Lydia's cheeks as her feelings overflow. "I'm so grateful that Brett is going to be okay. And I wish—" She lowers her feet and leans forward to extend a hand across the desk. "I wish Thomas were still alive and well. But you're a strong woman, Jen, stronger than I ever was. You're going to be fine, and your sons are going to grow into good, strong men."

In that moment, something in her words unlocks the frozen place within me. My feelings for Thomas have been confused over the last few months, but my love for my boys has never wavered. And they will feel this loss, not only today but through the years ahead.

For Bugs and Clay, I must pick myself up. For them, I can do what the sheriff expects me to do. And because Jesus asks me to bless those who hurt me, I will do the most difficult thing I can imagine for Thomas.

I stand and step around the desk to hug Lydia; then I leave the office and find Gerald in the preparation room. "Would you please call the hospital? Tell them you'll be picking up Thomas Graham. Services will be held at Fairlawn on—" I hesitate—"Wednesday?"

Gerald's eyes warm slightly, and the hint of a smile assures me that I'm doing the right thing. "Wednesday would be fine. Maybe one o'clock?"

"Yes. And, Gerald . . ."

He quirks a brow.

"May I help you? I'd like to do all I can for him."

A blush of pleasure warms his face. "Absolutely. I'd appreciate your help."

I step forward and lower my head to the old man's shoulder. "Thank you."

※※ ※※ ※※

Only in the emotional spectrum of marriage, I realize as I park the van outside the Pine Forest Cemetery, can a woman shift from being furious with her spouse to heartbroken for him in a matter of hours.

Bugs and Clay are with me. Mother and I gave them the news before lunch. As we expected, neither child felt much like eating. Both of them had questions; both immediately felt guilty.

"If we'd gone with him to Disney World," Clay said, "wouldn't he still be alive?"

I took his hand and tried to help him see past the pain. "You can't think about things like that. Your father was a good driver, but he was upset when he left us. He may have been distracted when he pulled out in front of that truck."

"If you'd gone with him, maybe he would have had the accident with you boys in the car," Mother pointed out.

Gerald replied that we can't control certain aspects of our lives any more than we can control the weather. "That's why we trust God," he said, smiling at my sons. "Even when we don't understand."

Gerald has given me a map of the available spaces at Pine Forest and suggested that Clay and Bugs help me pick out a burial plot for Thomas.

The paper crinkles in my hand as I ease out of the van. The boys open the small iron gate and enter the grassy area. Sprawling live oaks and a few pines border the property, but the acre within the fence is nothing but grass. Pine Forest is a memorial park, so there are no crypts or tombstones, just small brass markers and the occasional vase for flowers.

"Can we pick any place?" Clay says.

I shade my eyes with the map and look around. "Why don't you look for a spot near the fence? Maybe we can find a spot with shade."

The boys walk off and head toward the edge of the property.

I follow but take my time, wanting them to make the choice. It's a small thing, but they'll remember it.

Thomas Graham, of Falls Church, Virginia, will be buried in Mt.

Dora. With his parents deceased and his only sister living in Oregon, no one is likely to fuss.

I have spoken to Thomas's lawyer. He was shocked by my news, but he confirmed what I suspected—true to his pattern, my workaholic ex-husband kept his family responsibilities at the bottom of his priority list. "Some men think they have all the time in the world to handle this kind of thing," the lawyer tells me. "So you are still listed as executor of your ex-husband's will, and you and your sons are the beneficiaries of his life insurance policy."

Though it was difficult, I called Fiona to tell her about the funeral. The poor woman could barely speak, but when I asked if she wanted to attend the service, she wailed and said she didn't want to remember Thomas lying in a box.

So in two days, Bugs, Clay, Mom, Gerald, and I will bury Thomas.

Clay finds a vacant spot near the fence. "How about this, Mom?"

I walk over and study the plot. One area looks pretty much like another, so I glance to the left to see who Thomas's closest neighbor will be.

The brass nameplate makes me smile. I point to the grave marker. "Look at that. Maybe your father would like the idea of resting next to my great-uncle." I let my hand fall to the top of Bugs's head. "What do you think, kiddo?"

Bugs nods. "I like it."

I'm not certain how much the boys understand, and I know this one action isn't going to smooth their turbulent feelings about the argument, the divorce, and their father's death. But this is something we can do in this hour, and it feels right.

I turn to count rows. "All right—row four, last space on the right. I think your father would approve."

$\mathcal{B}$rett, Mother reports on Tuesday morning, suffered a concussion but will soon be released from the hospital. When the teenager comes home, Mom takes Clay and Bugs down to Lydia's house so they can hear about his adventures.

Lydia has promised to feed them lunch. The gesture is more than goodwill on her part; it's also subterfuge . . . because Gerald picked up Thomas last night. He is going to start the embalming soon, and I'm going to help him.

I never imagined that I'd be capable of putting on a rubber apron to embalm someone I loved, but when I see Thomas on the prep room table, I can't imagine *not* helping. I know this body intimately, every freckle and mole. I have loved it, cared for it, and slept with it by my side for thousands of long nights.

The body on the table doesn't make me queasy. I look at the scars and bruises from the accident and feel pity instead.

Gerald takes five rubber blocks from one of the cabinets and places the concave part of the blocks under Thomas's head, heels, and elbows. He pulls a wad of cotton from a box and gently lifts each eyelid, wiping the area beneath. He positions a curved piece of plastic on top of each eyeball and carefully closes the lids.

"Why?" I ask.

A half smile crosses his lined face. "Almost everything we'll do here is for the sake of the survivors. As the body desiccates, some tissues shrink. We don't want the eyes opening in the middle of the funeral."

As always, he makes sense. I watch as Gerald clamps Thomas's mouth shut, then tenderly lathers Thomas's face with shaving cream.

He lifts the razor and looks at me. "Would you like to do this?"

I blink away tears and take the razor. I move to Thomas's side and carefully hold his head with my left hand as I shave his jawline with my right.

Gerald keeps working as I slide the razor over cheekbones I have kissed a thousand times. A large bruise has discolored one cheek, and my heart twists at the sight of it.

As I concentrate on not cutting skin that can no longer heal, I am finally able to see why Gerald considers his work a ministry.

How do we show Jesus we love him? By doing things people cannot do for themselves. By restoring the appearance of one who has died so his children can say good-bye without suffering trauma.

By extending grace to one who has wronged us.

❧ ❧ ❧

Gerald pauses, an arterial hook in his hand. Jennifer appears to be lost in thought, but a smile ruffles her mouth as she shaves the face of the man who has brought so much heartache into her life.

Her expression is a miracle. As is her presence in this room.

He shakes his head as he slips the arterial hook into a neck incision. The woman may not realize it yet, but she is one step closer to fulfilling Ned's vision for Fairlawn.

Not many days ago, Gerald had been convinced that Ned was delusional when he decided to leave Fairlawn to Jennifer Graham. She came to Mt. Dora with only one thought in mind. She pushed Gerald to his limits, especially when she started making noises about turning the place into a prissified motel.

But he had prayed. And waited. And prayed again.

And now, in the Lord's mysterious timing, Fairlawn has opened its arms in Jennifer's hour of need.

❊❊ ❊❊ ❊❊

After a dinner of fried chicken, green beans, sweet potato casserole, country ham, and cherry pie—only a few of the dishes that have materialized in our kitchen, courtesy of folks from the church—Gerald and I descend the stairs to do the final work on Thomas.

The body I used to playfully pinch and poke is now as solid as stone. The mouth has been set in a gentle smile, the eyes permanently closed. The embalming fluid has done its work, and Gerald has done his, excusing me only when he did what he called the "cavity embalming."

Whatever it was, I trust Gerald enough to be glad I didn't see it.

Thomas lies on the table, his body tinged pink from the fluid in his veins. Gerald mixes iodine and alcohol in a beaker, then dips a flat brush into the mixture and coats the back of Thomas's pale hand with the solution. The color is a little dark, but Gerald assures me it will look natural in the chapel.

He hands me the brush. "Paint the back of the hands, the entire face, and the neck, down past the collar line. That's all you'll have to do."

While I apply color to Thomas's skin, Gerald cleans and clips my ex-husband's fingernails. Two gashes from the accident mar Thomas's chest, and I'm relieved to see that Gerald has stitched those with fine thread. The bruise on Thomas's cheek has been flushed away by the embalming fluid.

When I have finished, Gerald pulls a suit from the back of the door. "I picked this up at Penney's," he says, "since Thomas didn't have anything like this with him. The hotel clerk gave me everything else." He opens the paper bag and takes out a shirt, socks, and underwear.

I have done many things for my husband, but I never dreamed I would pull socks onto his lifeless feet.

Gerald shows me how to slit the shirt and suit down the back in order to dress the stiff body. A quick stitch at the middle of the collar holds the shirt together; then Gerald crosses Thomas's hands at his waist.

When he leaves to bring in the casket, I find myself staring at Thomas's face. I want to remember what he looked like for our sons' sake. I want to tell them about things they won't see in a photograph—about how Thomas's lips were quick to smile, his eyes apt to give away a surprise.

Gerald wheels in the casket and places it next to the embalming table, and together we lift Thomas and lower him into the coffin. While Gerald adjusts the position of the head, I take a satin box from my pocket.

Inside are my wedding band and my engagement ring. I will save the diamond ring; one day one of my sons might like to offer it to a young woman. But the wedding band will never be used again. Not by me, not by Bugs or Clay.

I take the golden circle from the box and slide it onto Thomas's pinky finger, then rest my hands upon his.

*W*ednesday morning dawns bright and hot. The flowers begin to arrive at nine, and soon their sweet perfume drifts upstairs. Bugs walks around holding his nose as if all the commotion is a colossal irritation, but I'm afraid the sights and smells of the impending funeral have upset Clay. He has shut himself in his room and will not come out.

I'm not sure how many people will come to the service. Thomas knows no one in Mt. Dora, and we've been living here only six weeks. I called Senator Barron's office Tuesday, hoping they would send a representative, and at ten-thirty Wednesday morning I learn that the office chief of staff is coming in by private jet. I'll be surprised if he arrives in time.

The senator Thomas sacrificed so much to serve has a schedule packed with meetings that cannot be postponed.

After lunch I go to my room, slip into my blue funeral dress, and apply a light dusting of makeup. I am surprised by the calm that rests like a mantle on my shoulders. I shed my tears yesterday; I said my farewells as I helped Gerald in the prep room.

Today I have to be strong for Clay and Bugs. Even if no one else shows up, I need to show my respect and love for their father. I do not want them to grow up thinking that love is impossible and marriage a waste of effort.

By the time I bring the boys downstairs at twelve-forty-five, the

west chapel is so crowded Gerald has to bring in folding chairs. At the organ, Ruby Masters plays hymns until everyone finds a seat.

Then Reverend Waters Scrugs, pastor of the Mt. Dora Community Church, moves to the simple wooden lectern. He welcomes everyone and thanks them for coming.

In the front row with Mother, Clay, and Bugs, I resist the temptation to turn around and study the crowd. Are they here because Thomas's death is a gossip-worthy event? Or did they come to support Gerald, who makes every service memorable?

Reverend Scrugs reads the Twenty-third Psalm and follows up with the beloved passage from the Gospel of John. "'Don't let your hearts be troubled. Trust in God, and trust also in me. There is more than enough room in my Father's home. If this were not so, would I have told you that I am going to prepare a place for you?'"

Honestly, I don't know if Thomas is in heaven or not. He went to church with us and called himself a Christian, but I don't know what that word meant to him. On the campaign trail, he was quick to say that Senator Barron believed America was a "Christian nation," but whether that translated into personal faith, I don't know.

The minister finishes reading the Scripture and steps back, the accepted cue for others to stand and speak.

What if no one says anything? I'd say something, but I don't trust my voice and I don't want to get up there and blubber. Mother has never had anything good to say about Thomas, and my boys are simply too young.

I glance at Gerald, hoping he'll say something, but he's studying the crowd, probably trying to figure out how the hastily chosen pallbearers can best maneuver the casket through all the extra chairs.

After an uncomfortable interval, the minister lifts his Bible, but he halts when an older man stands and walks forward, rocking down the aisle on stiff hips. He glances at Thomas in the coffin, then turns and faces the gathering.

The man lifts his hand in a stately salute. "I don't know the fellow behind me, and I'm not acquainted with his family, but I trust the folks of Mt. Dora. If they're burying somebody, I figure I need to support them."

The crowd chuckles softly, and I lean toward Lydia. "Who is that?"

She shakes her head. "I don't know."

"In the same way," the stranger continues, "I don't understand why this fellow was taken so suddenly, but I know we can trust the ways of God.

"I have known affliction in my years," he says, the lines in his face attesting to the truth in his words, "but I have never seen the godly forsaken nor their children begging for bread. I have known the hard grip of a Father who found me when I was lost and held me so tightly I thought he would leave fingerprints on my spine. As painful as his grip was, I have learned one thing: in times of suffering, God may hold me painfully close, but he will not let go."

The old man turns his bright gaze upon me. "That's how God is holding you and your boys, Mrs. Graham. Tightly. Painfully. But in love."

❧❧ ❧❧ ❧❧

Over the next few days, the boys and I make our peace with Thomas. Through Lydia, I learn that the crowd at Thomas's funeral came for our sakes, not for his. We are the people of Fairlawn, and Fairlawn belongs to the community.

So we now belong to Mt. Dora.

We never learned the identity of the old man who spoke at the funeral. Gerald didn't know him, nor did any of the Hatters, and he slipped out of town as quietly as he slipped in.

We buried Thomas in the westernmost plot of the fourth row, where the late afternoon sun will be filtered through the overhanging branches of a moss-festooned live oak.

After dinner on Saturday night, the boys and I set our dishes in the sink and walk down to the cemetery. Skeeter goes with us and chases butterflies as we put fresh flowers in a temporary vase. The plot looks bare without a marker, but the brass nameplate will arrive soon.

I wander through the cemetery, pretending not to listen as my boys stand at the foot of their father's grave. I hear them tell him about fishing with Gerald, Brett's recovery, and Grandma's bout with indigestion. I blink back tears as they tell him good night.

I can't help being struck by the irony—Thomas's unexpected death has, in a way, brought him closer to Clay and Bugs. The man who rarely found time to talk to his children is now being offered some of their deepest thoughts.

As we leave the cemetery, Bugs takes my right hand. That's not unusual, but I'm startled when Clay comes up and grips my left.

"Mom," he asks, not looking at me, "can you love and hate someone at the same time?"

I draw a deep breath. "Yes, I think you can."

"Is that wrong?"

We've reached the gate, but rather than release their hands, I stop on the grass. "Sometimes we hate because we are angry. When our anger fades away, the hate can disappear too."

I take a step back and kneel to speak to my sons on their level. "I know your daddy left you, but I also know he loved you. What we need to do, I think, is to be happy for his love and learn from his mistakes. One day you might have a little boy. If you do, remember how you're feeling right now. Maybe that'll help you be a better daddy for your son."

Bugs crinkles his nose, finding the idea of parenthood inconceivable, but Clay nods.

And as we walk to the van, I pray that faithful fathers are formed from such moments.

※ ※ ※

On Sunday afternoon, I leave the boys with Gerald and walk down to the cemetery alone. I need to make a different kind of peace with Thomas.

I pause at the rusty gate outside Pine Forest Cemetery. To my left, I can see the slightly rounded mound that marks Mavis Biddle's grave— Gerald says time will smooth things out.

I push at the gate, eliciting a rusty squeak from the hinges. An oak casts its shade over me while a squirrel pauses from his nut gathering to give me an inquisitive look. I stroll past graves old and new, moving from shade into sun and back into shade. At the end of the fourth row, I find the markers I am seeking: Marjorie Norris, Ned Norris, Thomas Graham.

No one has thought to place a bench at the end of this row; apparently not many people come here to converse. I sink to the cut sod blanketing Thomas's plot and curl my fingers into the grass.

How do I form the thoughts that have been stirring in my heart for days? All summer I felt the existence of a wall between my prayers and heaven. Now I realize the wall was of my own making.

I press my hands to my cheeks and inhale the scents of summer. "You said you were sorry, Thomas, when you left. I'm not sure what you meant, but I owe you an apology too. For months I've been telling the Lord that I'd forgive you if you apologized, but that was wrong of me. Forgiveness shouldn't come with strings attached.

"So I forgive you. For betraying my love, for leaving us, for all the pain and desperation. I don't know what I could have done to make you happier, but if there was something I could have done and didn't, I hope you'll forgive me for my blindness.

"I've learned something in the last few weeks: I was as caught up in my work as you were in yours. If we hadn't been forced to come here, I don't know that I would have had my eyes opened to that truth. So you see, if you hadn't left us, I might have awakened one day a few years from now and discovered that I didn't know our boys. The Lord has given them back to me . . . and Fairlawn has made us a family again. Even Mother and I have called a truce."

I fall silent as the gate creaks behind me. I hear the swish of grass, and a moment later a shadow overlaps mine.

"I thought I'd find you here."

I glance over my shoulder and see my mother with a small package in her hand. "Did you bring Thomas a present?"

"It's for you. A going-away gift."

I turn to face her. "Who's going away?"

"You don't need me anymore, Jen, and Fairfax is my home. I'll come to visit, but my Hatters need me, and I'll bet our choir director is about ready to bean Mildred Sackett. The woman can't find the harmony unless I'm singing in her ear." Mom stoops to press a small box into my hand. "It's nothing fancy. Just something I thought you could use."

I untie the ribbon and lift the lid. The cast-iron nameplate inside is shaped like a miniature Victorian painted in pink and gray. Beneath it, bold lettering spells out:

FAIRLAWN
Home to Jennifer, Gerald, Clay, and Bugs

I smile and stare past the horizon into my own thoughts. This gift cost Mother far more than money. She's realized what it has taken me some time to grasp: at Fairlawn, God has given me everything I need—a home, a family, and meaningful employment.

I've been blessed but not in the way I expected.

I stand and hug my mother. "It's beautiful. I'll mount it by the door as soon as I get home."

"You should let Clay do it. The boy's never going to learn to use a screwdriver if you do everything for him."

I'm tempted to chide her for telling me how to raise my children, but instead I stand back and smile into her eyes. "You might be right."

※ ※ ※

Joella closes her eyes as Jen jerks the steering wheel to the right and angles into a short parking space at the curb. Security is tight at the Orlando airport, and tempers are even tighter.

She ignores the stern expression of a guard in the center lane and turns to face her daughter. "You call me if anything comes up. You know I'll come back in a flash if you need me."

Jen grins and shoves the van into park. "You can stay if you want. I told you we'll always have a room with your name on it."

Joella shakes her head. "No, Fairlawn wears me out. I have to get back to the Hatters before the fall festival or Baroness Barbara Bee is liable to have our chapter selling crocheted toilet paper covers in the booth."

She leans toward her daughter and gives her a brief hug, then bites back tears. Who'd believe that a woman could change so much in such a short time? Jen was an absolute mess only a few weeks ago, but here she is, calm, confident, and content.

"Grandma, will they let you look in the cockpit?"

Joella turns to Bugs in the backseat. "I don't know, Bugsy. I've never asked. But come here, boy, and give me some sugar."

Bugs rolls his eyes, but he unsnaps his seat belt, moves forward, and throws his arms around her neck in a vise grip.

Joella holds him tight, remembering when Jen's hugs used to be this small and fierce.

"You'd better go, Mom." Jen squeezes Joella's arm. "You've still got to stand in those security lines."

"I know." Joella pulls back to give Bugs a smacky kiss on the cheek. Without looking at Jen, she slides out of the van and moves to the side door, then pulls out her suitcase.

Jen comes around, her hands in her pockets and a quizzical look on her face. "I don't know what we're going to do without you."

"Pshaw. You don't need me."

Jen startles as Bugs honks the horn; then she blows Joella a kiss. "Yes, Queen Snippy, we do. Hurry back."

※ ※ ※

Two weeks later, I am tackling my to-do list once again. Thomas's estate—which consisted of more than I'd imagined—has been translated into two college savings accounts and a deposit into our Fairlawn renovation fund. I'm still determined to refurbish Fairlawn, but we're not going to sell the property. We're going to live here and keep the home's legacy alive.

Now that I know we're staying, I'm using part of our inheritance to fence off a portion of the side lawn. Skeeter needs a safe place to run and play.

Clay and Bugs can't believe that summer is nearly over. I've enrolled both of them in Mt. Dora schools, and despite their grumbling, I think they're excited about making new friends.

The boys aren't the only ones going back to school. I've sent away for information on the mortuary program at the local community college, and I think I can complete my coursework within a year. In the meantime, Gerald says I can act as his apprentice and assist in the prep room.

The periwinkle in my flower beds has spread out and filled in the dead spots, and my new shingles look lovely in the glow of the setting sun. Last Saturday I climbed up on a ladder and polished the diamond-shaped window in the turret; now it sparkles with the brightness of our new hopes and dreams.

Coming here has taught me many things. I've learned that my marriage wasn't a mistake because it resulted in my sons, whom I love dearly. Life isn't a tragedy and neither is heartache. I have grown through it, and pain has taught me to depend more completely upon God.

Sometimes, when the boys bring up a happy memory of Thomas or I find myself missing Mother, I can almost feel God's fingerprints on my spine.

That's when I know he's holding me tight.

44

$\mathcal{G}$erald and I are sitting on the sofa with Skeeter snoring between us while the melodramatic *The Bold and the Beautiful* theme song spills from the television.

Gerald flips a page of *Mortuary Management.* "Do you think Brooke and Ridge will ever get married?"

"No way. Too predictable."

"You're probably right."

We sit there, as companionable as two puppies, while the house breathes in a moment of rare silence. Bugs and Clay have gone to the airport to provide moral support for Lydia, who is sending Brett back to California today.

They've been gone only a couple of hours, but I think Gerald misses them. He's grown accustomed to Clay's burping and Bugs's constant questions. He keeps glancing over his shoulder and squinting as if he's listening for the sound of a slammed car door or quick steps on the porch.

"The boys should be back around four." I curl into the corner of the sofa. "Maybe we can order a pizza for dinner."

"That'd be good. They'd like that."

I nod as the drama of Brooke and Ridge returns to the television.

"Did I tell you," Gerald says, "that I have a granddaughter?"

341

He has begun to mention his daughter now and then, but this is the first I've heard of a grandchild. "How old?"

He hesitates. "Eight, I think."

"Does she look like your daughter?"

A full minute passes before he answers. "I've never seen her."

I would ask why not, but something in his face closes and I know my questions won't be welcome. Not yet . . . but there's always tomorrow.

I stand when I hear the rumble of the mail truck on the street. "I'll be back."

I trot down the stairs and out to the mailbox, which has filled with catalogs and bills. I'm flipping through the stack when a black Beemer pulls up, churning the gravel on the driveway.

When the tinted window lowers, Daniel Sladen smiles at me. "The Hurricanes are scrimmaging the Panthers this afternoon," he says. "It's only a practice game, but I thought maybe you'd have some free time today."

Obviously the man hasn't seen my to-do list. I have a fence installer coming at three, and a county inspector due at four, and the cable guy is supposed to drop by today anytime between noon and six. I have dishes in the sink, and a stack of obits to read, and the boys will be ravenous when they come back from the airport.

But I could ask Gerald to fix the kids a snack. The dishes will wait, as will the obits. The inspector doesn't need me, Gerald can talk to the fence man, and the cable guy has been a no-show on two other appointment days.

Maybe it's my turn to be spontaneous.

I cock my index finger in Daniel's direction. "Will you give me five minutes? I need to brush my hair and grab my purse."

Daniel grins and shoves the gearshift into park. "I'll give you all the time you need."

About the Author

Christy Award winner **Angela Hunt** writes books for readers who have learned to expect the unexpected. With over three million copies of her books sold worldwide, she is the best-selling author of *The Tale of Three Trees*, *The Note*, *Unspoken*, and more than 100 other titles.

She and her youth pastor husband make their home in Florida with mastiffs. One of their dogs was featured on *Live with Regis and Kelly* as the second-largest canine in America.

Readers may visit her Web site at www.angelahuntbooks.com.

Discussion Questions

1. *Doesn't She Look Natural?* is the first of three novels featuring Jennifer Graham and the Fairlawn Funeral Home. Where do you think the author will take Jennifer and her family in subsequent books?

2. What are some of the major themes of this novel? Does the author use any symbols to illustrate those themes?

3. At one point, Jennifer says, "Only a stupid dog would run away from a boy who loved him, and only a selfish animal would stay away while we were all worried sick about him." Whom do you think she is really talking about in this passage?

4. In the first sentence, Jennifer tells us that she's developed a "crème brûlée" crust. How does this metaphor describe Jennifer as a person?

5. Is there anything in this story to which you can personally relate? Did you find yourself identifying with any of the characters?

6. What spiritual truth do you think the author meant to convey in this novel? Was that developed with the same care and attention as the characters and the plot?

7. Most of this story is told from Jennifer's viewpoint. How would it have been different if Joella or Gerald had been telling the story?

8. How important is the setting to this novel? Would it have worked as well if it had been set in a metropolitan area?

9. How does this book compare to others you've read by Angela Hunt? Do you see any similar themes or character traits?

10. At several points in the novel, Jennifer mentions surrender. How does this theme apply to the story? How does it apply in your life?

11. Have you ever been called to sacrifice a cherished dream? How painful was the experience, and what convinced you to do it?

In or Out of Season Strawberry Muffins

Ingredients:

¼ cup vegetable oil

½ cup milk

1 egg

2 teaspoon baking powder

½ teaspoon salt

½ cup sugar

1¾ cup all-purpose flour

1 cup chopped strawberries, fresh or frozen

Preheat oven to 375 degrees. Oil a muffin tin or use paper liners.

In a small bowl combine oil, milk, and egg. Beat lightly. In a large bowl mix flour, salt, baking powder, and sugar. Toss in chopped strawberries and stir to coat with flour. Pour in milk mixture and stir all together.

Fill muffin cups. Bake at 375 degrees for 25 minutes or until the tops bounce back from the touch. Cool 10 minutes and remove from pans.

Should make 8 muffins.

References

No novelist writes alone, and I owe a debt of gratitude to the following people and sources:

Henke, Roxanne. 2005. Personal correspondence.

Menager, Arlin D. 2001. *Embalming Is Not a Sport*. First Books.

Sacks, Terence J. 1997. *Opportunities in Funeral Services Careers*. Chicago: NTC Publishing Group.

Stair, Nancy L. 2002. *Choosing a Career in Mortuary Science and the Funeral Industry*. New York: The Rosen Publishing Group, Inc.

Wasson, Benna. April 11, 2006. Personal correspondence.

A special thanks to Randy Alcorn, whose book *Heaven* turned my thoughts toward things eternal; Nancy Rue for supplying me with the right lingo at the right moment; Karen Watson and Becky Nesbitt for a brainstorming session; my excellent editors Becky Nesbitt, Lorie Popp, and Dave Lambert; and to the dear Hatters of Heavenly Daze for allowing me to use their official royal names.

One final note: Mt. Dora is a real city in Lake County, Florida. If you have an opportunity to visit that lovely town, you will discover that many of the buildings, landmarks, and streets described in this novel actually exist. Others, however, do not. So please don't blame the city council if the Fairlawn Funeral Home is not where you think it should be.

Watch for the next book in the Fairlawn series . . .

She Always Wore Red

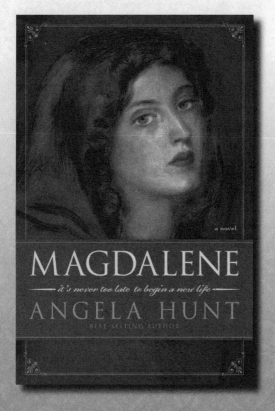

The Nativity Story—A novelization of the major motion picture. Best-selling author Angela Hunt presents a heartwarming adaptation of *The Nativity Story*. Hunt brings the story of Christ's birth to life with remarkable attention to detail and a pains-taking commitment to historical accuracy.

Also available in Spanish.

have you visited
tyndalefiction.com
lately?

Only there can you find:

- » books hot off the press
- » first chapter excerpts
- » inside scoops on your favorite authors
- » author interviews
- » contests
- » fun facts
- » and much more!

Sign up for your **free** newsletter!

Visit us today at: tyndalefiction.com